FAST AND LOOSE
and
THE BUCCANEERS

FAST and LOOSE
and
The BUCCANEERS
by
EDITH WHARTON

Edited and with an Introduction by
Viola Hopkins Winner

University Press of Virginia
Charlottesville and London

THE UNIVERSITY PRESS OF VIRGINIA
This Edition Copyright © 1993 by the Rector and Visitors
of the University of Virginia
First published 1993
Second printing 1993

Fast and Loose first published 1977
© Rector and Visitors of the University of Virginia

The Buccaneers first published 1938
Copyright, 1938, by D. Appleton-Century Company, Inc.

Library of Congress Cataloging-in-Publication Data

Wharton, Edith, 1862–1937.
[Fast and loose]
Fast and loose ; and, The buccaneers / by Edith Wharton ; edited
and with an introduction by Viola Hopkins Winner.
      p.   cm.
ISBN 0–8139–1482–5 (cloth).—ISBN 0–8139–1483–3 (paper)
I. Winner, Viola Hopkins.   II. Wharton, Edith, 1862–1937.
Buccaneers.   III. Title.
PS3545.H16F37   1993
813'.52—dc20   93–11207
                                                         CIP

Facing Fast and Loose *title page:*
Edith Newbold Jones in 1876.
(courtesy of the Clifton Waller Barrett
Collection of the Alderman Library, University of Virginia)

Facing The Buccaneers *title page:*
Edith Wharton about 1931.
(Courtesy of the Yale Collection of
American Literature, Beinecke Rare Book
and Manuscript Library, Yale University)

Printed in the United States of America

Contents

Introduction

From *Fast and Loose* to *The Buccaneers* Edith Wharton came full circle. She began *Fast and Loose* in the autumn of 1876, finishing it in January 1877, some weeks before her fifteenth birthday. It was published for the first time from her manuscript in 1977. In *The Buccaneers*, begun in late 1933 and published posthumously in 1938, she returned fictionally to the world of her early youth. The heroine is sixteen when the novel opens in the mid-1870s. There are other similarities. Both novels depict the manners and customs of the English aristocracy: the country house, the London season, the mating rituals. Both of the heroines are trapped in miserable marriages. Even the names of the principal lovers in the late work echo those in the earlier: Georgina ("Georgie") Rivers and Nan St George, Guy Hastings and Guy Thwarte. *The Buccaneers* is not a rewriting of *Fast and Loose*, but the juvenile novel she had written over fifty years before was fresh in her mind when she began to think about writing a novel on the subject of *The Buccaneers*. She had returned to *Fast and Loose* in the course of describing her earliest creative efforts in her memoir *A Backward Glance*, published in 1934, and *The Buccaneers* according to her publishing schedule was to be next on the list. The echoes and parallels between her first and last work were not coincidental.

Bringing the two works together enables us to look forward as well as to glance back. The extent to which *Fast and Loose* anticipates Edith Wharton's mature style and sense of life is remarkable. *The Buccaneers* resembles her previous works but also marks a new departure and a reflorescence

vii

of her imaginative powers after a decade of uncertain directions and, with some notable exceptions, literary decline. Both works pose interesting critical questions, and as front and end pieces to Edith Wharton's distinguished literary career, they claim our attention for the sake of the record. There is, however, ample reason for reviving these works on the grounds of literary merits; each on its own is more than merely readable. *Fast and Loose* is a spirited and witty performance. Scenes and characters from *The Buccaneers*, full of glints and gleams of Edith Wharton's narrative art at its best, linger in memory long after one has forgotten its flaws.

It is regrettable that Edith Wharton did not live to complete *The Buccaneers* and in a final form acceptable to her. For, as her literary executor, Gaillard Lapsley, observes in his afterword to the first edition, her novel "comprised some work as good as any she had ever done and some that she would never have allowed to appear as it stood." Although skeptics pointing to the sentimentality and tired diction of some of her later works may doubt that her artistic conscience was as sensitive as Lapsley believed, we may give her the benefit of the doubt that had she completed the book, she would have brought the bad in line with the good. Happily, in any event, it is not a mere fragment nor is it a rough first draft. On the contrary, she had finished the greater part of the novel and polished her prose as she went along. The manuscript breaks off in the midst of the twenty-ninth chapter, and according to a note in Edith Wharton's hand in the Beinecke Library, only three more chapters were projected to bring the novel to its conclusion. Moreover, unlike other unfinished novels such as Dickens's *Edwin Drood*, *The Buccaneers* does not leave its readers permanently suspended, depriving them of the basic satisfaction of learning how it was all meant to come out. Edith

Wharton's scenario for the book, outlining her thematic purpose and working out the plot to the end, has survived and is published here, as it was in the first edition, after the text of the novel.

Because Edith Wharton did not oversee the publication of her novel, it is especially important that the printed text accurately incorporate her latest revisions. Lapsley's text very nearly satisfies this requirement, and therefore we have reprinted it here, along with all of his deviations from her two final manuscript revisions. (For details on the textual problems and the list of variants, see below.) The deviations include typographical errors, omissions, and editorial emendations of the printed text. In effect, then, this is the first corrected edition of Edith Wharton's posthumously published novel, using the first-edition text and including a list of relevant corrections and revisions.

In her revisions to *Fast and Loose* (see below) the young author shows a precocious concern for verbal precision; her early and persistent jibes at her first sustained prose work suggest that she took it more seriously than she would have us believe she did or perhaps than she herself realized. In *A Backward Glance,* Wharton dismissed it lightly as a youthful jeu d'esprit. Unlike the poetry she was also writing in her adolescence, which she did not keep secret and which her mother had privately printed in a small volume in 1878, her novelette was not written to be circulated even in the family, but was instead "destined for the private enjoyment of a girl friend, and was never exposed to the garish light of print." The friend was most likely Emelyn Washburn, the daughter of the rector of the church Edith and her parents, Lucretia and George Frederic Jones, attended in New York, and the first near contemporary with whom Edith found intellectual companionship. From Emelyn, who was six years older than she and was to remain a lifelong friend, Edith could expect a sympathetic but also a sophisticated critical response.

To disarm such criticism or perhaps to respond to it, the young author wrote a series of mock reviews of her novelette, printed for the first time in the 1977 edition and reprinted here. Supposedly from the *Saturday Review,* the *Pall Mall Budget,* and the *Nation,* these reviews take the novelist to task for not fulfilling the promise of raciness raised by the title and for artistic ineptness. Aware that she had failed to realize her intentions, Edith converted her disappointment into a satiric performance at her own expense while simultaneously adopting a world-weary waspish tone parodying the style of American and English reviewers of the day.

More than twenty years later, when Wharton was beginning to publish professionally, she alluded humorously in a number of stories to *Fast and Loose* and to *Lucile,* the popular novel by Robert Lytton from which her epigraph and title originated, a book that she herself had obviously enjoyed in her youth. In her story "The Muse's Tragedy" (1899) the crude taste of the "perfectly beautiful" young woman whose mind is "all elbows" is indicated by her gift of *Lucile* to the great poet Rendle. In "April Showers" (1900), the first novel by the aspiring seventeen-year-old author, Theodora, ends with a quotation from the ending of *Fast and Loose.* Theodora is "almost sure" that she has written "a remarkable book," its "emotional intensity" compensating for its lack of "lightness of touch." A more explicit reference occurs in "Expiation" (1903), in which another would-be writer, Mrs. Fetheral, tries to launch her career with what she believes to be a daring novel exposing "the hollowness of social conventions." It does not create the sensation she had hoped for despite its racy title—*Fast and Loose.* Finally it does become a succès de scandale, but only because she has bribed the bishop of Ossining with a generous gift to the church to denounce it from his pulpit.

Despite the playfulness of Wharton's allusions to *Fast and Loose,* this recurring private joke at her own expense suggests that she had invested more of her literary aspirations in it than she publicly admitted. She was not an autobiographical writer of the confessional kind, like her writer Vance Weston in *Hudson River Bracketed* (1929), yet even in a work that owes as much as *Fast and Loose* does to the conventions of sentimental fiction, there is a biographical substratum. As R. W. B. Lewis observes, her "incipient vision" of the inevitable defeat of hopes and ideals in human undertakings was "based primarily upon her observation of her parents' life together." Similarly, the portrayal of Georgie's mother as a "nervous invalid, of the complainingly resigned sort" and as a widow who has lost not only her husband but all traces of beauty may be interpreted as a kind of wish-fulfilling dream, reflecting Edith's relationship with her powerful mother and ineffectual father. In a reversal of their roles in real life, the mother in the novelette is reduced to harmless passivity on her sofa, an object of ridicule, while Edith herself as Georgie is in full command. Moreover, the portrayal of Georgie on the one hand as a tomboy and on the other as a peaches-and-cream femme fatale may be taken as a reflection of Edith's desire to enjoy masculine freedom without sacrificing femininity, the potential conflict inherent in aspiring to excel in intellectual pursuits and to succeed as a debutante. Edith Jones's incompatible marriage to Edward Wharton was not a reenactment of Georgie's mercenary marriage to Lord Breton. Still, Georgie's description of Guy, whom she does *not* marry, as "the only man I ever knew who neither despises me nor is afraid of me" does suggest that scorn or fear was what Edith Jones, intellectually formidable and socially shy, thought young men felt about *her.* Her adolescent novel may be taken as psychologically prophetic insofar as she appears to have been drawn to "Teddy" because she felt safe with him from the challenge that marriage to someone who was more nearly her equal in intelligence and abilities would have posed.

Edith Jones's intellectual precocity and linguistic facility may be judged by the literary sources and models for *Fast and Loose.* In one of her reviews she ridicules the author for failing to make the novelette "as bad as Wilhelm Meister, Consuelo, & 'Goodbye Sweetheart'" combined. That she read Goethe's famous bildungsroman by fourteen shows not only a superior command of German but remarkable mental stamina. George Sand's romantic novel required no special linguistic effort, as she read French fluently—it is even possible that she may have learned to read French before English—but perhaps it called for endurance of another kind. She knew Italian well, colloquially more than literarily. Her pseudonym, "David Olivieri," and the French and Italian phrases sprinkled throughout the text came naturally as a result of her cosmopolitan upbringing. During most of her childhood, from the age of four to ten, the Jones family lived abroad, in Paris and in Rome, traveling in Germany and Spain as well.

Steeped in English and European literature and adept in their languages, she was not greatly influenced by American writers in her earliest fiction. She was familiar with genteel authors such as Washington Irving and Fitz-Greene Halleck, whose works were in her father's library, but she did not begin to write in the shadow of an American predecessor, unlike Henry James vis-à-vis Hawthorne. (In itself *Fast and Loose* disproves the lingering popular myth that she was James's disciple; she had discovered her own voice long before reading or meeting him.) That she nonetheless thought as an American in this novelette in which the main characters are all English is both obviously and subtly evident. There are telltale slips in idiom, such as when Egerton compares taking up with a woman to picking up a rattlesnake, and an overattention to social rank, such as calling attention to a guardsman's social status as a "Duke's son." The repeated reference to characters as "English"—for example, describing Mr. Graham as an "English merchant"—also stands out as an anomaly in a story that purports to be told from an English point of view. The most American characteristic of all may be that Edith Jones chose to use an English setting and characters: where else but in Europe could one imagine a young woman torn between love and a title, a brilliant social career, and great wealth? Clearly, at this stage in her life, Edith Wharton identified "literature" with the Old World.

As her epigraphs and literary echoes indicate, young Edith was particularly influenced by the poetry of Scott, Tennyson, and Browning, and by the fiction of Austen, Thackeray, and Trollope. Georgie's mother recalls the nervous, fussy invalid father in Austen's *Emma*. When Georgie, about to reveal that she is changing fiancés, warns her, "'Now, Mamma, I am going to shock you,'" Mrs. Rivers's reply is true to type: "'Oh, my dear, I hope not.'" Georgie reminds Egerton of Thackeray's Beatrix Esmond, and some of the other characters, in name at least, are straight from the pages of Trollope: Miss Priggett, the maid; Sir Ashley Patchem, the physician; Doublequick, the guardsman. Edith Jones's reading of eighteenth-century essays, poetry, and drama is reflected in the characterization of Lord Breton as a superannuated Regency buck. Courting Georgie, he conjures up "the ghost of what some might recall as a fascinating smile; but which was more like a bland leer to the eye unassisted by memory." The crisp, epigrammatic style owes not a little to the formal balance of thesis and antithesis characteristic of eighteenth-century prose.

According to *A Backward Glance,* Edith Jones's mother forbade her to read popular fiction, including Rhoda Broughton and "all the lesser novelists of the day." Either she was less dutiful or her mother was more relaxed than memory served, for not only did she read Broughton's *"Goodbye-Sweetheart!"* (1872) and *Lucile* (1860), by the lesser novelist Robert Lytton, they inspired her to emulation. Broughton, an English novelist born in 1840 who died in 1920, said of her own reputation that she began her career as Zola and was ending it as Miss Yonge, the epitome of Victorian gentility. While Broughton's novel is not brutally naturalistic, neither is it insipid or merely sentimental. The second half, much like that of *Fast and Loose,* is melodramatic; the death of Lucy, the heroine, by consumption is as arbitrary as Georgie's. But at first Lucy, like Georgie, is not the conventionally frail, submissive domestic angel; she is physically robust, outspoken, and sensual. The smell, look, and taste of things are palpably presented. Realistic touches undercut romanticism, as when the lovers set out from an inn where the smell of manure has permeated their tea. Though this kind of humble detail did not enter into her story of high life, Edith Jones adopted Broughton's short-hand method of setting the scene with a series of visual details much like stage directions, as well as her other dramatic tendencies such as subordinating narrative to dialogue.

The eponymous heroine of Robert Lytton's verse novel is "the belle of all places in which she is seen" (including Paris and Baden). She is upbraided by one of her suitors after she rejects him for playing "fast and loose thus with human despair," and our final glimpse of her is as Soeur Seraphine, a nun nursing her first lover's son, wounded in the Crimean War. In between are assignations by a waterfall in a wild landscape, duels and seductions (unconsummated), compromising letters, and bankruptcy—all occasioning disquisitions on Life, Time, and Sorrow. This romantic novel leavened with worldly epigrams must have impressed Edith Jones—as the parallels in plot and character types of *Fast and Loose*, her witty style, and the quotations from *Lucile* attest—but she did not imitate in her own sad story of a coquette its incidents of romantic adventure or its gothic touches. Guy goes "rapidly to the dogs" but of the "many modes of travelling on this road," his is not "the melodramatic one in which the dark-browed hero takes to murder, elopement, & sedition" nor does he take "the commonplace one" of "drinking, gambling & duelling" nor "the precipitate one of suicide." Instead "he seemed to grow careless of life, money & health, & to lose whatever faith & tenderness he had had in a sort of undefined skepticism." The author herself was moving toward psychological realism and satirical exposure of sentimentality. On occasion her characters wallow in tears, but her ironic detachment is evident early on, as when she describes Georgie crying her eyes "into the proper shade of pinkness." Premonitions of the "fine asperity" (James's phrase) so characteristic of Edith Wharton's mature work pervade her first fiction.

Thematically, *Fast and Loose* also foreshadows the later work. Georgie is the ancestor of all of Edith Wharton's sensitive, generous-minded "free spirits" trapped in a confining relationship: Lily Bart, Ralph Marvell, Ethan Frome, Newland Archer, Nan St George, to name a few. While Georgie's deathbed repentance is conventional, the treatment of the consequences of her decision to marry Lord Breton is characteristic of the mature author. Even as an adolescent she was predisposed to the fatalistic view of life so striking in her later fiction: the strokes of fate at times approach tragedy, as with the Eumenides-haunted end of Lily Bart, and sometimes they are merely ironic, as with Undine Spragg's final realization that the very means by which she has climbed the social ladder—divorce—will preclude her reaching the top. In *Fast and Loose* the inscrutable, often punitive, force governing human lives is manifest in Mrs. Graham's accident: "It is certain that in this world the smallest wires work the largest machinery in a wonderful way." If it had not been for her twisting her foot on the stairs, Guy would probably not have become engaged to Madeline. Thus, after Lord Breton dies and Georgie is free, Guy is not. By another twist of fate, Teresina, who in contrast to Georgie has married the poor young lover instead of the rich old suitor, is deserted by her husband. The marriage of the misogynist Jack Egerton to a "pale, melancholy, fascinating French Marquise" is a final ironic touch.

As an exercise in the craft of fiction, *Fast and Loose* shows considerable skill, and the list of her revisions (below) reveals the apprentice writer's awareness of special problems. Each chapter has organic unity yet advances the action. Too much happens overall, however, to be believable in the given span of time. Though enough time elapses for Georgie to become disillusioned with her marriage, there is not enough for Guy's disintegration. The announcement after two months that the young man's life has been ruined forever seems premature. Repeated tinkering with dates did not solve the problem but does indicate that Edith Jones knew that it takes more than telling the time to create the illusion of its flow.

Other revisions are in the direction of greater precision and concreteness, of "visibility." Edith's early European experience had shaped her sense of the beautiful, and the

Ruskin she read in her father's library in New York helped her learn how to look and how to translate visual impressions into prose. From her mother she inherited an eye for dress especially useful to the novelist of manners. Her description of Madeline setting out in a "gray walking dress, with a quantity of light blue veil floating about her leghorn hat & looped around her throat," is both precisely observed and characterizing. The cool, neutral, and harmonious colors and the ethereal veil convey her madonnalike purity and reserve. Similarly, feeling remorseful for having cast off Guy, Georgie catches a glimpse of herself in a pier glass. Her spirits revive: the sight of herself in a becoming riding habit consoles her and strengthens her resolve to marry Lord Breton. By indirection, the mirror incident reveals the ingenuous vanity that leads Georgie to marry a man who can materially sustain this image of herself. Overall, the description of the English scene is thin and sketchy, drawn it seems mostly from literary sources, whereas the depiction of the studio world of Rome, which Edith Jones knew at first hand, is evocative and rich in picturesque detail. It gives an inkling of the talent she would develop in painterly portrayal of people and places, manifested not just in her subsequent fiction but in her books on travel, gardens, and interior decoration.

Fast and Loose is fascinating as juvenilia—for what it reveals as a seedbed of style and thought brought to fruition in Edith Wharton's maturity. And it is also unique. No other work by her, I think it can be safely said, has its ebullience: a sense of joy in sheer creativity that quickens even the most lugubrious passages.

If *Fast and Loose* is a Victorian novel looking forward, *The Buccaneers* is a modern novel looking backwards. It takes place in Saratoga, New York City, and England from about 1873 to 1877, spanning the years of Edith Jones's early youth, from about the age of eleven to fifteen. As in *The Age of Innocence* (1920) and the *Old New York* stories (1924), the social world portrayed is partly hard-edged historical reconstruction and partly personal experience seen through a veil of nostalgia. The more the decades of cataclysmic change and of expatriation separated Edith Wharton from her youth, the more self-conscious she became as a social historian. We may see her concern about the accuracy of social detail from the questionnaire she sent to Frank Gray Griswold, an acquaintance eight years older than she, who had known at first hand the sporting and fashionable worlds of Saratoga and New York of the time. Among the questions (eight in all) was "To what clubs would the relatively unknown fathers of my fast girls belong? Was the Union still a fortress of old New Yorkers, or was there already a breach in the walls? I thought of them as successful Wall Street men, but not smart [fashionable]." He replied, "Manhattan Club (15th & 5th Ave.)" and "N.Y. Athletic Club," which Wharton incorporated in her text but eventually deleted. She also asked about the clothes that "an elderly Wall Street broker" would wear to a meet at Saratoga and about the balls at the United States Hotel (changed to the Grand Union in the novel) at Saratoga. While she did not immerse herself in scholarly research as she had for her Italian novel set in the eighteenth-century, *The Valley of Decision* (1902), she clearly sought in *The Buccaneers* to evoke time and place with the same historical veracity.

For the English setting of the 1870s Wharton drew on her own frequent visits to England. The romantic Arthurian motif was inspired by a visit in 1928 to Cornwall, where she wandered in the fog, much like Nan, on the ruins of the castle that was said to have been King Arthur's. Honourslove resembles Stanway, the house in Gloucestershire of Lord and Lady Elcho, whom she often visited. Her

xviii

familiarity with English country-house life served her well, evident especially in the description of the great houses of the Brightlingseas and of the Tintagels, modeled after Wilton House and Blenheim Palace. (The design for The Mount, Wharton's house at Lenox, Massachusetts, was based on Christopher Wren's Belton House, Lincolnshire, England.) Her lifelong interest in houses and gardens was professional and practical: *The Decoration of Houses* (1897) and *Italian Villas and Their Gardens* (1904) were pioneering books and are now regarded as classics of their kind. Besides The Mount, which was her creation from scratch, she adapted every house or apartment in which she lived in Newport, New York, Paris, St. Brice-sous-Forêt (in the environs of Paris), and Hyères to suit her purposes. In her fiction she used her architectural knowledge and taste in decor symbolically, poetically. Her houses mirror the people who inhabit them and their way of life: the tiny Miss March is epitomized by her tiny Mayfair house, as is the heavy hand of tradition and family pride by the duchess's sitting room at Longlands. On its walls "landscapes by the Dowager Duchess's great-aunts, funereal monuments worked in hair on faded silk, and photographs in heavy oak frames of ducal relatives, famous race-horses. Bishops in lawn sleeves, and undergraduates grouped about sporting trophies" jostle for space with the glorious Correggios. Whereas Allfriars is a place of "shabby vastness" and its owner, Lord Brightlingsea, scarcely knows one of its great pictures from another, Honourslove, as the name rather too obviously suggests, is "warm, cared-for, exquisitely intimate," and Guy has "a latent passion for every tree and stone of the beautiful old place." Nan "as a dweller in houses without histories" has never experienced this kind of attachment to place, but it was "familiar to her imagination." The mystic love of place saturated with the past is the correlative of their communion, of what Nan thinks of as "the *beyondness* of things."

Reconstructing English customs and manners in the 1870s, Wharton described rather more than she evoked, in contrast to her atmospheric recreation of the American scene, in which social detail is absorbed into the overall impressionistic picture. There is a touch too much explanation; references to the custom of afternoon tea and the backwardness of the gentry in installing modern conveniences such as gaslight and the telephone, for instance, have a guidebook ring, and an overconsciousness of social rank reminiscent of *Fast and Loose* suggests that, perhaps because she had never had a home in England, she was not quite at home there. On the other hand, the glimpses given of the Italian exiles and Pre-Raphaelites ring true, in part because it is the world of Laura Testvalley—the "insignificant" looking governess whose "eyebrows were so black and ironical." She is the most fully realized character in the novel and the last of the line of Wharton's vital and complex women that includes Lily Bart, Sophy Viner, and Ellen Olenska. Wharton's love and intimate knowledge of Italy and Italian history imbued her characterization of Laura and the Anglo-Italian aspect of the novel with feeling and life. And, on the whole, the device of mingling historical with fictional figures (the Rossettis with the Testavaglias, the duke of Argyll with the duke of Tintagel) succeeds in creating the ambience of the period and place.

The raw materials that inspired Edith Wharton's basic conception of the "transatlantic invaders" as well as individual characterization, scenes, and incidents were diverse, a mixture of fact and fiction. As Adeline Tintner has shown, the marriage of Nan to the duke and its unhappy consequences owed much in outline and in details to the much-publicized marriage (and its annulment) of Consuelo Vanderbilt to the duke of Marlborough. The exotic Brazilian heiress Conchita resembles Consuelo Yznaga, a friend of Edith Wharton's youth. In the early 1900s, after she had become the duchess of Manchester, they renewed their friendship. The idea for the Virginia reel, which figures prominently in the Christmas-party scene at Longlands, probably goes back to the famous Vanderbilt costume ball in New York in 1883. That ball ended at dawn with the unusual feature of the dancing of the reel. The post-Civil War phenomenon of American heiresses marrying into the European aristocracies, often English and usually impoverished, was, however, too widely recognized to permit assigning any single source. Among other instances, Edith Wharton almost certainly knew the New Yorker Lelia Wilson, who married the English diplomat Michael Herbert (eventually ambassador to the United States) and the other "marrying Wilsons," as she and her two sisters and brother were dubbed. The children of Melissa and Richard T. Wilson of Tennessee, they all made brilliant social marriages. Wilson, a Civil War profiteer, bought the Fifth Avenue house of "Boss" Tweed. This was perhaps the source for Colonel St George's purchase of the Madison Avenue house "built and decorated by one of the Tweed ring, who had come to grief earlier than his more famous fellow-criminals."

Among the specifically literary antecedents of *The Buccaneers*, the idea for the title may have come from John Esquemeling's *The Buccaneers of America* (1678), of which Edith Wharton owned a modern reprint (circa 1925). Adeline Tintner, who discovered Wharton's ownership of this book on pirates who marauded in the New World, suggests it may have sparked the idea of a reverse invasion by a band of adventuresses. A more closely related source is James's nouvelle *The Siege of London* (1883); not only the scheme to

xxi

bypass New York for London society but the imagery of the American girls as invaders launching their attack on the London citadel is a Jamesian echo, most specifically when Lizzy is described as "having come to lay siege to London." That the Tintagel's house is called Longlands, the name of the country house in James's nouvelle in which Nancy Headway launches her campaign, is either a sly allusion or a slip of memory. Also reminiscent of James is Miss March as "the oracle of transatlantic pilgrims in quest of a social opening." Like Maria Gostrey in *The Ambassadors,* she is an American expatriate who smoothes the way for Americans abroad, and like Miss Cutter in "Mrs. Medwin" she accepts gifts for her services, which she justifies as a way of keeping her house and herself "presentable." (In James's much harsher picture of the decadence of English society into which Americans bring fresh blood, Miss Cutter is driven by financial need to charge outright for her favors.)

The indebtedness of Edith Wharton to Proust suggested by Gaillard Lapsley in his afterword to the first edition is also significant. She read Proust too late in life to be deeply influenced by his style, aims, or approach, and the social worlds they depicted were too alien. Nevertheless in more than one respect, she was inspired by the second volume of *A la recherche du temps perdu.* The enchanting scene in which Laura is greeted at the station at Saratoga by the wagonload of girls is certainly indebted to the scene in which Marcel first encounters his young women in flower at the seaside resort of Balbec. More specifically, Proust was a source for the image in an earlier scene of the girls coming into the hotel dining room "arm-in-arm . . . like a branch hung with blossoms." These ascriptions do not detract from Edith Wharton's individuality. What she drew from Proust she made fully and organically her own. The revelry at the railway station foreshadows the sensuous joy and abandon of the Coreggio paintings of *The Earthly Paradise* at Long-lands. Her portrayal of the solidarity of the "fast girls," as she called them, was also influenced by Proust, but she worked out the theme in her own way. They are bound together like those of Proust's "little band" by their nubile beauty and careless egotism as well as by their social class. Like Proust's girls, they are the children of the new rich, "the 'new' coal and steel people." Two scenes illustrate this solidarity—the first in which Lizzy Elmsworth and Virginia St George help Conchita when she tries on her Assembly dress, even though they themselves have not been invited to the ball, and the second at the Runnymede cottage when Lizzy, giving up her own chance to marry Lord Seadown, comes to Virginia's rescue by announcing her friend's en-gagement to him. The design is further carried out when, on the strength of the bond of their past, Nan decides to somehow find the five hundred pounds to save Conchita from disaster.

The scene in which Conchita comes to Nan's room asking for money is a turning point in the novel: it precipitates the crisis in Nan's relations with the duke and leads to the renewal of her friendship with Guy and the eventual real-ization that she loves him, and it also brings to the fore the theme of personal happiness versus social responsibility, central to the novel. Conchita's "tirade" in response to Nan's suggestion that they return to New York, since all of their marriages "turned out a dreadful mistake," leads Nan to perceive how much she was attached to English life with its "layers and layers of rich deep background" and to won-der if it would be possible to "create for one's self a life out of all this richness, a life which should somehow make up for the poverty of one's personal lot." More the voice of Edith Wharton justifying her own expatriation and cul-tural preferences than a convincing representation of the character's thought, these reflections serve to distinguish Nan from Conchita, who scorns the "grotesque possibility" of returning to New York because of its social limitations. To her, "London's London, and London life the most exciting and interesting in the world." To Nan, "London society . . . had never had any attraction for her save as a splendid spectacle; and the part she was expected to play in that spectacle was a burden and not a delight." It is old England, not London, "which had gradually filled her veins and penetrated to her heart." And it is in comparison with England that she recalls "the thinness of the mental and moral air in her own home." Earlier, the day after the Christmas ball when the dowager duchess broke off her encounter with Nan so as not to keep their luncheon guests waiting, Nan concedes the value of discipline, of "rules and observances"; she begins "to see the use of having one's whims and one's rages submitted to some kind of control." In other words, we are meant to see Nan as having matured to the point of valuing order and discipline and as being willing to try to make a life for herself despite the almost total lack of rapport—both personal and cultural— between her and her husband. The miseries of her marriage in which she is expected to endure sexual relations for the sake of producing an heir prove too much for compromise.

Well-meaning and even kind in his way, Ushant is an emotional cipher. Ushant's limitations are symbolized by his name and by his one passion—clocks. Truly at ease only when winding or repairing clocks, he is humanly obtuse without a scintilla of imagination on how to manage the people on his estates or his wife. He can neither enter into Nan's "dreams and ambitions, in which a desire to better the world alternated with a longing for solitude and poetry" nor help her to find a meaningful place in his world. He has made the mistake of marrying Nan because he thought "she seemed too young and timid to have any opinions on any subject whatever" and so he could "form her," as he told his mother when he broke the news to her of his engagement. Her comment in reply that "women are not quite as simple as clocks" comes back to haunt him.

The scene in which the duke, having given Nan the five hundred pounds, goes to her bedroom expecting to exercise his conjugal rights is a marvel of economy and deftness. It is presented indirectly in the duke's own words the next morning, when he recounts the incident to the dowager duchess in the hope that "perhaps one woman can understand another where a man would fail..." He had gone to his wife's room that night with the thought that as "she'd gained her point about the money...she...er...would wish to show her gratitude." The dowager duchess's reply, "Naturally," and her subsequent remarks indicate that the duke's expectations were entirely within the realm of his moral rights and his wife's duty as understood by his society. While the dowager duchess is outraged at Nan's refusal, she, however, is also unsettled by it for "the light reflected back on her own past, and on the weary nights when she had not dared to lock her door..." Through her spoken response and her reflections, we see that while the duke acted according to an accepted moral code, unlike his mother he is too rigid and literal minded to imagine other points of view. The indirection of the narration does not diminish the sense conveyed of Nan's outrage and repugnance in her response to the duke's overture: "she refused, refused absolutely" and on the ground "that she hadn't understood I'd been driving a bargain with her." (In an earlier version of this scene, the language was stronger: "she said she was not for sale.")

The aforesaid scene without oversimplification both justifies and marks the beginning of Nan's liberation from a loveless dynastic marriage. The visit to Lady Glenloe's brings Nan together again with Laura and with Guy Thwarte. The extent to which Nan's ties to her husband have loosened and she has become involved with Guy are evident in the final extant chapter. She has herself asked to be invited to a party at the country house of her old friend Lizzy Elmsworth, knowing that Guy Thwarte is to be a guest.

Also on the guest list is Sir Blasker Tripp, "who of course belonged to Conchita Marable." Apparently Conchita moved on from "tender intimacies" with Miles Dawnly to the company of a very rich old man. This brings us back to the scene in which Conchita comes to Nan for money and also reveals to her that she has consoled herself for her misery in marriage with Miles Dawnly. Her parting words to Nan are especially relevant:

> "Nan," she said, almost solemnly, "don't judge me, will you, till you find out for yourself what it's like."
>
> "What what is like? What do you mean, Conchita?"
>
> "Happiness, darling," Lady Dick whispered.

Nan comes to know what it is like, but her happiness is not Conchita's kind. Her elopement with Guy, we have been prepared to believe, is to be a marriage of true minds as well as of the senses. The idealistic yet sensuous cast of their union is prefigured in the Honourslove scene on the terrace and more subtly resonates in the pictures and poetry of Rossetti and in *The Earthly Paradise* of the Coreggios. If Nan seems overidealized and Guy rather insubstantial, it is especially in comparison with the other "lovers," Laura and Sir Helmsley. Laura is an "adventuress" in the sense that she is not narrowly bound by social conventions and moral codes; she is a woman of the world. If she had been a man, as she says, "Dante Gabriel might not have been the only cross in the family." Sir Helmsley in turn is a man of the world, witty and artistic, and also irresponsible, eccentric, demanding. Neither he nor Laura are sentimentalized, whereas Nan and Guy come perilously close at times to the stereotypes of popular romance.

The projected conclusion in which Nan and Guy elope and presumably find "happiness" marks a striking change from Edith Wharton's usually pessimistic endings. It reflects not only the social changes that had taken place in the course of her lifetime from Victorianism to modernism, but the liberation and the sexual and intellectual fulfillment she had experienced in her love affair with Morton Fullerton. But examined more closely in relation to her previous work, we see that the implications of the ending of *The Buccaneers* are not unprecedented. Thus, the ending of *The Age of Innocence* raises the question of whether Newland Archer's adherence to the old New York code of honor justified the sacrifice of his personal happiness. He did the decent thing by not leaving his wife, but sitting on the bench outside of Ellen Olenska's Paris apartment and looking up at its shuttered windows, he is, like James's John Marcher in "The Beast in the Jungle," a man who has not lived. In *The Buccaneers* the conflict between social order and personal fulfillment is resolved in favor of the latter, but there is a price to be paid for happiness. For her part in acting on behalf of "the rights of the heart," in Edmund Wilson's phrasing, Laura is repudiated by Sir Helmsley and so forfeits the security and comfort, love and companionship, she would have had as his wife. He, in turn, is left embittered and estranged from his son. The scandal of the elopement is such that it seems unlikely that Guy can assume his place at Honourslove, his love of which had first drawn him to Nan. In this light, the ironic ending of *The Buccaneers* may be seen as linked with that of *Fast and Loose*.

Its moral realism marks the distance Edith Wharton traveled in her art and her sense of life in the full circle from her first to her last novel.

I wish to thank William Royall Tyler for his contribution to the first edition of *Fast and Loose* and his continued support. *Fast and Loose* is reprinted by permission of the author and the Watkins/Loomis agency. I am grateful for permission to publish manuscript material to the following: Lilly Library, Indiana University, Bloomington, Indiana; the Yale Collection of American Literature, Beinecke Rare Book and Manuscript Library, Yale University; the Clifton Waller Barrett Collection of the Alderman Library, University of Virginia. I am particularly indebted to Adeline R. Tintner for sharing her scholarly discoveries, to David Vander Meulen for textual advice, to Ginger Thornton for editorial assistance, and to Eleanor Dwight and Katherine Joslin for their encouragement and Whartonian wisdom.

V.H.W.

FAST AND LOOSE
and
THE BUCCANEERS

Fast and Loose.
A Novelette.
By
David Olivieri.

. . . "Let woman beware
How she plays fast & loose thus with human despair
And the storm in man's heart." *Robert Lytton*: Lucile.

Dedication
To
Cornélie

"[Donna] beata e bella" [*illegible*] Quinta.
(October 1876)

Fast and Loose—A Novelette

By David Olivieri

Chap. I. Hearts & Diamonds.

" 'Tis best to be off with the old love
Before you are on with the new!" *Song.*

A DISMAL AUTUMN AFTERNOON in the country. Without, a
soft drizzle falling on yellow leaves & damp ground; within,
two people playing chess by the window of the fire-lighted
drawing-room at Holly Lodge. Now, when two people play
chess on a rainy afternoon, tête-à-tête in a room with the door
shut, they are likely to be either very much bored, or rather
dangerously interested; & in this case, with all respect to romance, they appeared overcome by the profoundest ennui.
The lady—a girl of about 18, plump & soft as a partridge, with
vivacious brown eyes, & a cheek like a sun-warmed peach—
occasionally stifled a yawn, as her antagonist, curling a slight
blonde moustache (the usual sign of masculine perplexity) sat
absently meditating a move on which the game, in his eyes, appeared to depend; & at last, pushing aside her chair, she rose
& stood looking out of the window, as though even the dreary
Autumn prospect had more attraction for her than the handsome face on the other side of the chess-board. Her movement
seemed to shake her companion out of his reverie, for he rose
also, & looking over her shoulder, at the soft, misty rain, observed rather languidly, "Cheerful weather!" "Horrid!" said
the girl, stamping her foot. "I am dying of stagnation." "Don't

you mean to finish the game?" "If you choose. I don't care."
"Nor I—It's decidedly a bore." No answer. The bright brown
eyes & the lazy blue ones stared out of the window for the space
of five slow minutes. Then the girl said: "Guy!" "My liege!"
"You're not very amusing this afternoon." "Neither are you,
my own!" "Gallant for a lover!" she cried, pouting & turning
away from the window. "How can I amuse a stone wall? I
might talk all day!" She had a way of tossing her pretty little
head, & drawing her soft white forehead, that was quite irresistible. Guy, as the most natural thing in the world, put his
arm about her, but was met with a sharp, "Don't! You know
I hate to be taken hold of, Sir! Oh, I shall die of ennui if this
weather holds." Guy whistled, & went to lean against the fire-
place; while his betrothed stood in the middle of the room, the
very picture of "I-won't-be-amused" crossness. "Delightful!"
she said, presently. "Really, your conversation today displays
your wit & genius to a remarkable degree." "If I talk to you,
you scold, Georgie," said the lover, pathetically. "No, I don't!
I only scold when you twist your arms around me." "I can't
do one without the other!" Georgie laughed. "You *do* say nice
things, Guy! But you're a bore this afternoon, nevertheless."
"Isn't everything a bore?" "I believe so. Oh, I should be
another person galloping over the downs on Rochester!
'What's his name is himself again!' *Shall* we be able to hunt
tomorrow?" "Ask the clerk of the weather," said Guy, rather
dismally. "Guy! I do believe you're going to sleep! Doesn't it
rouse you to think of a tear 'cross country after the hounds?
Oh, Guy, a red coat makes my blood run faster!" "Does it?—
Georgie, have you got 'Je l'ai perdu'—the thing I sent you from
London?" "Yes—somewhere." "I am going to sing," said Guy.

4

"What a treat!" "As you don't object to my smoking, I thought you mightn't mind my singing." "Well," said Georgie, mischievously, "I don't suppose it *does* matter much which sense is offended. What are you going to sing?" Guy, without answering, began to hunt through a pile of music, & at last laid a copy of "The ballad to Celia" on the piano-rack. Georgie sat down, & while he leaned against the piano, struck a few prelude-chords; then he began to sing in a rich barytone, Ben Jonson's sweet old lines. At the end of the first stanza, Georgie shut the piano with a bang. "I will not play if you sing so detestably out of time, tune & everything. Do make yourself disagreeable in some less noisy way." "I think I shall make myself agreeable—by saying goodbye." "Very well, do!" "Georgie—what is the matter?" He took her little hand as he spoke, but she wrenched it away, stamping her foot again. "Dont & dont & dont! I'm as cross as I can be & I *won't* make friends!" she cried in a sort of childish passion, running away from him to the other end of the room. He stood for a moment, twirling his moustache; then, taking up his hat, said, "Goodbye." "Goodbye—Are you *very* angry?" she said, coming a step or two nearer, & looking up through her soft lashes. "No, I suppose not. I believe I have been boring you confoundedly." "I suppose I have been very cross." "Not more than I deserved, probably. I am going to London for a few days. Will you give me your hand for goodbye?" She stood still a moment, looking at him thoughtfully; then put out her hand. "Ah, Guy, I am a worthless little thing," she said, softly, as he took it. It was her left hand & a ring set with diamonds twinkled on it. "Worth all the world to me!" he answered; then lifted the hand to his lips & turned away. As his receding steps sounded through the hall, Georgie Rivers, taking a screen from the mantel-piece, sat down on the rug before the fire, with a thoughtful face out of which all the sauciness had vanished. As she watched the fire-light play on her ring, she began to think half-aloud as her childish fashion was; but Guy was cantering along the high road to West Adamsborough, & if there had been anyone to tell him what she said, he would [have] laughed—& [have] doubted it. As there was no one, however, Georgie kept her meditations to herself. "I know he thinks me a coquette," she whispered, leaning her head against her hand, "& he thinks I like to trifle with him—perhaps he is angry—(he looks very handsome when he is angry) but he doesn't know—how should he?—that I mean to break it off. I ought to have done it today, & I might have ended that beginning of a quarrel by giving him back the ring; but, oh dear, I wish—I wish I didn't care for him quite so much. He is so cool & handsome! And he is the only man I ever knew who neither despises me nor is afraid of me. Oh, Georgie, Georgie, you miserable little fool! I didn't mean to let him kiss my hand; he surprised me into it, just as he surprised me into accepting him. He always puts me off my guard, somehow! But it must be done. Perhaps I *am* in love with him, but I hope I haven't quite lost my common sense. It *must* be done, I say! I declare, I shall make an utter goose of myself in a minute! Where's that letter?" She put her hand into her pocket, & brought out an envelope, pompously sealed with a large coat of arms & motto; &, drawing out the folded sheet which it contained, slowly read aloud these words, written in a crabbed, old-fashioned hand:

6

My dear Miss Rivers: Ever since I was honoured by an introduction to you, my admiration for your charms & accomplishments has increased; & I have been sufficiently marked by your favour to hope that what I am about to say may not seem an entirely unwarrantable liberty. Although we are separated by many years, I do not perceive why that should be an obstacle to a happy union; & I therefore venture to beg that, if the profoundest admiration & respect can awaken responsive sentiments in your own bosom, you will honour me with your hand. I shall await with impatience your reply to my proposals, & am, my dear Miss Rivers, with deep esteem, Your faithful Servant

"Breton."

Georgie folded the letter again, & went on with her reflections in this wise. "I suppose I should have let him know that I was engaged to Guy, but it was so jolly to have an old Lord dangling about one, head over ears in love, &, figuratively speaking, going down on his noble, gouty knees every time one came into the room. And I really didn't think it would come to a climax so soon! I marked him by my favour, did I? And the poor old creature has got tipsy, like an old blue-bottle on a little drop of syrup. He is really in love with me! Me, Georgie Rivers, a wicked, fast, flirtatious little pauper—a lazy, luxurious coquette! Oh, Guy, Guy!—I mean, Oh, Lord Breton, Lord —ha? what's the matter?" For something dropped close by Georgie's ring, that sparkled as clearly in the fire-light as its own diamonds. "Crying! Crying! I thought I had no heart. I have always been told so. Ah, the horrid thing." She brushed the bright thing that was not a diamond away, but just then

7

her eyes brimmed over with two more, & she was obliged to dry them with her pocket handkerchief, talking on all the while. "This is too ridiculous. Georgie getting sentimental! Georgie booh-hoohing over a lover, when she's got a real, live Lord, with a deer-park, & a house in London & ever so much a year, at her feet! What else have I always wished for? But, come, I will think of it calmly. Say I am in love with Guy (if I have no heart, how can I love anybody?) say I am in love with him. He is poor, rather extravagant, lazy & just as luxurious as I am. Now, what should we live on? I should have to mend my clothes, & do the shopping, & I should never ride or dance or do anything worth living for any more; but there would be pinching & patching & starvation (politely called economy) & I should get cross, & Guy would get cross, & we should fight, fight, fight! Now—take the other side of the picture. First, Lord B. is really in love with me. Second, he is venerable, sleepy & fixed in his own ruts, & would give me twice as much liberty as a younger man; third, I should have three fine houses, plenty of horses & as many dresses as I could wear, (& I have a large capacity in that way!) & nothing to do but coquet with all the handsome boys whose heads I chose to turn; fourth, I should be Lady Breton of Lowood, & the first lady in the county! Hurrah!" As Georgie ended this resumé of the advantages of her ancient suitor, she clapped her hands together & jumped up from the hearth-rug. "It must be done. I am sure Guy & I could never be happy together, & I shall write & tell him so, the sooner the better. I suppose Mamma will be a little scandalized, but I can settle that. And when shall I ever have such a chance again?" She reopened Lord Breton's letter, read it for the third time, & then went up to the writing table that stood between the two windows. "The sooner the better, the sooner the better," she repeated, as she sat down & took out a sheet of paper stamped with the Rivers crest. She dipped her pen in ink, dated the blank sheet—& then paused a moment, with contracting eye-brows. "No. I suppose that I must write to Guy first. What shall I say? It is so hard . . . I . . . hush, you little idiot! Are you going to change your mind again?" With this self-addressed rebuke, she re-dipped her pen, & began to write hastily—

Dear Guy: I am sure we can never be happy as anything but friends, & I send you back the ring which will be far better on someone else's hand. You will get over your fancy, & I shall Always be, Your Affectionate Cousin G.R.

To Guy Hastings Esqr.

It was soon over, & she laid the pen down & pushed the paper away quickly, covering her eyes with her hand. The clock, striking the hour on the chimney-piece, roused her with a start. "I suppose I had better take this ring off," she said, slowly, gazing at the hoop of diamonds. "There is no use in hesitating—or the battle is lost. There—what is it, a ring? It will be replaced by another (with bigger diamonds) tomorrow afternoon." She drew it off hurriedly, as though the operation were painful, & then looked at her unadorned hand. "You change owners, poor little hand!" she said softly. Then she kissed the ring & laid it away. After that it was easier to go on with her next note, though she wrote two copies before she was satisfied that it was proper to be sent to the great Lord Breton. The note finally ran thus:

My dear Lord Breton: I was much flattered by your offer, which I accept, remaining Yours truly (I shall be at home tomorrow afternoon.) Georgina Rivers.

"Like answering a dinner-invitation," commented Georgie; "but I can't make it longer. I don't know what to say!"

Chap. II.   Enter Lord Breton.

"Auld Robin Gray cam 'a courtin' me." *Lady Barnard.*

LET IT BE UNDERSTOOD by the reader, in justice to Miss
Rivers, that, before she despatched the note with which our
last chapter closes, she shewed it to her mother. As she had
expected, that lady offered some feeble opposition to her
daughter's bold stroke. It was early the next morning & Mrs.
Rivers—a nervous invalid, of the complainingly resigned sort
—was still in her bedroom, though the younger members of
the family, Kate, Julia & Tom, had breakfasted & been called
to their lessons, by Miss Blackstone, their governess. Georgie
therefore found her mother alone, when she entered with the
answer to Lord Breton's letter in her hand; & it was easy, after
one glance at the small figure on the couch, with faded hair,
pink lids & yielding wrinkles about the mouth, to see why,
though "Mamma would be a little scandalized" it would be
easy to "settle that." If Mrs. Rivers had ever been a beauty
much mourning & malady had effaced all traces thereof from
her gentle, sallow face framed in a heavy widow's cap; she was
one of those meek, shrinking women who seem always overwhelmed by their clothes, & indeed by circumstances in general. She greeted her daughter's entrance with a faint smile, &
observed in a thin, timid voice "that it was a beautiful morning." "Yes," said Georgie, kissing her, "jolly for hunting. How

did you sleep, little Mamma?" "Oh, well enough, my dear—
as well as I could have hoped," said Mrs. Rivers, sighing. "Of
course Peters forgot my sleeping-draught when he went into
West Adamsborough yesterday, but what else could I expect?"
"I am very sorry! The man never had his proper allowance of
brains." "Nay, my dear, I do not complain." "But I do," said
Georgie, impatiently. "I hate to be resigned!" "My child!"
"You know I do, Mamma. But I want to speak to you now.
Will Payson be coming in for anything?" "Indeed I can't tell,
my dear." (Mrs. Rivers was never in her life known to express
a positive opinion on any subject.) "Very well, then" said
Georgie, "I will make sure." She locked the door, & then came
& sat down at her mother's feet. "Now, Mamma, I am going
to shock you," she said. "Oh, my dear, I hope not." "But I tell
you that I am," persisted Georgie. "Now listen. I have decided
that I shouldn't be happy with Guy, & I have written to tell
him so." Mrs. Rivers looked startled. "What has happened,
my love?" she asked anxiously. "I hope you have not been
quarrelling. Guy is a good boy." "No, we have not been quarrelling—at least, not exactly. But I have thought it all over.
Guy & I would never get on. And I am going to accept Lord
Breton!" "Good gracious, my dear!" cried Mrs. Rivers, in
mingled horror & admiration at her daughter's sudden decision. "But what will Guy say? . . . Have you reflected? . . ." "I
have set Guy free; therefore I am at liberty to accept Lord
Breton." "But—so soon? I don't understand," said poor Mrs.
Rivers, in humble perplexity. "Of course the engagement will
not be announced at once; but Lord Breton's letter requires an
answer & I have written it." She handed the note to her mother,
who looked over it with her usual doubtful frown, but whose

only comment was a meek suggestion that it was very short. "I can't write four pages to say I'll accept him," said Georgie, sharply; & Mrs. Rivers, reflecting that her unusual crossness was probably due to concealed agitation, only said mildly, "but poor Guy." "Why do you pity Guy, Mamma? He will be rid of me, & if he *is* really in love with me—why, men get over those things very quickly." "But I cannot help thinking, my dear . . ." "Don't, Mamma!" cried Georgie, passionately, "don't think. I have made up my mind, & if you talk all day you can only make me cry." The last word was almost a sob, & Georgie turned sharply away from her mother. "I am afraid you are unhappy, darling child." "Why should I be?" burst out Georgie, with sudden fierceness. "Don't be so foolish Mamma! Why should I be unhappy? It is my own choice, & I don't want to be pitied!" She ran out of the room as she ended, & Mrs. Rivers' anxious ears heard her bedroom door slam a moment later. The note was sent duly, that morning; & in the afternoon the various members of the family saw, from their respective windows, Lord Breton of Lowood ride up to the door of Holly Lodge. Georgie, with an unusual colour in her face, which was set off by the drooping ruffle of lace about her soft throat, came in to her mother's room for a kiss & a word or two. Now that Guy's ring had really been sent back, she seemed to have nerved herself to go through the day resolutely; & with a quick, firm step, & her head higher than its wont she went downstairs to meet her suitor. Lord Breton was leaning against the mantel-piece where Guy had stood yesterday; & it would have been hard to find a greater contrast to that handsome young gentleman than Georgie's noble lover. Fifty-eight years of what is commonly called hard living had left heavy traces on what in its day was known as a fine figure; & in the Lord Breton whom some few could remember as "that gay young buck" the present generation saw nothing but a gray gouty old gentleman, who evidently enjoyed his port wine & sherry generously. He came forward as Georgie entered, & bending over her hand (it was not the hand that Guy had kissed) said, pompously: "I need not say how deeply I feel the honour you confer on me, Miss Rivers. This is indeed a happy day!" "Thank you," said Georgie, with a wild desire to draw her hand away; "you are very kind, Lord Breton." "No, no," returned his lordship affably; "I only rejoice in being allowed to call mine a young lady so abundantly endowed with every charm as Miss Rivers—as—May I call you Georgina?" Georgie started; no one had ever called her by her name, preferring the boyish abbreviation which seemed to suit her lively, plump prettiness best; but, after all, it was better he should not call her as Guy did. Georgina was more suitable for the future Lady Breton. "You have won the right to do so," she said, as she sat down, & Lord Breton took a chair opposite, at an admiring distance. "A most precious right," he replied, conjuring up the ghost of what some might recall as a fascinating smile; but which was more like a bland leer to the eye unassisted by memory. "Let me assure you," he continued, "that I know how little a man of my advanced years deserves to claim the attention of a young lady in the lovely bloom of youth; but—ahem— I hope that the name, the title—& above all the respect & esteem which I lay at her feet may compensate—" he paused, & evidently wondered that Georgie did not reply to this sublime condescension; but as she was silent, he was forced to take up the thread of his speech. "As I said in my letter, you will

remember, Miss . . . Ah . . . Georgina—as I said in my letter,
I do not see why difference of age should be an obstacle to a
happy union; & as—ahem—& since your views so happily coin-
cide with mine, permit me to—to adorn this lovely hand with
—a—with—" here Lord Breton, finding that his eloquence had
for the moment run dry, supplied the lack of speech by action,
& producing a brilliant ruby set in large diamonds, slipped it
on Georgie's passive hand. "I hope you will accept this, as a
slight token of—of . . ." "It is very beautiful," said Georgie,
colouring with pleasure, as the dark fire of the ruby set off the
whiteness of her hand. "You are most generous. But you will
forgive me if I do not wear it, at least in public. I should prefer
not to have the engagement announced at once." Lord Breton
looked justly astonished, as he might have done if a crossing-
sweeper to whom he had tossed a shilling had flung it back in
his face. "May I ask why this—this secrecy must be preserved?"
he said, in a tone of profound, but suppressed, indignation; remembering, just in time, that though the wife is a legitimate
object of wrath, it is wise to restrain one's self during court-
ship. "I am going to shew you what a spoiled child I am, by
refusing to tell you," said Georgie, putting on an air of imperious mischievousness to hide her growing agitation, "& I
know you will humour me. I am so used to having my own
way, that it might be dangerous to deprive me of it!" If she
had not said this with a most enchanting smile, naughty & yet
appealing, Lord Breton might not have been so easily ap-
peased; but being charmed with this pretty display of wilful-
ness (as men are apt to be before marriage) & concluding that
her mother might have something to do with the obstruction
she would not name, he only said, with a bow, "The loss is on

my side, however! I shall count the days until I can proclaim to the world what a prize I have won." Georgie laughed; a sweet, little bird-like laugh, which was as resistless as her pout. "You pay me so many compliments that I shall be more spoiled than ever! But you will not have to wait long, I promise you." "No waiting can be very long while I am privileged to enjoy your companionship," said Lord Breton, rising to the moment triumphantly. "Oh, for shame! Worse & worse!" cried Georgie. "But I think Mamma is in the study. Won't you come in & see her?"

Chap. III. Jilted.

―――― "There can be no reason
Why, when quietly munching your dry-toast & butter
Your nerves should be suddenly thrown in a flutter
At the sight of a neat little letter addressed
In a woman's handwriting." *Robert Lytton*: Lucile.

GUY HASTINGS WAS FINISHING an unusually late breakfast
at his favourite resort in London, Swift's Club, St. James St.,
on the morning after his parting with Georgie, when a note
addressed in her well-known hand, with its girlish affectation
of masculiness, was handed to him by a Club servant. Although he was surprised that she should have written so soon,
(she seldom, during his trips to London, wrote to him at all)
he was not excited by any stronger emotion than surprise &
slight curiosity, for the words that passed between them the
day before had appeared to him nothing more than a lover's
quarrel developed by bad weather & ennui & he was too well
accustomed to unaccountable phases in his cousin's April character to imagine that anything serious could be its consequence.
A man, however, who is as deeply in love as Guy was, does not
have a letter in the beloved one's handwriting long unopened;
& though a pile of other envelopes "To Guy Hastings Esqr."
were pushed aside until fuller leisure after breakfast, he broke
Georgie's seal at once. One glance at the hurriedly written

lines sufficed to change the aspect of life completely. At first there came a sense of blank bewilderment, followed, upon reflection, by indignation at this undeserved slight; & these emotions combined were enough to make him turn from the breakfast-table, thrusting the package which contained the ring into his breast-pocket, to escape from the clatter & movement of the breakfast room. One might have supposed that every member of the club would be off shooting, fishing, hunting or travelling at this unfashionable time, but of course, as Guy went down to take refuge in the reading-room he was fastened upon by a veteran club bore, who talked to him for half an hour by the clock, while all the time Georgie's note was burning in his pocket. At last the bore discovered that he had an engagement, & with deep regret (more for Guy's sake than his own) was obliged to break off in the midst of an Indian anecdote; but he was replaced almost immediately by Capt. Doublequick of the _____th, who always had a new scandal to feast his friends on, & now for dearth of listeners, came to tell Guy the fullest details of "that affair with young Wiggins & the little French Marquise." This delectable history, embellished with the Capt.'s usual art, lasted fully another half hour; & Guy was in the last stages of slow torture when the unconscious Doublequick espied a solitary man at the other end of the room who had *not* heard all about "young Wiggins." Left to himself, Guy, with the masculine instinct of being always as comfortable as possible, settled himself in an armchair, & reread Georgie's note, slowly, carefully & repeatedly, as though he fancied it might be an optical delusion after all. But it was one of Georgie's virtues to write a clear hand. The cruel words were there, & remained the same, read them as he would. At last, as he sat half-stupidly staring at the few lines, a purpose formed itself within him to write at once & ask the meaning of them. Think as he would, he could not remember having, by word or act, justified Georgie in sending him such a letter; & he concluded that the best thing & the simplest he could do, was to demand an explanation. He loved her too deeply & reverently to believe that she could mean to throw him over thus; he thought he knew the depths & shallows of her character, & though he was not blind to her faults, he would never have accused her, even in the thought, of such unwarranted heartlessness. Having determined, then, on this first step, he called for pen & paper, & after tearing up several half-written sheets, folded & sealed this letter.

What have I done to deserve the note I got from you this morning? Why do you send the ring back? God knows I love you better than anyone on earth, & if I am at fault, it is ignorantly. If you have found out you don't care for me, tell me so—but for Heaven's sake don't throw me over in this way without a word of explanation. G.H.
Miss Rivers. Holly Lodge, Morley-near-W. Adamsbro.

Every one of those few words came straight from Guy's heart; for Georgie Rivers had been his one "grande passion," & his love for her perhaps the noblest, strongest feeling he was capable of. Indeed, I am disposed to think that the life of "a man about town" (the life which Guy had led since his college days five years before) is apt to blunt every kind of feeling into a well-bred monotone of ennui, & it is a wonder to me that he had preserved so strong & intact the capacity of really "falling in love." Of course, he had had a dozen little affaires de coeurs here & there before his heart was really touched; a man who lives as fast & free as Guy Hastings had done, seldom escapes without "the least little touch of the spleen"—but he had outgrown them one after another as people do outgrow those inevitable diseases, until the fatal malady seized him in the shape of his pretty cousin. His love for her had influenced his whole life, & blent itself into his one real talent, for painting, so that he sketched her bewitching little head a thousand & one times, & looked forward in the future, after his marriage, to turning his brush to account, selling his pictures high, &, in the still dimmer To-be becoming an R.A. How many an idle amateur has dreamed in this fashion! Meanwhile, he had enjoyed himself, made love to her, & lived neither better nor worse than a hundred other young men of that large class delightful for acquaintance, but dangerous for matrimony, whom susceptible young ladies call "fascinating" & anxious mothers "fast." Now, though like takes to like, it is seldom that two people of the same social tastes fall in love with each other; Mr. Rapid, who has been in all the escapades going, & connected with a good many of the most popular scandals, is attracted by Miss Slow, just out of a religious boarding-school, with downcast eyes & monosyllabic conversation; Miss Rapid, who has always been what Punch calls "a leetle fast," settles down to domesticity with good, meek-minded Mr. Slow. Such is the time-honoured law of contrasts. But Guy Hastings & Georgie were one of those rare exceptions said to prove the rule which they defy. If Guy had tasted the good things of life generously, his cousin was certainly not wanting in a spice of fastness. Yet these two sinners fell mutually in love at first sight, & remained in that ecstatic condition until Georgie's un-

accountable note seemed to turn the world temporarily up-
side-down. That unaccountable note! After answering it &
calling for a servant to post his answer, he thrust it away in his
pocket, & since "there was no help for it," resolved to make
the best of the matter by forgetting it as quickly as possible.
There are few young men who do not turn with an instinct of
abhorrence from the contemplation of anything painful; &
some possess the art of "drowning dull care" completely. Guy,
however, could not shake his disagreeable companion off; &
he must have shewed it in his face, for as he was leaving the
club, in the forlorn hope of finding some note or message from
Georgie at his rooms, a familiar voice called out "Hullo, Guy
Fawkes, my boy! I didn't know you were in town! Had a row?
What makes your mustachios look so horridly dejected?"
"Jack Egerton!" exclaimed Guy, turning to face the speaker, a
short, wiry-built little man with reddish whiskers & honest
gray eyes, who laid a hand on his shoulder, & gravely scanned
him at arm's length. Guy laughed rather uneasily. No man
likes to think that another has guessed his inmost feelings at
first sight. "Yes," said Egerton, slowly, "your Fortunatus purse
has run out again, & Poole has too much sense to send that
blue frock coat home, or you've had a row about some pretty
little votary of the drama, & been O jolly thrashed—or—
Araminta, or Chloe or Belinda (we won't say which) has been
shewing you some charming phase in her character usually
reserved for post-nuptial display. Come now, Knight of the
Dolorous Visage, which is it?" Jack Egerton (commonly
called Jack-All, from his wonderful capacity for doing everything, knowing everybody & being everywhere) although by
some years Guy's senior, had known him at Cambridge (poor

Jack was there through several sets of new men) & had struck up a warm friendship with him which nothing since had shaken. Egerton shared Guy's artistic inclinations, & was like him "a man about town," & a general favourite, so that the similarity of their life had thrown them together ever since they forsook the shade of Alma Mater, Jack steering the "young Duke" as he always called Guy, out of many a scrape, & Guy replenishing Jack's purse when his own would allow of such liberality. Guy then, who would not have betrayed himself to any other living man, found it a great relief to unburden his woes to Jack Egerton, knowing that he possessed the rare talent of keeping other people's secrets as jealously as his own. "Hang it, there *is* a row," said the lover, pulling the dejected moustache. "But for Heaven's sake come out of this place. We shall be seized upon by some proses in a minute. Come along." He ran his arm through Egerton's, & the two sallied forth into the streets, making for the deserted region of Belgravia. It was not until they were in the most silent part of that dreary Sahara between the iron railings of a Duke who was off in Scotland, & the shut windows of an Earl who had gone to Italy, that Jack, who knew his companion "au fond," broke the silence by, "Well, my boy?" Guy glared suspiciously at a dirty rag-picker who was expressing to himself & his rag-bag the deepest astonishment "that them two young swells should be 'ere at this time o' year"; but even that innocent offender soon passed by, & left him secure to make his confession in entire privacy. "Look here" he said, taking Georgie's note from his pocket & handing it to Egerton. (Although the engagement between them, which had been of short duration, was kept private, he was shrewd enough to guess that his friend

knew of it.) Jack, leaning against the Duke's railings, perused
the short letter slowly; then folded it up & relieved himself by
a low whistle. "Well?" groaned Guy, striking his stick sharply
against His grace's area-gate, "What do you think of that? Of
course you know that we were engaged, & she always said she
cared for me, & all that—until *that* thing came this morning."
Jack looked meditatively at his friend. "I beg pardon," he said,
slowly, "but did you have a row when you last saw her?" "No,
upon my honour none that I was conscious of! It was yesterday
—beastly weather, you remember, & we were a little cross, but
we made it up all right—at least, I thought so." "Of course you
thought so," said Jack, calmly; "The question is, who provoked
the quarrel?" "God knows—if there was a quarrel—I did not.
I would go to the ends of the earth for her, Jack!" "Then—
excuse me again, old boy—then *she* tried to pick a quarrel?"
Guy paused—it seemed treason to breathe a word against his
lady, & yet he could not but recall how strange her behaviour
had been—"I—I believe I bored her," he stammered, not caring to meet Jack's eyes. "Did she tell you so?" "Well—yes; but,
you know, she often chaffs, & I thought—I thought . . ." "You
thought it was a little love-quarrel to kill time, eh?" said Jack,
in his short, penetrating way. "Well, my dear boy, so it might
have been, but I don't think it was." "What do you think
then?" said Guy, anxiously. "Don't be afraid to tell me, old
fellow." "Look here, then. You are a handsome young gaillard
—just the sort that women like, the worse luck for you!—& I
haven't a doubt your cousin (she shall not be named) fell in
love with you. But—taking a slight liberty with the proverb—
"fall in love in haste, repent at leisure"—How much have you
got to support a wife on?" "Deucedly little," said Guy, bit-

terly. "Exactly. And you like to live like a swell, & have plenty of money to pitch in the gutter, when society requires it of you. Now, I dare say your cousin knows this." "Well?" "Well—& she has more good sense & just as much heart as most young ladies of our advanced civilization. She has had the wit to see what you, poor fool, sublimely overlooked—that what is comfort for one is pinching for two (or—ahem! three)—& the greater wit to tell you so before it is too late." Jack paused, & looked Guy directly in the face. "Do you understand?" "I don't know . . . I . . . for Heaven's sake, Jack, out with it," groaned the lover. Jack's look was of such deep, kindly pity as we cast on a child, whom we are going to tell that its goldfish is dead or its favourite toy broken. "My poor boy," he said, gently, "don't you see that you have been—jilted?"—

Chap. IV. The End of the Idyl.

"Through you, whom once I loved so well—
Through you my life will be accursed."

GEORGIE HAD JUST COME home from a ride to the meet with
Lord Breton, on the day after her engagement to that venerable
peer, when her mother called to her that there was a letter on
her table upstairs in Guy's handwriting. Georgie changed
colour; she had not expected this, & had thought to cast off
"the old love" more easily. It came now like a ghost that steals
between the feaster & his wine-cup; a ghost of old wrongs that
he thought to have laid long ago but that rises again & again
to cast a shadow on life's enjoyments. Georgie, however, determined to take the bull by the horns, & went up to her room
at once; but she paused a moment before the pier-glass to smile
back at the reflection of her trim figure in the dark folds of a
faultless habit, & crowned by the most captivating little "top-
per" from under which a few little brown curls *would* escape,
despite the precaution which Georgie of course *always* took to
brush them back into their place. Then, setting her saucy, rose-
bud mouth firmly, she turned from the glass & opened Guy's
letter. If she had not been very angry at his having written at
all, she might have been in danger of giving Lord Breton the
slip, & coming back to her first choice; for she did love Guy,
though such a poor, self-despising thing as love could have no

legitimate place in the breast of the worldly-wise Miss Rivers! But she *was* angry with Guy, & having read his appeal tore it up, stamped her foot & nearly broke her riding-whip in the outburst of her rage. After that, she locked her door, & threw herself into what she called her "Crying-chair"; a comfortable, cushioned seat which had been the confidante of many a girlish fit of grief & passion. Having cried her eyes into the proper shade of pinkness, all the while complaining bitterly of Guy's cruelty & the hardness of the world, & her own unhappy fate, she began to think that his letter must nevertheless be answered, & having bathed her injured lids and taken an encouraging look at Lord Breton's ruby flashing on her left hand, she wrote thus:

My dear Guy: I don't think I deserved your reproaches, or, if I did, you must see that I am not worth your love. But I will tell you everything plainly. Knowing (as I said before) that we could never be happy together, I have engaged myself to Lord Breton. You will thank me some day for finding our feelings out & releasing you before it was too late—though of course I expect you to be angry with me now. Believe me, I wish that we may always be friends; & it is for that reason that I speak to you so frankly. My engagement to Lord Breton will not be announced yet. With many wishes for your happiness, Yours

"Georgina" Rivers.
To Guy Hastings Esqr. Swift's Club, Regent St. London W.

Georgie was clever & politic enough to know that such desperate measures were the only ones which could put an end to this unpleasant matter; but she was really sorry for Guy

& wanted to make the note as kind & gentle as possible. Perhaps Guy felt the sting none the less that it was so adroitly sheathed in protestations of affection & unworthiness. He was alone in the motley apartment, half-studio, half smoking-room & study, which opened off his bedroom at his London lodgings. He had not had the heart to stay at the Club after he had breakfasted; but pocketed Georgie's note (which was brought to him there) & went home at once. Inevitable business had detained him in town the day before, but he had determined to run down to West Adamsborough that morning, having prepared Georgie by his note. Now his plans, & indeed his whole life, seemed utterly changed. There comes a time in the experience of most men when their faith in womankind is shaken pretty nearly to its foundations; & that time came to Guy Hastings as he sat by his fire, with a bust of Pallas (adorned by a Greek cap & a faded blue breast-knot) presiding over him, & read his dismissal. But here I propose to spare my reader. I suppose every lover raves in the same rhetoric, when his mistress plays him false, & when to you, Sylvia, or you, Damon, that bitter day comes, you will know pretty accurately how Guy felt & what Guy said. Let us, then, pass over an hour, & reenter our hero's domain with Jack Egerton, who, at about 11 o'clock, gave his sharp, short rap at the door of that sanctum. "Who the devil is it?" said Guy, savagely, starting at the sound. "Your Mentor." "Jack?—Confound you!—Well, come in if you like." "I do like, most decidedly," said Egerton briskly, sending a puff of balmy Havana smoke before him as he entered. "What's the matter *now*? I've been at Swift's after you, & didn't half expect to find you moping here." "I don't care where I am," said Guy with a groan. "Sit down. What is the use of living?" "Shall I answer you from a scientific, theological or moral point of view?" "Neither. Don't be a fool." "Oh," with a slight shrug, "I thought you might like me to keep you company." Guy growled. "I don't know whether you want to be kicked or not," he said, glaring at poor Jack, "but I feel deucedly like trying it." "Do, my dear fellow! If it will shake you out of this agreeable fit of the dumps I shall feel that it is not paying too dearly." Guy was silent for a moment; then he picked up Georgie's letter & held it at arm's length, before his friend. "Look there," he said. Jack nodded. "My death warrant." He stooped down & pushed it deep into the smouldering coals—it burst into a clear flame, & then died out & turned to ashes. "Woman's love," observed Jack sententiously. Jack was a boasted misogynist, & if he had not pitied Guy from the depths of his honest heart, might have felt some lawful triumph in the stern way in which his favourite maxim, "Woman is false" was brought home to his long unbelieving friend; such a triumph as that classic bore, Mentor, doubtless experienced when Telemachus broke loose from the rosy toils of Calypso. "There," he continued. "If you have the pluck to take your fancy—your passion—whatever you choose to call it, & burn it as you burned that paper, I have some hopes for you." Guy sat staring absently at the red depths of the falling fire. "Did a woman ever serve you so, Jack?" he asked, suddenly, facing about & looking at Egerton sharply; but Jack did not flinch. "No," he said in a voice of the profoundest scorn; "I never gave one of them a chance to do it. You might as well say, did I ever pick up a rattle-snake, let it twist round my arm & say: 'Bite!' No, decidedly not!" "Then you believe that all women are the same?" "What else have I always preached to

28

you?" cried Jack, warming with his favourite subject. "What does Pope say? 'Every woman is at heart a rake'! And Pope knew 'em. And I know 'em. Look here; your cousin is not the only woman you've had to do with. How did the others treat you? Ah—I remember the innkeeper's daughter that vacation in Wales, my boy!" "Don't," said Guy reddening angrily. "It was my own fault. I was only a boy, & I was a fool to think I cared for the girl—that's nothing. *She* is the only woman I ever loved!" "So much the better. The more limited one's experience, the less harm it will do. Only guard yourself from repeating such a favourite folly." "There's no danger of that!" "I hope not," said Egerton. "But I have got a plan to propose to you. After such a little complaint as you have been suffering from, change of scene & climate is considered the best cure. Come to Italy with me, old fellow!" "To Italy!" Guy repeated. "When? How soon?" "The day after tomorrow." "But—I—I meant—I hoped . . . to see her again." Jack rapped the floor impatiently with his stick. "What? Expose yourself to the contempt & insult, or still worse, the pity, of a woman who has jilted you? For Heaven's sake, lad, keep hold of your senses!" "You think I oughtn't to go, then?" said Guy, anxiously. "Go! —out of the fryingpan into the fire I should call it," stormed Jack, pacing up & down the littered room. "No. He must be a poor-spirited fellow who swims back for salvation to the ship that his pitched him overboard! No. Come abroad with me, as soon as you can get your traps together, & let the whole thing go to the deuce as fast as it can." Jack paused to let his words take effect; & Guy sat, with his head leaning on his hand, still studying the ruins of the fire. At last he sprang up & caught his shrewd-headed friend by the hand. "By Jove,

Jack, you're right. What have we got to live for but our art? Come along. Let's go to Italy—tomorrow, if you can, Jack!" And go they did, the next day. As his friends used to say of him, "Jack's the fellow for an emergency." His real, anxious affection for Guy, & his disinterested kind-heartedness conquered every obstacle to so hasty & unexpected a departure; & four days after he parted with Georgie in the drawingroom of Holly Lodge, Guy Hastings was on his way to Calais, looking forward, through the distorting spectacles of a disappointed love, to a long, dreary waste of life which was only one degree better than its alternative, the utter chaos of death.

Chap. V. Lady Breton of Lowood.

"A sorrow's crown of sorrow is remembering happier things."
Tennyson: Locksley Hall.

IT IS SOMETIMES WONDERFUL to me how little it takes to
make people happy. How short a time is needed to bury a
grief, how little is needed to cover it! What Salvandy once said
in a political sense, "Nous dansons sur un volcan," is equally
true of life. We trip lightly over new graves & gulfs of sorrow
& separation; we piece & patch & draw together the torn woof
of our happiness; yet sometimes our silent sorrows break
through the slight barrier we have built to ward them off, &
look us sternly in the face—

A month after Guy Hastings & Egerton started on their
wanderings southward, Miss Rivers' engagement to Lord
Breton of Lowood was made known to the fashionable
world, & a month after that (during which the fashionable
world had time to wag its tongue over the nine-day's wonder
of the old peer's being caught by that "fast little chit") Georgie became Lady Breton. As a county paper observed: "The
brilliant espousals were celebrated with all the magnificence
of wealth directed by taste." Georgie, under her floating mist
of lace went up the aisle with a slow step, & not a few noticed
how intensely pale she was; but when she came out on her
husband's arm her colour had revived & she walked quickly

& bouyantly. Of course Mrs. Rivers was in tears; & Kate & Julia, in their new rôle of bridemaids fluttered about everywhere; & Miss Blackstone put on a gown of Bismarck-coloured poplin (her favourite shade) & a bonnet of surprising form & rainbow tints, in honour of the occasion. But perhaps the real moment of Georgie's triumph was when the carriage rolled through the grand gateways of Lowood, & after long windings through stately trees & slopes of shaven lawn, passed before the door of her new home. Her heart beat high as Lord Breton, helping her to descend, led her on his arm through the wide hall lined by servants; she felt now that no stakes would have been too high to win this exquisite moment of possessorship. A fortnight after this brought on the bright, busy Christmas season; & as Lord Breton was desirous of keeping it festively, invitations were sent out right & left. Georgie, although perhaps she had not as much liberty as she had dreamed, found her husband sufficiently indulgent, unless his express wishes were crossed; when, as the game-keeper once remarked, "His lordship were quite *piq*nacious." She enjoyed, too, the character of Lady Bountiful, & the tribute of obsequious flattery which everybody is ready to pay to the mistress of a hospitable house; but it was not long before she felt that these passing triumphs, which her girlish fancy had exaggerated, palled on her in proportion as they became an understood part of her life; praise loses half its sweetness when it is expected. At first she would not confess to herself the great want that seemed to be growing undefinably into her life; but as the gulf widened, she could not overlook it. There is but one Lethe for those who are haunted by a life's mistake; & Georgie plunged into it. I have hinted that she had had a reputation for fastness in her unmarried days; this reputation, which grew as much out of a natural vivacity & daring as out of anything marked in her conduct, grew to be a truth after she became Lady Breton. She dashed into the crowd to escape the ghosts that peopled her solitude with vague reproaches; & as the incompleteness of her mischosen life grew upon her day by day it gave new impetus to the sort of moral opium-eating which half-stifled memory. Lord Breton did not care to stay her; he took a certain pride in the glitter that his young wife's daring manners carried with them; for in pretty women, fastness has always more or less fascination. And Georgie had to perfection the talent of being "fast." She was never coarse, never loud, never disagreeably masculine; but there was a resistless, saucy élan about her that carried her a little beyond the average bounds laid for a lady's behaviour. It seemed as though her life never stood still, but rushed on with the hurry & brawl of the streamlet that cannot hide the stones clogging its flow. Altogether, she fancied herself happy; but there were moments when she might have said, with Miss Ingelow: "My old sorrow wakes & cries"; moments when all the hubbub of the present could not drown the low reproach of the past. It was a very thin partition that divided Georgie from her skeleton.

One day, when the last Christmas guests had departed from Lowood, & the new relay had not arrived, Lord Breton, who was shut up with a sharp attack of gout, sent a servant to Georgie's dressing-room, to say that he would like to see my lady. She came to him at once, for even his company, & his slow, pompous speeches, were better than that dreadful solitude; although gout did not sweeten his temper. "My dear," he said, "seeing that ivory chess-board in the drawing-room yesterday suggested to me an occupation while I am confined to my chair. I used to be a fair player once. Will you kindly have the board brought up?" As it happened, Georgie had not played a game of chess since the afternoon of her parting with Guy, & her husband's words, breaking upon a train of sad thought (she had been alone nearly all day) jarred her strangely. "Chess!" she said, with a start. "Oh, I—I had rather not. Excuse me. I hate chess. Couldn't we play something else?" Lord Breton looked surprised. "Is the game so repugnant to you that I may not ask you to gratify me this afternoon?" he asked, serenely; & Georgie felt almost ashamed of her weakness. "I beg your pardon," she said. "I play very badly, & could only bore you." "I think I can instruct you," said Lord Breton, benignly; mistaking her aversion for humility, & delighted at the display of this wife-like virtue. "Oh, no, indeed. I am so stupid about those things. And I don't like the game." "I hoped you might conquer your dislike for my sake. You forget that I lead a more monotonous existence than yours, when confined by this unfortunate malady." Lord Breton's very tone spoke unutterable things; but if Georgie could have mastered her feeling, the spirit of opposition alone would have been enough to prick her on now. "I am sorry," she said, coldly, "that my likes & dislikes are not under better control. I cannot play chess." "You cannot, or will not?" "Whichever you please," said Georgie, composedly. Lord Breton's wrath became evident in the contraction of his heavy brows; that a man with *his* positive ideas about wifely submission, & marital authority, should have his reproofs answered thus! "I do not think," he observed, "that you consider what you are saying." "I seldom

34

do," said Georgia, with engaging frankness. "You know I am quite incorrigible." "I confess, Lady Breton, I do not care for such trifling." "I was afraid I was boring you. I am going to drive into Morley. Shall I order you any books from the library?" enquired Georgie, graciously. But as she rose to go, Lord Breton's ire burst out. "Stay!" he exclaimed, turning red up to his rough eye-brows. "I repeat, Lady Breton, that I do not think you know what you are saying. This trivial evasion of so simple [a] request displeases me; & I must again ask you to sacrifice part of your afternoon to the claims of your husband." Georgie, who [was] standing with her hand on the door, did not speak; but her eyes gave him back flash for flash. "Will you oblige me by ringing for the chess-board?" continued Lord Breton, rigidly. "Certainly. Perhaps you can get Williamson to play with you," said Georgie, pulling the bell. (Williamson was my lord's confidential valet.) "I beg your pardon. I believe I have already asked *you* to perform that function, Lady Breton." "And I believe that I have already refused," said Georgie, regaining her coolness in proportion as her husband grew more irate. At this moment, Williamson appeared, & Lord Breton ordered him to bring up the chess-board. When he was gone, Georgie saw that matters had gone too far for trifling. She had set her whole, strong will against playing the game, & she resolved that Lord Breton should know it at once. "I do not suppose," she said, looking him directly in the face, "that you mean to drive me into obeying by force. Once for all, I cannot & I will not, do as you ask me. You have insulted me by speaking to me as if I were a perverse child, & not the head of your house; but I don't mean to lose my temper. I know that gout is very trying." With this Parthian shot, she turned & left the room. Lord Breton, boiling with rage, called after her—but what can a man tied to his chair with the gout do against a quick-witted strategist in petticoats? Lord Breton began to think that this wife-training was, after all, not mere child's play. This was the first declaration of open war; but it put Lord Breton on the alert, & spurred Georgie into continual opposition. After all, she said to herself, quarrelling was better than [the] heavy monotony of peace; Lord Breton was perhaps not quite such a bore when worked into a genuine passion, as when trying to be ponderously gallant. Poor Georgie! When she appeared on her husband's arm at the county balls & dinners in the flash of her diamonds & the rustle of her velvet & lace, it seemed a grand thing to be Lady Breton of Lowood; but often, after those very balls & dinners, when she had sent her hundred-eyed maid away, & stood before the mirror taking off her jewels, she felt that, like Cinderella, after one of those brief triumphs, she was going back to the ashes & rags of reality.

Chap. VI. At Rome.

"I & he, Brothers in art." *Tennyson.*

A LARGE STUDIO on the third floor of a Roman palazzo; a
room littered & crowded & picturesque in its disorderliness, as
only a studio can be. A white cast of Aphrodite relieved by a
dull tapestry background representing a wan Susannah dip-
ping her foot in the water, while two muddy-coloured elders
glare through a time-eaten bough; an Italian stove surmounted
by a coloured sporting print, a Toledo blade & a smashed
Tyrolean hat; in one corner a lay-figure with the costumes of
a nun, a brigand, a sultana & a Greek girl piled on indis-
criminately; in another an easel holding a large canvas on
which was roughly sketched the head of a handsome contadina.
Such was the first mixed impression which the odd furnishing
of the room gave to a newcomer; although a thousand lesser
oddities, hung up, artist-fashion, everywhere, made a background of bright colours for these larger objects. It was a soft
February day, & the window by which Guy Hastings sat (he
was lounging on its broad, uncushioned sill) was opened; so
that the draught blew the puffs from his cigarette hither &
thither before his face. Jack Egerton, who shared the studio
with him, was painting before a small easel, adding the last
crimson touches to a wild Campagna sunset, & of course they
kept the ball flying between them pretty steadily, as the one

37

worked & the other watched. "That will be a success," observed Guy, critically. "For whom did you say it was painted?" "A fellow named Graham, an English merchant, with about as much knowledge of art as you & I have of roadmaking. But it is such a delightful rarity to sell a picture, that I don't care who gets it." "How did he happen to be trapped?" Jack laughed. "Why, I met him at your handsome Marchese's the other day, & she made a little speech about my superhuman genius, which led him to take some gracious notice of me. I hinted that he might have seen one of my pictures (that confounded thing that Vianelli's had for a month) in a shop-window on the Corso, & he remembered it, & enquired the price. 'Very sorry' said I, 'but the thing is sold. To an English Earl, an amateur, whose name I am not at liberty to mention.' He gobbled the bait at once, ordered this at a splendid price, & I ran down to Vianelli's, let him into my little game, told him to send the picture home at once, & then sent some flowers to the Marchese!" Guy laughed heartily at his friend's ruse, & then observed, "I wish you had mentioned that *I* had some pictures which I would part with as a favour." "By degrees, my boy, by degrees. He will come to the studio, to see this chef-d'oeuvre, & then you shall be introduced as a painter of whose fame he has of course etc., etc. By the way, I shouldn't wonder if he came today." Guy knocked the ashes off his cigarette & got up from his seat. "I thought Teresina would have come this morning," he said, "but I hope she won't. She gets so confoundedly frightened when anybody comes in, & one feels like such a fool." "Guy!" said Egerton, suddenly, laying down his brush. "Well, old fellow?" "Are you going to make an ass of yourself?" "Not that I know of. How do you mean?" Guy stood opposite his friend, & looked him frankly in the face. "I mean," said Jack, resuming his work, "Are you going to fancy yourself in love with this pretty little peasant, & get into no end of a scrape?" "I don't know." "Well, then, be warned. What is the saying? Le jeu ne vaut pas la chandelle." "Very likely not. But . . . Ah, here she is. I know that tremulous little knock." Guy opened the door as he spoke, to admit a contadina, in holyday dress, with a gold chain about her soft olive throat & a clean white head-dress above her lustrous braids pinned with a silver dagger. She could not have been more than 16 years old, & was of that purest type of the Roman peasant which is so seldom met with nowadays. Her large, languid blue-black eyes were so heavily fringed that when she looked downward (as she almost always did, from an instinct of fawn-like timidity) they scarcely gleamed through their veil; & there was not a tinge of colour in the transparent olive cheek which made her full, sensitive mouth look all the redder as it parted on a row of pearl-white teeth, when Guy greeted her with his usual gentle gayety. It was no wonder that Jack had his fears. Little Teresina, with her trembling shyness & her faint smiles, & her low, sweet Italian, was a more dangerous siren than many an accomplished woman of the world. "I expected you" said Guy, smiling, as she stepped timidly into the room; & speaking in Italian, which Jack, as he bent quietly over his work, wished more than ever to understand. "Look here," Guy continued, pointing to the sketched head in the corner, "I have not touched it since because I knew I could not catch those eyes or that sweet, frightened smile without looking at you again." As he spoke, he moved the easel out into its place, & began to collect his brushes, while Teresina went

quietly to place herself in a large, carved armchair raised on a
narrow daïs. When Guy had finished his preparations, & arranged the light to his complete satisfaction, he sprang up on
the daïs, with an old red cloth on his arm & stretched it at
Teresina's feet. "Now, piccola," he said, standing at a critical
distance, "let us see if you are properly posed. Wait a minute.
So." He came close to her, adjusted a fold in her dress & moved
her soft, frightened hand a little. "Are you so much afraid of
me, cara?" he asked, smiling, as he felt it tremble. "I am not
very hard to please, am I?" Teresina shook her head. "There,"
said Guy, "that is right, now. Only lift up those wonderful
lashes. I do not want to paint the picture of a blind contadina,
do I?" All this, spoken in a soft tone which was natural to Guy
when addressing any woman, made poor Jack groan inwardly
at his own stupidity in not understanding that sweet pernicious
language that sounded like perpetual love-making! Having
perfected Teresina's attitude, Guy sat down before his canvas,
& began to paint; every now & then saying something to pro-
voke the soft, monosyllables that he liked so well. "Where did
you get that fine gold necklace, piccola?" he asked, beginning
to paint it in with a few preparatory touches. "It is not mine.
It belongs to la madre," said Teresina. "She wore it at her wedding." "Ah, & perhaps you will wear it at yours. Should you
like to get married, Teresina?" "I don't know," said Teresina,
slowly. "La madre wants me to marry Pietro (the carpenter,
you know) but I would rather kill myself!" There was a flash
in the soft velvet eyes, that made Guy pause in undisguised
admiration; but it died in an instant, & no art of his brush or
palette could hope to reflect it. "Is there anyone else you would

like to marry, Teresina?" She was silent; & he repeated his question. "Why do you ask me, Signore?" said the girl, dropping her lids. "I wish you would go on painting." Guy was not a little astonished at this outburst; & went on with his work quietly, to Jack's intense relief. After about an hour of silence (Jack was obstinately dumb during Teresina's presence in the studio, believing that those infernal models could understand anything a fellow said) a round knock at the door made Guy breathe a low "confound it!" Egerton called "Come in," & the next moment a portly gentleman, unmistakably English from top to toe, stood on the threshold. "Mr. Graham!" said Jack, rising. "You find me at work on the last touches of your little thing. Let me present my friend, Mr. Hastings, whose fame of course . . . I need not say. . . . Mr. Graham bowed, & was very much honoured by an introduction to Mr. Hastings. Mr. Graham spoke in a satisfied, important voice. Mr. Graham had the uneasy, patronizing air of a man who stands higher than his level, & is not quite sure of his footing. "You see," Jack continued, lightly, moving a chair forward for his august visitor, "that we painters are not quite such idle fellows as the world makes us out to be. Hastings & I take advantage of this fine light for our work." "So I observe," said Mr. Graham, with a bow. "I see you've nearly done my order—a very nice little bit (as you artists would say) a very nice little bit." As Mr. Graham spoke, his eye wandered about the motley room, & in its course rested on Teresina. As Guy had said, she got "so confoundedly frightened" when any stranger was present; it was the first year she had been hired as a model, & the miserable life had not yet rubbed off her girlish bloom. When she met Mr. Graham's scrutinizing eyes, her lashes drooped & a soft crimson stole over her neck & face, making her lovelier than ever; "let me go, Signore," she whispered to Guy, who had approached her to rearrange some detail in her dress. Then, without a word, she slipped down from her elavation, & stole quickly out of the room, still followed by Mr. Graham's gaze. "A model, eh? A very pretty little girl, Mr. Hastings. And a very nice picture—a very good likeness." Mr. Graham threw his head back critically & fancied, worthy man, that he had been eminently calculated to discriminate justly in art. "Have you been long at that, eh?" he continued, nodding towards the picture. "Two sittings," said Guy, shortly; he was vexed that this intrusion had put his shy bird to the flight, & could not abide this goodnatured bourgeois patronage which Jack laughed at & professed to like as a study of character. "A very pretty, sweet little girl," said Mr. Graham, who had a weighty way of repeating his remarks as if they were too precious to pass at once into oblivion. "But I am told that those models haven't much character, Mr. Hastings, eh?" "A common mistake," Guy returned coldly. "Ah!" said Mr. Graham. But Jack's effusive politeness flattered him more than the stern reserve of Jack's handsome, sulky friend; & Guy was left to himself, while the merchant & Egerton talked together. It was not until the former rose to go, that he was again drawn into the circle of conversation. "I hope we shall see you at our apartment, no. 2 via _____, Mr. Egerton. You—Mr. Hastings— you also, Sir. I shall be happy to introduce my wife & daughter. I shall have my little commission tomorrow, then? Good morning to you, gentlemen." And Mr. Graham marched out

with what (he flattered himself) was a ducal elegance of manner & carriage. When the door was shut, Guy relieved himself of, "I hate your confounded shopkeepers!" "Every man
who buys my pictures is my brother," exclaimed Jack, dra-
matically, "whatever be his station in life!" "Odd—because I
never knew one of your brothers to do such an ingenuous
thing!" observed Guy, gathering up his brushes. "Guy, my
boy! You're getting sarcastic." "Very likely. I am going to the
deuce by grande vitesse." "Why don't you stop at a station by
the way?" said Egerton, rising with a yawn from his easel. "It
would be a pity to reach your destination so soon." "What does
it matter?" returned Guy, bitterly, turning away to stare out
of the window. "A good deal, my boy, to some people." I might
have thought so once," said Guy very low. Jack was silent; he
lighted his cigar & leaned back in a medieval armchair puffing
meditatively. After a while he said, "Are you falling in love
with Teresina?" Guy started. "No," he said, "I don't think I
am falling in love with anybody. If I have any heart left, I
haven't enough for that. Poor little Teresina!" "Why do you
pity her?" said Jack, sharply. "Because she is young &—I believe—sincere." "Pity such virtues don't last longer in persons
of her class!" said Egerton." "But you've got her in your head.
Now, what are you going to do with her?" "Paint her." "Nonsense!" Jack jumped up & laid a hand on his friend's shoulder.
"Look here, my boy," he said, in his quick way, "since you left
London with me last Autumn you have been doing your best
to shew what I have always said—that there is nothing like a
woman for ruining a man's life. In short, you have been going
rapidly to the dogs. Well; I am not a parson either, & I don't

care to preach. But, for Heaven's sake, don't give way one instant to another woman! If, as you say, this child is innocent & honest, leave her so. Don't let those confounded soft eyes twist you into the idea that you're in love." "Poor little Teresina!" said Guy again.

Chap. VII. The Luckiest Man in London.

"Oh, to be in England, now that April's there."
Robert Browning: Dramatic Lyrics.

AS THE WARM ROMAN WINTER melted into Spring, Jack
Egerton felt growing upon him the yearning which the poet
expressed above; excepting that he would have transposed the
month & made it May, or, in other words, "the season." In
short, he got a little tired of his painting & the Bohemianism
of his life in Rome; & would have been only too glad if he
could have carried Guy off with him. But Guy would not go.
His love had not been of the slight sort which can be cast off
like a dress out of fashion, at the right time; & he dreaded being
within reach of the possibility of seeing his cousin again. As
it is with many another young man of like class & habits, the
warp in his love had warped his life; an undertone of bitterness
ran habitually through it now, which Jack had striven in vain
to destroy. Guy had decided to spend the Summer in Alp-
climbing; but he intended to stay on in Rome until the end of
April, so that Jack, who started homeward in the early part of
that month, left him still there. Jack got back to England in
time to pay several duty visits to his relations in the country;
but the opening season found him in London again, ready, as
the phrase is, for everything "going." Everybody was glad to
see "Jack-All" back again; but his welcome at Swift's was per-

haps the warmest & the most heartily gratifying that he got. "Hullo, melancholy Jacques!" cried some familiar voice as Jack stalked into the reading room one mild May evening. "Back from Rome, eh? An R.A. yet?" More than one took up the chorus; & Jack found himself surrounded by a group of laughing flâneurs, all asking questions, "chaffing," & regaling the newcomers with town news. "How's Hastings?" said a tall Life-Guardsman (a Duke's son) who had joined in the circle of talk over the broadcloth shoulder of a wiry little Viscount. "Didn't Hastings go to Rome with you?" "Of course he did," said the Viscount, who knew everybody. "Don't you know, Hasty was so awfully gone on old Breton's wife, & she jilted him—didn't she, Jack? Stunning little woman!" "Yes," said someone else, "Hasty was entirely done up by that. It *was* hard lines." "Has Hasty gone in regularly for painting?" enquired the Life Guard's man; & staunch Jack, who had not answered a word to this volley, turned the subject dexterously. "Yes. He has joined the Alpine Club." "Instead of the Royal Academy?" "Whoever made that witticism ought to be black-balled," said the Viscount. "Can't you give Jack full swing, all of you?" "By all means! Fire away, old boy. How many women are you in love with, how many pictures have you sold & how many people have you quarrelled with?" "I am in love with as many women as I was before," said our stout misogynist, "& I have sold two pictures" ("Why did you make him perjure himself?" observed the Viscount parenthetically) "& I have quarrelled with everybody who didn't buy the rest." There was a general laugh; & just then Lord Breton (who was one of the Patriarchs of the Club) came up & caught sight of Jack. "Ha! Mr. Egerton. I understood you were in Italy," said his lordship condescendingly. "Have you been long in town? If you have no prior engagement, dine with me tomorrow night at 8." And Lord Breton passed on with a bow, while Jack stood overwhelmed by this sudden condescension. "By Jove," said the Lifeguardsman as the old peer passed out of hearing, "I believe you're the luckiest man in London!" "Why?" said Jack, amused. "Why! Don't you know that you're going to dine with the fastest, handsomest, most bewitching woman in town? Don't you know that everybody's mad over Lady Breton?" "Yes!" added the Viscount. "Tom Fitzmore of the _____th & little Lochiel (Westmoreland's son, you know) had a row about her that might have ended seriously if the Duchess of Westmoreland hadn't found out & gone down on her knees to her eldest hope, imploring him to give it up. Lochiel is a muff, & went off to Scotland obediently, but Fitzmore was furious." "They say Monsieur is as watchful as a dragon & as jealous as an old woman, but she plays her cards too cleverly for him," resumed my lord Lifeguardsman. "I've danced with her once, & by Jove! it's like moving on air with a lot of roses & soft things in your arms." "And how she sings!" cried the Viscount, waxing warm. "I swear, it's a pity she's a lady. She'd make a perfect actress." "But old B. ('Beast' they call him you know—'Beauty & the Beast')," explained the other, "is awfully suspicious & never lets her sing except to a roomfull of dowagers & ugly men." "Thanks!" observed the quick-witted Viscount. "*I've* heard her sing twice." "Which proves the truth of my statement," quoth the Lifeguardsman coolly, lounging off towards another group, while the little nobleman, in a deep note of mock ferocity called after him for an explanation. This was not the last that Jack heard of

Lady Breton's praises. The next day he went to see a friend, a
brother-artist (whose fame, however, exceeded Jack's) & saw
on his easel the head of a woman with a quantity of white lace
& pearls folded about a throat as round & soft as a Hebe's. Her
soft, chesnut-brown hair fell in resistless little rings & wave-
lets about a low white arch of forehead, beneath which two
brilliant hazel eyes, with curly fringes, glanced out with a half-
defiant, half-enticing charm. The features, which had no es-
pecial regularity, were redeemed by the soft peachbloom on
either rounded cheek, & the whole face made piquant by a
small nose, slightly "tip-tilted," & a dimple in the little white
chin. Although Jack could find no real beauty in the lines of
the charmingly-poised head, some nameless fascination arrested his eyes; & he stood before the picture so long that the
artist, who was just then busy with another portrait called out,
"What! Are *you* losing your heart too, Benedick?" "Who is
it?" said Jack. "What! don't you—It's the handsomest—no, not
the handsomest, nor the most beautiful, nor the prettiest,
woman in London; but, I should say, the most fascinating.
Isn't that face irresistible? That is Lady Breton!" Jack started;
perhaps he for the first time fully understood what had darkened Guy Hastings' life. "Yes," continued his friend, enthusiastically, "she is the sensation of the season. And no wonder!
There is a perfect magic about her, which, I see by your face,
I have been fortunate enough to reflect in part on my canvas.
But if you knew her!" "I am going to dine there tonight," said
Jack turning away, his admiration changed to a sort of loathing, as he thought of the destruction those handsome eyes had
wrought. "Are you? Let me congratulate you. You're the
luckiest man in London," cried the portrait-painter, uncon-

sciously repeating the words which had hailed Jack's good-fortune at Swift's the night before. "And this," thought Egerton, "is what a woman gets for spoiling a man's life!" Nevertheless, prompted by a certain curiosity (which Jack was careful to call a natural interest in the various phases of human nature, since to confess the desire of seeing a woman—even the woman whom all London was raving about—would have been high-treason to his cherished misogynism)—actuated, I say, by this feeling, he looked forward rather impatiently to the evening which was to introduce him to the famous Lady Breton; &, as he was ushered by a resplendent Jeames up the velvet-spread staircase of her Belgravian mansion, was aware of that pleasurable sensation with which an ardent play-goer awaits the lifting of the curtain upon the first scene of a new drama. How the curtain lifted, what scenes it disclosed, & how unexpectedly it fell, our next chapter will reveal.

Chap. VIII. Jack the Avenger.

"I have a heart tho' I have played it false." *Old Play.*

LADY BRETON WAS LEANING against the chimney-piece in her splendid drawing-room, hung with violet satin, & illuminated by sparkling chandeliers. Her black velvet dress set off the neatly-moulded lines of her figure, which seemed to have gained in height & stateliness since her unmarried days in Holly Lodge; & the low, square-cut bodice revealed a bosom the whiter by contrast to a collar of rubies clasped closely about the throat. She was watching, half-absently, the flash of her rings, as she leaned her chin upon one drooping hand; & was so absorbed in some silent reverie, that she scarcely noticed the pompous entrance of her lord & master, until that noble gentleman observed, "I have asked Egerton to dine here to-night. I believe you know him." "I?" said Georgie, starting slightly. "N—no—I do not know him." But she *did* know that he was Guy's friend & travelling companion. "A very gentlemanly fellow, & of good family," said Lord Breton, graciously, "though an artist." A moment later, &, fortunately for his peace of mind, just too late to catch these words, Mr. Egerton was announced. Lord Breton went ponderously through an introduction to "Lady Breton, my friend Mr. Egerton"; & then he found himself sitting in a very easy chair, with only a velvet-covered tea-table between himself & the most popular woman in London. Certainly, the charm of her face, her tone, her gesture, was irresistible. Her ease was so engaging, there was such a pretty spice of freedom in her speech & manner, her coquetry was so artless & original, that Jack had surely succumbed if he had not seen in this fascinating Lady Breton the destroyer of his friend's happiness. Ten minutes later, after another stray man, a distant relative of Lord Breton's, had made his appearance in dinner-array, Egerton had the whitest of hands lying on his coat-sleeve & was leading his hostess to the dining-room, in a very delightful frame of mind. The parti quarré was kept alive, during the elaborate courses of the dinner, by Lady Breton's vivacity; & as she employed herself in drawing Jack out (Jack was a clever talker) the two kept a constant flow of words circulating. Every moment, as he watched her & heard her voice, the fascination & the loathing increased together. In truth, Georgie had laid herself out to conquer this clever friend of Guy's; & she in part succeeded. When at last she rose, with her rich draperies falling about her & a deeper flush on her cheek, & swept out of the room, a dullness fell on the three men which Lord Breton's sublimity was not likely to relieve. Jack was glad when the time which etiquette orders to be devoted to nuts & wine (Lord Breton's wine was by no means contemptible) was over, & the gentlemen went to the drawing-room to join Georgie; nor was his pleasure impaired by the fact that Lord Breton soon challenged his other guest to a game of billiards. "Let us stay here, Mr. Egerton," said Georgie, with a smile. "It always makes my head ache to see Lord Breton play billiards. You don't mind staying?" Jack protested. "Ah! I see you are like all other men—you always flatter." "How can we help it when there is so much to flatter?" "That is a doubtful compliment, but I will take it at its best, as one must everything in this life. Do you take tea, Mr. Egerton?" Jack had an old-maid's passion for the fragrant brew, & watched with no small enjoyment the quick movements of Georgie's pretty hand as she filled & sweetened his cup. "There! You have got to pay for my services by getting up to fetch it, since you *will* plant yourself at the other end of the room," she said, laughing, as she handed it to him. "Thanks. I find that English tea is a different thing from Roman tea," said Jack, leaning back luxuriously, so that he could watch her as she sat opposite, in a charming négligeé attitude, as easy as his own. "But one doesn't go to Rome for tea! At least, I believe not," she said, taking up her cup. "What does one go to Rome for?" returned Jack; "as I sit here, in this charming drawing-room, with London on every side, I wonder how anyone can care to go abroad?" "Really," said Georgie, smiling, "your words have a double entendre. Is it my drawing-room, Mr. Egerton, or London that makes it hard to go abroad?" "To those who have the happiness of knowing you, I should say—both." "Unanswerable! Compliments always are —But do tell me, Mr. Egerton, if you have seen my cousin Guy—Mr. Hastings, lately?" She said it lightly, easily, in the tone she had used to rally & amuse him a moment before; there was no change in voice, or manner. Jack was disagreeably startled out of his train of lazy enjoyment; in the charm of her presence he had nearly forgotten his loyalty to Guy, but the lightness of her tone as she named him, brought all the horror jarringly back. He changed in a moment from the mere drawing room lounger, with a flattering repartee for every remark, into the stout friend & the "good hater." He was our old Jack Egerton again. For a moment he did not answer her; & as she appeared absorbed in the contemplation of the fan which she was opening & furling, perhaps she did not see the angry flash in his honest gray eyes. When he spoke she did look up, & with undisguised astonishment in her pretty face. "I think, Lady Breton," said Jack, sternly, "that you should be able to answer your own question." "What *can* you mean, Mr. Egerton? Why do you speak in that solemn oracular manner?" "Excuse me, Lady Breton," returned Jack; "I cannot speak in any other tone of my friend!" "Than the solemn & oracular?" said Georgie, mischievously. "You must pardon me," Egerton answered gravely," If I ask you not to speak so lightly on a subject which . . . which . . ." "Pray go on, Mr. Egerton," she said, in a low, taunting voice; & it urged him on, before he knew it, to utter the truth. "I believe," he returned quickly, "that we are speaking at cross-purposes, but since you give me permission I *will* go on & tell you frankly that I cannot sit still and listen to such mere trifling with his name from the woman who has ruined Guy Hastings' life." Her colour deepened, but her voice was quite controlled as she said, "I do not think I gave you permission to insult me." "Nor did I mean to insult you, Lady Breton; if I have, order me out of your drawing-room at once—but I must speak the truth." "Since when have you developped this virtue, Mr. Egerton? Well—" she set her lips slightly, "go on. I will listen to the truth." "You have heard what I said," Jack answered, coldly. "Let me see"—Jack noticed that she composed herself by an effort—"that I had ruined Guy—Mr. Hastings' life." "As you must ruin the life of any man who has the misfortune to love you. You know your power." "Well—suppose I do. Did you come from Rome to tell me this, Mr. Egerton?" she said, bitterly. "No. And I see that I shall repent having told you," said Jack. "Let us talk of something else." "Not at all! Since you broached the subject, it shall be your penalty to go on with it as long as I choose." "Are you so unused to the truth, Lady Breton, that even such harsh truths as these are acceptable?" "Perhaps." She paused, playing with her fan; then, suddenly, flashing one of her superb looks at him; "How you despise me!" she said. "You think I cared nothing for—for him?" "I cannot think that if you had cared for him, you would have thrown him over." "Ah—you know nothing of women!" "I believe" said Jack, very low, "I know too much of them." "And you despise them all, do you not?" she cried. "Yet—I have a heart." "My friend did not find it so," said Jack, pitilessly. Her eyes flashed; & she bit her lip (the blood had fled from her whole face) before she could answer. "How do you know that you are not wronging me?" "If I am wronging you, why is my friend's life cursed?" he exclaimed. "No, Lady Breton! The wrong is on your side, & when I think of him, & of what he might have been, I cannot help telling you so." Her agitation had increased perceptibly, & she rose here, as if to find a vent for it in the sudden movement. Jack could not help thinking how her pallour altered her. There ran through his head, half unconsciously, the wonderful words that describe Beatrix Esmond when she finds her guilt discovered: "The roses had shuddered out of her cheeks; she looked quite old." He waited for Georgie to speak. "What he might have been," she repeated slowly. "What have I done? What have I done?" "You have very nearly broken his heart." She gave a little cry, & put her hand against her breast. "Don't! Don't!" she said, wildly.

"I *did* love him, I *did* care—I believe my heart is nearly broken too!" She tried to steady her voice, & went on hurriedly. "I was young & silly & ambitious. I fancied I didn't care, but I did— did. I have suffered too, & the more bitterly because what you say is true. I *have* wronged him!" She sank down on a chair, hiding her face in her hands, & Jack, who had not expected this passionate outburst, was not a little appalled by what he had brought about. But it was too late now to undo it; Georgie was thoroughly shaken out [of] her habitual artificial composure. The mask had fallen off, & oh, how sadly, sadly human were the features behind it! "And you," she went on, "are the first who has dared to tell me what *I* have felt so long! I could almost thank you—" She paused once more, & Jack knew that her tears were falling, though she screened her face with one lifted hand. "Instead of that," he said, "you must forgive my frankness—my impertinence, rather—in speaking to you in this way." "No—no. I think I feel better for it," she almost whispered. "But one thing more. Does he—does he think of me as you do?" "Do not ask me," said Jack, gently. "I think of you with nothing but pity." "And he—he despises me? He thinks I do not care for him? Oh—it will break my heart. And yet," she went on, with a moan, "what else have I deserved? Oh, my folly, my folly! But *you* believe I do love him? You see how wretched, how—" She did not notice, that, as she spoke, leaning toward Jack with her hand half outstretched, Lord Breton's voice was sounding near the door; but Jack did. "Yes," he said, composedly, taking up an album, "these photographs are charming. Have you seen the last of the Princess of Wales?" Georgie's tact would ordinarily have exceeded his; but she had been carried far beyond external observances, &

could only sit silent, with white, compressed lips as the gentleman entered. When Lord Breton came up to the tea-table, however, she rose, & said: "Will you excuse me? I do not feel quite well—it is very warm. Will you give me your arm?" She took her husband's arm & he led her to the door. "Lady Breton's delicate health is a continual source of anxiety to me," he explained as he came back. But circumstantial evidence was against Jack, & there was a scowl of suspicion beneath my lord's heavy politeness. A few days later, Egerton called at the house, but my lady was out; & although he saw her several times at balls & drums & races, always resplendent & always surrounded by a faithful retinue of adorers, he had no opportunity of exchanging a word with her.

Chap. IX. Madeline Graham.

"The lady, in truth, was young, fair & gentle."
Robert Lytton: Lucile.

SINCE HIS PARTING with Georgie Rivers, & the disappointment of his love, Guy Hastings had been, as Jack expressed it:
"going rapidly to the dogs." Now there are many modes of
travelling on this road; the melodramatic one in which the
dark-browed hero takes to murder, elopement, & sedition;
the commonplace one in which drinking, gambling & duelling
are prominent features; the precipitate one of suicide; & finally
that one which Guy himself had chosen. He did not kill himself, as we have seen, nor did he run away with anyone, or fight
a duel, or drink hard; but he seemed to grow careless of life,
money & health, & to lose whatever faith & tenderness he had
had in a sort of undefined skepticism. Perhaps this least perceptible is yet the most dangerous way of "going to the dogs"; it is
like the noiseless dripping of lime-water which hardens the
softest substance into stone. Guy's life was no longer sweet to
him. He felt himself sliding away from all ties of kindliness &
affection, & did not care to stay his course; he thought his heart
was withered & that nothing could revive it. Perhaps the first
thing that came near touching it, & shewed that it had any
vitality left, was Teresina. Not that he loved her; Jack need
not have been anxious on that score. But there is a dangerous

57

sort of interest & pity which may too easily be mistaken for love, & which Guy felt towards the little contadina. She appealed to the heart he thought dead by her shyness & her soft, leaning temper; & to his eye by the rich, languid beauty which could in no way bring to his mind another kind of prettiness with which his bitterest memories were associated. He painted the girl over & over again, & interested himself in her; but whatever danger might have been in store was warded off by a confession that Teresina made one April morning, with blushes & tears, to the Signore. She was in love, poor little soul, with Matteo, old Giovanni the blacksmith's son; but Matteo was poor, & Teresina's parents had destined her to be the wife of the rich carpenter, Pietro. So she told Guy; & her story so completely enlisted his sympathy that he not only went to see the Padre & bribed him largely to let Teresina marry where her heart was, but wrote to Mr. Graham, who had bought one of his pictures, & got a nice little sum from the generous merchant. This was some time after Jack's departure, & a week after Guy left Rome for his Summer wanderings in Switzerland, followed by the gratitude of two honest peasant hearts.

The soft July day, a little more than two months after this, he was walking along the old covered bridge at Interlaken, when the sound of voices reached him from the other end, & a moment later a stout, fair lady, who seemed to move in an English atmosphere, so clear was her nationality, appeared with a girl by her side. The girl was tall & élancée, & bore an unmistakeable resemblance to the elder lady; & a few yards behind them Guy espied the florid, whiskered countenance of Mr. Graham. The merchant was the first to speak his recognition, in his usual loud tones, while the ladies fell back a little, & the girl began to sketch with her parasol. "Mr. Hastings here!" exclaimed Mr. Graham. "This is a surprise! Been here long, eh? Mrs. Graham, my dear, this is Mr. Hastings, the gentleman who painted that pretty little face you make so much of; this is my daughter, Mr. Hastings." These introductions over, Guy perforce turned his steps & recrossed the bridge with the family party. He talked to Mrs. Graham, while the girl walked behind with her father; but his quick artist's eye had taken in a glance the impression that she was thin, but well-built, & exquisitely blonde, with large blue eyes, almost infantine in their innocent sweetness. She spoke very little, & seemed retiring & unaffected; & he noticed that her voice was low & musical. As for Mrs. Graham, she may best be described as being one of a large class. She was comely & simple-mannered, intensely proud of her husband & her daughter, & satisfied with life altogether; one of those dear, commonplace souls, without wit or style, but with an abundance of motherliness that might cover a multitude of fashionable defects. Guy was universally polite to women, but Mrs. Graham's bland twaddle about hôtels, scenery & railway carriages (the British matron's usual fund of conversation when taking a relaxation from housekeeping on the continent) was not very absorbing, & his eyes wandered continually towards her daughter—Madeline, her father had called her. He wondered why the name suited her soft, blonde beauty so well; he wondered if she were as refined as she looked; & indulged in so many of those lazy speculations which a young man is apt to lavish on a beautiful girl, that Mrs. Graham's account of their journey over the Cornice was almost entirely lost to his inattentive ears. Finally, as they drew near home, Madeline stopped to fill her hands with flowers, & he picked up her sunshade, falling back by her side to admire her nosegay. This young gentleman —who would have called himself "a man of the world" & thought he knew woman-kind pretty well, from the actress to the Duchess—had never seen before the phenomenon of an unsophisticated English beauty among the better classes. "I think that ladies' hands were made for gathering flowers," he observed. "It is the prettiest work they can do." Madeline blushed; "It is the pleasantest work, I think," she said, in her clear, shy tones, bending her tall head over her field-blossoms. Guy thought of "The Gardener's Daughter," & wondered whether her golden hair was as pale & soft as Madeline Graham's. "But you can paint them," the girl added. "How I envy you!" "If you are so fond of flowers, you should learn to paint them yourself, Miss Graham," said Guy. "Ah—if I could. I don't think I have any talent." "You must let me find that out," he returned, smiling. "I should like to teach you." Madeline blushed again; indeed, every passing emotion made her colour change & waver exquisitely. Guy liked to watch the wildrose flush deepen & fade on the pure cheek beside him; it was a study in itself to make an artist happy. "You know," he went on, "all talents are not developped at once, but lie dormant until some magic touch awakens them. Your love for flowers may help you to find out that you are an artist." "I am very fond of pictures," said Madeline, simply. "I love the Madonna heads with their soft, sweet eyes & blue hoods. But then, you know, I am no judge of art—Papa is." At another time, Guy would have smiled at this daughterly illusion; now it only struck him as a very rare & pretty thing. "One does not need to be a judge of art to love it," he said. "The discrimination comes later; but the love is inborn." She lifted her wide blue eyes shyly to his face. "I suppose you have both," she said, gravely. "Very little of either, I am afraid," said Guy, smiling. "I am little more than an amateur, you know." Just then, Mr. Graham, who had gone forward with his wife, called Madeline. "Come, come, my dear. It is getting damp & we must be off to our hotel. Our paths divide, here, eh? Mr. Hastings. Come & see us." "Goodbye," said Madeline, with a smile. "Goodbye," he answered; "shall you be at home tomorrow afternoon?" "Yes. I believe so. Shall we not, Mamma?" "What, my dear? Yes," nodded Mrs. Graham. "Do come, Mr. Hastings. It's a little dull for Madeline here." And they parted, Guy lifting his hat, & lingering a moment to watch them on their way. "A very nice young fellow, eh?" said Mr. Graham, as Madeline slipped her hand through his arm. "Excellent family. Excellent family." "And so polite," cried Mrs. Graham. "I declare he talked beautifully." "I think he is very handsome," said Madeline, softly. "And how clever he is, Papa." "Clever, eh? Yes—yes; a rising young fellow. And very good family." "But it's a wonder to me he took any notice of you, Maddy," observed Mrs. Graham. "Those handsome young men in the best society don't care for anything under an Earl's wife." "But he is a gentleman, Mamma!" said Madeline with a blush. The next afternoon, a servant was sent up to Mr. Graham's apartments at the Hôtel Belvidere with a card; which a maid carried into an inner room, where the following dialogue went on while the Hôtel servant waited. "Mr. Hastings, Mamma—what shall I do?" "See him, love. I am not suffering much." "Oh, Mamma, I can't leave you alone!" "With Priggett, my dear? Of course. Perhaps he might know of a physician." "Of course,

Mamma! I will see him. Ask the man to shew Mr. Hastings up." And when Guy was ushered into the stiffly-furnished sitting room a pale young lady with her crown of golden hair somewhat disturbed & her white dress rumpled, came forward to meet him. "Oh, Mr. Hastings . . ." "Has anything happened, Miss Graham?" The tears were hanging on Madeline's lashes & her quiet manner was changed for a trembling agitation. "Mamma has sprained her ankle," she said, "& Papa is away. He went to the Lauterbrunnen this morning, & an hour ago Mamma slipped on the staircase—" she ended rather abruptly by pressing her handkerchief to her eyes. "My dear Miss Graham, how unfortunate! Have you sent for a physician? Can I do anything for you?" "Oh, thanks," said Madeline, "we have got the maid & I have bound her ankle up, but we didn't know where to find a physician." "How lucky that I came!" Guy exclaimed. "I believe there is no good native doctor, but Sir Ashley Patchem is at my Hôtel & I will go back at once." "Oh, thank you, thank you!" Madeline could scarcely control her tears, as she held her hand out. "May I come back & see if I can help you in any other way?" Guy said, as he took it; & then he was gone, at a quick pace. Half an hour later, the famous London physician was in Mrs. Graham's room at the Hôtel Belvidere. "A very slight sprain, I assure you," he said, as Madeline followed him anxiously into the sitting-room. "Don't disturb yourself. Only have this sent for at once." He put a prescription in her hand, & as he left the room Guy came in again. "I am so much relieved," said Madeline, "& I don't know how to thank you." "What does Sir Ashley say?" "It is very slight, not at all dangerous. I am so thankful! But this prescription . . . I suppose one of the servants . . ." "Let me take

it," said Guy. Then, glancing at his watch; "Mr. Graham ought
to be here shortly, but you will send for me in case of need,
Miss Graham? Are you sure that I can do nothing else?" "You
have done so much," Madeline answered, with a smile. "No, I
think everything is arranged, & as you say Papa will be here
soon." "I will not delay the prescription, then. Goodbye, Miss
Graham!" "Goodbye." She held out her hand again, as to a
friend, & again he took it & pressed it for an instant. As he
walked homeward in the soft Summer dusk, he had the pleasant feeling of a man who knows that he has gained the admiration & gratitude of a pretty, interesting girl by an easy
service just at the right time. No man wins his way so easily
as he who has the good luck to prove himself "a friend in
need"; & Guy felt that in one day he had come nearer to
Madeline Graham than months of casual acquaintance could
have brought him.

Chap. X. At Interlaken.

"Through those days
Youth, love & hope walked smiling hand in hand."
Old Play.

IT IS CERTAIN that in this world the smallest wires work the largest machinery in a wonderful way. The twist that Mrs. Graham's foot took on the Hôtel staircase, led gradually up a ladder of greater events to a most unexpected climax, & influenced her daughter's life as the most carefully laid plans could perhaps not have done. Strangely & wonderfully, "Dieu dispose." The Grahams had not intended to remain over a week at Interlaken, & had all their Summer plans arranged after the approved tourist fashion. These plans Mrs. Graham's sprained ankle of course overset. Slight at the accident was, it tied her to her couch for five weeks at the least; & all that could be done was to accept the circumstances & engage the best rooms which the Hôtel Belvidere could offer, for that length of time. Mr. Graham was thoroughly disgusted. "To be mewed up in this hole," he complained to Hastings, "with nothing to do but look at the mountains out of one's bedroom windows. In fact, though the continent is very pleasant for a change & very nice to travel in, England's the place to be quiet in!" "Yes, I agree with you," said Guy; "but I hope this unfortunate accident won't frighten you off to England?" Mr.

Graham shook his head despondently! "I wish it could, my dear Hastings, I wish it could. But, you see, our Madeline is too delicate for the rough English weather, & as we've got to choose between Nice & Rome of course we'll go to Rome again." As for Madeline, she accepted the change with youthful adaptability, invented fancy-work for her mother, collected flowers, played on the rattling Hôtel piano which had been moved into her sitting-room, & took long walks with her father & Mr. Hastings. These walks, indeed, were the pleasantest part of her quiet, contented days; Mr. Hastings talked so well & got her such pretty wild-flowers, she said simply to her mother. And Mrs. Graham sighed. Madeline was a good, dutiful girl, & full of worship for her father; but perhaps she was not sorry when, on the morning which had been chosen for a long pilgrimage, Mr. Graham got some business letters which required immediate answers, & announced at the breakfast table that he could not go. "Oh, what a pity, John," said Mrs. Graham, from the sofa. "It is such a beautiful day, & Maddy has been counting on this walk." Madeline looked studiously at her plate, but the pink was beginning to flutter up into her cheek. "Nonsense!" said Mr. Graham. "Madeline shall go, of course. What do you suppose Hastings wants with an old fellow like me, eh? No, no, Mother; Madeline shall go & they will be only too glad to be rid of me." "Oh, Papa!" murmured Madeline. But when Guy Hastings appeared an hour later, she was ready in her gray walking dress, with a quantity of light blue veil floating about her leghorn hat & looped around her throat. There was a slight flush on her face, & she had never looked more lovely. "This morning was made for a walk," said Guy, as he stood by Mrs. Graham's couch. "But the one we

have planned is long. I hope we shall not tire Miss Graham."
"Oh, no," said Madeline, coming up, "but—Papa can't come
this morning." "Mr. Graham has some business letters to at-
tend to," explained Mrs. Graham. Guy glanced at Madeline;
"You are dressed," he said: "won't you trust to my guidance?"
Madeline stood still, blushing; but just then Mr. Graham came
in, & overhearing Guy's words, said warmly: "Yes, indeed she
will! Take good care of her, Hastings. I say, she will be glad
to have her old father out of the way." "Oh, Papa," said
Madeline again. So the two started out, Guy carrying her
flower-basket & shawl, through the sunny morning weather.
A handsome couple they made; & as they walked through the
Hôtel garden together, a Russian princess, who was taking an
early airing, observed to her little French secretary: "that those
English were fiancées; she could see it." As they reached the
gate, a little child who was racing after a hoop, stumbled & fell
crying across their path; & Madeline stooped down & picked
him up very tenderly. "Are you hurt?" "Not very much,
Madame," said the child; & Madeline felt the blood flying into
her face, & wondered whether Guy were very much vexed at
having her mistaken for his wife. On through the sunny morning weather: who can tell of that walk, with all its pretty little
incidents, & surprises & adventures? It was such a pastoral as
drops now & then between the tragedies & farces of life.
Madeline was perfectly happy; & if Guy was not as happy as
she, he was in a better mood than he had been for many a day,
& the bright morning air, the beautiful scenery, the sweet
English face at his side, warmed him more & more into hearty
enjoyment. As they walked, the flower-basket was filled with
new trophies; & when they reached their destination, Guy

spread Madeline's shawl under a nut-tree, & sat down by her side to sketch. "Why not take a drawing lesson today?" he said, as she watched him pointing his pencils & making his slight preparations. "I think one could learn anything in such beautiful weather." "I had rather watch you," said Madeline, "& you know I have to arrange my flowers too. Oh, what a beautiful day!" "Perfect. I didn't know what an attractive little nook Interlaken is before." "And you are going tomorrow?" asked Madeline, dropping her lashes. "I think so. Every artist is at heart a wanderer—begging Pope's pardon for taking such a liberty with his line. There, Miss Graham, what do you think of those outlines?" "How quick you are! Oh, how cleverly you have done it." Guy laughed. "Such injudicious praise as yours would soon spoil me," he said. "I suppose so," Madeline returned naively. "You know I am so ignorant." Guy went on with his sketch; he revelled in the deep, luxurious Summer silence, the whisper of the leaves above his head, the easy consciousness that if he did lift his eyes from his work they would meet nothing less in harmony with the radiant day than Madeline Graham's fair, sweet face bent above her flowers. Now & then, as the sketch grew beneath his quick pencil, she offered her shy criticism or her shyer praise; but for the most part they were silent, as though afraid by word or movement to break the spell of peacefulness that had fallen upon them. It was not until they had again reached the gate of the Hôtel garden, that either reverted to Guy's coming departure. "I am glad that our last walk has been so pleasant," he said. "I wonder how many more walks you will take after I am gone." "You are really going?" He saw the colour creep upwards, & the long lashes tremble. "I had intended to go," he answered, leaning against the gate. "I suppose—I suppose it has grown dull," murmured Madeline. "It has grown so pleasant that I wish I had not reached my limit," said Guy. "When a man proposes to spend two days at a place, & lengthens his visit to nearly two weeks, as I have done, he must begin to consider how much time he has left for the rest of his tour." "We shall miss you," ventured Madeline, overwhelmed with blushes. "Papa, I mean, will . . ." "Won't *you* miss me?" said Guy, very low. Madeline's half-averted cheek turned a deeper crimson; her heart was beating stormily, & everything seemed to swim before her. "I don't know," she whispered, tremblingly. In any other person, at any other time, such an answer would have been bête; in Madeline Graham, with the sunset light striking her pale golden braids, & the church-bells coming softly through the sweet evening air, as they stood by the gate, it seemed to Guy Hastings very sweet & musical. "If I thought you would miss me I should be almost glad to go," he said, quietly. "And yet, I do not know why I go. It is so peaceful here, that I feel as if life were worth a little—if I go, I shall probably do my best to tumble down a ravine." Madeline lifted her blue eyes in wonderment; she had never heard him speak so before. "Yes," he went on, "You do not know what it is to feel that everything is worthless & heartless, as I have done. I envy you. I almost wish that I were going to stay here." He paused; &, moved by the weary sadness which his voice & words had for the first time betrayed, Madeline gathered heart to say, holding out her hand: "I don't understand, but I am very sorry for you. You must have had a disappointment. Stay here." And Guy stayed; why not? As he had said, life seemed worth a little in this friendly atmosphere of peace, & in

Madeline's society. An inexpressible charm, which he scarcely acknowledged to himself, made her society pleasant; the quiet, Arcadian days were an utter contrast to the dash & hurry of his unsatisfied life; he had found a palmtree in the desert-sand & he sat down to rest. As for Madeline, on the day when she met Guy in the covered bridge, that mysterious thing called "love at first sight" had entered in & taken possession of her heart. His manner had, indeed, a great fascination for all; & he was unusually gentle & serious with Madeline; then he was handsome, & Madeline, though she was not, like her Papa, a judge of art, had the good taste common to most girls, to admire a handsome face. As for those words of his by the gate, to say that she was a woman is to say that they aroused her sympathy & admiration as nothing else could have done, & raised Guy into a suffering hero. Nothing could be purer & more childlike than Madeline's passion; it blent with her life like a strain of sweet music, in which as yet there were no jarring chords; there was nothing noisy or turbulent about it. So the Summer stole on through balmy days & short, warm nights; Guy lingered at Interlaken, & Madeline saw him daily. He certainly treated her with marked admiration, & both Mr. & Mrs. Graham were not slow to draw their conclusions therefrom; but he spoke no word of love, &, as the happy days passed, seemed inclined to remain "half her lover, all her friend." Nor did Madeline feel the want of a closer appeal to her heart. The present was all-sufficient. Why should this pastoral ever end, or if it was to end, why should she not enjoy it the more fully now? Her love for Guy was as yet almost too idealized & abstract to demand a reciprocation. Enough that he was by her side, & that he was glad to be there. Mr. Graham, too, was quite easy on the subject. Madeline was a pretty girl, & Hastings was evidently very much gone on her; he was of good family & she had money enough for both; no match could be more desirable, & none seemed more likely to prosper. It was natural that they should like to spin out their courtship-days; young people have the whole world before them, & are never in a hurry. But Mrs. Graham was not so well-pleased with the turn affairs had taken. "Don't be so confident, John," she said, anxiously. "I had rather trust Maddy with a good, honest business man than one of these fine, fast young fellows. Very likely he is only amusing himself; what does he want with a merchant's daughter? No, no; it will come to nothing & if it goes on much longer the child's heart will be broken. I have heard stories enough about Mr. Hastings & his set, & I don't believe in one of them!" "Nonsense!" said Mr. Graham, angrily. He had set his heart on the match & these warnings of his wife's, which he could not in his heart despise, made him uneasy.

Chap. XI. The End of the Season.

"Adieu, bal, plaisir, amour! On disait: Pauvre Constance!
Et on dansait jusqu'au Jour chez l'ambassadeur de France."
Delavigne.

ON A CERTAIN EVENING near the close of those busy, rushing
summer months which Londoners call "the season," Lady
Breton was sitting alone in the long, luxurious dressing-room
which opened off her satin-hung boudoir. She wore one of
those mysterious combinations of lace & ribands & soft folds
called a wrapper, & as she leaned back rather wearily in her
deep-arm-chair, her slippered feet were stretched out to meet
the glow of the small wood-fire crackling on the hearth. There
was no other light in the room, but the fire-flash, unless a certain dull twilight gleam through the dark folds of the curtains,
deserves such a name; for my lady had given orders not to be
disturbed, adding that she would ring for the lamps. But in
the soft, flickering of the flames, that rose & fell fitfully, it
was a very white & mournful face that sank back in the shadow
of the crimson cushion; a face in which there was no discernible
trace of the rosy, audacious Georgie Rivers whom we used to
know. Nor was it the splendid, resistless Lady Breton who had
taken London by storm that Summer; but only a very miserable little personage, occasionally breaking the twilight hush
of the warm room with a heavy, aching cough, that made her

lean shivering nearer the pleasant blaze. In fact, Georgie had at last broken down, in body & mind, under the weight of her bitter mistake; which all her triumphs & her petty glories seemed only to make bitterer, with a sense of something empty & unsatisfied, lower than the surface-gayety of the ball-room. The pang had deepened & deepened, driving her farther into the ceaseless rush of society with the vain hope of losing her individual sorrow there; no one was gayer than Lady Breton. But at home, in the grand house, with its grave servants & its pictures & treasures, that was no more hope of forgetting than abroad. Any sympathy that might eventually have grown up between the old lord & his young wife, had been frozen by Georgie's persistent indifference to him; & whatever love his worn-out old heart had at first lavished on her, was lost in the nearer interests of a good dinner or an amusing play. Lord Breton, in short, relapsed entirely into his bachelor-habits, & was only with his wife, or conscious of her existence when she presided at his table, or entered a ball-room at his side. He was not ungenerous; he allowed her plenty of liberty & still had a comfortable pleasure in feeling that he was the possessor of the most charming woman in London—but day by day, she became less a part of his life. And still at her heart clung the love that she had despised of old, & whose unconquerable reality she was learning now—too late. Jack Egerton's reproaches seemed to have been the last drop in her cup of shame & bitterness—again & again came the wretched, haunting thought that she had lost Guy's esteem forever, & nothing could win back the place in his heart that she had sold so cheap. So she mused on in the closing darkness, over the fire-light, & it was 8 o'clock when she rang for her maid, who came in with the lamps & a bottle of cough-syrup for my lady. Georgie rose wearily from her seat, drawing a soft shawl close about her shoulders; &, as the maid stood waiting for orders, said between her painful coughing: "I shall dress for the ball now, Sidenham." "But, my lady," the woman answered, "you have had no dinner." "No, I did not want any, thanks. It is time to dress." "But—my lady," persisted the maid, "your cough is so bad . . . indeed, my lady . . ." Georgie interrupted her with an impatient movement. "My white dress, Sidenham. Have the flowers come home?" "Yes, my lady." And the process of the toilette began. Sidenham had a real attachment for her mistress, but she knew that my lady could brook no questioning of her will, & being a good servant, went about her duty obediently. Lord Breton had dined out that evening, but at about 9.30, as Sidenham was putting the last touches to Georgie's hair, he knocked unexpectedly at the dressing-room door, & then came in, in his evening dress. "I hoped you were in bed by—good Heavens!" he exclaimed, as Georgie rose in her glistening satin. "You don't mean to say that you are going out tonight?" Sidenham, shaking out my lady's train, looked volumes of sympathy at my lord. "Oh, certainly," returned Georgie, unconcernedly. "It is the Duchess of Westmoreland's ball tonight, you know." "But this is madness—madness. Your cough was much worse today—such exposure at night would be extremely dangerous." Georgie was clasping her diamonds, with her back turned towards him, & merely shrugged her white shoulders slightly. "Let me dissuade you," Lord Breton continued, with real anxiety. "Surely it is little to forfeit one ball—the last of the season—for one's health's sake. Your physician would certainly not advise such imprudence, such abso-

lute risk." "Very likely," said Georgie, nonchalantly, "but
—'when the cat's away the mice will play,' you know." "I
know that going out tonight would be folly on your part; let
me beg you to desist from it." "My white fan, Sidenham. I
presume," said Georgie, turning to face her husband as she
spoke, "that I shall have your escort?" "I am going to the
ball." "And yet" she continued lightly, "you wish to exile me
from it? I should die of ennui in half an hour alone here!"
"Then—then, may I offer you my company?" he said, eagerly,
taking the cloak from Sidenham's hands. "Let us give up the
ball, Georgina." Georgie was really moved; such a demonstra-
tion was so unusual on Lord Breton's part, that it could not
fail to touch her. But it was not her rôle to shew this. "No indeed!" she replied, clasping her bracelet, & coming closer to
him. "Why should either of us be sacrificed? Instead of suicide
for one, it would be—murder for both! Please put my cloak
on." "You go then?" said Lord Breton, coldly, with a gathering
frown. "Oh, yes. As you say, it is the last ball of the season.
Tomorrow I shall do penance." And drawing her cloak close,
with a suppressed cough, she swept out of the room. The
Duchess of Westmoreland's ball, at Lochiel House, was a very
grand & a very brilliant affair, & a very fitting finale to one
of the gayest seasons that people could recall. Everybody (that
is, as her Grace expressively said, "everybody that is anybody")
was there; & the darling of the night was, as usual, the fascinating Lady Breton. White as her white dress, unrelieved by
a shade of colour, she came in on her husband's arm; people
remembered afterwards, how strangely, deadly pale she was.
But she danced continually, talked & laughed with everyone
more graciously than ever, & raised the hearts of I don't know

how many desponding lovers by her charming gayety & good-nature. She was resting after the last quadrille, when the Duke of Westmoreland himself, came up to her, with the inexpressibly relieved air of a model host who, having done his duty by all the ugly dowagers in the room, finds himself at liberty to follow his own taste for a few moments. "I don't think" he said, answering Georgie's greeting "that you have seen the Duchess's new conservatories. Will you let me be your cicerone?" "How did you guess, Duke," she returned, gaily "that I was longing to escape from the heat & light? Do take me, if I am not carrying you off from any more—agreeable—duty!" "My duty is over," said the Duke, smiling. "But you are coughing tonight, Lady Breton, & I cannot allow you to go into the cooler air without a wrap." Signing to a servant, he sent for a soft fur mantle, & having folded it carefully about Georgie's shoulders, led her on his arm through the long & brilliant suites. Followed by many an envious & many an admiring eye, she walked on with her proud step, talking lightly & winningly to her noble escort, until they reached the folding doors of the great conservatories. The Duke led her in, & they paused on the threshold looking down the green vista of gorgeous tropical plants. The gay dance-music came like a soft echo from the distant ball-room, mingling with the clear tinkle of fountains that tossed their spray amid the branching ferns & palm-trees on which the Chinese lanterns swung from the ceiling, shed an unreal, silvery glow. For a moment neither spoke; then Georgie looked up at her host with a bright smile. "Fairyland!" she exclaimed. "No one shall persuade me that this is the work of anyone less ethereal than Queen Mab herself! Is it real? Will it last?" "I hope so," his Grace answered, laughing; "it would be a pity that her Elfin Majesty's work should vanish in a single night." "Only, as children say, 'it is too good to be true,' " said Georgie, merrily. "At least, to us lesser mortals, who are not accustomed to all the marvels of Lochiel House." "Will you come on a little further?" said the Duke, well-pleased. "I want to shew you some rare ferns. Here they are." And so they passed along the aisle of mingled green, in the soft moonlike radiance; pausing here & there to admire or discuss the Duke's favourite specimens. At the end of the long, cool bower a broad ottoman stood in a recess filled with ferns; & Georgie asked to sit down before entering the next conservatory. "You are tiring yourself, Lady Breton?" asked the Duke, anxiously, sitting down beside her, & drawing the mantle, which had slipped down, over her shoulder. "No, not tired, indeed," she answered, "but half dizzy with so much beauty. I must sit still to be able to enjoy it perfectly—sit still, & drink it in." "It is a relief after the crowded rooms," assented his Grace. "I was longing to be here all the evening." "I cannot wonder. Do you know, Duke," said Georgie, laughing, "if I were disposed to be sentimental I should say that I envied the gardener who has these conservatories in charge more than anyone in Lochiel House!" The Duke echoed her laugh. "If it suits you to be sentimental just now, Lady Breton, the gardener—an old protégé of mine—is a very fit subject. He has a romance attached to him." "Better & better!" cried Georgie. "He can come in here & dream of it!" "I daresay though—poor fellow!—he would rather forget it," said the Duke. Georgie started slightly, & a strange look came into her eyes. "Oh, if we could but forget," she half-whispered; then, in a different tone: "but what of the gardener? I will not let you off with

that story; you must play Princess Scheherazade, Duke!"
"Most obediently, though poor Watson probably never intended his poor little love-affair to serve such a grand purpose.
Well—'anything, but to the purpose' is my motto, Lady Breton, so here is the whole romance. Watson came into my
father's service as a lad & rose to be one of the undergardeners
down at Morley Towers. There he wooed my mother's maid,
a pretty young woman, who in the end spoiled two lives by
her ambition.—Are you ill, Lady Breton?" "No, no," said
Georgie, hastily, playing nervously with her bouquet, "please
go on. I am quite impatient." "Watson," continued the Duke,
"was successful in his suit, & the wedding was arranged, much
to the poor fellow's happiness—for he was as genuinely in
love, Lady Breton," said the Duke, with slight sarcasm, "as any
gentleman would have been—the wedding, I say, was arranged, when my father brought home a fine French valet,
who got a larger salary, & had altogether a higher seat in the
synagogue, than Watson. The bride, whose head was turned
by the attentions of this more fascinating rival, gave Watson
the slip—jilted him, and—great Heavens! You are faint, Lady
Breton—what is it?" The bouquet had slipped from Georgie's
powerless hands, & she could scarcely answer, as the Duke
bent over her, "it will be over—in a moment—" "Let me call
someone," said his Grace, anxiously; but she shook her head,
& whispered faintly, "No, no . . . Do not call . . . it will be
over . . ." "I will get you some wine. Can you wait here alone?"
She gave a little, frightened cry & caught his hand wildly.
"Don't leave me! I . . . I . . . am better . . . now. I don't want
anything . . . Take me away, Duke!" Sorely perplexed, he
helped her to rise, & giving her his arm, led her very slowly

back through the conservatory. She had evidently rallied her strength for the effort, for though she did not trust herself to speak, her step was almost steady; & at last, to the Duke's intense relief, they reached the doors. The room on which the conservatory opened was hung with pictures & during the earlier part of the evening had been deserted for the other end of the suite; but the crowd had taken a new turn now & people were thronging in, to fill the interval before supper. Once or twice in his anxious progress through the crush the Duke was arrested, & not a few astonished glances met Lady Breton's white, suffering face; but they had nearly gained a door leading by a back way to the cloak-room, when his Grace felt the cold hand slip from his arm, & Georgie fell backward fainting. In an instant they were ringed in by a startled, eager crowd; but the Duke, lifting the slight, unconscious form in his arms, refused peremptorily all offers for assistance, & despatching a messenger for Lord Breton, himself carried Georgie into a dressing-room, out of reach of the bustle & curiosity of his officious guests.

Chap. XII. Poor Teresina.

"When pain & anguish wring the brow, a ministering Angel thou!"
                                              Scott: "Marmion."

THE RETURNING WINTER found Guy Hastings again at
Rome, in the old studio which he & Egerton had shared the
year before; but Jack was still in England, though he wrote in
the expectancy of joining his Telemachus in the early Spring.
Meanwhile Guy, on settling down in his Winter quarters, began to apply himself with real assiduity to his art. He painted
a successful picture which was bought by an Italian connoisseur; & inspirited by this piece of good fortune, grew more &
more attached to the great work he had heretofore treated as
play. He had lost his utter recklessness in this deepening interest, & a new & softening influence seemed to have entered
into his imbittered life since the happy weeks at Interlaken.
This influence was not the less tender or pleasant that it was
somehow connected with a pair [of] sweet, childlike blue eyes
& a low voice full of shy music. Little did Madeline, cherishing
the secret of her first love in silence, guess the innocent change
she had worked in her hero; & perhaps Guy himself scarcely
realized her quiet power. When the Grahams came back to
Rome however, the intercourse which had charmed the Interlaken days, was renewed; Guy was always welcomed in their
apartment, & many a little breakfast or supper was given in

their honour in his sunny studio. Mr. Graham, too, discovered
that Madeline's portrait must be painted; & twice a week she
& her mother would knock at Guy's door, until, when the last
coat of varnish was dry & the picture sent home, he grew to
miss the timid rap & the pleasant hour that ensued & to discover that it had been, unconsciously, the brightest part of his
day. Madeline's frail health grew stronger, & her shy laugh
gayer; & though one parent was far from satisfied with the
cause, both could not but rejoice over the effect of this change.
Altogether, the Winter was a happy, if a quiet one to the few
with whom our story is most concerned; & as the days slipped
by, they forged the imperceptible links of interest & sympathy
which were drawing Guy nearer to Madeline. One of these
links was brought about by a little personage who by this time
had nearly dropped out of Guy's remembrance, although her
face was reflected on more than one canvas hung upon his
studio wall. He was hurrying homeward near dusk on a soft
day toward the end of January, & taking a short cut to the
Piazza _____, struck a little, out of the way street, apparently
quite deserted in the waning light. The houses were old &
ruinous, & if Guy had found time to pause, their tumbling
picturesqueness would have delighted his artist-eye; but as it
was, he was in too great haste to notice anything, until at a
turn in the street he nearly stumbled across a little drooping
figure huddled against a broken flight of steps. Bending down
in astonishment, he asked in Italian what was the matter.
There was no answer, or movement, & he repeated his question
more anxiously. Just then a coarse-faced woman came swinging down the street bare-headed, & paused in astonishment to
see the handsome Signore Inglese bending over a little, cower-

ing contadina with her face hidden. "Eh, she won't move, Signore," said the woman, grinning. "She's been there these three hours." "Is she dead?" asked Guy, pityingly. "Dead? Santa Maria! No, not she. Maybe she is crazy." "You cannot leave her here," said Guy; "if she is alive she should be taken in somewhere." The woman shrugged her shoulders. "I tell you, she won't move. I don't know who she is." "Poverina!" said Guy, very low; but he had scarcely spoken when a tremor shot through the crouching form at his feet, & a faint little cry reached him. "Signore—it is Teresina!" "Teresina," repeated Guy in amazement. "Are you ill? What is the matter?" "Eh," said the woman, staring, "The Signore knows her, then?" "What has happened?" Guy continued, as a burst of sobs answered his questions. "Will you get up, Teresina, & let me carry you into some house?" But she did not lift her hidden face, nor move from her cowering attitude. Guy was in sore perplexity. He could not leave her, not knowing whether she was ill or frightened in some way; & the woman who had been watching him with an expression of sleepy surprise on her heavy face ran off here in pursuit of a brown-legged little boy who was scampering toward the Piazza. Just then, as Guy was gazing doubtfully down the crooked street, two people appeared moving quickly against the dark sunset glow; one a short, plain-faced little woman, with the indefinable air of an English servant—the other tall, & blonde, with soft blue eyes & her hands full of flowers. "Miss Graham!" exclaimed Guy, as she recognized him with a start & a deepening blush. "What is the matter?" said Madeline, glancing with surprise towards Teresina while Priggett, the maid, hung back with a disapproving stare. "Who is that poor creature, Mr. Hastings?

Why," she continued suddenly, "it must be your little peasant
—Teresina!" "So it is," said Guy, "& I cannot find whether she
is ill or only unhappy. She will not move, & I cannot get her to
answer my questions." "Poor thing!" and Madeline, regardless
of the dirty cobble-stones & her own soft, pretty dress, knelt
down beside Teresina; & began to speak in her sweet, shy Italian. "Will you not tell us if you are suffering?" she said; "we
are so sorry for you & we cannot leave you here." "Miss—" said
Priggett in an agony, "Miss, it's growing very dark." "Never
mind, Priggett. Mr. Hastings, will you hold these flowers,
please?" & putting her roses into his hand, she quietly slipped
her arm about Teresina & raised the poor little drooping head
tenderly. "I do not think she is in pain—speak to her, Mr.
Hastings." Guy bent over her & said a few soothing words; &
Madeline, still kneeling by her side, asked again very gently:
"What is it, Teresina?" "Tell the Signora," urged Guy. "She
is very kind & wants to help you." Teresina was still sobbing,
but less violently & now she made no attempt to hide her face;
& in a few moments they caught a little, trembling answer.
"I am hungry." "Poor thing—poor thing—" said Madeline,
through her tears. "Have you no home?" She gave a little
shriek & tried to hide her face, repeating passionately "No, no,
no!" "She is not fit to answer any questions," said Madeline.
"Mr. Hastings, she must be carried into some house at once &
taken care of." The woman who had stared at Guy came back
just then from her chase to the piazza; & calling her, they persuaded her to let Teresina be taken into her house close by.
Guy lifted the poor, fainting creature in his arms & Madeline
followed, for once regardless of Priggett's indignant glances,
while the woman led the way up some tumbling steps into a

wretched little room. The night had fallen when, having left some money & sundry directions, they turned once more into the lonely street, Madeline shyly accepting Guy's escort home. "I will go & see the poor thing tomorrow," she said, her sweet voice full of pity. "I think she has had a great blow. She does not seem really ill—only exhausted." "She could not be under kinder care—poor child!" said Guy, thoughtfully. "I cannot understand what has happened. She was happily married to her lover last year—as you know." "He may have died. How lonely she seemed! O poor, poor thing—it makes me feel almost guilty to think how loved & happy I am while others . . ." Madeline brushed away her tears hastily, & for a few moments neither spoke. The next morning found Priggett & her young mistress hurrying down the same obscure street, laden with baskets & shawls, towards the house into which Teresina had been carried. She was still lying on the low bed where they had left her the night before, her great eyes wide with grief, her childish face haggard with lines of suffering. "She won't eat much, Signora," said Giovita, the woman of the house, as Madeline bent anxiously over the bed, "but I think she'll be better soon, poor fanciulla!" Teresina turned her eyes to the fair, pitying face that stooped above her. "You are the beautiful Signora," she whispered, "that came to me last night. The Signore Inglese said you would be kind." Madeline's colour brightened softly; he called her kind! "I want to be your friend, Teresina," she answered; "for he has told me a great deal about you, & we are both so sorry for you!" Teresina sighed. A new contentment was entering into her eyes as they met those other eyes, pure & tender as a guardian Angel's. "You look like one of the Saints in the great pictures," she murmured dreamily.

"It was at Easter—I saw it—the saint with the white face like yours." "Never mind that, Teresina," Madeline said gently. "I want you to tell me why you were so hungry & unhappy & all alone in the street last night. Do not be afraid to tell me. If you have no friends, I want to help you & take care of you." "I have no friends," Teresina whispered, still gazing up at Madeline. "Oh, I am so unhappy, Signora . . . I ran away to starve all alone . . . I could not kill myself . . ." she shuddered & hid her face with a burst of sobs. At first Madeline could win no more from her, but gradually, as she sat by the wretched bedside, she learned the story of Teresina's sorrow. She had been married—poor child!—to her sweetheart, Matteo, & they had been so happy, until Matteo could get no work, & grew harsh & reckless. Teresina was unhappy, & cried because he did not love her any more—& the bambino died of the fever, & Matteo got worse & worse. Still there was no work, & Teresina was ill at home—Matteo said he could not feed her. He used to go out all day, & one day he did not come back— she never saw him again, & she knew that he had deserted her. "Oh, it was so lonely without the bambino," ended the poor little wife, through her tears. "I could not bear to go home, for the Madre is dead & the Padre was so angry when I married Matteo—& I did not want anything but to run away & hide my- self—& die." But she did not die; Madeline felt a new interest in her after this & watched & comforted her tenderly; & in a few days she was strong enough to be moved from the wretched house to the Graham's apartment. They sent for her father, a rough old peasant who would have nothing to do with her, & cursed her for marrying against his will. Teresina begged with passionate tears not to go back to him; & Madeline had grown so attached to her that she easily prevailed on her father to keep the poor child at least for the present. On Teresina's part there had sprung up a blind adoration of the beautiful Signorina who was the Signore Inglese's friend; she asked nothing but to stay with her always & serve her & follow her like a dog. Guy was not a little interested in the fate of his poor little model; & Madeline's kindness to her won him more & more. Few girls, he thought, would have behaved as nobly, as impulsively & as tenderly as Madeline had done. And so it was that Teresina's misfortune revealed to him the earnest, quiet beauty of this shy English girl's character, & made him think more & more seriously every day that in this world of sin & folly & darkness there are after all some pure spirits moving, like sun-gleams in a darkened chamber.

Chap. XIII. Villa Doria-Pamfili.

"If thou canst reason, sure thou dost not love." *Old Play.*

ON ONE OF THOSE delicious languid days of Spring that follow in the footsteps of the short Roman Winter, the Grahams drove out to spend a long afternoon at the Villa Doria-Pamfili, where the violets & anemones were awake in every hollow, & the trees putting on their tenderest silver-green. Guy rode by the side of the carriage, having breakfasted that morning with its occupants & engaged to join them again in the afternoon. Day by day Madeline's society had grown sweeter & more needful to him, her soft presence effacing as nothing else could the bitter past. Great sorrows cast long shadows; & in reality the gloom of his disappointed love still hung darkly over Hastings' life; but it was a softened gloom when he was at Madeline's side, losing his heart-loneliness in her sunny companionship. When a man marries without falling in love he always has at hand an elaborate course of reasoning to prove beyond all doubt the advisableness of the step he takes; & some such process was occupying Guy's thoughts as he trotted along on his chesnut, Rienzi, beside the Grahams' carriage. Since his engagement had been broken he had, as we have said, felt all hope & interest in life slipping away from his empty grasp; & now that he had met & known Madeline it struck him with what renewed dreariness he would return to his old, reckless ways when their paths divided. More than once he had dreamed of his motley studio with a fair figure moving continually about it, or a soft, flushed face bending over him as he worked; & had wondered if life would not get a new zest with some-one beside him to be cherished & worked for until death. Madeline's peculiar innocence & shy simplicity had soothed him in contrast to the gay, wilful charms with which his most cruel recollections were united; he thought that here was a shrinking, clinging creature who would need his tender pro-tection & look up to him always for the help & love that another had despised. In short, on that sweet Spring afternoon, the impressions & reflections of the whole Winter had nearly resolved themselves into a determination to ask Madeline for his wife, when the whole party reached the gates of the Villa Doria. Giving Rienzi over to his groom, Guy stood by the car-riage to help Madeline & her mother out; & then they all strolled along through the beautiful princely grounds. Made-line's passion for flowers was very pretty that day; prettier than ever it seemed to Hastings, as she bent down to fill her hands with violets, or ran on in search of a new blossom under the greening boughs. Oh, the sunshiny peacefulness of that long Spring afternoon, under the soft Italian sky, with the wood-flowers underfoot & the tree-branches closing above, bubbling over with the earliest bird-music of the new-drest year! They wandered on in the delicious Spring-time idleness that had fallen upon them all; now & then resting on a bench in some quiet alley or soft, violet-sown slope, or pausing to ad-mire a beautiful view—all forgetting that even in the Villa Doria-Pamfili, on a Heavenly day of Spring, the hours will fly & the sun stoop to the west. Strolling along by Madeline's side, carrying her sunshade & her cloak, Guy recalled Robert Spencer's bright words: "How lightly falls the foot of Time That only treads on flowers!" He repeated them to her, adding as he glanced down at his feet, "literally true here, is it not, Miss Graham? You trample a violet at every step." "Oh, I am so sorry for them!" said Madeline, earnestly; "but what can I do? My hands are quite full." She was standing still, in her floating white dress, framed by rising boughs, & holding a great mass of the balmy purple treasures. Guy Hastings had never seen a fairer picture in a fairer setting. "If I had my pallette & canvas here, Miss Graham, I should paint you as you stand, for a Proserpine." "I am glad you haven't then," returned Madeline, laughing, "for I should be longing to escape in search of some more flowers, & how tired I should get, standing so long." "You will be tired now if you don't rest a little," said Guy. They were standing near an old grey stone bench, hidden in tree-shadows, with a cushioning of deep moss & anemones around it. "Let us sit down, Miss Graham," he continued. "You are dropping your violets at every step & my practical mind suggests that they should be tied together to prevent further loss." Madeline laughed, & sat down while he quietly folded her cloak about her, & then took his place at her side. Mr. and Mrs. Graham had walked on slowly, & were presently lost among the trees; but neither Guy nor Madeline noticed this—which is perhaps scarcely surprising. It suited Hastings very well to be sitting there, holding the violets, while Madeline's soft hands took them from him one by one & bound them carefully together; he had never found her quite so lovely as on that golden afternoon. "Am I to have none as a reward for my help?" he asked, as she took the last violets to

88

add to her bunch. "You are very miserly with your treasures, Miss Graham." "Because I don't think you love them as well as I do," she said, smiling. "But you did hold them very well, & here is your reward." She handed him two or three, with her soft blush, & he was very near kissing the white ungloved hand that offered them. But reflecting that so sudden a proceeding might startle his shy damsel, & break up the sweet, idle course of their tête à tête, he wisely refrained, & only thanked her as he put the violets in his coat. "I shall wear them as my Legion of honour," he added, smiling. "But they will fade so soon! Do you know," said Madeline, glancing up into the handsome blue eyes bent on her face, & then looking quickly downward with a blush, as if she had read some secret there too subtle to be put into words—"do you know, it always makes me a little sad—foolishly, I suppose—to gather flowers, when I think of that." "Gather ye roses while ye may!" hummed Guy, laughing. "I don't think the flowers are to be pitied, Miss Graham." "Why not?" said Madeline, very low. "Why not? Because— I put myself in their place & judge their feelings by—my own." Madeline's heart beat quicker, & she sprang up suddenly. "Where is Papa, Mr. Hastings? I think . . ." Guy caught her hand. "Stay, Miss Graham," he said as she rose. "Before you go, I want to say a few words to you. Will you hear me?" He led her quietly back to her shady seat, & sat down beside her again, leaning forward to catch sight of her half-turned face & dropped lashes. "I do not know," he went on, in his low, winning voice, "what right I have to say these words, or to expect an answer; for I feel, day by day, as I watch you, so young, so happy, so beautiful—pardon me—I feel how little I can give in return for what your kindness has encouraged me to ask."

He spoke with a calm grave gentleness as far removed from the anxious, entangled faltering of a lover as if he had been offering friendly criticism or long-prepared advice. Madeline's only answer was the rising crimson on her cheek; & he continued, in the same quiet, undisturbed tones: "I told you once that there was little interest or happiness left in my life—a wasted life I fear it has been!—but since I have known you, Miss Graham, it has seemed as though an Angel were beckoning me back to a new existence—a more peaceful one than I have ever known." He paused. His eyes had wandered from the flushed face at his side to the golden streaks of sunset barring the soft Western sky. It seemed to Madeline as if the wild, hot beating of her heart must drown her voice; she could not speak. "You know—you must know—" he said presently, "how miserably little I have to offer—the battered remains of a misspent life! Heaven forbid that I should claim the same right as another man to this little hand, (let me hold it). Heaven forbid that I should call myself worthy of the answer I have dared to hope for!" She had half-risen again, with a faint attempt to free her hand; but he rose also, & quietly drew her closer. "Madeline, can you guess that I want to ask you to be my wife?" He had possession of both her hands, & she did not struggle but only stood before him with eyes downcast & burning cheeks. "Will you give me no answer, Madeline?" he said, gently. There was a faint movement of her tremulous lips, & bending down he caught a soft, fluttering "Yes." He lifted her right hand to his lips & for a moment neither spoke. Then Madeline said, in a frightened, half-guilty voice, "Oh, let us go to Papa." "They are coming to us," returned Guy, still detaining her, as he caught sight of Mr. & Mrs. Graham

moving slowly towards them under the shadowy ilex-clumps.
"Why do you want to run away from me, Madeline? I have
the right to call you so now, have I not?" "Yes," she murmured, still not daring to meet his kind, searching eyes. "But,
come, please, let us go & meet them. I . . . I must tell Mamma,
you know . . ." "One moment. I have another right also, dear
one!" He stooped & kissed her quickly as he spoke, then drawing her trembling hand through his arm, led her forward to
the advancing couple under the trees. Madeline's tearful confusion alone would have betrayed everything to her mother's
quick eyes. "Oh, Mamma, Mamma," she cried, running to Mrs.
Graham & hiding her face. Guy came up, in his quiet easy way,
looking frankly into the mother's rosy, troubled face. "I have
asked Madeline to be my wife," he said, "& she has consented."
"Maddy, Maddy," cried Mrs. Graham, tearfully, "is it so, my
dear?" But Mr. Graham was disposed to view things more
cheerfully, & while the mother & daughter were weeping in
each other's arms, shook Hastings' hand with ill-concealed delight. "She is our only one, Hastings, & we could not trust you
with a dearer thing, but—there, I won't exactly say 'No'!" "Believe me," Guy returned, "I know how precious is the treasure
I have dared to ask for. I shall try to make myself worthy of
her by guarding her more tenderly than my own life—if indeed you consent. . . ." Madeline turned a shy, appealing glance
at Mr. Graham as she stood clinging to her mother. "Eh, Maddy?" said the merchant, goodnaturedly, "what can the old
father say, after all? Well—I don't know how to refuse. We
must think, we must think." "Madeline," said Hastings, bending over her, "will you take my arm to the carriage?" They did
not say much as they walked along in the dying sunset light;

but a pleasant sense of possessorship came over Guy as he felt the shy hand lying on his arm—& who can sum up the wealth of Madeline's silent happiness? And so they passed through the gates, & the Spring twilight fell over Villa Doria-Pamfili.

Chap. XIV. Left Alone.

"Death, like a robber, crept in unaware."
Old Play. (From the Spanish)

THREE SLOW WEEKS of illness followed Georgie's imprudence at Lochiel House; & in September when she began to grow a little better, she was ordered off to the Mediterranean for the Winter. She scarcely regretted this; the trip in Lord Breton's yacht would be pleasant, & any change of scene welcome for a time—but as far as her health was concerned, she cared very little for its preservation, since life in every phase grew more hopelessly weary day by day. Favourable winds made their passage short & smooth, but when they reached the Mediterranean Georgie was too poorly to enjoy the short cruise along its coast which had been planned, & they made directly for Nice. After a few dreary days of suffering at a Hôtel, Lord Breton gave up all idea of prolonging his yachting & by his physician's advice moved at once into a small sunny villa where Georgie could have perfect quiet for several months. She was very ill again, & it was long before she recovered from the exhaustion of the journey. Even when she began to grow better & lie on her lounge or creep downstairs, it was a cheerless household; for Lord Breton, cut off by recurring attacks of gout from any exercise or amusement that the town might have afforded, grew daily more irritable &

gloomy. Nor did Georgie attempt at first to rouse herself for
his sake; it was hard enough, she thought, to be shut up forever
face to face with her own unquenchable sorrow & remorse. It
did not occur to her that wherever her heart might be, her
duty lay with her husband. She learned this one March day, as
we do learn all our great heart-lessons, suddenly & plainly. Her
physician had been to see her, & in taking leave said very gravely: "in truth, Lady Breton, I am just now more anxious about
your husband's welfare than your own. He suffers a great deal,
& needs constant distraction. You will excuse my saying,
frankly, that I think the loneliness, the want of—may I say
sympathy? in his life, is preying upon him heavily. I cannot
tell you to be easy, where I see such cause for anxiety." These
words—grave & direct, as a good physician's always are—affected Georgie strangely. Could it be that he too suffered, &
felt a bitter want in his life? she questioned herself. Could it
be that she had failed in her duty? that something more was
demanded of her? And with this there came over her with a
great rush, the thought of her own selfish absorption & neglect. Had he not, after all, tried to be a kind & a generous
husband? Had she not repulsed him over & over again? In
that hour of sad self-conviction the first unselfish tears that
had ever wet her cheek sprang to Georgie Breton's eyes. Remorse had taken a new & a more practical form with her. For
once she saw how small, how base & petty had been her part
in the great, harmonious drama of life; how mean the ends
for which she had made so great a sacrifice; how childish the
anger & disappointment she had cherished—how self-made
the fate against which she had railed. She had looked forward
that day to a drive, the chief pleasure & excitement of her

monotonous hours; but ringing the bell, she countermanded her carriage, & went downstairs to her husband's room. Lord Breton was sitting helpless in his arm-chair, the sun dazzling his eyes through the unshaded window, & his newspapers pushed aside as if whatever interest they contained had long ago been exhausted. He looked up with some surprise when Georgie entered with her slow, feeble step, & crossing the room quietly dropped the Venetian shade. "Thank you," he said. "The sun was blinding. I hope you are feeling better to-day, Georgina?" "Oh, yes, I think so," she returned with a brave effort at gaiety, as she sank down in a low chair. "But I am afraid you are suffering. I . . . I am awfully sorry." Lord Breton's amazement waxed stronger. He even forgave the slang in which this unusual sympathy was clothed. "My pain is not very great," he replied, affably, "& I think has been slightly alleviated thanks to Dr. W. I hope soon to be released from my imprisonment." "You *must* be bored," assented Georgie, then added suddenly as a new thought struck her: "I think you said once you liked . . . you were fond of playing chess. I . . . shall we play a game today?" Lord Breton wondered if the world were upsidedown. "Yes," he said, even more affably, "I was once a good player, & it has always been a favourite pastime of mine. I never proposed it to you, as I understood that—that you had a peculiar aversion to the game." Georgie turned scarlet. "That is nothing," she said, hastily. "I think there is a board in the sitting-room. I will ring." She sent for the board, & the contest immediatly began. How was it that in this new impulse of self-sacrifice Georgie began to lose the lonely weight of her sorrow, & brighten herself in proportion as her efforts dispersed Lord Breton's moody dullness? They were both good players, but Georgie being the quicker-witted would have won had her tact not shewn her that she could please Lord Breton better by allowing herself to be defeated. It was quite late when the game ended, & Georgie had absolutely forgotten her drive; but her husband had not. "Surely you are going out today, Georgina?" he said. "You should have gone earlier, indeed. I fear I unintentionally detained you . . ." "Not at all!" she returned, promptly. "I had not meant to go." "Nevertheless you should take advantage of the favourable weather. It is not yet too late." "I had rather stay here, please," said Georgie, but Lord Breton would not hear of it. He ordered the carriage, & she went up to dress with a lighter heart than she carried for many a day. As she came down again, some impulse made her enter her husband's room. "There is nothing I can do for you in the town?" she asked. "No, nothing at all, nothing at all," returned Lord Breton in a gratified voice. "Be careful of the evening air. You are well-wrapped?" "Oh, yes," she said, lingering. "I shall not be long gone. Goodbye." "Goodbye." She took a short drive in the mild Spring air, & came back, strengthened & freshened, before sundown. Strangely enough, there was no one to help her from the carriage but Sidenham, who always accompanied her; & in the hall she was met by her physician. A sudden foreboding rushed through her mind as she saw him coming towards her. "What is it?" she said faintly. He gave his arm & led her quietly into the empty salon. "Sit down, Lady Breton. Compose yourself, for Heaven's sake," he said. "Lord Breton is—very ill." She looked at him in a dazed way. "I—I don't think I understand," she gasped. "Your husband is very dangerously ill," said the physician again. "How can that be? He was much better when I went out—tell me, tell me!" Sidenham had brought a glass of wine, which she swallowed hurriedly at a sign from the doctor. "Now tell me," she repeated, wildly. "My dear Lady Breton, try to quiet yourself. You say he seemed better—in better spirits—when you went out?" "Yes—I thought so." "So his servant tells me," the physician continued gently. "He said he had not seen his master in such good spirits since he came to Nice.—Compose yourself—Take some more wine. —Half an hour ago I was sent for—" he paused, & in that pause she snatched at the truth he was trying gently to postpone. "He is dead?" she whispered. "Tell me at once. I am calm." "He has been taken from us," the physician answered, his voice tremulous with emotion. "Taken from us without suffering, thank God! His servant went into his room & found him . . . dead. I was sent for at once." "Go on," said Georgie, in a low voice, fixing her tearless eyes on his earnest, pitying face. "I can hear all. He died without . . . pain?" "Entirely. Nothing could have been more sudden or painless." For a little while neither spoke; then Georgie rose suddenly. "Take me to him," she said, in the same calm voice. "Take me, please." "Can you bear it— so soon, Lady Breton?" "Take me," she repeated. "I told him I would come back soon!" She put her hand on the doctor's arm, & he led her out across the hall in silence; but at the door of her husband's room she fainted suddenly, & fell back as she had done at Lochiel House. They carried her up to her room, & it was long before her consciousness could be restored. When she was roused from her stupour it changed into wild fever & delirium, & for nearly a week after Lord Breton's sad & quiet funeral, she lay raving and moaning on her darkened bed. The fever was quieted at last, but she was terribly weakened & even when her mind returned scarcely realized that she had entered into the first days of her widowhood. It was talked of all over Nice, how the old English peer, Lord Breton of Lowood, had been carried off suddenly by the gout, while his wife was out driving; how rich & haughty he was; & how she, poor young creature, delicate, bright & beautiful, & just 21, had been left there in the sunny Mediterranean town, far from friends & home, with no one but her physician & her servants to care for her or to comfort her—had been left there—alone. But perhaps no one quite guessed all the peculiar bitterness that those words contained when, with her returning consciousness they dawned upon Georgie—"left alone."

Chap. XV. A Summons.

"Could ye come back to me, Douglas, Douglas,
   In the old likeness that I knew!" *Miss Mulock*: "Douglas."

LORD BRETON DIED early in March; & it was three weeks later
that Guy Hastings, returning from a certain eventful visit to
Villa Doria-Pamfili which I have recorded in a previous chapter, found awaiting him at his studio a black-bordered letter
with a Nice postmark. If he had not recognized the writing,
this post-mark would have told him in an instant that it was
from Georgie; for though all intercourse had ceased between
them he had heard through some English friends that she was
passing the Winter at Nice. The black edge & black seal of the
envelope, united to the well-known manuscript, were a deep
shock; & it was several minutes before he could compose himself sufficiently to read the letter.

"Nice, March ____[th]*—Dear Guy, I should never venture to
write this if I did not feel sure that I shall not live very long.
Since Lord Breton's death I have been much worse, they say;
but I only know that my heart is breaking, & that I* must *see
you once for goodbye. If you can forgive all the wrong I have
done you—what bitter suffering it has brought me since!—
come to me as soon as possible. Georgie."*

99

Hastings could scarcely read the end of the few, trembling lines for the tears that blinded him. Those heart-broken, pleading words seemed to melt away in an instant all the barriers of disappointment & wounded pride, & to wake up the old estranged love that was after all not dead—but sleeping! He scarcely noticed the mention of Lord Breton's death, which reached him now for the first time—he only felt that Georgie was dying, that she had been unhappy & that she loved him still. Then there came a rebellious cry against the fate that reunited them only to part once more. Why must she die when a new promise of brightness was breaking through the storm of life? Why must she die when he was there once more to shield & cherish her as he had dreamed long ago? She should not die! Life must revive with reviving happiness, & the shadow of death wane in the sunrise of their joy. So he raved, pacing his lonely studio, through the long hours of the evening until in the midst of the incoherent flood of thought that overwhelmed him, there flashed suddenly the harsh reality that he had for the moment lost. What if Georgie lived? *He was not free!* How the self-delusion, the hasty mistake of that day, started up cruelly before him in this new light. It was he, then, who had been unfaithful & impatient, & she who had loved on through all, to this cruel end. Thus he reproached himself, as the hopeless cloud of grief closed around him once more. I know not what wild temptations hurried through his mind in that terrible night's struggle. A faint fore-hint of dawn was climbing the gray Orient when at last he threw himself on his bed to seize a few hours sleep before he brought the resolutions of this night into action. He had decided that come what would, he must see Georgie at once—even though it were for the last time, & only to return into the deeper desolation which his error had brought upon him. In this last revolution of feeling he had almost entirely lost sight of the fact that Georgie was dying, & that even in the case of his being free, their parting was inevitable. It seemed to him now that his madness (as he called it in his hopeless self-reproach) had alone exiled him from a renewed life of love & peace with the girl of his heart. He had forgotten, in the whirl of despairing grief, that the shadow of the Angel of Death fell sternly between him & Georgie. When after a short, unrestful sleep he rose & dressed, the morning sun was high over Rome; & he found he had no time to lose if he should attempt to start for Civita Vecchia by the early train. He would not breakfast, but thinking that the early air might freshen him for his long journey, walked immediatly to the Grahams' apartment. He had meant to ask for Mr. Graham, but when he reached the door his heart failed, & he merely told the servant he would not disturb him. Taking one of his cards, he wrote on it hurriedly in pencil: "I am called suddenly to Nice for a few days. Cannot tell when I will be back. Start this morning via Civita Vecchia." He left this for Madeline, knowing that any more elaborate explanation of the object of his journey would be useless; & an hour later he was on his way to Civita Vecchia to meet a steamer to Genoa. The weary, interminable hours drew slowly towards the night; but it seemed to Hastings that the sad journey would never come to an end. When he reached Nice the next morning after a day & a night of steady travel, the strain of thought & fatigue had been so great that he was scarcely conscious of his surroundings, & having driven to the nearest Hôtel went at once up to his room to rest, if indeed rest were possible. A blinding headache had come on, & he was glad to lie on the bed with his windows darkened until the afternoon. He had almost lost the power of thinking now; a dull, heavy weight of anguish seemed to press down destroying all other sensation. When at last he felt strong enough to rouse himself, he rang for a servant & enquired for Lady Breton's villa in the hope that someone in the Hôtel might direct him thither—for poor Georgie, in her hasty note, had forgotten to give her address. Lord Breton's death had made too much noise in Nice for his residence to remain unknown; but Guy, not feeling as well as he had fancied, sat down & wrote a few lines asking when he should find Georgie prepared for him— & despatched these by the servant. It was a great relief when, about an hour later, a note was brought back in the meek, ladylike handwriting of Mrs. Rivers, who had of course joined her daughter on Lord Breton's death. *Dear Guy,* it ran, *We think our darling Georgie is a little better today, but not strong enough to see you. If she is no worse tomorrow, can you come in the afternoon at about four o'clock? This is a time of great anxiety for us all, which I am sure you must share. My poor child longs to see you. Your loving Cousin, M.A. Rivers.*

Hastings scarcely knew how that miserable day passed. He had intended writing to Mr. Graham, but he had lost all power of self-direction, & the one absorbing thought that pressed upon him drowned every lesser duty in its vortex of hopeless pain. Early the next morning he sent to the Villa to enquire after Georgie, & word was brought that my lady was no worse, so that a faint hope began to buoy him up as the hours crept on towards the time appointed for their meeting. His agitation was too intense for outward expression, & he was quite calm when at four o'clock he started out on foot through the sunny streets. It was not a long way to the white villa in its fragrant rose-garden; & before long a servant dressed in black had ushered him into the cool salon where a slight, pink-eyed personage in heavier black than of old, came tearfully forward to meet him. "She will be so glad to see you, Guy," wept poor Mrs. Rivers. "She said you were to come at once. Are you ready? This is the way."

Chap. XVI. Too Late.

"Tis better to have loved & lost
Than never to have loved at all." *Tennyson.* In Memoriam.

GUY FOLLOWED MRS. RIVERS in silence as she led the way across the polished hall & up a short flight of stairs. Leaving him a moment in a small, sunny boudoir bright with pictures & flowers, she went on into an inner room where there was a faint sound of voices. Returning a moment later, she came up & laid an appealing hand of his arm. "You will be careful, dear Guy, not to agitate her? She is so easily excited, so weak, poor darling! Come now." She threw the door open, standing back for him to enter the room, & then closed it softly upon him. It was a large room, with two windows through which the mellow afternoon sunlight streamed; & beside one of these windows, in a deep, cushioned arm-chair Georgie sat with a pale, expectant face. So fragile, so sad & white she looked that he scarcely knew her as he crossed the threshold; then she held out her thin little hand & called softly: "Guy!" It was the old voice; that at least had not changed! He came forward almost blindly, & felt his hand grasped in the soft, trembling fingers on which his parting kiss had fallen more than a year ago. He could not speak at first, & she too was silent; both lost in the intensity of their emotion. "Sit down beside me," she said at last, still clasping his hand gently; & then he looked up again

& met the wide, burning hazel eyes brimmed with tears. "Oh, Guy," she cried, "I never thought to see you again. Have you come to forgive me?" "Do not talk of that," he answered with an effort. "Only tell me that you are stronger, that you will be well soon." She shook her head quietly. "I cannot tell you that; & I *must* tell you how I have suffered through my folly—my wicked folly." Her tears were falling softly, but she made no attempt to hide them. "I think," she went on, still holding Guy's hand, "that the thought—which pursued me always & everywhere—of the wrong I did you, has killed me. When I look back at the hours of shame & suffering I have passed, I almost wonder I lived through them—I almost feel glad to die! Surely, surely there never was so wicked & miserable a creature in the world—I shudder at the mere thought of my hard, silly selfishness." She paused, her voice broken by a sob; then hurried on, as if to relieve herself of a great weight. "Oh, Guy, it would not have been so bad if all this time I had not—cared; but I did. There was no one like you—no one with whom I could feel really happy as with you. Then I thought I would drown all these sad recollections by going into society; but under all the gayety & the noise, Guy, my heart ached—ached so cruelly! Listen a moment longer. When I thought how you must despise me & hate me, I felt like killing myself. I seemed to have been such a traitor to you, although you were the only man I ever loved! I gave up all thought of seeing you again until—until I heard them say I was dying, & then I got courage, remembering how tender & how generous you always were— & as I lay there after the fever left me, I could think nothing but: 'I must see Guy, I must be forgiven,' over & over again." Her voice failed again, & she leaned back among her cushions.

"And you came," she continued, presently, "you came though I had wronged you & insulted you and—and deserved nothing but your contempt. You have come to forgive me!" "Hush, dearest," Guy answered, struggling to master his voice, "try to forget everything that is past. Let us be happy—for a little while." "Oh, I am so happy," she cried; "perhaps, after all, then, you did not think of me quite so hardly—as I deserved. Perhaps—you understood a little—you felt sorry—" "My dearest," he answered, passionately; "I did more; I—loved you." A new light seemed to flash over her face; he could feel the hand that clasped his tighten & tremble. "Don't—don't," she gasped, in a voice full of pain, "it can't be true—don't try to love me—I—I only meant to be forgiven." "Forgiven!" said Guy, with a sudden bitterness, "it is I who need to be forgiven, if there is forgiveness in Heaven or earth for such folly & madness as have been mine! Oh, Georgie darling, I think I have been in a horrible dream." Startled by the sudden wildness of his words, Georgie lifted her eyes full of sorrowful questioning to his. "What is it, Guy? Are we all to be unhappy?" And then, in a few, broken words of shame & self-reproach, he told her how when all the hope & sacredness of life was slipping from him, he had met Madeline, & thinking that such a pure presence might hallow his days, & recall him from the reckless path to which despair had beckoned him, had asked her to be his wife. When he ended, Georgie sat quite still, a grave pity shining in the eyes that seemed too large for her little, wasted face. "I am so glad, Guy," she said, in her sweet, tremulous tone, still clasping his hand; "so glad that I may die without that dreadful thought of having spoiled your life as well as my own. Oh, Guy, I am quite happy now! I am sure she must be good & gentle, because you are fond of her; & I am sure she will be a good wife to you, because—no one could help it." She paused a moment, but he could not trust himself to speak, & gathering strength, she went on with touching earnestness, "Guy, you will be good to her, will you not? And you will make her home pleasant, & forget everything that is gone for her sake? And kiss her, Guy, on her wedding-day, from some one who calls herself her sister. Do you promise?" "Anything, dearest girl," he answered, brokenly. She smiled; one of those rare, brilliant smiles that to his tear-dimmed eyes made her face as the face of an Angel. "My own brave Guy," she whispered. "And you will go back to your painting, & your work— & when I am dead, no one will say 'She ruined his life.'" "They will say, dearest, that if forgiving love & tenderness could wash out his folly, when he thought that nothing but despair was left in life, she did so as no one else could." "Hush, Guy, hush," she faltered, as he kissed the trembling hand laid on his own, "you pain me. I do not deserve so much. I do not deserve to die so happy—so unspeakably happy." "To die!" he repeated, passionately. "Darling, do [not] say that—I had almost forgotten! They said you were better." She shook her head, again with that sweet, flitting smile. "It is better you should know, Guy—& indeed all is best! I have not courage to live, if I had the strength. But you must go back to a braver & a happier life, & then to die will be like going to sleep with the consciousness that the day is over, & when I wake there will be . . . no more sorrow & regrets. . . ." There was a long pause. The clock ticked steadily; the afternoon sunshine waned, & the sand in an hour-glass on the table trickled its last grains through to mark the ended hour. Guy sat clasping the little wasted fingers,

& leaning his face against his hand in the hopeless silence of grief. At last Georgie, bending towards him, spoke, very tenderly & quietly: "Look Guy; the twilight is coming. We must say goodbye." "Goodbye?" he echoed vaguely, only half-startled out of his bitter dream by the strangely calm, low words. "For the last time," Georgie went on, drawing her hand softly away. "Oh, Guy, say again before you go that you forgive me everything—everything." He had risen, dazzled by his tears, & turned to the window that she might not see his white face & quivering lips; he could not answer. "Guy, Guy," she repeated passionately, "you forgive me? Guy, come closer; bend down, so, that I may see your face—for it is growing dark. Say 'I forgive you,' Guy!" "I—forgive you." Once more the old, radiant smile, transfiguring her pale features as health & enjoyment had never done, answered his broken words. "Thank you—that is all I wanted," she whispered, gazing up into the haggard face bent over her. "If you knew, Guy, how happy I am ... now...." Silence again. "Now kiss me, Guy, & bid me goodnight." Almost childishly, she held up her little, trembling lips; & stifling back his anguish he stooped & kissed them solemnly. "Guy, goodnight." "Goodnight . . . my Love! my Love!—"

. . . . .

Someone led him gently from the room; & he knew that he had seen the face of his beloved for the last time on earth. The next morning word was brought him that Georgie had passed very quietly with the dawn, "to where, beyond these voices, there is Peace."

Chap. XVII. Afterwards.

"—But who that has loved forgets?" *Old Song.*

FIVE YEARS, FRUITFUL in many a silent change, have passed since the life-chronicle which filled these pages, closed with Georgie Breton's peaceful death; fruitful in so great changes, that before parting with the different persons who have filled our story-world, it is tempting to take one last glance into their altered lives & households, that we may carry away with us the memory, not of what they were, but of what they are. The villa at Nice in which Lord Breton & his young wife died has passed into other hands; but the story of the old English Lord's death, followed so soon & so tragically by that of the beautiful milady, still clings to it, & marks it with a peculiar interest. As for Mrs. Rivers, on her eldest daughter's death she returned at once to the seclusion of Holly Lodge, where she spends her time in tears & retirement, overwhelmed by her crape trimmings, overwhelmed by the education of her children, & by everything, poor lady, which comes in her way. A distant cousin of the late Lord Breton's (a grave married man with a large family) has inherited his title & his estates; & there are three blooming, marrigeable girls at Lowood; for whom the new Lord & Lady Breton are continually giving croquet-parties, dinners & balls in the hope that the eligible young men of the county may be attracted thither, & discover their charms. Mr.

and Mrs. Graham have come back to England too, & have bought a pretty, well-kept little place not far from London, whose walls are adorned with many foreign works of art, collected during their memorable tour on the continent. The honest couple live very quietly, keeping occasional feast-days when the postman leaves at the door a thick blue envelope with a foreign stamp; an envelope containing a pile of close-written sheets beginning "Darling Mamma & Papa" & ending "Your own loving daughter, Madeline." And with what pride will they shew you a photograph, which was enclosed in one of these very letters, of a little, earnest, bright-eyed man of two or three, on the back of which a loving hand has written "Baby's picture." One more English household calls our attention before we wander back for the last time to Italian skies; a comfortable London house in a pleasant neighbourhood, near all the clubs. Jack Egerton is established there; our Bohemian Jack, who has come into a nice fortune in the course of these last years, & has also met with a pale, melancholy, fascinating French Marquise, who so far disturbed his cherished theories of misogynism, that a very quiet wedding was the result of their intimacy, & who now presides with a tact, a grace, & a dignity of which he may well be proud, at his friendly table. So we leave him; to turn once more before parting, to a familiar, though now a changed scene—the old studio on the third floor of the Roman palazzo, where in the old days, Hastings & Egerton lounged & painted. A Signore Inglese has rented the whole floor now; & that Signore is Guy. The studio is essentially as it was; but the glamour of a woman's presence has cast the charm of order & homelikeness over its picturesque chaos, & the light footsteps of a woman cross & recross the floor as Hastings sit[s] at his easel in the sunshine. For, as will have been divined, Guy has fulfilled Georgie's latest prayer, & for nearly five years Madeline Graham has been his wife. They spend their Winters always in Rome, for the sake at once of Madeline's health & Hastings' art-studies; & there is a younger Guy who is beginning to toddle across the studio floor to his father's knee, guided by a little, blushing velvet-eyed Italian Nurse whom he has been taught to call Teresina. Guy works harder than of old, & is on a fair road to fame. He has not forgotten his old friend & Mentor, Egerton, but I doubt if he will ever accept the constant invitations to England which kind-hearted Jack sends him. For there are certain memories which time cannot kill, & change cannot efface. So Madeline is happy in a sunny, peaceful household; in returning health, & new & pleasant duties; in the most beautiful boy that mother ever sung to sleep or woke with a laughing kiss; & in a husband, who is the soul of grave courtesy & kindness. But Guy Hastings' heart is under the violets on Georgie's grave.

The End.

Contents

The End.

Begun in the Autumn of 1876 at Pencraig, Newport; finished
January 7th 1877 at New York.

"Fast and Loose—A Novelette" by David Olivieri

(*From* The Saturday Review)

It is a melancholy study of human nature to observe the suicidal passion for novel-writing of a certain numerous class of harmless fanatics who, without having a grain of literary talent or training, avail themselves of the freedom of the press to inundate a long suffering public with yellow-coloured volumes of twaddling romance. Among the latest of these deluded self-murderers we may mention (with peculiar compassion for his case seems indeed desperate) the author of "Fast & Loose," a gentleman(?) revelling in the sumptuous name of David Olivieri—a combination suggesting vividly the statuary in the Groves of Blarney, "bold Neptune, Plutarch, & Nicodemus." On first opening the pages of this "novelette," (let us be thankful it is no more) we are impressed with an idea of dashing fastness, & expect to find in a hero named Guy Hastings, who belongs to Swift's Club & has had "a dozen little affaires de coeur," the darling type of the "bold bad man" of modern literature. The very title suggests something desperate. Who is fast? What is loose? Apparently the author's well-meant intention was that everybody & everything should be fast & loose. In the very first chapter, the charming heroine describes herself as "a wicked, fast, flirtatious little pauper—a lazy, luxurious coquette!" Guy is again hopefully mentioned as "belonging to that large class whom anxious mothers call fast," &

we feel a thrill of greedy expectation when we hear that he "lived neither better nor worse than a hundred other young men" belonging to the same class. Furthermore, Guy's friend Egerton informs us that he is "not a parson either & doesn't care to preach"; & on our first introduction to Lord Breton, the peer of the story, we fondly dream to perceive the vestiges of a courtly roué of the old school. Such are the great hopes that Mr. Olivieri raises in the bosoms of his too-confident readers. We prophesy 128 pages of racy trash & are glad to think we shall be wasting our time agreeably. How is it then, that the hero evaporates into a vascillating sentimentalist who, though he is ostentatiously & repeatedly labelled as "going to the Dogs," takes so quiet & respectable a road to that mysterious goal that we have an irrepressible desire to push him on a little faster? How is it that the heroine, who, we are anxiously informed, is the fastest woman in London, does nothing that would have raised a blush on the rigid countenance of an elderly Quakeress? How is it that Lord Breton melts into a harmless gourmet, & Egerton gloomily moralizes, though he so sternly refuses to preach? It is plain, before we are well-launched on this ocean of vice, that Mr. Olivieri's talent does not lie in the painting of publicans & sinners. Nor is he more successful in the angelical contrast which he offers to the heroine's worldliness, in the person of Madeline Graham. If Madeline be Mr. Olivieri's conception of innocence, we no longer have any difficulty in understanding the motives which prompted Herod to the Massacre of the Innocents. Between these two representatives of Virtue & Vice (as Mr. Olivieri understands them) Hastings oscillates gently; until, being thrown over by Vice, he flies for salvation from some rather vague moral danger, to the willing arms of Virtue. But it would be cruel to Mr. Olivieri to take the last gloss from his gingerbread by revealing the intricacies of the thrilling plot which connects the lives of the individuals whose characters we have taken the liberty so frankly to handle. We content ourselves by saying in a sweeping summary, that whatever character Mr. Olivieri hopefully attempts to pourtray, we lose before long all the boundaries of its individuality, & find ourselves towards the welcome last page involved in a chaos of names apparently all seeking their owners. Guy might as well be Madeline, & vice versa. The Pharisees & the publicans (to continue our Biblical figure) sit down at meat together, & when they arise it seems that the mutual contact must have effaced whatever distinctive marks they originally possessed.

From the Pall Mall Budget

... And in concluding our survey of the melancholy band of nonentities which form the dramatis personae of this dolorous tale, our eye rests with pain & astonishment on the multilated, useless, unfinished picture of the Italian peasant-girl Teresina. It is evidently the author's first intention to make the hero fall indiscreetly & ruinously in love with this pretty little negative —but again Mr. Olivieri's unaesthetical morality conquers; he leaves Teresina & Guy intact, & in the end marries both in a lawful & prosaic way. Teresina's marriage is indeed followed by a tragedy of sickness & desertion; but a tragedy evidently concocted by Mr. Olivieri to get the poor girl off his hands & make way for Hastings' third & sickliest goddess, Madeline Graham...

From The Nation

... In short, in such a case, it is false charity to reader & writer to mince matters. The English of it is that every character is a failure, the plot a vacuum, the style spiritless, the dialogue vague, the sentiments weak, & the whole thing a fiasco. Is not —the disgusted reader is forced to ask—is not Mr. Olivieri very, very like a sick-sentimental school-girl who has begun her work with a fierce & bloody resolve to make it as bad as Wilhelm Meister, Consuelo, & "Goodbye Sweetheart" together, & has ended with a blush, & a general erasure of all the naughty words which her modest vocabulary could furnish? ...

THE
BUCCANEERS

By
EDITH WHARTON

D. APPLETON-CENTURY COMPANY
INCORPORATED
NEW YORK 1938 LONDON

BOOK I

I

IT was the height of the racing-season at Saratoga.

The thermometer stood over ninety, and a haze of sun-powdered dust hung in the elms along the street facing the Grand Union Hotel, and over the scant triangular lawns planted with young firs, and protected by a low white rail from the depredations of dogs and children.

Mrs. St George, whose husband was one of the gentlemen most interested in the racing, sat on the wide hotel verandah, a jug of iced lemonade at her elbow and a palmetto fan in one small hand, and looked out between the immensely tall white columns of the portico, which so often reminded cultured travellers of the Parthenon at Athens (Greece). On Sunday afternoons this verandah was crowded with gentlemen in tall hats and frock-coats, enjoying cool drinks and Havana cigars, and surveying the long country street planted with spindling elms; but today the gentlemen were racing, and the rows of chairs were occupied by ladies and young girls listlessly awaiting their return, in a drowsy atmosphere of swayed fans and iced refreshments.

Mrs. St George eyed most of these ladies with a melancholy disfavour, and sighed to think how times had changed since she had first—some ten years earlier— trailed her crinolined skirts up and down that same verandah.

Mrs. St George's vacant hours, which were many, were filled by such wistful reflexions. Life had never been easy, but it had certainly been easier when Colonel St George devoted less time to poker, and to Wall Street; when the children were little, crinolines were still worn, and Newport had not yet eclipsed all rival watering-places. What, for instance, could be prettier, or more suitable for a lady, than a black alpaca skirt looped up like a window-drapery above a scarlet serge underskirt, the whole surmounted by a wide-sleeved black poplin jacket with ruffled muslin undersleeves, and a flat "pork-pie" hat like the one the Empress Eugenie was represented as wearing on the beach at Biarritz? But now there seemed to be no definite fashions. Everybody wore what they pleased, and it was as difficult to look like a lady in those tight perpendicular polonaises bunched up at the back that the Paris dress-makers were sending over as in the outrageously low square-cut evening gowns which Mrs. St George had viewed with disapproval at the Opera in New York. The fact was, you could hardly tell a lady now from an actress, or—er—the other kind of woman; and society at Saratoga, now that all the best people were going to Newport, had grown as mixed and confusing as the fashions.

Everything was changed since crinolines had gone out and bustles come in. Who, for instance, was that new woman, a Mrs. Closson, or some such name, who had such a dusky skin for her auburn hair, such a fat body for her small uncertain feet, and who, when she wasn't strumming on the hotel piano, was credibly reported by the domestics to lie for hours on her bedroom sofa

smoking—yes, *smoking* big Havana cigars? The gentlemen, Mrs. St George believed, treated the story as a
good joke; to a woman of refinement it could be only a
subject for painful meditation.

Mrs. St George had always been rather distant in her
manner to the big and exuberant Mrs. Elmsworth who
was seated at this moment near by on the verandah. (Mrs.
Elmsworth was always "edging up.") Mrs. St George was
instinctively distrustful of the advances of ladies who
had daughters of the age of her own, and Lizzy Elmsworth, the eldest of her neighbour's family, was just about
the age of Virginia St George, and might by some (those
who preferred the brunette to the very blond type) be
thought as handsome. And besides, where did the Elmsworths come from, as Mrs. St George had often asked
her husband, an irreverent jovial man who invariably
replied: "If you were to begin by telling me where *we*
do!"...so absurd on the part of a gentleman as well-
known as Colonel St George in some unspecified district
of what Mrs. St George called the Sa-outh.

But at the thought of that new dusky Closson woman
with the queer-looking girl who was so ugly now, but
might suddenly turn into a beauty (Mrs. St George had
seen such cases), the instinct of organized defence awoke
in her vague bosom, and she felt herself drawn to Mrs.
Elmsworth, and to the two Elmsworth girls, as to whom
one already knew just how good-looking they were
going to be.

A good many hours of Mrs. St George's days were
spent in mentally cataloguing and appraising the
physical attributes of the young ladies in whose com-

pany her daughters trailed up and down the verandahs, and waltzed and polka-ed for hours every night in the long bare hotel parlours, so conveniently divided by sliding doors which slipped into the wall and made the two rooms into one. Mrs. St George remembered the day when she had been agreeably awestruck by this vista, with its expectant lines of bent-wood chairs against the walls, and its row of windows draped in crimson brocatelle heavily festooned from overhanging gilt cornices. In those days the hotel ball-room had been her idea of a throne-room in a palace; but since her husband had taken her to a ball at the Seventh Regiment Armoury in New York her standards had changed, and she regarded the splendours of the Grand Union almost as contemptuously as the arrogant Mrs. Eglinton of New York, who had arrived there the previous summer on her way to Lake George, and after being shown into the yellow damask "bridal suite" by the obsequious landlord, had said she supposed it would do well enough for one night.

Mrs. St George, in those earlier years, had even been fluttered by an introduction to Mrs. Elmsworth, who was an older habituée of Saratoga than herself, and had a big showy affable husband with lustrous black whiskers, who was reported to have made a handsome fortune on the New York Stock Exchange. But that was in the days when Mrs. Elmsworth drove daily to the races in a high barouche sent from New York, which attracted perhaps too much attention. Since then Mr. Elmsworth's losses in Wall Street had obliged his wife to put down her barouche, and stay at home on the hotel verandah with the other ladies, and she now no longer inspired Mrs. St George with awe or envy. Indeed, had it not been for this new Closson danger Mrs. Elmsworth in her present situation would have been negligible; but now that Virginia St George and Lizzy Elmsworth were "out" (as Mrs. St George persisted in calling it, though the girls could not see much difference in their lives)— now that Lizzy Elmsworth's looks seemed to Mrs. St George at once more to be admired and less to be feared, and Mabel, the second Elmsworth girl, who was a year older than her own youngest, to be too bony and lantern-jawed for future danger, Mrs. St George began to wonder whether she and her neighbour might not organize some sort of joint defence against new women with daughters. Later it would not so much matter, for Mrs. St George's youngest, Nan, though certainly not a beauty like Virginia, was going to be what was called fascinating, and by the time her hair was put up the St George girls need fear no rivalry.

Week after week, day after day, the anxious mother had gone over Miss Elmsworth's points, comparing them one by one with Virginia's. As regards hair and complexion, there could be no doubt; Virginia, all rose and pearl, with sheaves of full fair hair heaped above her low forehead, was as pure and luminous as an apple-blossom. But Lizzy's waist was certainly at least an inch smaller (some said two), Lizzy's dark eyebrows had a bolder curve, and Lizzy's foot—ah, where in the world did an upstart Elmsworth get that arrogant instep? Yes; but it was some comfort to note that Lizzy's complexion was opaque and lifeless compared to Virginia's, and that her fine eyes showed temper, and would be likely to frighten the young men away. Still, she had to an alarming degree what was called "style", and Mrs. St George suspected that in the circles to which she longed to introduce her daughters style was valued even more highly than beauty.

These were the problems among which her thoughts moved during the endless sweltering afternoon hours, like torpid fish turning about between the weary walls of a too-small aquarium. But now a new presence had invaded that sluggish element. Mrs. St George no longer compared her eldest daughter and Lizzy Elmsworth with each other; she began to compare them both with the newcomer, the daughter of the unknown Mrs. Closson. It was small comfort to Mrs. St George (though she repeated it to herself so often) that the Clossons were utterly unknown, that though Colonel St George played poker with Mr. Closson, and had what the family called "business connections" with him, they were nowhere near the stage when it becomes a pleasing duty for a man to introduce a colleague to his family. Neither did it matter that Mrs. Closson's own past was if anything obscurer than her husband's, and that those who said she was a poor Brazilian widow when Closson had picked her up on a business trip to Rio were smiled at and corrected by others, presumably better informed, who suggested that *divorcée* was the word, and not widow. Even the fact that the Closson girl (so called) was known not to be Closson's daughter, but to bear some queer exotic name like Santos-Dios ("the Colonel says that's not swearing, it's the language," Mrs. St George explained to Mrs. Elmsworth when they talked the new-comers over)—even this was not enough to calm Mrs. St George. The girl, whatever her real name, was known as Conchita Closson; she addressed as "Father" the non-committal pepper-and-salt-looking man who joined his family over Sundays at the Grand Union; and it was of no use for Mrs. St George to say to herself that Conchita was plain and therefore negligible, for she had the precise kind of plainness which, as mothers of rival daughters know, may suddenly blaze into irresistible beauty. At present Miss Closson's head was too small, her neck was too long, she was too tall and thin, and her hair—well, her hair (oh, horror!) was nearly red. And her skin was dark, under the powder which (yes, my dear—at eighteen!) Mrs. St George was sure she ap-plied to it; and the combination of red hair and sallow complexion would have put off anybody who had heard a description of them, instead of seeing them trium-phantly embodied in Conchita Closson. Mrs. St George shivered under her dotted muslin ruffled with Valen-ciennes, and drew a tippet edged with swansdown over her shoulders. At that moment her own daughters, Vir-ginia and Nan, wandered by, one after the other; and the sight somehow increased Mrs. St George's irritation.

"Virginia!" she called. Virginia halted, seemed to hesitate as to whether the summons were worth heeding, and then sauntered across the verandah toward her mother.

"Virginia, I don't want you should go round any more with that strange girl," Mrs. St George began.

Virginia's sapphire eyes rested with a remote indiffer-

ent gaze on the speaker's tightly buttoned bronze kid
boots; and Mrs. St George suddenly wondered if she
had burst a buttonhole.

"What girl?" Virginia drawled.

"How do I know? Goodness knows who they are. Your
pa says she was a widow from one of those South American countries when she married Mr. Closson—the
mother was, I mean."

"Well, if he says so, I suppose she was."

"But some people say she was just divorced. And I
don't want my daughters associating with that kind of
people."

Virginia removed her blue gaze from her mother's
boots to the little mantle trimmed with swansdown. "I
should think you'd roast with that thing on," she remarked.

"Jinny! Now you listen to what I say," her mother
ineffectually called after her.

Nan St George had taken no part in the conversation;
at first she had hardly heeded what was said. Such
wrangles between mother and daughter were of daily,
almost hourly, occurrence; Mrs. St George's only way of
guiding her children was to be always crying out to them
not to do this or that. Nan St George, at sixteen, was
at the culminating phase of a passionate admiration for
her elder sister. Virginia was all that her junior longed
to be: perfectly beautiful, completely self-possessed,
calm and sure of herself. Nan, whose whole life was a
series of waves of the blood, hot rushes of enthusiasm,
icy chills of embarrassment and self-depreciation, looked
with envy and admiration at her goddess-like elder. The

only thing she did not quite like about Virginia was
the latter's tone of superiority with her mother; to get
the better of Mrs. St George was too easy, too much like
what Colonel St George called "shooting a bird sitting".
Yet so strong was Virginia's influence that in her presence Nan always took the same tone with their mother,
in the secret hope of attracting her sister's favourable
notice. She had even gone so far as to mime for Virginia
(who was no mimic) Mrs. St George looking shocked at
an untidy stocking ("mother wondering where we were
brought up"), Mrs. St George smiling in her sleep in
church ("mother listening to the angels"), or Mrs. St
George doubtfully mustering new arrivals ("mother
smelling a drain"). But Virginia took such demonstra-
tions for granted, and when poor Nan afterward, in an
agony of remorse, stole back alone to her mother, and
whispered through penitent kisses: "I didn't mean to
be naughty to you, Mamma," Mrs. St George, raising a
nervous hand to her crimped *bandeaux,* would usually
reply apprehensively: "I'm sure you didn't, darling;
only don't get my hair all in a muss again."

Expiation unresponded to embitters the blood, and
something within Nan shrank and hardened with each
of these rebuffs. But she now seldom exposed herself to
them, finding it easier to follow Virginia's lead and
ignore their parent's admonitions. At the moment, however, she was actually wavering in her allegiance to
Virginia. Since she had seen Conchita Closson she was
no longer sure that features and complexion were
woman's crowning glory. Long before Mrs. St George
and Mrs. Elmsworth had agreed on a valuation of the

newcomer Nan had fallen under her spell. From the day when she had first seen her come whistling around the corner of the verandah, her restless little head crowned by a flapping Leghorn hat with a rose under the brim, and dragging after her a reluctant poodle with a large red bow, Nan had felt the girl's careless power. What would Mrs. St George have said if one of her daughters had strolled along the verandah whistling, and dragging a grotesque-looking toy-shop animal at her heels? Miss Closson seemed troubled by no such considerations. She sat down on the upper step of the verandah, pulled a lump of molasses candy from her pocket, and invited the poodle to "get up and waltz for it"; which the uncanny animal did by rising on his hind legs and performing a series of unsteady circles before his mistress while she licked the molasses from her fingers. Every rocking-chair on the verandah stopped creaking as its occupant sat upright to view the show. "Circus performance!" Mrs. St George commented to Mrs. Elmsworth; and the latter retorted with her vulgar laugh: "Looks as if the two of 'em were used to showing off, don't it?"

Nan overheard the comments, and felt sure the two mothers were mistaken. The Closson girl was obviously unaware that any one was looking at her and her absurd dog; it was that absence of self-consciousness which fascinated Nan. Virginia was intensely self-conscious; she really thought just as much as her mother of "what people would say"; and even Lizzy Elmsworth, though she was so much cleverer at concealing her thoughts, was not really simple and natural; she merely affected unaffectedness. It frightened Nan a little to find herself thinking these things; but they forced themselves upon her, and when Mrs. St George issued the order that her daughters were not to associate with "the strange girl" (as if they didn't all know her name!) Nan felt a rush of anger. Virginia sauntered on, probably content to have shaken her mother's confidence in the details of her dress (a matter of much anxious thought to Mrs. St George); but Nan stopped short.

"Why can't I go with Conchita if she wants me to?"

Mrs. St George's faintly withered pink turned pale. "If she *wants you to?* Annabel St George, what do you mean by talking to me that way? What on earth do you care for what a girl like that *wants?*"

Nan ground her heels into the crack between the verandah boards. "I think she's lovely."

Mrs. St George's small nose was wrinkled with disdain. The small mouth under it drooped disgustedly. She was "mother smelling a drain".

"Well, when that new governess comes next week I guess you'll find she feels just the way I do about those people. And you'll have to do what *she* tells you, anyhow," Mrs. St George helplessly concluded.

A chill of dismay rushed over Nan. The new governess! She had never really believed in that remote bogey. She had an idea that Mrs. St George and Virginia had cooked up the legend between them, in order to be able to say "Annabel's governess", as they had once heard that tall proud Mrs. Eglinton from New York, who had stayed only one night at the hotel, say to the landlord: "You must be sure to put my daughter's governess in the room next to her." Nan had never believed that the affair of the governess would go beyond talking; but now she seemed to hear the snap of the handcuffs on her wrists.

"A governess—me?"

Mrs. St George moistened her lips nervously. "All stylish girls have governesses the year before they come out."

"I'm not coming out next year—I'm only sixteen," Nan protested.

"Well, they have them for two years before. That Eglinton girl had."

"Oh, that Eglinton girl! She looked at us all as if we weren't there."

"Well, that's the way for a lady to look at strangers," said Mrs. St George heroically.

Nan's heart grew black within her. "I'll kill her if she tries to interfere with me."

"You'll drive down to the station on Monday to meet her," Mrs. St George shrilled back, defiant. Nan turned on her heel and walked away.

II

THE Closson girl had already disappeared with her dog, and Nan suspected that she had taken him for a game of ball in the rough field adjoining the meagre grounds of the hotel. Nan went down the steps of the porch, and crossing the drive espied the slim Conchita whirling a ball high overhead while the dog spun about frantically at her feet. Nan had so far exchanged only a few shy words with her, and in ordinary circumstances would hardly have dared to join her now. But she had reached an acute crisis in her life, and her need for sympathy and help overcame her shyness. She vaulted over the fence into the field and went up to Miss Closson.

"That's a lovely dog," she said.

Miss Closson flung the ball for her poodle, and turned with a smile to Nan. "Isn't he a real darling?"

Nan stood twisting one foot about the other. "Have you ever had a governess?" she asked abruptly.

Miss Closson opened with a stare of wonder the darkly fringed eyes which shone like pale aquamarines on her small dusky face. "Me? A governess? Mercy, no—what for?"

"That's what I say! My mother and Virginia have cooked it up between them. I'm going to have one next week."

"Land's sake! You're not? She's coming here?" Nan nodded sulkily.

"Well—" Conchita murmured.

"What'll I do about it—what would you?" Nan burst out, on the brink of tears.

Miss Closson drew her lids together meditatively; then she stooped with deliberation to the poodle, and threw the ball for him again.

"I said I'd kill her," broke from Nan in a hoarse whisper.

The other laughed. "I wouldn't do that; not right off, anyhow. I'd get round her first."

"Get round her? How can I? I've got to do whatever she wants."

"No, you haven't. Make her want whatever *you* want."

"How can I? Oh, can I call you Conchita? It's such a lovely name. Mine's Annabel, really, but everybody calls me Nan... Well, but how can I get round that governess? She'll try to make me learn lists of dates ... that's what she's paid for."

Conchita's expressive face became one grimace of disapproval. "Well, I should hate that like castor-oil. But perhaps she won't. I knew a girl at Rio who had a governess, and she was hardly any older than the girl, and she used to ... well, carry messages and letters for her, the governess did ... and in the evening she used to slip out to ... to see a friend ... and she and the girl knew all each other's secrets; so you see they couldn't tell on each other, neither one of them couldn't..."

"Oh, I see," said Nan, with a feigned air of knowingness. But she was suddenly conscious of a queer sensation in her throat, almost of physical sickness. Conchita's laughing eyes seemed whispering to her through half-drawn lids. She admired Conchita as much as ever—but she was not sure she liked her at that moment.

Conchita was obviously not aware of having produced an unfavourable impression. "Out in Rio I knew a girl who got married that way. The governess carried her notes for her... Do you want to get married?" she asked abruptly.

Nan flushed and stared. Getting married was an inexhaustible theme of confidential talk between her sister and the Elmsworth girls; but she felt herself too young and inexperienced to take part in their discussions. Once, at one of the hotel dances, a young fellow called Roy Gilling had picked up her handkerchief, and refused to give it back. She had seen him raise it meaningly to his young moustache before he slipped it into his pocket; but the incident had left her annoyed and bewildered rather than excited, and she had not been sorry when soon afterward he rather pointedly transferred his attentions to Mabel Elmsworth. She knew Mabel Elmsworth had already been kissed behind a door; and Nan's own sister Virginia had too, Nan suspected. She herself had no definite prejudices in the matter; she simply felt unprepared as yet to consider matrimonial plans. She stooped to stroke the poodle, and answered, without looking up: "Not to anybody I've seen yet."

The other considered her curiously. "I suppose you like love-making better, eh?" She spoke in a soft drawl, with a languid rippling of the Rs.

Nan felt her blood mounting again; one of her quick blushes steeped her in distress. Did she—didn't she—

like "love-making", as this girl crudely called it (the others always spoke of it as flirting)? Nan had not been subjected to any warmer advances than Mr. Gilling's, and the obvious answer was that she didn't know, having had no experience of such matters; but she had the reluctance of youth to confess to its youthfulness, and she also felt that her likes and dislikes were no business of this strange girl's. She gave a vague laugh and said loftily: "I think it's silly."

Conchita laughed too; a low deliberate laugh, full of repressed and tantalizing mystery. Once more she flung the ball for her intently watching poodle; then she thrust a hand into a fold of her dress, and pulled out a crumpled packet of cigarettes. "Here—have one! Nobody'll see us out here," she suggested amicably.

Nan's heart gave an excited leap. Her own sister and the Elmsworth girl already smoked in secret, removing the traces of their indiscretion by consuming little highly perfumed pink lozenges furtively acquired from the hotel barber; but they had never offered to induct Nan into these forbidden rites, which, by awful oaths, they bound her not to reveal to their parents. It was Nan's first cigarette, and while her fingers twitched for it she asked herself in terror: "Suppose it should make me sick right before her?"

But Nan, in spite of her tremors, was not the girl to refuse what looked like a dare, nor even to ask if in this open field they were really safe from unwanted eyes. There was a clump of low shrubby trees at the farther end, and Conchita strolled there and mounted the fence-rail, from which her slender uncovered ankles dangled gracefully. Nan swung up beside her, took a cigarette, and bent toward the match which her companion proffered. There was an awful silence while she put the forbidden object to her lips and drew a frightened breath; the acrid taste of the tobacco struck her palate sharply, but in another moment a pleasant fragrance filled her nose and throat. She puffed again, and knew she was going to like it. Instantly her mood passed from timidity to triumph, and she wrinkled her nose critically and threw back her head, as her father did when he was tasting a new brand of cigar. "These are all right—where do you get them?" she inquired with a careless air; and then, suddenly forgetful of the experience her tone implied, she rushed on in a breathless little-girl voice: "Oh, Conchita, won't you show me how you make those lovely rings? Jinny doesn't really do them right, nor the Elmsworth girls either."

Miss Closson in turn threw back her head with a smile. She drew a deep breath, and removing the cigarette from her lips, curved them to a rosy circle through which she sent a wreath of misty smoke-rings. "That's how," she laughed, and pushed the packet into Nan's hands. "You can practice at night," she said good-humouredly, as she jumped from the rail.

Nan wandered back to the hotel, so much elated by her success as a smoker that her dread of the governess grew fainter. On the hotel steps she was further re-assured by the glimpse, through the lobby doors, of a tall broad-shouldered man in a Panama hat and light gray suit who, his linen duster over his arm, his portmanteaux at his feet, had paused to light a big cigar and

shake hands with the clerk. Nan gave a start of joy. She
had not known that her father was arriving that afternoon, and the mere sight of him banished all her cares.
Nan had a blind faith in her father's faculty for helping
people out of difficulties—a faith based not on actual experience (for Colonel St George usually dealt with difficulties by a wave of dismissal which swept them into
somebody else's lap), but on his easy contempt for
feminine fusses, and his way of saying to his youngest
daughter: "You just call on me, child, when things want
straightening out." Perhaps he would straighten out
even this nonsense about the governess; and meanwhile
the mere thought of his large powerful presence, his big
cologne-scented hands, his splendid yellow moustache
and easy rolling gait, cleared the air of the cobwebs in
which Mrs. St George was always enveloped.

"Hullo, daughter! What's the news?" The Colonel
greeted Nan with a resounding kiss, and stood with one
arm about her, scrutinizing her lifted face.

"I'm glad you've come, father," she said, and then
shrank back a little, fearful lest a whiff of cigarette
smoke should betray her.

"Your mother taking her afternoon nap, I suppose?"
the Colonel continued jovially. "Well, come along with
me. See here, Charlie" (to the clerk), "send those things
right along to my room, will you? There's something in
them of interest to this young lady."

The clerk signalled to a black porter, and preceded
by his bags the Colonel mounted the stairs with Nan.

"Oh, father! It's lovely to have you! What I want to
ask you is—"

But the Colonel was digging into the depths of one of the portmanteaux and scattering over the bed various parts of a showy but somewhat crumpled wardrobe. "Here now; you wait," he puffed, pausing to mop his broad white forehead with a fine cambric handkerchief. He pulled out two parcels, and beckoned to Nan. "Here's some fancy notions for you and Jinny; the girl in the store said it was what the Newport belles are wearing this summer. And this is for your mother, when she wakes up." He took the tissue-paper wrappings from a small red-morocco case and pressed the spring of the lid. Before Nan's dazzled eyes lay a diamond brooch formed of a spray of briar-roses. She gave an admiring gasp. "Well, how's that for style?" laughed her father.

"Oh, father—" She paused, and looked at him with a faint touch of apprehension.

"Well?" the Colonel repeated. His laugh had an emptiness under it, like the hollow under a loud wave; Nan knew the sound. "Is it a present for mother?" she asked doubtfully.

"Why, who'd you think it was for—not you?" he joked, his voice slightly less assured.

Nan twisted one foot about the other. "It's terribly expensive, isn't it?"

"Why, you critical imp, you—what's the matter if it is?"

"Well, the last time you brought mother a piece of jewelry there was an all-night row after it, about cards or something," said Nan judicially.

The Colonel burst out laughing, and pinched her chin. "Well, well! You fear the Greeks, eh, do you? How does it go? *Timeo Danaos. . .*"

"What Greeks?"

Her father raised his handsome ironic eyebrows. Nan knew he was proud of his far-off smattering of college culture, and wished she could have understood the allusion. "Haven't they even taught you that much Latin at your school? Well, I guess your mother's right; you *do* need a governess."

Nan paled, and forgot the Greeks. "Oh, father; that's what I wanted to speak to you about—"

"What about?"

"That governess. I'm going to hate her, you know. She's going to make me learn lists of dates, the way the Eglinton girl had to. And mother'll fill her up with silly stories about us, and tell her we mustn't do this, and we mustn't say that. I don't believe she'll even let me go with Conchita Closson, because mother says Mrs. Closson's divorced."

The Colonel looked up sharply. "Oh, your mother says that, does she? She's down on the Clossons? I supposed she would be." He picked up the morocco case and examined the brooch critically. "Yes; that's a good piece; Black, Starr and Frost. And I don't mind telling you that you're right; it cost me a pretty penny. But I've got to persuade your mother to be polite to Mrs. Closson—see?" He wrinkled up his face in the funny way he had, and took his daughter by the shoulders. "Business matter, you understand—strictly between ourselves. I need Closson; got to have him. And he's fretted to death about the way all the women cold-shoulder his wife. . . I'll tell you what, Nan; suppose you and I form a league, defensive and offensive? You help me to talk round your mother, and get her to be decent to Mrs. Closson, and persuade the others to be, and to let the girl go round with all of you; and I'll fix it up with the governess so you don't have to learn too many dates."

Nan uttered a cry of joy. Already the clouds were lifting. "Oh, father, you're perfectly grand! I knew everything would be all right as soon as you got here! I'll do all I can about mother—and you'll tell the governess I'm to go round all I like with Conchita?" She flung herself into the Colonel's comforting embrace.

III

MRS. ST GEORGE, had she looked back far enough, could have recalled a time when she had all of Nan's faith in the Colonel's restorative powers; when to carry her difficulties to him seemed the natural thing, and his way of laughing at them gave her the illusion that they were solved. Those days were past; she had long been aware that most of her difficulties came from the Colonel instead of being solved by him. But she admired him as much as ever—thought him in fact even handsomer than when, before the Civil War, he had dawned on her dazzled sight at a White Sulphur Springs ball, in the uniform of a captain·of militia; and now that he had become prominent in Wall Street, where life seemed to grow more feverish every day, it was only natural that he should require a little relaxation, though she deplored its always meaning poker and whisky, and sometimes, she feared, the third element celebrated in the song. Though Mrs. St George was now a worried middle-aged woman with grown-up daughters, it cost her as much to resign herself to this as when she had first found in her husband's pocket a letter she was not meant to read. But there was nothing to be done about it, or about the whisky and poker, and the visits to establishments where game and champagne were served at all hours, and gentlemen who had won at roulette or the races supped in meretricious company.

All this had long since been part of Mrs. St George's consciousness, yet she was half consoled, when the Colonel joined his family at Long Branch or Saratoga, by the knowledge that all the other worried and middle-aged wives in the long hotel dining-room envied her her splendid husband.

And small wonder, thought Mrs. St George, contemptuously picturing the gentlemen those ladies had to put up with: that loud red-faced Elmsworth, who hadn't yet found out that big lumps of black whisker were no longer worn except by undertakers, or the poor dyspeptic Closson, who spent such resigned and yawning hours beside the South American woman to whom he was perhaps not married at all. Closson was particularly obnoxious to Mrs. St George; much as she despised Mrs. Closson, she could almost have pitied her for having nothing better to show as a husband—even if he was that, as Mrs. St George would add in her confidential exchanges with Mrs. Elmsworth.

Even now, though of late the Colonel had been so evasive and unsatisfactory, and though she wasn't yet sure if he would turn up for the morrow's races, Mrs. St George reflected thankfully that if he *did* she wouldn't have to appear in the hotel dining-room with a man about whom a lady need feel apologetic. But when, after her siesta, as she was re-arranging her hair before going back to the verandah, she heard his laugh outside of her door, her slumbering apprehensions started up. "He's too cheerful," she thought, nervously folding away her dressing-gown and slippers; for when the Colonel was worried he was always in the highest spirits.

"Well, my dear! Thought I'd surprise the family, and see what you were all up to. Nan's given me a fairly good report, but I haven't run down Jinny yet." He laid a hand on his wife's graying blond hair, and brushed her care-worn forehead with the tip of his moustache; a ritual gesture which convinced him that he had kissed her, and Mrs. St George that she had been kissed. She looked up at him with admiring eyes.

"That governess is coming on Monday," she began. At the moment of his last successful "turn-over", a few months earlier, his wife had wrung from him the permission to engage a governess; but now she feared a renewal of the discussion about the governess's salary, and yet she knew the girls, and Nan especially, must have some kind of social discipline. "We've got to have her," Mrs. St George added.

The Colonel was obviously not listening. "Of course, of course," he agreed, measuring the room with his large strides (his inability to remain seated was another trial to his sedentary wife). Suddenly he paused before her and fumbled in his pocket, but produced nothing from it. Mrs. St George noted the gesture, and thought: "It's the coal bill! But he *knew* I couldn't get it down any lower..."

"Well, well, my dear," the Colonel continued, "I don't know what you've all been up to, but I've had a big stroke of luck, and it's only fair you three girls should share in it." He jerked the morocco case out of another pocket. "Oh, Colonel," his wife gasped as he pressed the spring. "Well, take it—it's for you!" he joked.

Mrs. St George gazed blankly at the glittering spray; then her eyes filled, and her lip began to tremble. "Tracy ..." she stammered. It was years since she had called him by his name. "But you oughtn't to," she protested, "with all our expenses. . . It's too grand—it's like a wedding present. . ."

"Well, we're married, ain't we?" The Colonel laughed resonantly. "There's the first result of my turn-over, madam. And I brought the girls some gimcracks too. I gave Nan the parcel; but I haven't seen Jinny. I suppose she's off with some of the other girls."

Mrs. St George detached herself from ecstatic contemplation of the jewel. "You mustn't spoil the girls, Colonel. I've got my hands full with them. I want you to talk to them seriously about not going with that Closson girl. . ."

Colonel St George blew a faint whistle through his moustache, and threw himself into the rocking-chair facing his wife's. "Going with the Closson girl? Why, what's the matter with the Closson girl? She's as pretty as a peach, anyhow."

"I guess your own daughters are pretty enough without having to demean themselves running after that girl. I can't keep Nan away from her." Mrs. St George knew that Nan was the Colonel's favourite, and she spoke with an inward tremor. But it would never do to have this fashionable new governess (who had been with the Russell Parmores of Tarrytown, and with the Duchess of Tintagel in England) imagine that her new charges were hand in glove with the Clossons.

Colonel St George tilted himself back in his chair,

felt for a cigar and lit it thoughtfully. (He had long since taught Mrs. St George that smoking in her bedroom was included among his marital rights.) "Well," he said, "what's wrong with the Clossons, my dear?"

Mrs. St George felt weak and empty inside. When he looked at her in that way, half laughing, half condescending, all her reasons turned to a puff of mist. And there lay the jewel on the dressing-table—and timorously she began to understand. But the girls must be rescued, and a flicker of maternal ardour stirred in her. Perhaps in his large careless way her husband had simply brushed by the Clossons without heeding them.

"I don't know any of the particulars, naturally. People *do* say ... but Mrs. Closson (if that's her name) is not a woman I could ever associate with, so I haven't any means of knowing. .."

The Colonel gave his all-effacing laugh. "Oh, well—if you haven't any means of knowing, we'll fix that up all right. But I've got business reasons for wanting you to make friends with Mrs. Closson first; we'll investigate her history afterward."

Make friends with Mrs. Closson! Mrs. St George looked at her husband with dismay. He wanted her to do the thing that would most humiliate her; and it was so important to him that he had probably spent his last dollar on this diamond bribe. Mrs. St George was not unused to such situations; she knew that a gentleman's financial situation might at any moment necessitate compromises and concessions. All the ladies of her acquaintance were inured to them; up one day, down the next, as the secret gods of Wall Street decreed. She measured her husband's present need by the cost of the probably unpaid for jewel, and her heart grew like water.

"But, Colonel—"

"Well, what's wrong with the Clossons, anyhow? I've done business with Closson off and on for some years now, and I don't know a squarer fellow. He's just put me on to a big thing, and if you're going to wreck the whole business by turning up your nose at his wife..."

Mrs. St George gathered strength to reply: "But, Colonel, the talk is that they're not even married..."

Her husband jumped up and stood before her with flushed face and irritated eyes. "If you think I'm going to let my making a big rake-off depend on whether the Clossons had a parson to tie the knot, or only the town-clerk..."

"I've got the girls to think of," his wife faltered.

"It's the girls I'm thinking of, too. D'you suppose I'd sweat and slave down town the way I do if it wasn't for the girls?"

"But I've got to think of the girls they go with, if they're to marry nice young men."

"The nice young men'll show up in larger numbers if I can put this deal through. And what's the matter with the Closson girl? She's as pretty as a picture."

Mrs. St George marvelled once more at the obtuseness of the most brilliant men. Wasn't that one of the very reasons for not encouraging the Closson girl?

"She powders her face, and smokes cigarettes..."

"Well, don't our girls and the two Elmsworths do as much? I'll swear I caught a whiff of smoke when Nan kissed me just now."

Mrs. St George grew pale with horror. "If you'll say that of your daughters you'll say anything!" she protested.

There was a knock at the door, and without waiting for it to be answered Virginia flew into her father's arms. "Oh, father, how sweet of you! Nan gave me the locket. It's too lovely; with my monogram on it—and in diamonds!"

She lifted her radiant lips, and he bent to them with a smile. "What's that new scent you're using, Miss St George? Or have you been stealing one of your papa's lozenges?" He sniffed and then held her at arm's-length, watching her quick flush of alarm, and the way in which her deeply fringed eyes pleaded with his.

"See here, Jinny. Your mother says she don't want you to go with the Closson girl because she smokes. But I tell her I'll answer for it that you and Nan would never follow such a bad example—eh?"

Their eyes and their laugh met. Mrs. St George turned from the sight with a sense of helplessness. "If he's going to let them smoke now..."

"I don't think your mother's fair to the Closson girl, and I've told her so. I want she should be friends with Mrs. Closson. I want her to begin right off. Oh, here's Nan," he added, as the door opened again. "Come along, Nan; I want you to stick up for your friend Conchita. You like her, don't you?"

But Mrs. St George's resentment was stiffening. She could fight for her daughters, helpless as she was for herself. "If you're going to rely on the girls to choose who they associate with! They say the girl's name isn't Closson at all. Nobody knows what it is, or who any of them are. And the brother travels round with a guitar tied with ribbons. No nice girls will go with your daughters if you want them seen everywhere with those people."

The Colonel stood frowning before his wife. When he frowned she suddenly forgot all her reasons for opposing him, but the blind instinct of opposition remained. "You wouldn't invite the Clossons to join us at supper tonight?" he suggested.

Mrs. St George moistened her dry lips with her tongue. "Colonel—"

"You won't?"

"Girls, your father's joking," she stammered, turning with a tremulous gesture to her daughters. She saw Nan's eyes darken, but Virginia laughed—a laugh of complicity with her father. He joined in it.

"Girls, I see your mother's not satisfied with the present I've brought her. She's not as easily pleased as you young simpletons." He waved his hand to the dressing-table, and Virginia caught up the morocco box. "Oh, mother—is this for *you?* Oh, I never saw anything so beautiful! You must invite Mrs. Closson, just to see how envious it makes her. I guess that's what father wants you to do—isn't it?"

The Colonel looked at her sympathetically. "I've told your mother the plain truth. Closson's put me on to a good thing, and the only return he wants is for you ladies to be a little humane to his women-folk. Is that too unreasonable? He's coming today, by the afternoon train, bringing two young fellows with him, by the way—his step-son and a young Englishman who's been working out in Brazil on Mrs. Closson's estancia. The son of an Earl, or something. How about that, girls? Two new dancing-partners! And you ain't any too well off in that line, are you?" This was a burning question, for it was common knowledge that, if their dancing-partners were obscure and few, it was because all the smart and eligible young men of whom Virginia and the Elmsworths read in the "society columns" of the newspapers had deserted Saratoga for Newport.

"Mother knows we generally have to dance with each other," Virginia murmured sulkily.

"Yes—or with the beaux from Buffalo!" Nan laughed.

"Well, I call that mortifying; but of course, if your mother disapproves of Mrs. Closson, I guess the young fellows that Closson's bringing'll have to dance with the Elmsworth girls instead of you."

Mrs. St George stood trembling beside the dressing-table. Virginia had put down the box, and the diamonds sparkled in a sunset ray that came through the slats of the shutters.

Mrs. St George did not own many jewels, but it suddenly occurred to her that each one marked the date of a similar episode. Either a woman, or a business deal—something she had to be indulgent about. She liked trinkets as well as any woman, but at that moment she wished that all of hers were at the bottom of the sea. For each time she had yielded—as she knew she was going to yield now. And her husband would always think that it was because he had bribed her...

THE BUCCANEERS

The re-adjustment of seats necessary to bring together the St George and Closson parties at the long hotel supper-table caused a flutter in the room. Mrs. St George was too conscious of it not to avoid Mrs. Elmsworth's glance of surprise; but she could not deafen herself to Mrs. Elmsworth's laugh. She had always thought the woman had an underbred laugh. And to think that, so few seasons ago, she had held her chin high in passing Mrs. Elmsworth on the verandah, just as she had done till this very afternoon—and how much higher!—in passing Mrs. Closson. Now Mrs. Elmsworth, who did not possess the art of the lifted chin, but whispered and nudged and giggled where a "lady" would have sailed by —now it would be in her power to practise on Mrs. St George these vulgar means of reprisal. The diamond spray burned like hot lead on Mrs. St George's breast; yet through all her misery there pierced the old thrill of pride as the Colonel entered the dining-room in her wake, and she saw him reflected in the other women's eyes. Ah, poor Mrs. Elmsworth, with her black-whiskered undertaker, and Mrs. Closson with her cipher of a husband—and all the other ladies, young or elderly, of whom not one could boast a man of Colonel St George's quality! Evidently, like Mrs. St George's diamonds, he was a costly possession, but (unlike the diamonds, she suspected) he had been paid for—oh, how dearly!—and she had a right to wear him with her head high.

But in the eyes of the other guests it was not only the Colonel's entrance that was reflected. Mrs. St George saw there also the excitement and curiosity occasioned by the re-grouping of seats, and the appearance, behind

Mrs. Closson—who came in with her usual somnambu-
list's walk, and thick-lashed stare—of two young men, two
authentic new dancers for the hotel beauties. Mrs. St
George knew all about them. The little olive-faced velvet-
eyed fellow, with the impudently curly black hair, was
Teddy de Santos-Dios, Mr. Closson's Brazilian step-son,
over on his annual visit to the States; the other, the short
heavy-looking young man with a low forehead pressed
down by a shock of drab hair, an uncertain mouth under
a thick drab moustache, and small eyes, slow, puzzled,
not unkindly yet not reliable, was Lord Richard Marable, the impecunious younger son of an English Marquess, who had picked up a job on the Closson estancia,
and had come over for his holiday with Santos-Dios. Two
"foreigners", and certainly ineligible ones, especially the
little black popinjay who travelled with his guitar—but,
after all, dancers for the girls, and therefore not wholly
unwelcome even to Mrs. St George, whose heart often
ached at the thought of the Newport ball-rooms, where
black coat-tails were said to jam every doorway; while at
Saratoga the poor girls—

Ah, but there they were, the girls!—the privileged
few whom she grouped under that designation. The
fancy had taken them to come in late, and to arrive all
together; and now, arm-in-arm, a blushing bevy, they
swayed across the threshold of the dining-room like a
branch hung with blossoms, drawing the dull middle-
aged eyes of the other guests from lobster salad and fried
chicken, and eclipsing even the refulgent Colonel—
happy girls, with two new dancers for the week-end,
they had celebrated the unwonted wind-fall by extra

touches of adornment: a red rose in the fold of a fichu, a loose curl on a white shoulder, a pair of new satin slippers, a fresh *moiré* ribbon.

Seeing them through the eyes of the new young men Mrs. St George felt their collective grace with a vividness almost exempt from envy. To her, as to those two foreigners, they embodied "the American girl", the world's highest achievement; and she was as ready to enjoy Lizzy Elmsworth's brilliant darkness, and that dry sparkle of Mab's, as much as her own Virginia's roses, and Nan's alternating frowns and dimples. She was even able to recognize that the Closson girl's incongruous hair gilded the whole group like a sunburst. Could Newport show anything lovelier, she wondered half-bitterly, as she seated herself between Mr. Closson and young Santos-Dios.

Mrs. Closson, from the Colonel's right, leaned across the table with her soft ambiguous smile. "What lovely diamonds, Mrs. St George! I wish I hadn't left all mine in the safe at New York!"

Mrs. St George thought: "She means the place isn't worth bringing jewels to. As if she ever went out anywhere in New York!" But her eyes wandered beyond Mrs. Closson to Lord Richard Marable; it was the first time she had ever sat at table with any one even remotely related to a British nobleman, and she fancied the young man was ironically observing the way in which she held her fork. But she saw that his eyes, which were sand-coloured like his face, and sandy-lashed, had found another occupation. They were fixed on Conchita Closson, who sat opposite to him; they rested on her unblinkingly, immovably, as if she had been a natural object, a landscape or a cathedral, that one had travelled far to see, and had the right to look at as long as one chose. "He's drinking her up like blotting-paper. I thought they were better brought up over in England!" Mrs. St George said to herself, austerely thankful that he was not taking such liberties with *her* daughters ("but men always know the difference," she reflected), and suddenly not worrying any longer about how she held her fork.

IV

MISS LAURA TESTVALLEY stood on the wooden platform of the railway station at Saratoga Springs, N. Y., and looked about her. It was not an inspiriting scene; but she had not expected that it would be, and would not have greatly cared if it had. She had been in America for eighteen months, and it was not for its architectural or civic beauties that she had risked herself so far. Miss Testvalley had small means, and a derelict family to assist; and her successful career as a governess in the households of the English aristocracy had been curtailed by the need to earn more money. English governesses were at a premium in the United States, and one of Miss Testvalley's former pupils, whose husband was attached to the British Legation in Washington, had recommended her to Mrs. Russell Parmore, a cousin of the Eglintons and the van der Luydens—the best, in short, that New York had to offer. The salary was not as high as Miss Testvalley had hoped for; but her ex-pupil at the Legation had assured her that among the "new" coal and steel people, who could pay more, she would certainly be too wretched. Miss Testvalley was not sure of this. She had not come to America in search of distinguished manners any more than of well-kept railway stations; but she decided on reflection that the Parmore household might be a useful spring-board, and so it proved. Mrs. Russell Parmore was certainly very distinguished, and so were her pallid daughter and her utterly rubbed-out husband; and how could they know that to Miss Testvalley they represented at best a *milieu* of retired Colonials at Cheltenham, or the household of a minor canon in a cathedral town? Miss Testvalley had been used to a more vivid setting, and accustomed to social dramas and emotions which Mrs. Russell Parmore had only seen hinted at in fiction; and as the pay was low, and the domestic economies were painful (Mrs. Russell Parmore would have thought it ostentatious and vulgar to live largely), Miss Testvalley, after conscientiously "finishing" Miss Parmore (a young lady whom Nature seemed scarcely to have begun), decided to seek, in a different field, ampler opportunities of action. She consulted a New York governesses' agency, and learned that the "new people" would give "almost anything" for such social training as an accomplished European governess could impart. Miss Testvalley fixed a maximum wage, and in a few days was notified by the agency that Mrs. Tracy St George was ready to engage her. "It was Mrs. Russell Parmore's reference that did it," said the black-wigged lady at the desk as they exchanged fees and congratulations. "In New York that counts more than all your Duchesses"; and Miss Testvalley again had reason to rate her own good sense at its just value. Life at the Parmores', on poor pay and a scanty diet, had been a weary business; but it had been worth while. Now she had in her pocket the promise of eighty dollars a month, and the possibility of a more exciting task; for she understood that the St Georges were very "new", and the prospect of comparing the

manners and customs of the new and the not-new might
be amusing. "I wonder," she thought ironically, "if the
Duchess would see the slightest difference..." the
Duchess meaning always *hers*, the puissant lady of Tintagel, where Miss Testvalley had spent so many months
shivering with cold, and bandaging the chilblains of the
younger girls, while the other daughters, with their particular "finishing" duenna, accompanied their parents
from one ducal residence to another. The Duchess of
Tintagel, who had beaten Miss Testvalley's salary well-
nigh down to the level of an upper house-maid's, who
had so often paid it after an embarrassingly long delay,
who had been surprised that a governess should want a
fire in her room, or a hot soup for her school-room
dinner—the Duchess was now (all unknown to herself)
making up for her arrears toward Miss Testvalley. By
giving Mrs. Parmore the chance to say, when she had
friends to dine: "I happen to know, for instance, that at
Tintagel Castle there are only open fires, and the halls
and corridors are not heated at all", Miss Testvalley had
gained several small favours from her parsimonious employer: and by telling her, in the strictest confidence,
that their Graces had at one time felt a good deal of
anxiety about their only son—oh, a simple sweet-natured
young man if ever there was one; but then, the temptations which beset a Marquess!—Miss Testvalley had obtained from Mrs. Parmore a letter of recommendation
which placed her at the head of the educational sisterhood in the United States.

Miss Testvalley needed this, and every other form of
assistance she could obtain. It would have been difficult

for either Mrs. Parmore or the Duchess of Tintagel to imagine how poor she was, or how many people had (or so she thought) a lien on her pitiful savings. It was the penalty of the family glory. Miss Testvalley's grandfather was the illustrious patriot, Gennaro Testavaglia of Modena, fomenter of insurrections, hero of the Risorgimento, author of those once famous historical novels, *Arnaldo da Brescia* and *La Donna della Fortezza,* but whose fame lingered in England chiefly because he was the cousin of the old Gabriele Rossetti, father of the decried and illustrious Dante Gabriel. The Testavaglias, fleeing from the Austrian inquisition, had come to England at the same time as the Rossettis, and contracting their impossible name to the scope of English lips, had intermarried with other exiled revolutionaries and antipapists, producing sons who were artists and agnostics, and daughters who were evangelicals of the strictest pattern, and governesses in the highest families. Laura Testvalley had obediently followed the family tradition; but she had come after the heroic days of evangelical great ladies who required governesses to match; competition was more active, there was less demand for drawing-room Italian and prayerful considerations on the Collects, and more for German and the natural sciences, in neither of which Miss Testvalley excelled. And in the intervening years the mothers and aunts of the family had grown rheumatic and impotent, the heroic old men lingered on in their robust senility, and the drain on the younger generation grew heavier with every year. At thirty-nine Laura had found it impossible, on her English earnings, to keep the grandmother (wife of the Risorgimento hero), and to aid her own infirm mother in supporting an invalid brother and a married sister with six children, whose husband had disappeared in the wilds of Australia. Laura was sure that it was not her vocation to minister to others, but she had been forced into the task early, and continued in it from family pride —and because, after all, she belonged to the group, and the Risorgimento and the Pre-Raphaelites were her chief credentials. And so she had come to America.

At the Parmores' she had learned a good deal about one phase of American life, and she had written home some droll letters on the subject; but she had suspected from the first that the real America was elsewhere, and had been tempted and amused by the idea that among the Wall Street *parvenus* she might discover it. She had an unspoiled taste for oddities and contrasts, and nothing could have been more alien to her private sentiments than the family combination of revolutionary radicalism, Exeter Hall piety, and awestruck reverence for the aristocratic households in which the Testvalley governesses earned the keep of their ex-carbonari. "If I'd been a man," she sometimes thought, "Dante Gabriel might not have been the only cross in the family." And the idea obscurely comforted her when she was correcting her pupils' compositions, or picking up the dropped stitches in their knitting.

She was used to waiting in strange railway stations, her old black beaded "dolman" over her arm, her modest horse-hair box at her feet. Servants often forget to order the fly which is to fetch the governess, and the lady herself, though she may have meant to come to the station, is not infrequently detained by shopping or calling. So Miss Testvalley, without impatience, watched the other travellers drive off in the spidery high-wheeled vehicles in which people bounced across the humps and ruts of the American country roads. It was the eve of the great race-week, and she was amused by the showy garb of the gentlemen and the much-flounced elegance of their ladies, though she felt sure Mrs. Parmore would have disdained them.

One by one the travellers scattered, their huge "Saratogas" (she knew that expression also) hoisted into broken-down express-carts that crawled off in the wake of the owners; and at last a new dust-cloud formed down the road and floated slowly nearer, till there emerged from it a lumbering vehicle of the kind which Miss Testvalley knew to be classed as hotel hacks. As it drew up she was struck by the fact that the driver, a small dusky fellow in a white linen jacket and a hat-brim of exotic width, had an orange bow tied to his whip, and a beruffled white poodle with a bigger orange bow perched between himself and the shabby young man in overalls who shared his seat; while from within she felt herself laughingly surveyed by two tiers of bright young eyes. The driver pulled up with a queer guttural cry to his horses, the poodle leapt down and began to dance on his hind legs, and out of the hack poured a spring torrent of muslins, sash-ends, and bright cheeks under swaying hat-brims. Miss Testvalley found herself in a circle of nymphs shaken by hysterical laughter, and as she stood there, small, brown, interrogative, there swept through her mind a shred of verse which Dante Gabriel used to be fond of reciting:

Whence came ye, merry damsels, whence came ye,
So many and so many, and such glee?

and she smiled at the idea that Endymion should greet her at the Saratoga railway station. For it was clearly in search of her that the rabble rout had come. The dancing nymphs hailed her with joyful giggles, the poodle sprang on her with dusty paws, and then turned a somersault in her honour, and from the driver's box came the twang of a guitar and the familiar wail of: *Nita, Juanita, ask thy soul if we must part?*

"No, certainly not!" cried Miss Testvalley, tossing up her head toward the driver, who responded with doffed sombrero and hand on heart. "That is to say," she added, "if my future pupil is one of the young ladies who have joined in this very flattering welcome."

The enchanted circle broke, and the nymphs, still hand in hand, stretched a straight line of loveliness before her. "Guess which!" chimed simultaneously from five pairs of lips, while five deep curtsies swept the platform; and Miss Testvalley drew back a step and scanned them thoughtfully.

Her first thought was that she had never seen five prettier girls in a row; her second (tinged with joy) that Mrs. Russell Parmore would have been scandalized by such an exhibition, on the Saratoga railway platform, in full view of departing travellers, gazing employés, and delighted station loafers; her third that, whichever of the beauties was to fall to her lot, life in such company would be infinitely more amusing than with the Parmores. And still smiling she continued to examine the mirthful mocking faces.

No dominant beauty, was her first impression; no proud angelic heads, ready for coronets or halos, such as she was used to in England; unless indeed the tall fair girl with such heaps of wheat-coloured hair and such gentian-blue eyes—or the very dark one, who was too pale for her black hair, but had the small imperious nose of a Roman empress . . . yes, those two were undoubtedly beautiful, yet they were not beauties. They seemed rather to have reached the last height of prettiness, and to be perched on that sunny lower slope, below the cold divinities. And with the other three, taken one by one, fault might have been found on various counts; for the one in the striped pink and white organdy, though she looked cleverer than the others, had a sharp nose, and her laugh showed too many teeth; and the one in white, with a big orange-coloured sash the colour of the poodle's bow (no doubt she was his mistress) was sallow and red-haired, and you had to look into her pale starry eyes to forget that she was too tall, and stooped a little. And as for the fifth, who seemed so much younger—hardly more than a child—her small face was such a flurry of frowns and dimples that Miss Testvalley did not know how to define her.

"Well, young ladies, my first idea is that I wish you were all to be my pupils; and the second—" she paused, weighed the possibilities and met the eyes—"the second is that this is Miss Annabel St George, who is, I believe, to be my special charge." She put her hand on Nan's arm.

"How did you know?" burst from Nan, on the shrill note of a netted bird; and the others broke into laughter.

"Why, you silly, we told you so! Anybody can see you're nothing but a baby!"

Nan faced about, blazing and quivering. "Well, if I'm a baby, what I want is a nurse, and not a beastly English governess!"

Her companions laughed again and nudged each other; then, abashed, they glanced at the newcomer, as if trying to read in her face what would come next.

Miss Testvalley laughed also. "Oh, I'm used to both jobs," she rejoined briskly. "But meanwhile hadn't we better be getting off to the hotel? Get into the carriage, please, Annabel," she said with sudden authority.

She turned to look for her trunk; but it had already been shouldered by the nondescript young man in over-alls, who hoisted it to the roof of the carriage, and then, jumping down, brushed the soot and dust off his hands. As he did so Miss Testvalley confronted him, and her hand dropped from Nan's arm.

"Why—Lord Richard!" she exclaimed; and the young man in overalls gave a sheepish laugh. "I suppose at home they all think I'm in Brazil," he said in an uncertain voice.

"I know nothing of what they think," retorted Miss Testvalley drily, following the girls into the carriage. As they drove off, Nan, who was crowded in between Mab Elmsworth and Conchita, burst into sudden tears.

"I didn't mean to call you 'beastly'," she whispered, stealing a hand toward the new governess; and the new governess, clasping the hand, answered with her undaunted smile: "I didn't hear you call me so, my dear."

V

MRS. ST GEORGE had gone to the races with her husband—an ordeal she always dreaded and yet prayed for. Colonel St George, on these occasions, was so handsome, and so splendid in his light racing suit and gray top hat, that she enjoyed a larger repetition of her triumph in the hotel dining-room; but when this had been tasted to the full there remained her dread of the mysterious men with whom he was hail-fellow-well-met in the paddock, and the dreadful painted women in open carriages, who leered and beckoned (didn't she see them?) under the fringes of their sunshades.

She soon wearied of the show, and would have been glad to be back rocking and sipping lemonade on the hotel verandah; yet when the Colonel helped her into the carriage, suggesting that if she wanted to meet the new governess it was time to be off, she instantly concluded that the rich widow at the Congress Springs Hotel, about whom there was so much gossip, had made him a secret sign, and was going to carry him off to the gambling rooms for supper—if not worse. But when the Colonel chose his arts were irresistible, and in another moment Mrs. St George was driving away alone, her heart heavy with this new anxiety superposed on so many others.

When she reached the hotel all the frequenters of the verandah, gathered between the columns of the porch, were greeting with hysterical laughter a motley group who were pouring out of the familiar vehicle from which Mrs. St George had expected to see Nan descend with the dreaded and longed-for governess. The party was headed by Teddy de Santos-Dios, grotesquely accoutred in a hotel waiter's white jacket, and twanging his guitar to the antics of Conchita's poodle, while Conchita herself, the Elmsworth sisters and Mrs. St George's own two girls, danced up the steps surrounding a small soberly garbed figure, whom Mrs. St George instantly identified as the governess. Mrs. Elmsworth and Mrs. Closson stood on the upper step, smothering their laughter in lace handkerchiefs; but Mrs. St George sailed past them with set lips, pushing aside a shabby-looking young man in overalls who seemed to form part of the company.

"Virginia—Annabel," she gasped, "what is the meaning . . . Oh, Miss Testvalley—what *must* you think?" she faltered with trembling lips.

"I think it very kind of Annabel's young friends to have come with her to meet me," said Miss Testvalley; and Mrs. St George noted with bewilderment and relief that she was actually smiling, and that she had slipped her arm through Nan's.

For a moment Mrs. St George thought it might be easier to deal with a governess who was already on such easy terms with her pupil; but by the time Miss Testvalley, having removed the dust of travel, had knocked at her employer's door, the latter had been assailed by new apprehensions. It would have been comparatively simple to receive, with what Mrs. St George imagined to be the dignity of a Duchess, a governess used to such ceremonial; but the disconcerting circumstances of Miss Testvalley's arrival, and the composure with which she met them, had left Mrs. St George with her dignity on her hands. Could it be—? But no; Mrs. Russell Parmore, as well as the Duchess, answered for Miss Testvalley's unquestionable respectability. Mrs. St George fanned herself nervously.

"Oh, come in. Do sit down, Miss Testvalley." (Mrs. St George had expected some one taller, more majestic. She would have thought Miss Testvalley insignificant, could the term be applied to any one coming from Mrs. Parmore.) "I don't know how my daughters can have been induced to do anything so—so undignified. Unfortunately the Closson girl—." She broke off, embarrassed by the recollection of the Colonel's injunctions.

"The tall young girl with auburn hair? I understand that one of the masqueraders was her brother."

"Yes; her half-brother. Mrs. Closson is a Brazilian"—but again Mrs. St George checked the note of disparagement. "Brazilian" was bad enough, without adding anything pejorative. "The Colonel—Colonel St George—has business relations with Mr. Closson. I never met them before. . ."

"Ah," said Miss Testvalley.

"And I'm sure my girls and the Elmsworths would never. . ."

"Oh, quite so; I understood. I've no doubt the idea was Lord Richard's."

She uttered the name as though it were familiar to her, and Mrs. St George caught at Lord Richard. "You knew him already? He appears to be a friend of the Clossons."

"I knew him in England; yes. I was with Lady Brightlingsea for two years—as his sisters' governess."

Mrs. St George gazed awestruck down this new and resonant perspective. "Lady Brittlesey?" (It was thus that Miss Testvalley had pronounced the name.)

"The Marchioness of Brightlingsea; his mother. It's a very large family. I was with two of the younger daughters. Lady Honoria and Lady Ulrica Marable. I think Lord Richard is the third son. But one saw him at home so very seldom. . ."

Mrs. St George drew a deep breath. She had not bargained for this glimpse into the labyrinth of the peerage, and she felt a little dizzy, as though all the Brightlingseas and the Marables were in the room, and she ought to make the proper gestures, and didn't even know what to call them without her husband's being there to tell her. She wondered whether the experiment of an English governess might not after all make life too complicated. And this one's eyebrows were so black and ironical.

"Lord Richard," continued Miss Testvalley, "always has to have his little joke." Her tone seemed to dismiss him, and all his titled relations with him. Mrs. St George was relieved. "But your daughter Annabel—perhaps," Miss Testvalley continued, "you would like to give me some general idea of the stage she has reached in her different studies?" Her manner was now distinctly professional, and Mrs. St George's spirits drooped again. If only the Colonel had been there—as he would have been, but for that woman! Or even Nan herself...Mrs. St George looked helplessly at the governess. But suddenly an inspiration came to her. "I have always left these things to the girls' teachers," she said with majesty.

"Oh, quite—" Miss Testvalley assented.

"And their father; their father takes a great interest in their studies—when time permits..." Mrs. St George continued. "But of course his business interests...which are enormous..."

"I think I understand," Miss Testvalley softly agreed.

Mrs. St George again sighed her relief. A governess who understood without the need of tiresome explanations—was it not more than she had hoped for? Certainly Miss Testvalley looked insignificant; but the eyes under her expressive eyebrows were splendid, and she had an air of firmness. And the miracle was that Nan should already have taken a fancy to her. If only the other girls didn't laugh her out of it! "Of course," Mrs. St George began again, "what I attach most importance to is that my girls should be taught to—to behave like ladies."

Miss Testvalley murmured: "Oh, yes. Drawing-room accomplishments."

"I may as well tell you that I don't care very much for the girls they associate with here. Saratoga is not what it used to be. In New York of course it will be different. I hope you can persuade Annabel to study."

She could not think of anything else to say, and the governess, who seemed singularly discerning, rose with a slight bow, and murmured: "If you will allow me..."

Miss Testvalley's room was narrow and bare; but she had already discovered that the rooms of summer hotels in the States were all like that; the luxury and gilding were reserved for the public parlours. She did not much mind; she had never been used to comfort, and her Italian nature did not crave it. To her mind the chief difference between the governess's room at Tintagel, or at Allfriars, the Brightlingsea seat, and those she had occupied since her arrival in America, was that the former were larger (and therefore harder to heat) and were furnished with threadbare relics of former splendour, and carpets in which you caught your heel; whereas at Mrs. Parmore's, and in this big hotel, though the governess's quarters were cramped, they were neat and the furniture was in good repair. But this afternoon Miss Testvalley was perhaps tired, or oppressed by the heat, or perhaps only by an unwonted sense of loneliness. Certainly it was odd to find one's self at the orders of people who wished their daughters to be taught to "behave like ladies". (The alternative being—what, she wondered? Perhaps a disturbing apparition like Conchita Closson.)

At any rate, Miss Testvalley was suddenly aware of a sense of loneliness, of far-away-ness, of a quite unreasonable yearning for the dining-room at the back of a certain shabby house at Denmark Hill, where her mother, in a widow's cap of white crape, sat on one side of the scantily filled grate, turning with rheumatic fingers the pages of the Reverend Frederick Maurice's sermons, while, facing her across the hearth, old Gennaro Testavaglia, still heavy and powerful in his extreme age, brooded with fixed eyes in a big parchment-coloured face, and repeated over and over some forgotten verse of his own revolutionary poems. In that room, with its chronic smell of cold coffee and smouldering coals, of Elliman's liniment and human old age, Miss Testvalley had spent some of the most disheartening hours of her life. *"Le mie prigioni,"* she had once called it; yet was it not for that detested room that she was homesick!

Only fifteen minutes in which to prepare for supper! (She had been warned that late dinners were still unknown in American hotels.) Miss Testvalley, setting her teeth against the vision of the Denmark Hill dining-room, went up to the chest of drawers on which she had already laid out her modest toilet appointments; and there she saw, between her yellowish-backed brush and faded pincushion, a bunch of freshly gathered geraniums and mignonette. The flowers had certainly not been there when she had smoothed her hair before waiting on Mrs. St George; nor had they, she was sure, been sent by that lady. They were not bought flowers, but flowers lovingly gathered; and some one else must have entered in Miss Testvalley's absence, and hastily deposited the humble posy.

The governess sat down on the hard chair beside the bed, and her eyes filled with tears. Flowers, she had noticed, did not abound in the States; at least not in summer. In winter, in New York, you could see them banked up in tiers in the damp heat of the florists' windows; plumy ferns, forced lilac, and those giant roses, red and pink, which rich people offered to each other so lavishly in long white card-board boxes. It was very odd; the same ladies who exchanged these costly tributes in mid-winter lived through the summer without a flower, or with nothing but a stiff bed of dwarf foliage plants before the door, or a tub or two of the inevitable hydrangeas. Yet some one had apparently managed to snatch these flowers from the meagre border before the hotel porch, and had put them there to fill Miss Test-valley's bedroom with scent and colour. And who could have done it but her new pupil?

Quarter of an hour later Miss Testvalley, her thick hair re-braided and glossed with brilliantine, her black merino exchanged for a plum-coloured silk with a cro-chet lace collar, and lace mittens on her small worn hands, knocked at the door of the Misses St George. It opened, and the governess gave a little "oh!" of surprise. Virginia stood there, a shimmer of ruffled white droop-ing away from her young throat and shoulders. On her heaped-up wheat-coloured hair lay a wreath of corn-flowers; and a black velvet ribbon with a locket hanging from it intensified her fairness like the black stripe on a ring-dove's throat.

"What elegance for a public dining-room!" thought Miss Testvalley; and then reflected: "But no doubt it's her only chance of showing it."

Virginia opened wondering blue eyes, and the gov-erness explained: "The supper-bell has rung, and I thought you and your sister might like me to go down with you."

"Oh—" Virginia murmured; and added: "Nan's lost her slipper. She's hunting for it."

"Very well; shall I help her? And you'll go down and excuse us to your mamma?"

Virginia's eyes grew wider. "Well, I guess mother's used to waiting," she said, as she sauntered along the corridor to the staircase.

Nan St George lay face downward on the floor, poking with a silk parasol under the wardrobe. At the sound of Miss Testvalley's voice she raised herself sulkily. Her small face was flushed and frowning. ("None of her sister's beauty," Miss Testvalley thought.) "It's there, but I can't get at it," Nan proclaimed.

"My dear, you'll tumble your lovely frock—"

"Oh, it's not lovely. It's one of Jinny's last year's organdies."

"Well, it won't improve it to crawl about on the floor. Is your shoe under the wardrobe? Let me try to get it. My silk won't be damaged."

Miss Testvalley put out her hand for the sunshade, and Nan scrambled to her feet. "You can't reach it," she said, still sulkily. But Miss Testvalley, prostrate on the floor, had managed to push a thin arm under the wardrobe, and the parasol presently re-appeared with a little bronze slipper on its tip. Nan gave a laugh.

"Well, you *are* handy!" she said.

Miss Testvalley echoed the laugh. "Put it on quickly, and let me help you to tidy your dress. And, oh dear, your sash is untied—." She spun the girl about, re-tied the sash and smoothed the skirt with airy touches; for all of which, she noticed, Nan uttered no word of thanks.

"And your handkerchief, Annabel?" In Miss Testvalley's opinion no lady should appear in the evening without a scrap of lace-edged cambric, folded into a triangle and held between gloved or mittened finger-tips. Nan shrugged. "I never know where my handker-chiefs are—I guess they get lost in the wash, wandering round in hotels the way we do."

Miss Testvalley sighed at this nomadic wastefulness. Perhaps because she had always been a wanderer herself she loved orderly drawers and shelves, and bunches of lavender between delicately fluted under-garments.

"Do you always live in hotels, my dear?"

"We did when I was little. But father's bought a house in New York now. Mother made him do it because the Elmsworths did. She thought maybe, if we had one, Jinny'd be invited out more; but I don't see much difference."

"Well, I shall have to help you to go over your linen," the governess continued; but Nan showed no interest in the offer. Miss Testvalley saw before her a cold im-patient little face—and yet. . .

"Annabel," she said, slipping her hand through the girl's thin arm, "how did you guess I was fond of flowers?"

The blood rose from Nan's shoulders to her cheeks, and a half-guilty smile set the dimples racing across her face. "Mother said we'd acted like a lot of savages, get-ting up that circus at the station—and what on earth would you think of us?"

"I think that I shall like you all very much; and you especially, because of those flowers."

Nan gave a shy laugh. "Lord Richard said you'd like them."

"Lord Richard?"

"Yes. He says in England everybody has a garden, with lots of flowers that smell sweet. And so I stole them from the hotel border... He's crazy about Conchita, you know. Do you think she'll catch him?"

Miss Testvalley stiffened. She felt her upper lip lengthen, though she tried to smile. "I don't think it's a question that need concern us, do you?"

Nan stared. "Well, she's my greatest friend—after Jinny, I mean."

"Then we must wish her something better than Lord Richard. Come, my dear, or those wonderful American griddle-cakes will all be gone."

Early in her career Miss Testvalley had had to learn the difficult art of finding her way about—not only as concerned the tastes and temper of the people she lived with, but the topography of their houses. In those old winding English dwellings, half fortress, half palace, where suites and galleries of stately proportions abruptly tapered off into narrow twists and turns, leading to unexpected rooms tucked away in unaccountable corners, and where school-room and nurseries were usually at the far end of the labyrinth, it behoved the governess to blaze her trail by a series of private aids to memory. It was important, in such houses, not only to know the way you were meant to take, but the many you were expected to avoid, and a young governess turning too often down the passage leading to the young gentlemen's wing, or getting into the way of the master of the house in his dignified descent to the breakfast-room, might suddenly have her services dispensed with. To any one thus trained the simple plan of an American summer hotel offered no mysteries; and when supper was over and, after a sultry hour or two in the red and gold ball-room, the St George ladies ascended to their apartments, Miss Testvalley had no difficulty in finding her way up another flight to her own room. She was already aware that it was in the wing of the hotel, and had noted that from its window she could look across into that from which, before supper, she had seen Miss Closson signal to her brother and Lord Richard, who were smoking on the gravel below.

It was no business of Miss Testvalley's to keep watch on what went on in the Closson rooms—or would not have been, she corrected herself, had Nan St George not spoken of Conchita as her dearest friend. Such a tie did seem to the governess to require vigilance. Miss Closson was herself an unknown quantity, and Lord Richard was one only too well-known to Miss Testvalley. It was therefore not unnatural that, after silence had fallen on the long corridors of the hotel, the governess, finding sleep impossible in her small suffocating room, should put out her candle, and gaze across from her window at that from which she had seen Conchita lean.

Light still streamed from it, though midnight was past, and presently came laughter, and the twang of Santos-Dios's guitar, and a burst of youthful voices joining in song. Was her pupil's among them? Miss Testvalley could not be sure; but soon, detaching itself from Teddy de Santos-Dios's reedy tenor, she caught the hoarse barytone of another voice.

Imprudent children! It was bad enough to be gathered at that hour in a room with a young man and a guitar; but at least the young man was Miss Closson's brother, and Miss Testvalley had noticed, at the supper-table, much exchange of civilities between the St Georges and the Clossons. But Richard Marable—that was inexcusable, that was scandalous! The hotel would be ringing with it tomorrow. . .

Ought not Miss Testvalley to find some pretext for knocking at Conchita's door, gathering her charges back to safety, and putting it in their power to say that their governess had assisted at the little party? Her first impulse was to go; but governesses who act on first impulses seldom keep their places. "As long as there's so much noise," she thought, "there can't be any mischief . . ." and at that moment, in a pause of the singing, she caught Nan's trill of little-girl laughter. Miss Testvalley started up, and went to her door; but once more she drew back. Better wait and see—interfering might do more harm than good. If only some exasperated neighbour did not ring to have the rejoicings stopped!

At length music and laughter subsided. Silence followed. Miss Testvalley, drawing an austere purple flannel garment over her night-dress, unbolted her door and stole out into the passage. Where it joined the main corridor she paused and waited. A door had opened half way down the corridor—Conchita's door—and the governess saw a flutter of light dresses, and heard subdued laughter and good nights. Both the St George and Elmsworth families were lodged below, and in the weak glimmer of gas she made sure of four girls hurrying toward her wing. She drew back hastily. Glued to her door she listened, and heard a heavy but cautious step passing by, and a throaty voice humming "Champagne Charlie". She drew a breath of relief, and sat down before her glass to finish her toilet for the night.

Her hair carefully waved on its pins, her evening prayer recited, she slipped into bed and blew out the light. But still sleep did not come, and she lay in the sultry darkness and listened, she hardly knew for what. At last she heard the same heavy step returning cautiously, passing her door, gaining once more the main corridor—the step she would have known in a thousand, the step she used to listen for at Allfriars after midnight, groping down the long passage to the governess's room.

She started up. Forgetful of crimping-pins and bare feet, she opened her door again. The last flicker of gas had gone out, and secure in the blackness she crept after the heavy step to the corner. It sounded ahead of her half way down the long row of doors; then it stopped, a door opened . . . and Miss Testvalley turned back on leaden feet. . .

Nothing of that fugitive adventure at Allfriars had ever been known. Of that she was certain. An ill-conditioned youth, the boon companion of his father's grooms, and a small brown governess, ten years his elder, and known to be somewhat curt and distant with every one except her pupils and their parents—who would ever have thought of associating the one with the other? The episode had been brief; the peril was soon over; and when, the very same year, Lord Richard was solemnly banished from his father's house, it was not because of his having once or twice stolen down the school-room passage at undue hours; but for reasons so far more deplorable that poor Lady Brightlingsea, her reserve utterly broken down, had sobbed out on Miss Testvalley's breast: "Anything, anything else I know his father would have forgiven." (Miss Testvalley wondered . . .)

VI

WHEN Colonel St George bought his house in Madison Avenue it seemed to him fit to satisfy the ambitions of any budding millionaire. That it had been built and decorated by one of the Tweed ring, who had come to grief earlier than his more famous fellow-criminals, was to Colonel St George convincing proof that it was a suitable setting for wealth and elegance. But social education is acquired rapidly in New York, even by those who have to absorb it through the cracks of the sacred edifice; and Mrs. St George had already found out that no one lived in Madison Avenue, that the front hall should have been painted Pompeian red with a stencilled frieze, and not with naked Cupids and humming birds on a sky-blue ground, and that basement dining-rooms were unknown to the fashionable. So much she had picked up almost at once from Jinny and Jinny's school-friends; and when she called on Mrs. Parmore to enquire about the English governess, the sight of the Parmore house, small and simple as it was, completed her disillusionment.

But it was too late to change. The Colonel, who was insensitive to details, continued to be proud of his house; even when the Elmsworths, suddenly migrating from Brooklyn, had settled themselves in Fifth Avenue he would not admit his mistake, or feel the humiliation of the contrast. And yet what a difference it made to a lady to be able to say "Fifth Avenue" in giving her address to Black, Starr and Frost, or to Mrs. Connelly, the fashionable dress-maker! In establishments like that they classed their customers at once, and "Madison Avenue" stood at best for a decent mediocrity.

Mrs. St George at first ascribed to this unfortunate locality her failure to make a social situation for her girls; yet after the Elmsworths had come to Fifth Avenue she noted with satisfaction that Lizzy and Mabel were not asked out much more than Virginia. Of course Mr. Elmsworth was an obstacle; and so was Mrs. Elsmworth's laugh. It was difficult—it was even painful—to picture the Elmsworths dining at the Parmores' or the Eglintons'. But the St Georges did not dine there either. And the question of ball-going was almost as discouraging. One of the young men whom the girls had met at Saratoga had suggested to Virginia that he might get her a card for the first Assembly; but Mrs. St George, when sounded, declined indignantly, for she knew that in the best society girls did not go to balls without their parents.

These subscription balls were a peculiar source of bitterness to Mrs. St George. She could not understand how her daughters could be excluded from entertainment for which one could buy a ticket. She knew all about the balls from her hair-dresser, the celebrated Katie Wood. Katie did everybody's hair, and innocently planted dagger after dagger in Mrs. St George's anxious breast by saying: "If you and Jinny want me next Wednesday week for the first Assembly you'd better say so right off, because I've got every minute bespoke already from three o'clock on", or: "If you're invited to the opening night of the Opera, I might try the new chignon with the bunch of curls on the left shoulder", or worse still: "I suppose Jinny belongs to the Thursday Evening Dances, don't she? The débutantes are going to wear wreaths of apple-blossom or rose-buds a good deal this winter—or forget-me-not would look lovely, with her eyes."

Lovely, indeed. But if Virginia had not been asked to belong, and if Mrs. St George had vainly tried to have her own name added to the list of the Assembly balls, or to get a box for the opening night of the Opera, what was there to do but to say indifferently: "Oh, I don't know if we shall be here—the Colonel's thinking a little of carrying us off to Florida if he can get away . . ." knowing all the while how much the hair-dresser believed of that excuse, and also aware that, in speaking of Miss Eglinton and Miss Parmore, Katie did not call them by their Christian names. . .

Mrs. St George could not understand why she was subjected to this cruel ostracism. The Colonel knew everybody—that is, all the gentlemen he met down town, or at his clubs, and he belonged to many clubs. Their dues were always having to be paid, even when the butcher and the grocer were clamouring. He often brought gentlemen home to dine, and gave them the best champagne and Madeira in the cellar; and they invited him back, but never included Mrs. St George and Virginia in their invitations.

It was small comfort to learn one day that Jinny and

Nan had been invited to act as Conchita Closson's brides-maids. She thought it unnatural that the Clossons, who were strangers in New York, and still camping at the Fifth Avenue Hotel, should be marrying their daughter before Virginia was led to the altar. And then the bride-groom!—well, everybody knew that he was only a younger son, and that in England, even in the great aristocratic families, younger sons were of small account unless they were clever enough to make their own way—an ambition which seemed never to have troubled Dick Marable. Moreover, there were dark rumours about him, reports of warning discreetly transmitted through the British Legation in Washington, and cruder tales among the clubs. Still, nothing could alter the fact that Lord Richard Marable was the son of the Marquess of Brightlingsea, and that his mother had been a Duke's daughter—and who knows whether the Eglintons and Parmores, though they thanked heaven their dear girls would never be exposed to such risks, were not half envious of the Clossons? But then there was the indecent haste of it. The young people had met for the first time in August; and they were to be married in November! In good society it was usual for a betrothal to last at least a year; and among the Eglintons and Parmores even that time-allowance was thought to betray an undue haste. "The young people should be given time to get to know each other," the mothers of Fifth Avenue de-creed; and Mrs. Parmore told Miss Testvalley, when the latter called to pay her respects to her former employer, that she for her part hoped her daughter would never consent to an engagement of less than two years. "But

I suppose, dear Miss Testvalley, that among the people you're with now there are no social traditions."

"None except those they are making for themselves," Miss Testvalley was tempted to rejoin; but that would not have been what she called a "governess's answer", and she knew a governess should never be more on her guard than when conversing with a former employer. Especially, Miss Testvalley thought, when the employer had a long nose with a slight droop, and pale lips like Mrs. Parmore's. She murmured that there were business reasons, she understood; Mr. Closson was leaving shortly for Brazil.

"Ah, so they *say*. But of course, the rumours one hears about this young man . . . a son of Lord Brightlingsea's, I understand? But, Miss Testvalley, you were with the Brightlingseas; you must have known him?"

"It's a very big family, and when I went there the sons were already scattered. I usually remained at Allfriars with the younger girls."

Mrs. Parmore nodded softly. "Quite so. And by that time this unfortunate young man had already begun his career of dissipation in London. He *has* been dissipated, I believe?"

"Lately I think he's been trying to earn his living on Mr. Closson's plantation in Brazil."

"Poor young man! Do his family realize what a deplorable choice he has made? Whatever his past may have been, it's a pity he should marry in New York, and leave it again, without having any idea of it beyond what can be had in the Closson set. If he'd come in different circumstances, we should all have been so happy... Mr. Parmore would have put him down at his clubs... he would have been invited everywhere... Yes, it does seem unfortunate... But of course no one knows the Clossons."

"I suppose the young couple will go back to Brazil after the marriage," said Miss Testvalley evasively.

Mrs. Parmore gave an ironic smile. "I don't imagine Miss Closson is marrying the son of a Marquess to go and live on a plantation in Brazil. When I took Alida to Mrs. Connelly's to order her dress for the Assembly, Mrs. Connelly told me she'd heard from Mrs. Closson's maid that Mr. Closson meant to give the young couple a house in London. Do you suppose this is likely? They can't keep up any sort of establishment in London without a fairly large income; and I hear Mr. Closson's position in Wall Street is rather shaky."

Miss Testvalley took refuge in one of her Italian gestures of conjecture. "Governesses, you know, Mrs. Parmore, hear so much less gossip than dress-makers and ladies'-maids; and I'm not Miss Closson's governess."

"No; fortunately for you! For I believe there were rather unpleasant rumours at Saratoga. People were bound to find a reason for such a hurried marriage... But your pupils have been asked to be bridesmaids, I understand?"

"The girls got to know each other last summer. And you know how exciting it is, especially for a child of Annabel St George's age, to figure for the first time in a wedding procession."

"Yes. I suppose they haven't many chances... But shouldn't you like to come upstairs and see Alida's Assembly dress? Mrs. Connelly has just sent it home, and your pupils might like to hear about it. White tulle, of course—nothing will ever replace white tulle for a débutante, will it?"

Miss Testvalley, after that visit, felt that she had cast in her lot once for all with the usurpers and the adventurers. Perhaps because she herself had been born in exile, her sympathies were with the social as well as the political outcasts—with the weepers by the waters of Babylon rather than those who barred the doors of the Assembly against them. Describe Miss Parmore's white tulle to her pupils, indeed! What she meant—but how accomplish it?—was to get cards for the Assembly for Mrs. St George and Virginia, and to see to it that the latter's dress outdid Miss Parmore's as much as her beauty over-shadowed that young woman's.

But how? Through Lord Richard Marable? Well, that was perhaps not impossible... Miss Testvalley had detected, in Mrs. Parmore, a faint but definite desire to make the young man's acquaintance, even to have him on the list of her next dinner. She would like to show him, poor young fellow, her manner implied, that there are houses in New York where a scion of the English aristocracy may feel himself at home, and discover (though, alas, too late!) that there are American girls comparable to his own sisters in education and breeding.

Since the announcement of Conchita's engagement, and the return of the two families to New York, there had been a good deal of coming and going between the

St George and Closson households—rather too much to suit Miss Testvalley. But she had early learned to adapt herself to her pupils' whims while maintaining her authority over them, and she preferred to accompany Nan to the Fifth Avenue Hotel rather than let her go there without her. Virginia, being "out", could come and go as she pleased; but among the Parmores and Eglintons, in whose code Mrs. St George was profoundly versed, girls in the school-room did not walk about New York alone, much less call at hotels, and Nan, fuming yet resigned—for she had already grown unaccountably attached to her governess—had to submit to Miss Testvalley's conducting her to the Closson apartment, and waiting below when she was to be fetched. Sometimes, at Mrs. Closson's request, the governess went in with her charge. Mrs. Closson was almost always in her sitting-room, since leaving it necessitated encasing her soft frame in stays and a heavily whale-boned dress; and she preferred sitting at her piano, or lying on the sofa with a novel and a cigarette, in an atmosphere of steam-heat and heavily scented flowers, and amid a litter of wedding presents and bridal finery. She was a good-natured woman, friendly and even confidential with everybody who came her way, and when she caught sight of Miss Testvalley behind her charge, often called to her to come in and take a look at the lovely dress Mrs. Connelly had just sent home, or the embossed soup-tureen of Baltimore silver offered by Mr. Closson's business friends. Miss Testvalley did not always accept; but sometimes she divined that Mrs. Closson wished to consult her, or to confide in her, and, while her pupil joined the other girls, she would clear the finery from a chair and prepare to receive Mrs. Closson's confidences—which were usually connected with points of social etiquette, indifferent to the lady herself, but preoccupying to Mr. Closson.

"He thinks it's funny that Dick's family haven't cabled, or even written. Do they generally do so in England? I tell Mr. Closson there hasn't been time yet— I'm so bad about answering letters myself that I can't blame anybody else for not writing! But Mr. Closson seems to think it's meant for a slight. Why should it be? If Dick's family are not satisfied with Conchita, they will be when they see her, don't you think so?" Yes, certainly, Miss Testvalley thought so. "Well, then— what's the use of worrying? But Mr. Closson is a business man, and he expects everybody to have business habits. I don't suppose the Marquess is in business, is he?"

Miss Testvalley said no, she thought not; and for a moment there flickered up in Mrs. Closson a languid curiosity to know more of her daughter's future relatives. "It's a big family, isn't it? Dick says he can never remember how many brothers and sisters he has; but I suppose that's one of his jokes. . . He's a great joker, isn't he; like my Ted! Those two are always playing tricks on everybody. But how many brothers and sisters are there, really?"

Miss Testvalley, after a moment's calculation, gave the number as eight; Lord Seadown, the heir, Lord John, Lord Richard—and five girls; yes, there were five girls. Only one married as yet; the Lady Camilla. Her own charges, the Ladies Honoria and Ulrica, were now out; the other two were still in the school-room. Yes; it was a large family—but not so very large, as English families went. Large enough, however, to preoccupy Lady Brightlingsea a good deal—especially as concerned the future of her daughters.

Mrs. Closson listened with her dreamy smile. Her attention had none of the painful precision with which Mrs. St George tried to master the details of social life in the higher spheres, nor of the eager curiosity gleaming under Mrs. Parmore's pale eyelashes. Mrs. Closson really could not see that there was much difference between one human being and another, except that some had been favoured with more leisure than others—and leisure was her idea of heaven.

"I should think Lady Brightlingsea would be worn out, with all those girls to look after. I don't suppose she's had much time to think about the boys."

"Well, of course she's devoted to her sons too."

"Oh, I suppose so. And you say the other two sons are not married?" No, not as yet, Miss Testvalley repeated.

A flicker of interest was again perceptible between Mrs. Closson's drowsy lids. "If they don't either of them marry, Dick will be the Marquess some day, won't he?"

Miss Testvalley could not restrain a faint amusement. "But Lord Seadown is certain to marry. In those great houses it's a family obligation for the heir to marry."

Mrs. Closson's head sank back contentedly. "Mercy! How many obligations they all seem to have. I guess Conchita'll be happier just making a love-match with Lord Richard. He's passionately in love with her, isn't he?" Mrs. Closson pursued with her confidential smile. "It would appear so, certainly," Miss Testvalley rejoined.

"All I want is that she should be happy; and he *will* make her happy, won't he?" the indulgent mother concluded, as though Miss Testvalley's words had completely re-assured her.

At that moment the door was flung open, and the bride herself whirled into the room. "Oh, mother!" Conchita paused to greet Miss Testvalley; her manner, like her mother's, was always considerate and friendly. "You're not coming to take Nan away already, are you?" Re-assured by Miss Testvalley, she put her hands on her hips and spun lightly around in front of the two ladies.

"Mother! Isn't it a marvel?—It's my Assembly dress," she explained, laughing, to the governess.

It was indeed a marvel; the money these American mothers spent on their daughters' clothes never ceased to astonish Miss Testvalley; but while her appreciative eye registered every costly detail her mind was busy with the incredible fact that Conchita Closson—"the Closson girl" in Mrs. Parmore's vocabulary—had contrived to get an invitation to the Assembly, while her own charges, who were so much lovelier and more loveable. . . But here they were, Virginia, Nan, and Lizzy Elmsworth, all circling gaily about the future bride, applauding, criticizing, twitching as critically at her ruffles and ribbons as though these were to form a part of their own adornment. Miss Testvalley, looking closely, saw no trace of envy in their radiant faces, though Virginia's was perhaps a trifle sad. "So they've not been invited to the ball, and Conchita *has*," she reflected, and felt a sudden irritation against Miss Closson.

But the irritation did not last. This was Mrs. Parmore's doing, the governess was sure; to secure Lord Richard she had no doubt persuaded the patronesses of the Assembly—that stern tribunal—to include his fiancée among their guests. Only—how had she, or the others, managed to accept the idea of introducing the fiancée's mother into their hallowed circle? The riddle was answered by Mrs. Closson herself. "First I was afraid I'd have to take Conchita—just imagine it! Get up out of my warm bed in the middle of the night, and rig myself up in satin and whale-bones, and feathers on my head—they say I'd have had to wear feathers!" Mrs. Closson laughed luxuriously over this plumed and armoured vision. "But luckily they didn't even invite me. They invited my son instead—it seems in New York a girl can go to a ball with her brother, even to an Assembly ball . . . and Conchita was so crazy to accept that Mr. Closson said we'd better let her. . ."

Conchita spun around again, her flexible arms floating like a dancer's on her outspread flounces. "Oh, girls, it's a perfect shame you're not coming too! They ought to have invited all my bridesmaids, oughtn't they, Miss Testvalley?" She spoke with evident good will, and the governess reflected how different Miss Parmore's view would have been, had she been invited to an exclusive entertainment from which her best friends were omitted. But then no New York entertainment excluded Miss Parmore's friends.

Miss Testvalley, as she descended the stairs, turned the problem over in her mind. She had never liked her girls (as she already called them) as much as she did at that moment. Nan, of course, was a child, and could comfort herself with the thought that her time for ball-going had not yet come; but Virginia—well, Virginia, whom Miss Testvalley had not altogether learned to like, was behaving as generously as her sister. Her quick hands had displaced the rose-garland on Conchita's shoulder, re-arranging it in a more becoming way. Conchita was careless about her toilet, and had there been any malice in Virginia she might have spoilt her friend's dress instead of improving it. No act of generosity appealed in vain to Miss Testvalley, and as she went down the stairs to the hotel entrance she muttered to herself: "If I only could—if I only knew how!"

VII

SHE was so busy with her thoughts that she was startled by the appearance, at the foot of the stairs, of a young man who stood there visibly waiting.

"Lord Richard!" she exclaimed, almost as surprised as when she had first recognized him, disguised in grimy overalls, at the Saratoga station.

Since then she had, of necessity, run across him now and then, at the St Georges' as well as at Mrs. Closson's; but if he had not perceptibly avoided her, neither had he sought her out, and for that she was thankful. The Lord Richard chapter was a closed one, and she had no wish to re-open it. She had paid its cost in some brief fears and joys, and one night of agonizing tears; but perhaps her Italian blood had saved her from ever, then or after, regarding it as a moral issue. In her busy life there was no room for dead love-affairs; and besides, did the word "love" apply to such passing follies? Fatalistically, she had registered the episode and pigeon-holed it. If ever she were to know an abiding grief it must be caused by one that engaged the soul.

Lord Richard stood before her awkwardly. He was always either sullen or too hearty, and she hoped he was not going to be hearty. But perhaps since those days life had formed him. . .

"I saw you go upstairs just now—and I waited."

"You waited? For me?"

"Yes," he muttered, still more awkwardly. "Could I speak to you?"

Miss Testvalley reflected. She could not imagine what he wanted, but experience told her that it would almost certainly be something disagreeable. However, it was not her way to avoid issues—and perhaps he only wanted to borrow money. She could not give him much, of course ... but if it were only that, so much the better. "We can go in there, I suppose," she said, pointing to the door of the public sitting-room. She lifted the *portière*, and finding the room empty, led the way to a ponderous rosewood sofa. Lord Richard shambled after her, and seated himself on the other side of the table before the sofa.

"You'd better be quick—there are always people here receiving visitors."

The young man, thus admonished, was still silent. He sat sideways on his chair, as though to avoid facing Miss Testvalley. A frown drew the shock of drab hair still lower over his low forehead, and he pulled nervously at his drab moustache.

"Well?" said Miss Testvalley.

"I—look here. I'm no hand at explaining ... never was. .. But you were always a friend of mine. .."

"I've no wish to be otherwise."

His frown relaxed slightly. "I never know how to say things. .."

"What is it you wish to say?"

"I—well, Mr. Closson asked me yesterday if there was any reason why I shouldn't marry Conchita."

His eyes still avoided her, but she kept hers resolutely on his face. "Do you know what made him ask?"

"Well, you see—there's been no word from home. I rather fancy he expected the governor to write, or even to cable. They seem to do such a lot of cabling in this country, don't they?"

Miss Testvalley reflected. "How long ago did you write? Has there been time enough for an answer to come? It's not likely that your family would cable."

Lord Richard looked embarrassed; which meant, she suspected, that his letter had not been sent as promptly as he had let the Clossons believe. Sheer dilatoriness might even have kept him from sending it at all. "You have written, I suppose?" she enquired sternly.

"Oh, yes, I've written."

"And told them everything—I mean about Miss Closson's family?"

"Of course," he repeated, rather sulkily. "I haven't got much of a head for that kind of thing; but I got Santos-Dios to write it all out for me."

"Then you'll certainly have an answer. No doubt it's on the way now."

"It ought to be. But Mr. Closson's always in such a devil of a hurry. Everybody's in a hurry in America. He asked me if there was any reason why my people shouldn't write."

"Well—is there?"

Lord Richard turned in his chair, and glanced at her with an uncomfortable laugh. "You must see now what I'm driving at."

"No, I don't. Unless you count on me to re-assure the Clossons?"

"No—. Only, if they should take it into their heads to question you. . ."

She felt a faint shiver of apprehension. To question her—about what? Did he imagine that any one, at this hour, and at this far end of the world, would disinter that old unhappy episode? If this was what he feared, it meant her career to begin all over again, those poor old ancestors of Denmark Hill without support or comfort, and no one on earth to help her to her feet. . . She lifted her head sternly. "Nonsense, Lord Richard—speak out."

"Well, the fact is, I know my mother blurted out all that stupid business to you before I left Allfriars—I mean about the cheque," he muttered half-audibly.

Miss Testvalley suddenly became aware that her heart had stopped beating by the violent plunge of relief it now gave. Her whole future, for a moment, had hung there in the balance. And after all, it was only the cheque he was thinking of. Now she didn't care what happened! She even saw, in a flash, that she had him at a disadvantage, and her past fear nerved her to use her opportunity.

"Yes, your mother did, as you say, blurt out something. . ."

The young man, his elbows on the table, had crossed his hands and rested his chin on them. She knew what he was waiting for—but she let him wait.

"I was a poor young fool—I didn't half know what I was doing. . . My father was damned hard on me, you know."

"I think he was," said Miss Testvalley.

Lord Richard lifted his head and looked at her. He hardly ever smiled, but when he did his face cleared, and became almost boyish again, as though a mask had been removed from it. "You're a brick, Laura—you always were."

"We're not here to discuss my merits, Lord Richard. Indeed you seem to have doubted them a moment ago." He stared, and she remembered that subtlety was always lost on him. "You imagined, knowing that I was in your mother's confidence, that I might betray it. Was that it?"

His look of embarrassment returned. "I—you're so hard on a fellow. . ."

"I don't want to be hard on you. But, since you suspected I might tell your secrets, you must excuse my suspecting *you*—"

"Me? Of what?"

Miss Testvalley was silent. A hundred thoughts rushed through her brain—preoccupations both grave and trivial. It had always been thus with her, and she could never see that it was otherwise with life itself, where unimportant trifles and grave anxieties so often darkened the way with their joint shadows. At Nan St George's age, Miss Testvalley, though already burdened with the care and responsibilities of middle life, had longed with all Nan's longing to wear white tulle and be invited to a ball. She had never been invited to a ball, had never worn white tulle; and now, at nearly forty, and scarred by hardships and disappointments, she still felt that early pang, still wondered what, in life, ought to be classed as trifling, and what as grave. She looked again at Lord Richard. "No," she said, "I've only one stipulation to make."

He cleared his throat. "Er—yes?"

"Lord Richard—are you truly and sincerely in love with Conchita?"

The young man's sallow face crimsoned to the roots of his hair, and even his freckled hands, with their short square fingers, grew red. "In love with her?" he stammered. "I . . . I never saw a girl that could touch her. . . ."

There was something curiously familiar about the phrase; and she reflected that the young man had not renewed his vocabulary. Miss Testvalley smiled faintly. "Conchita's very charming," she continued. "I wouldn't for the world have anything—anything that I could prevent—endanger her happiness."

Lord Richard's flush turned to a sudden pallor. "I— I swear to you I'd shoot myself sooner than let anything harm a hair of her head."

Miss Testvalley was silent again. Lord Richard stirred uneasily in his chair, and she saw that he was trying to interpret her meaning. She stood up and gathered her old beaded dolman about her shoulders. "I mean to believe you, Lord Richard," she announced abruptly. "I hope I'm not wrong."

"Wrong? God bless you, Laura." He held out his blunt hand. "I'll never forget—never."

"Never forget your promise about Conchita. That's all I ask." She began to move toward the door, and slowly, awkwardly, he moved at her side. On the threshold she turned back to him. "No, it's not all—

there's something else." His face clouded again, and his look of alarm moved her. Poor blundering boy that he still was! Perhaps his father *had* been too hard on him.

"What I'm going to ask is a trifle . . . yet at that age nothing is a trifle. . . Lord Richard, I'll back you up through thick and thin if you'll manage to get Miss Closson's bridesmaids invited to the Assembly ball next week."

He looked at her in bewilderment. "The Assembly ball?"

"Yes. They've invited you, I know; and your fiancée. In New York it's considered a great honour—almost" (she smiled) "like being invited to Court in England. . .

"Oh, come," he interjected. "There's nothing like a Court here."

"No; but this is the nearest approach. And my two girls, the St Georges, and their friends the Elmsworths, are not very well-known in the fashionable set which manages the Assemblies. Of course they can't all be invited; and indeed Nan is too young for balls. But Virginia St George and Lizzy Elmsworth ought not to be left out. Such things hurt young people cruelly. They've just been helping Conchita to arrange her dress, knowing all the while they were not going themselves. I thought it charming of them. . ."

Lord Richard stood before her in perplexity. "I'm dreadfully sorry. It is hard on them, certainly. I'd forgotten all about that ball. But can't their parents—?"

"Their parents, I'm afraid, are the obstacle."

He bent his puzzled eyes on the ground, but at length light seemed to break on him. "Oh, I see. They're not in the right set? They seem to think a lot about sets in the States, don't they?"

"Enormously. But as you've been invited—through Mrs. Parmore, I understand—and Mr. de Santos-Dios also, you two, between you, can certainly get invitations for Virginia and Lizzy. You can count on me, Lord Richard, and I shall count on you. I've never asked you a favour before, have I?"

"Oh, but I say—I'd do anything, of course. But how the devil can I, when I'm a stranger here?"

"Because you're a stranger—because you're Lord Richard Marable. I should think you need only ask one of the patronesses. Or that clever monkey Santos-Dios will help you, as he has with your correspondence." Lord Richard reddened. "In any case," Miss Testvalley continued, "I don't wish to know how you do it; and of course you must not say that it's my suggestion. Any mention of that would ruin everything. But you must get those invitations, Lord Richard."

She held him for a second with her quick decisive smile, just touched his hand, and walked out of the hotel.

New York society in the 'seventies was a nursery of young beauties, and Mrs. Parmore and Mrs. Eglinton would have told any newcomer from the old world that he would see at an Assembly ball faces to outrival all the court-beauties of Europe. There were rumours, now and then, that others even surpassing the Assembly standard had been seen at the Opera (on off-nights, when the fashionable let, or gave away, their boxes, or at such promiscuous annual entertainments as the Charity ball, the Seventh Regiment ball, and so on. And of late, more particularly, people had been talking of a Miss Closson, daughter or step-daughter of a Mr. Closson, who was a stock-broker or railway-director—or was he a coffee planter in South America? The facts about Mr. Closson were few and vague, but he had a certain notoriety in Wall Street and on the fashionable race-courses, and had now come into newspaper prominence through the engagement of his daughter (or step-daughter) to Lord Richard Marable, a younger son of the Marquess of Brightlingsea... (No, my dear, you must pronounce it Brittlesey.) Some of the fashionable young men had met Miss Closson, and spoken favourably, even enthusiastically, of her charms; but then young men are always attracted by novelty, and by a slight flavour of, shall we say fastness, or anything just a trifle off-colour?

The Assembly ladies felt it would be surprising if any Miss Closson could compete in loveliness with Miss Alida Parmore, Miss Julia Vandercamp, or, among the married, with the radiant Mrs. Casimir Dulac, or Mrs. Fred Alston, who had been a van der Luyden. They were not afraid, as they gathered on the shining floor of Delmonico's ball-room, of any challenge to the supremacy of these beauties.

Miss Closson's arrival was, nevertheless, awaited with a certain curiosity. Mrs. Parmore had been very clever about her invitation. It was impossible to invite Lord Richard without his fiancée, since their wedding was to take place the following week; and the ladies were eager to let a scion of the British nobility see what a

New York Assembly had to show. But to invite the Closson parents was obviously impossible. No one knew who they were, or where they came from (beyond the vague tropical background), and Mrs. Closson was said to be a *divorcée*, and to lie in bed all day smoking enormous cigars. But Mrs. Parmore, whose daughter's former governess was now with a family who knew the Clossons, had learned that there was a Closson step-son, a clever little fellow with a Spanish name, who was a great friend of Lord Richard's, and was to be his best man; and of course it was perfectly proper to invite Miss Closson with her own brother. One or two of the more conservative patronesses had indeed wavered, and asked what further concessions this might lead to; but Mrs. Parmore's party gained the day, and rich was their reward, for at the eleventh hour Mrs. Parmore was able to announce that Lord Richard's sisters, the Ladies Ulrica and Honoria, had unexpectedly arrived for their brother's wedding, and were anxious, they too—could anything be more gratifying?—to accompany him to the ball.

Their appearance, for a moment, over-shadowed Miss Closson's; yet perhaps (or so some of the young men said afterward) each of the three girls was set off by the charms of the others. They were so complementary in their graces, each seemed to have been so especially created by Providence, and adorned by coiffeur and dress-maker, to make part of that matchless trio, that their entrance was a sight long remembered, not only by the young men thronging about them to be introduced but by the elderly gentlemen who surveyed them from a distance with critical and reminiscent eyes. The patron-esses, whose own daughters risked a momentary eclipse, were torn between fears and admiration; but after all these lovely English girls, one so dazzlingly fair, the other so darkly vivid, who framed Miss Closson in their contrasting beauty were only transient visitors; and Miss Closson was herself soon to rejoin them in England, and might some day, as the daughter-in-law of a Marquess, remember gratefully that New York had set its social seal on her.

No such calculations troubled the dancing men. They had found three new beauties to waltz with—and how they waltzed! The rumour that London dancing was far below the New York standard was not likely to find credit with any one who had danced with the Ladies Marable. The tall fair one—was she the Lady Honoria? —was perhaps the more harmonious in her movements; but the Lady Ulrica, as befitted her flashing good looks, was as nimble as a gipsy; and if Conchita Closson polka-ed and waltzed as well as the English girls, these surpassed her in the gliding elegance of the square dances.

At supper they were as bewitching as on the floor. Nowhere in the big supper-room, about the flower-decked tables, was the talk merrier, the laughter louder (a shade too loud, perhaps?—but that may have been the fault of the young men), than in the corner where the three girls, enclosed in a dense body-guard of admirers, feasted on champagne and terrapin. As Mrs. Eglinton, with some bitterness, afterward remarked to Mrs. Parmore, it was absurd to say that English girls had no conversation, when these charming creatures had chattered all night like magpies. She hoped it would teach their own girls that there were moments when a little innocent *abandon* was not unsuitable.

In the small hours of the same night a knock at her door waked Miss Testvalley out of an uneasy sleep. She sat up with a start, and lighting her candle beheld a doleful little figure in a beribboned pink wrapper.

"Why, Annabel—aren't you well?" she exclaimed, setting down her candle beside the Book of Common Prayer and the small volume of poems which always lay together on her night-table.

"Oh, don't call me Annabel, please! I can't sleep, and I feel so lonely. . ."

"My poor Nan! Come and sit on the bed. What's the matter, child? You're half frozen!" Miss Testvalley, thankful that before going to bed she had wound her white net scarf over her crimping-pins, sat up and drew the quilt around her pupil.

"I'm not frozen; I'm just lonely. I *did* want to go to that ball," Nan confessed, throwing her arms about her governess.

"Well, my dear, there'll be plenty of other balls for you when the time comes."

"Oh, but will there? I'm not a bit sure; and Jinny's not either. She only got asked to this one because Lord Richard fixed it up. I don't know how he did it; but I suppose those old Assembly scare-crows are such snobs—"

"Annabel!"

"Oh, bother! When you know they are. If they hadn't

been, wouldn't they have invited Jinny and Lizzy long ago to all their parties?"

"I don't think that question need trouble us. Now that your sister and Lizzy Elmsworth have been seen they're sure to be invited again; and when your turn comes..."

Suddenly she felt herself pushed back against her pillows by her pupil's firm young hands. "Miss Testvalley! How can you talk like that, when you know the only way they got invited—"

Miss Testvalley, rearing herself up severely, shook off Nan's clutch. "Annabel! I've no idea how they were invited; I can't imagine what you mean. And I must ask you not to be impertinent."

Nan gazed at her for a moment, and then buried her face among the pillows in a wild rush of laughter.

"Annabel!" the governess repeated, still more severely; but Nan's shoulders continued to shake with mirth.

"My dear, you told me you'd waked me up because you felt lonely. If all you wanted was some one to giggle with, you'd better go back to bed, and wait for your sister to come home."

Nan lifted a penitent countenance to her governess. "Oh, she won't be home for hours. And I promise I won't laugh any more. Only it *is* so funny! But do let me stay a little longer; please! Read aloud to me, there's a darling; read me some poetry, won't you?"

She wriggled down under the bed-quilt, and crossing her arms behind her, laid her head back against them, so that her brown curls overflowed on the pillow. Her face had grown wistful again, and her eyes were full of entreaty.

Miss Testvalley reached out for *Hymns Ancient and Modern*. But after a moment's hesitation she put it back beside the prayer-book, and took up instead the volume of poetry which always accompanied her on her travels.

"Now listen; listen very quietly, or I won't go on." Almost solemnly she began to read.

> *"The blessèd damozel leaned out*
> *From the gold bar of Heaven:*
> *Her eyes were deeper than the depth*
> *Of waters stilled at even;*
> *She had three lilies in her hand,*
> *And the stars in her hair were seven."*

Miss Testvalley read slowly, chantingly, with a rich murmur of vowels, and a lingering stress on the last word of the last line, as though it symbolized something grave and mysterious. *Seven...*

"That's lovely," Nan sighed. She lay motionless, her eyes wide, her lips a little parted.

> *"Her robe, ungirt from clasp to hem,*
> *No wrought flowers did adorn,*
> *But a white rose of Mary's gift..."*

"I shouldn't have cared much for that kind of dress, should you? I suppose it had angel sleeves, if she was in heaven. When I go to my first ball I want to have a dress that *fits;* and I'd like it to be pale blue velvet, embroidered all over with seed-pearls, like I saw..."

"My dear, if you want to talk about ball-dresses, I should advise you to go to the sewing-room and get the maid's copy of *Butterick's Magazine*," said Miss Testvalley icily.

"No, no! I want to hear the poem—I do! Please read it to me, Miss Testvalley. See how good I am."

Miss Testvalley resumed her reading. The harmonious syllables flowed on, weaving their passes about the impatient young head on the pillow. Presently Miss Testvalley laid the book aside, and folding her hands continued her murmur of recital.

> *"And still she bowed herself and stooped*
> *Out of the circling charm;*
> *Until her bosom must have made*
> *The bar she leaned on warm . . ."*

She paused, hesitating for the next line, and Nan's drowsy eyes drifted to her face. "How heavenly! But you know it all by heart."

"Oh, yes; I know it by heart."

"I never heard anything so lovely. Who wrote it?"

"My cousin, Dante Gabriel."

"Your own cousin?" Nan's eyes woke up.

"Yes, dear. Listen:

> *"And the lilies lay as if asleep*
> *Along her bended arm . . .*

> *"The sun was gone now; the curled moon*
> *Was like a little feather . . ."*

"Do you mean to say he's your very own cousin? Aren't you madly in love with him, Miss Testvalley?"

"Poor Dante Gabriel! My dear, he's a widower, and very stout—and has caused all the family a good deal of trouble."

Nan's face fell. "Oh—a widower? What a pity... If I had a cousin who was a poet I should be madly in love with him. And I should desert my marble palace to flee with him to the isles of Greece."

"Ah—and when are you going to live in a marble palace?"

"When I'm an ambassadress, of course. Lord Richard says that ambassadresses... Oh, darling, don't stop! I do long to hear the rest... I do, really..."

Mis Testvalley resumed her recital, sinking her voice as she saw Nan's lids gradually sink over her questioning eyes till at last the long lashes touched her cheeks. Miss Testvalley murmured on, ever more softly, to the end; then, blowing out the candle, she slid down to Nan's side so gently that the sleeper did not move. "She might have been my own daughter," the governess thought, composing her narrow frame to rest, and listening in the darkness to Nan's peaceful breathing.

Miss Testvalley did not fall asleep herself. She lay speculating rather nervously over the meaning of her pupil's hysterical burst of giggling. She was delighted that Lord Richard had succeeded in getting invitations to the ball for Virginia and Lizzy Elmsworth; but she could not understand why Nan regarded his having done so as particularly droll. Probably, she reflected, it was because the invitations had been asked for and obtained without Mrs. St George's knowledge. Everything was food for giggles when that light-hearted company were together, and nothing amused them more than to play a successful trick on Mrs. St George. In any case, the girls had had their evening—and a long evening it must have been, since the late winter dawn was chilling the windows when Miss Testvalley at length heard Virginia on the stairs.

Lord Richard Marable, as it turned out, had underrated his family's interest in his projected marriage. No doubt, as Miss Testvalley had surmised, his announcement of the event had been late in reaching them; but the day before the wedding a cable came. It was not, however, addressed to Lord Richard, or to his bride, but to Miss Testvalley, who, having opened it with surprise (for she had never before received a cable) read it in speechless perplexity.

"Is she black his anguished mother Selina Brightlingsea."

For some time the governess pored in vain over this cryptic communication; but at last light came to her, and she leaned her head back against her chair and laughed. She understood just what must have happened. Though there were two splendid globes, terrestrial and celestial, at opposite ends of the Allfriars library, no one in the house had ever been known to consult them; and Lady Brightlingsea's geographical notions, even measured by the family standard, were notoriously hazy. She could not imagine why any one should ever want to leave England, and her idea of the continent was one enormous fog from which two places called Paris and Rome indistinctly emerged; while the whole western hemisphere was little more clear to her than to the fore-runners of Columbus. But Miss Testvalley remembered that on one wall of the Vandyke saloon, where the family sometimes sat after dinner, there hung a great tapestry, brilliant in colour, rich and elaborate in design, in the foreground of which a shapely young Negress flanked by ruddy savages and attended by parakeets and monkeys was seen offering a tribute of tropical fruits to a lolling divinity. The housekeeper, Miss Testvalley also remembered, in showing this tapestry to visitors, on the day when Allfriars was open to the public, always designated it as "The Spanish Main and the Americas—" and what could be more natural than that poor bewildered Lady Brightlingsea should connect her son's halting explanations with this instructive scene?

Miss Testvalley pondered for a long time over her reply; then, for once forgetting to make a "governess's answer", she cabled back to Lady Brightlingsea: "No, but comely."

BOOK II

VIII

ON a June afternoon of the year 1875 one of the biggest carriages in London drew up before one of the smallest houses in Mayfair—the very smallest in that exclusive quarter, its occupant, Miss Jacqueline March, always modestly averred.

The tiny dwelling, a mere two-windowed wedge, with a bulging balcony under a striped awning, had been newly painted a pale buff, and freshly festooned with hanging pink geraniums and intensely blue lobelias. The carriage, on the contrary, a vast old-fashioned barouche of faded yellow, with impressive armorial bearings, and coachman and footman to scale, showed no signs of recent renovation; and the lady who descended from it was, like her conveyance, large and rather shabby though undeniably impressive.

A freshly starched parlour-maid let her in with a curtsey of recognition. "Miss March is in the drawing-room, my lady." She led the visitor up the narrow stairs and announced from the threshold: "Please, Miss, Lady Brightlingsea."

Two ladies sat in the drawing-room in earnest talk. One of the two was vaguely perceived by Lady Brightlingsea to be small and brown, with burning black eyes which did not seem to go with her stiff purple poplin and old-fashioned beaded dolman.

The other lady was also very small, but extremely fair

and elegant, with natural blond curls touched with gray, and a delicate complexion. She hurried hospitably forward.

"Dearest Lady Brightlingsea! What a delightful surprise!— You're not going to leave us, Laura?"

It was clear that the dark lady addressed as Laura was meant to do exactly what her hostess suggested she should not. She pressed the latter's hand in a resolute brown kid glove, bestowed a bow and a slanting curtsey on the Marchioness of Brightlingsea, and was out of the room with the ease and promptness of a person long practised in self-effacement.

Lady Brightlingsea sent a vague glance after the retreating figure. "Now who was that, my dear? I seem to know. . ."

Miss March, who had a touch of firmness under her deprecating exterior, replied without hesitation: "An old friend, dear Lady Brightlingsea, Miss Testvalley, who used to be governess to the Duchess's younger girls at Tintagel."

Lady Brightlingsea's long pale face grew still vaguer. "At Tintagel? Oh, but of course. It was I who recommended her to Blanche Tintagel. . . Testvalley? The name is so odd. She was with us, you know; she was with Honoria and Ulrica before Madame Championnet finished them."

"Yes. I remember you used to think well of her. I believe it was at Allfriars I first met her."

Lady Brightlingsea looked plaintively at Miss March. Her face always grew plaintive when she was asked to squeeze one more fact—even one already familiar—into her weary and over-crowded memory. "Oh, yes . . . oh, yes!"

Miss March, glancing brightly at her guest, as though to re-animate the latter's failing energy, added: "I wish she could have stayed. You might have been interested in her experiences in America."

"In America?" Lady Brightlingsea's vagueness was streaked by a gleam of interest. "She's been in America?"

"In the States. In fact, I think she was governess to that new beauty who's being talked about a good deal just now. A Miss St George—Virginia St George. You may have heard of her?"

Lady Brightlingsea sighed at this new call upon her powers of concentration. "I hear of nothing but Americans. My son's house is always full of them."

"Oh, yes; and I believe Miss St George is a particular friend of Lady Richard's."

"Very likely. Is she from the same part of the States—from Brazil?"

Miss March, who was herself a native of the States, had in her youth been astonished at enquiries of this kind, and slightly resentful of them; but long residence in England, and a desire to appear at home in her adopted country, had accustomed her to such geography as Lady Brightlingsea's. "Slightly farther north, I think," she said.

"Ah? But they make nothing of distances in those countries, do they? Is this new young woman rich?" asked Lady Brightlingsea abruptly.

Miss March reflected, and then decided to say: "According to Miss Testvalley the St Georges appear to live in great luxury."

Lady Brightlingsea sank back wearily. "That means nothing. My daughter-in-law's people do that too. But the man has never paid her settlements. Her step-father, I mean—I never can remember any of their names. I don't see how they can tell each other apart, all herded together, without any titles or distinctions. It's unfortunate that Richard did nothing about settlements; and now, barely two years after their marriage, the man says he can't go on paying his step-daughter's allowance. And I'm afraid the young people owe a great deal of money."

Miss March heaved a deep sigh of sympathy. "A bad coffee-year, I suppose."

"That's what he says. But how can one tell? Do you suppose those other people would lend them the money?"

Miss March counted it as one of the many privileges of living in London that two or three times a year her friend Lady Brightlingsea came to see her. In Miss March's youth a great tragedy had befallen her—a sorrow which had darkened all her days. It had befallen her in London, and all her American friends—and they were many—had urged her to return at once to her home in New York. A proper sense of dignity, they insisted, should make it impossible for her to remain in a society where she had been so cruelly, so publicly offended. Miss March listened, hesitated—and finally remained in London. "They simply don't know," she explained to an American friend who also lived there, "what they're asking me to give up." And the friend sighed her assent.

"The first years will be difficult," Miss March had continued courageously, "but I think in the end I shan't be sorry." And she was right. At first she had been only a poor little pretty American who had been jilted by an eminent nobleman; yes, and after the wedding-dress was ordered—the countermanding of that wedding-dress had long been one of her most agonizing memories. But since the unhappy date over thirty years had slipped by; and gradually, as they passed, and as people found out how friendly and obliging she was, and what a sweet little house she lived in, she had become the centre of a circle of warm friends, and the oracle of transatlantic pilgrims in quest of a social opening. These pilgrims had learned that Jacky March's narrow front door led straight into the London world, and a number had already slipped in through it. Miss March had a kind heart, and could never resist doing a friend a good turn; and if her services were sometimes rewarded by a cheque, or a new drawing-room carpet, or a chinchilla tippet and muff, she saw no harm in this way of keeping herself and her house in good shape. "After all, if my friends are kind enough to come here, I want my house and myself, tiny as we both are, to be presentable."

All this passed through Miss March's active mind while she sat listening to Lady Brightlingsea. Even should friendship so incline them, she doubted if the St George family would be able to come to the aid of the young Dick Marables, but there might be combinations, arrangements—who could tell? Laura Testvalley might enlighten her. It was never Miss March's policy to oppose a direct refusal to a friend.

"Dear Lady Brightlingsea, I'm so dreadfully distressed at what you tell me."

"Yes. It's certainly very unlucky. And most trying for my husband. And I'm afraid poor Dick's not behaving as well as he might. After all, as he says, he's been deceived."

Miss March knew that this applied to Lady Richard's money and not to her morals, and she sighed again. "Mr. St George was a business associate of Mr. Closson's at one time, I believe. Those people generally back each other up. But of course they all have their ups and downs. At any rate I'll see, I'll make enquiries. . ."

"Their ways are so odd, you know," Lady Brightlingsea pursued. It never seemed to occur to her that Miss March was one of "them", and Miss March emitted a murmur of sympathy, for these new people seemed as alien to her as to her visitor. "So very odd. And they speak so fast—I can't understand them. But I suppose one would get used to that. What I *cannot* see is their beauty—the young girls, I mean. They toss about so—they're never still. And they don't know how to carry themselves." She paused to add in a lower tone: "I believe my daughter-in-law dances to some odd instrument—quite like a ballet dancer. I hope her skirts are not as short. And sings in Spanish. Is Spanish their native language still?"

Miss March, despairing of making it clear to Lady Brightlingsea that Brazil was not one of the original Thirteen States, evaded this by saying: "You must remember they've not had the social training which only a Court can give. But some of them seem to learn very quickly."

"Oh, I hope so," Lady Brightlingsea exclaimed, as if clutching at a floating spar. Slowly she drew herself up from the sofa-corner. She was so tall that the ostrich plumes on her bonnet might have brushed Miss March's ceiling had they not drooped instead of towering. Miss March had often wondered how her friend managed to have such an air of majesty when everything about her flopped and dangled. "Ah—it's their secret," she thought, and rejoiced that at least she could recognize and admire the attribute in her noble English friends. So many of her travelling compatriots seemed not to understand, or even to perceive, the difference. They were the ones who could not see what she "got out" of her little London house, and her little London life.

Lady Brightlingsea stood in the middle of the room, looking uncertainly about her. At last she said: "We're going out of town in a fortnight. You must come down to Allfriars later, you know."

Miss March's heart leapt up under her trim black satin bodice. (She wore black often, to set off her still fair complexion.) She could never quite master the excitement of an invitation to Allfriars. In London she did not expect even to be offered a meal; the Brightlingseas always made a short season, and there were so many important people whom they had to invite. Besides, being asked down to stay in the country, *en famille,* was really much more flattering—more intimate. Miss March felt herself blushing to the roots of her fair curls. "It's so kind of you, dear Lady Brightlingsea. Of course you know there's nothing I should like better. I'm never as happy anywhere as at Allfriars."

Lady Brightlingsea gave a mirthless laugh. "You're not like my daughter-in-law. She says she'd as soon spend a month in the family vault. In fact she'd never be with us at all if they hadn't had to let their house for the season."

Miss March's murmur of horror was inarticulate. Words failed her. These dreadful new Americans—would London ever be able to educate them? In her confusion she followed Lady Brightlingsea to the landing without speaking. There her visitor suddenly turned toward her. "I wish we could marry Seadown," she said.

This allusion to the heir of the Brightlingseas was a fresh surprise to Miss March. "But surely—in Lord Seadown's case it will be only too easy," she suggested with a playful smile.

Lady Brightlingsea produced no answering smile. "You must have heard, I suppose, of his wretched entanglement with Lady Churt. It's much worse, you know, than if she were a disreputable woman. She costs him a great deal more, I mean. And we've tried everything... But he won't look at a nice girl..." She paused, her wistful eyes bent entreatingly on Miss March's responsive face. "And so, in sheer despair, I thought perhaps, if this friend of my daughter-in-law's is rich, really rich, it might be better to try... There's something about these foreigners that seems to attract the young men."

Yes—there was, as Jacky March had reason to know. Her own charm had been subtler and more discreet, and in the end it had failed her; but the knowledge that she had possessed it gave her a feeling of affinity with this new band of marauders, social aliens though they were: the wild gipsy who had captured Dick Marable, and her young friends who, two years later, had come out to look over the ground, and do their own capturing.

Miss March, who was always on her watch-tower, had already sighted and classified them; the serenely lovely Virginia St George, whom Lady Brightlingsea had singled out for Lord Seadown, and her younger sister Nan, negligible as yet compared with Virginia, but odd and interesting too, as her sharp little observer perceived. It was a novel kind of invasion, and Miss March was a-flutter with curiosity, and with an irrepressible sympathy. In Lady Brightlingsea's company she had quite honestly blushed for the crude intruders; but freed from the shadow of the peerage she felt herself mysteriously akin to them, eager to know more of their plans, and even to play a secret part in the adventure.

Miss Testvalley was an old friend, and her arrival in London with a family of obscure but wealthy Americans had stirred the depths of Miss March's social curiosity. She knew from experience that Miss Testvalley would never make imprudent revelations concerning her employers, much less betray their confidence; but her shrewd eye and keen ear must have harvested, in the transatlantic field, much that would be of burning interest to Miss March, and the latter was impatient to resume their talk. So far, she knew only that the St George girls were beautiful, and their parents rich, yet that fashionable New York had rejected them. There was much more to learn, and there was also this strange outbreak of Lady Brightlingsea's to hint at, if not reveal, to Miss Testvalley.

It was certainly a pity that their talk had been interrupted by Lady Brightlingsea; yet Miss March would not for the world have missed the latter's visit, and above all, her unexpected allusion to her eldest son. For years Miss March had carried in her bosom the heavy weight of the Marable affairs, and this reference to Seadown had thrown her into such agitation that she sat down on the sofa and clasped her small wrinkled hands over her anxious heart. Seadown to marry an American—what news to communicate to Laura Testvalley!

Miss March rose and went quickly to her miniature writing-desk. She wrote a hurried note in her pretty flowing script, sealed it with silver-gray wax, and rang for the beruffled parlour-maid. Then she turned back into the room. It was crowded with velvet-covered tables and quaint corner-shelves, all laden with photographs in heavy silver or morocco frames, surmounted by coronets, from the baronial to the ducal—one, even, royal (in a place of honour by itself, on the mantel). Most of these photographs were of young or middle-aged women, with long necks and calm imperious faces, crowned with diadems or nodded over by court feathers. "Selina Brightlingsea", "Blanche Tintagel", "Elfrida Marable", they were signed in tall slanting hands. The hand-writing was as uniform as the features, and nothing but the signatures seemed to differentiate these carven images. But in a corner by itself (pushed behind a lamp at Lady Brightlingsea's arrival) was one, "To Jacky from her friend Idina Churt", which Miss March now drew forth and studied with a furtive interest. What chance had an untaught transatlantic beauty against this reprehensible creature, with her tilted nose and impertinent dark fringe? Yet, after studying the portrait for a while, Miss March, as she set it down, simply murmured: "Poor Idina."

IX

IN the long summer twilight a father and son were pacing the terrace of an old house called Honourslove, on the edge of the Cotswolds. The irregular silver-gray building, when approached from the village by a drive winding under ancient beech-trees, seemed, like so many old dwellings in England, to lie almost in a hollow, screened to the north by hanging woods, and surveying from its many windows only its own lawns and trees; but the terrace on the other front overlooked an immensity of hill and vale, with huddled village roofs and floating spires. Now, in the twilight, though the sky curved above so clear and luminous, everything below was blurred, and the spires were hardly distinguishable from the tree-trunks; but to the two men strolling up and down before the house long familiarity made every fold of the landscape visible.

The Cotswolds were in the blood of the Thwartes, and their rule at Honourslove reached back so far that the present baronet, Sir Helmsley Thwarte, had persuaded himself that only by accident (or treachery—he was given to suspecting treachery) had their title to the estate dropped out of Domesday.

His only son, Guy, was not so sure; but, as Sir Helmsley said, the young respect nothing and believe in nothing, least of all in the validity of tradition. Guy did, however, believe in Honourslove, the beautiful old place which had come to be the first and last article of the family creed. Tradition, as embodied in the ancient walls and the ancient trees of Honourslove, seemed to him as priceless a quality as it did to Sir Helmsley; and indeed he sometimes said to himself that if ever he succeeded to the baronetcy he would be a safer and more vigilant guardian than his father, who loved the place and yet had so often betrayed it.

"I'd have shot myself rather than sell the Titian," Guy used to think in moments of bitterness. "But then my father's sure to outlive me—so what's the odds?"

As they moved side by side that summer evening it would have been hard for a looker-on to decide which had the greater chance of longevity; the heavy vigorous man approaching the sixties, a little flushed after his dinner and his bottle of Burgundy, but obliged to curb his quick stride to match his son's more leisurely gait; or the son, tall and lean, and full of the balanced energy of the hard rider and quick thinker.

"You don't adapt yourself to the scene, sir. It's an insult to Honourslove to treat the terrace as if it were the platform at Euston, and you were racing for your train."

Sir Helmsley was secretly proud of his own activity, and nothing pleased him better than his son's disrespectful banter on his over-youthfulness. He slackened his pace with a gruff laugh.

"I suppose you young fellows expect the gray-beards to drag their gouty feet and lean on staves, as they do in *Oedipe-roi* at the *Français*."

"Well, sir, as your beard's bright auburn, that strikes

me as irrelevant." Guy knew this would not be unwelcome either; but a moment later he wondered if he had not overshot the mark. His father stopped short and faced him. "Bright auburn, indeed? Look here, my dear fellow, what is there behind this indecent flattery?" His voice hardened. "Not another bill to be met—eh?"

Guy gave a short laugh. He *had* wanted something, and had perhaps resorted to flattery in the hope of getting it; but his admiration for his brilliant and impetuous parent, even when not disinterested, was sincere.

"A bill—?" He laughed again. That would have been easier—though it was never easy to confess a lapse to Sir Helmsley. Guy had never learned to take his father's tropical fits of rage without wincing. But to make him angry about money would have been less dangerous; and, at any rate, the young man was familiar with the result. It always left him seared, but still upright; whereas. . .

"Well?"

"Nothing, sir."

The father gave one of his angry "foreign" shrugs (reminiscent of far-off Bohemian days in the Quartier Latin), and the two men walked on in silence.

There were moments during their talks—and this was one—when the young man felt that, if each could have read the other's secret mind, they would have found little to unite them except a joint love of their house and the land it stood on. But that love was so strong, and went so deep, that it sometimes seemed to embrace all the divergences. Would it now, Guy wondered? "How the devil shall I tell him?" he thought.

The two had paused, and stood looking out over the lower terraces to the indistinct blue reaches beyond. Lights were beginning to prick the dusk, and every roof which they revealed had a name and a meaning to Guy Thwarte. Red Farm, where the famous hazel copse was, Ausprey with its decaying Norman church, Little Ausprey with the old heronry at the Hall, Odcote, Sudcote, Lowdon, the ancient borough with its market-cross and its rich minster—all were thick with webs of memory for the youth whose people had so long been rooted in their soil. And those frail innumerable webs tightened about him like chains at the thought that in a few weeks he was to say goodbye to it all, probably for many months.

After preparing for a diplomatic career, and going through a first stage at the Foreign Office, and a secretaryship in Brazil, Guy Thwarte had suddenly decided that he was not made for diplomacy, and braving his father's wrath at this unaccountable defection had settled down to a period of hard drudgery with an eminent firm of civil engineers who specialized in railway building. Though he had a natural bent for the work he would probably never have chosen it had he not hoped it would be a quick way to wealth. The firm employing him had big contracts out for building railways in Far Eastern and South American lands, and Guy's experience in Brazil had shown him that in those regions there were fortunes to be made by energetic men with a practical knowledge of the conditions. He preferred making a fortune to marrying one, and it was clear that sooner or later a great deal of money would be needed to save Honourslove and keep it going. Sir

Helmsley's financial ventures had been even costlier than his other follies, and the great Titian which was the glory of the house had been sold to cover the loss of part of the fortune which Guy had inherited from his mother, and which, during his minority, had been in Sir Helmsley's imprudent hands. The subject was one never touched upon between father and son, but it had imperceptibly altered their relations, though not the tie of affection between them.

The truth was that the son's case was hardly less perplexing than the father's. Contradictory impulses strove in both. Each had the same love for the ancient habitation of their race, which enchanted but could not satisfy them, each was anxious to play the part fate had allotted to him, and each was dimly conscious of an inability to remain confined in it, and painfully aware that their secret problems would have been unintelligible to most men of their own class and kind. Sir Helmsley had been a grievous disappointment to the county, and it was expected that Guy should make up for his father's short-comings by conforming to the accepted standards, should be a hard rider, a good shot, a conscientious landlord and magistrate, and should in due time (and as soon as possible) marry a wife whose settlements would save Honourslove from the consequences of Sir Helmsley's follies.

The county was not conscious of anything incomprehensible about Guy. Sir Helmsley had dabbled dangerously in forbidden things; but Guy had a decent reputation about women, and it was incredible that a man so tall and well set-up, and such a brilliant point-

to-point rider, should mess about with poetry or painting. Guy knew what was expected of him, and secretly
agreed with his observers that the path they would have
him follow was the right one for a man in his situation.
But since Honourslove had to be saved, he would rather
try to save it by his own labour than with a rich woman's
money.

Guy's stage of drudgery as an engineer was now over,
and he had been chosen to accompany one of the members
of the firm on a big railway-building expedition in South
America. His knowledge of the country, and the fact
that his diplomatic training had included the mastering
of two or three foreign languages, qualified him for the
job, which promised to be lucrative as well as adven-
turous, and might, he hoped, lead to big things. Sir
Helmsley accused him of undergoing the work only for
the sake of adventure; but, aggrieved though he was
by his son's decision, he respected him for sticking to
it. "I've been only a brilliant failure myself," he had
grumbled at the end of their discussion; and Guy had
laughed back: "Then I'll try to be a dingy success."

The memory of this talk passed through the young
man's mind, and with it the new impulse which, for
the last week, had never been long out of his thoughts,
and now threatened to absorb them. Struggle as he
would, there it was, fighting in him for control. "As if
my father would ever listen to reason!" But was this
reason? He leaned on the balustrade, and let his mind
wander over the rich darkness of the country-side.

Though he was not yet thirty, his life had been full
of dramatic disturbances; indeed, to be the only son of

Sir Helmsley Thwarte was in itself a potential drama.
Sir Helmsley had been born with the passionate desire
to be an accomplished example of his class: the ideal
English squire, the model landowner, crack shot, leader
and champion in all traditionally British pursuits and
pleasures; but a contrary streak in his nature was perpetually driving him toward art and poetry and travel,
odd intimacies with a group of painters and decorators
of socialistic tendencies, reckless dalliance with ladies,
and a loud contempt for the mental inferiority of his
county neighbours. Against these tendencies he waged
a spasmodic and unavailing war, accusing and excusing
himself in the same breath, and expecting his son to
justify his vagaries, and to rescue him from their results. During Lady Thwarte's life the task had been less
difficult; she had always, as Guy now understood, kept
a sort of cold power over her husband. To Guy himself
she remained an enigma; the boy had never found a
crack through which to penetrate beyond the porcelain-
like surface of her face and mind. But while she lived
things had gone more smoothly at Honourslove. Her
husband's oddest experiments had been tried away from
home, and had never lasted long; her presence, her
power, her clear conception of what the master of
Honourslove ought to be, always drew him back to her
and to conformity.

Guy summed it up by saying to himself: "If she'd
lived the Titian never would have gone." But she had
died, and left the two men and their conflicting tendencies alone in the old house. . . Yes; she had been the right
mistress for such a house. Guy was thinking of that now,

and knew that the same thought was in his father's mind, and that his own words had roused it to the pitch of apprehension. Who was to come after her? father and son were both thinking.

"Well, out with it!" Sir Helmsley broke forth abruptly.

Guy straightened himself with a laugh. "You seem to expect a confession of bankruptcy or murder. I'm afraid I shall disappoint you. All I want is to have you ask some people to tea."

"Ah—? Some 'people'?" Sir Helmsley puffed dubiously at his cigar. "I suppose they've got names and a local habitation?"

"The former, certainly. I can't say as to the rest. I ran across them the other day in London, and as I know they're going to spend next Sunday at Allfriars I thought—"

Sir Helmsley Thwarte drew the cigar from his lips, and looked along it as if it were a telescope at the end of which he saw an enemy approaching.

"Americans?" he queried, in a shrill voice so unlike his usual impressive barytone that it had been known to startle servants and trespassers almost out of their senses, and even in his family to cause a painful perturbation.

"Well—yes."

"Ah—" said Sir Helmsley again. Guy proffered no remark, and his father broke out irritably: "I suppose it's because you know how I hate the whole spitting tobacco-chewing crew, the dressed-up pushing women dragging their reluctant backswoodsmen after them, that you suggest polluting my house, and desecrating our last few days together, by this barbarian invasion—eh?"

There had been a time when his father's outbursts, even when purely rhetorical, were so irritating to Guy that he could meet them only with silence. But the victory of choosing his career had given him a lasting advantage. He smiled, and said: "I don't seem to recognize my friends from your description."

"Your friends—your friends? How many of them are there?"

"Only two sisters—the Miss St Georges. Lady Richard would drive them over, I imagine."

"Lady Richard? What's she? Some sort of West Indian octoroon, I believe?"

"She's very handsome, and has auburn hair."

Sir Helmsley gave an angry laugh. "I suppose you think the similarity in our colouring will be a tie between us."

"Well, sir, I think she'll amuse you."

"I hate women who try to amuse me."

"Oh, she won't try—she's too lazy."

"But what about the sisters?"

Guy hesitated. "Well, the rumour is that the eldest is going to marry Seadown."

"Seadown—marry Seadown? Good God, are the Brightlingseas out of their minds? It was well enough to get rid of Dick Marable at any price. There wasn't a girl in the village safe from him, and his father was forever buying people off. But Seadown—Seadown marry an American! There won't be a family left in England without that poison in their veins."

Sir Helmsley walked away a few paces and then returned to where his son was standing. "Why do you want these people asked here?"

"I—I like them," Guy stammered, suddenly feeling as shamefaced as a guilty school-boy.

"Like them!" In the darkness, the young man felt his father's nervous clutch on his arm. "Look here, my boy —you know all the plans I had for you. Plans—dreams, they turned out to be! I wanted you to be all I'd meant to be myself. The enlightened landlord, the successful ambassador, the model M.P., the ideal M.F.H. The range was wide enough—or ought to have been. Above all, I wanted you to have a steady career on an even keel. Just the reverse of the crazy example I've set you."

"You've set me the example of having too many talents to keep any man on an even keel. There's not much danger of my following you in that."

"Let's drop compliments, Guy. You're a gifted fellow; too much so, probably, for your job. But you've more persistency than I ever had, and I haven't dared to fight your ideas because I could see they were more definite than mine. And now—"

"Well, sir?" his son queried, forcing a laugh.

"And now—are you going to wreck everything, as I've done so often?" He paused, as if waiting for an answer; but none came. "Guy, why do you want those women here? Is it because you've lost your head over one of them? I've a right to an answer, I think."

Guy Thwarte appeared to have none ready. Too many thoughts were crowding through his mind. The first was: "How like my father to corner me when anybody with a lighter hand would have let the thing pass unnoticed! But he's always thrown himself against life head foremost. . ." The second: "Well, and isn't that what I'm doing now? It's the family folly, I suppose. . . Only, if he'd said nothing. . . When I spoke I really hadn't got beyond . . . well, just wanting to see her again . . . and now. . ."

Through the summer dark he could almost feel the stir of his father's impatience. "Am I to take your silence as an answer?" Sir Helmsley challenged him.

Guy relieved the tension with a laugh. "What nonsense! I ask you to let me invite some friends and neighbours to tea. . ."

"To begin with, I hate these new-fangled intermediate meals. Why can't people eat enough at luncheon to last till dinner?"

"Well, sir, to dine and sleep, if you prefer."

"Dine and sleep? A pack of strange women under my roof?" Sir Helmsley gave a grim laugh. "I should like to see Mrs. Bolt's face if she were suddenly told to get their rooms ready! Everything's a foot deep in dust and moths, I imagine."

"Well, it might be a good excuse for a clean-up," rejoined his son good-humouredly. But Sir Helmsley ignored this.

"For God's sake, Guy—you're not going to bring an American wife to Honourslove? I shan't shut an eye tonight unless you tell me."

"And you won't shut an eye if I tell you 'yes'?"

"Damn it, man—don't fence."

"I'm not fencing, sir; I'm laughing at your way of

jumping at conclusions. I shan't take any wife till I get back from South America; and there's not much chance that this one would wait for me till then—even if I happened to want her to."

"Ah, well. I suppose, this last week, if you were to ask me to invite the devil I should have to do it."

From her post of observation in the window of the housekeeper's room, Mrs. Bolt saw the two red cigar-tips pass along the front of the house and disappear. The gentlemen were going in, and she could ring to have the front door locked, and the lights put out everywhere but in the baronet's study and on the stairs.

Guy followed his father across the hall, and into the study. The lamp on the littered writing-table cast a circle of light on crowded book-shelves, on Sienese predellas, and bold unsteady water-colours and charcoal-sketches by Sir Helmsley himself. Over the desk hung a small jewel-like picture in a heavy frame, with D. G. Rossetti inscribed beneath. Sir Helmsley glanced about him, selected a pipe from the rack, and filled and lit it. Then he lifted up the lamp.

"Well, Guy, I'm going to assume that you mean to have a good night's sleep."

"The soundest, sir."

Lamp in hand, Sir Helmsley moved toward the door. He paused—was it voluntarily?—half way across the room, and the lamplight touched the old yellow marble of the carved mantel, and struck upward to a picture above it, set in elaborate stucco scrolls. It was the portrait of a tall thin woman in white, her fair hair looped under a narrow diadem. As she looked forth from the dim background, expressionless, motionless, white, so her son remembered her in their brief years together. She had died, still young, during his last year at Eton—long ago, in another age, as it now seemed. Sir Helmsley, still holding the lifted lamp, looked up too. "She was the most beautiful woman I ever saw," he said abruptly—and added, as if in spite of himself: "But utterly unpaintable; even Millais found her so."

Guy offered no comment, but went up the stairs in silence after his father.

X

THE St George girls had never seen anything as big as the house at Allfriars except a public building, and as they drove toward it down the long avenue, and had their first glimpse of Inigo Jones's most triumphant expression of the Palladian dream, Virginia said with a little shiver: "Mercy—it's just like a gaol."

"Oh, no—a palace," Nan corrected.

Virginia gave an impatient laugh. "I'd like to know where you've ever seen a palace."

"Why, hundreds of times, I have, in my dreams."

"You mustn't tell your dreams. Miss Testvalley says nothing bores people so much as being told other people's dreams."

Nan said nothing, but an iron gate seemed to clang shut in her; the gate that was so often slammed by careless hands. As if any one could be bored by such dreams as hers!

"Oh," said Virginia, "I never saw anything so colossal. Do you suppose they live all over it? I guess our clothes aren't half dressy enough. I told mother we ought to have something better for the afternoon than those mauve organdies."

Nan shot a side-glance at the perfect curve of her sister's cheek. "Mauve's the one colour that simply murders me. But nobody who sees *you* will bother to notice what you've got on."

"You little silly, you, shut up... Look, there's Conchita and the poodle!" cried Virginia in a burst of reassurance. For there, on the edge of the drive, stood their friend, in a crumpled but picturesque yellow muslin and flapping garden hat, and a first glance at her smiling waving figure assured the two girls of her welcome. They sprang out, leaving the brougham to be driven on with maid and luggage, and instantly the trio were in each other's arms.

"Oh, girls, girls—I've been simply pining for you! I can't believe you're really here!" Lady Richard cried, with a tremor of emotion in her rich Creole voice.

"Conchita! Are you really glad?" Virginia drew back and scanned her anxiously. "You're lovelier than ever; but you look terribly tired. Don't she look tired, Nan?"

"Don't talk about me. I've looked like a fright ever since the baby was born. But he's a grand baby, and they say I'll be all right soon. Jinny, darling, you can't think how I've missed you both! Little Nan, let me have a good look at you. How big your eyes have grown... Jinny, you and I must be careful, or this child will crowd us out of the running..."

Linked arm in arm, the three loitered along the drive, the poodle caracoling ahead. As they approached the great gateway, Conchita checked their advance. "Look, girls! It *is* a grand house, isn't it?"

"Yes; but I'm not a bit afraid any more," Nan laughed, pressing her arm.

"Afraid? What were you afraid of?"

"Virginia said you'd be as grand as the house. She

didn't believe you'd be really glad to see us. We were scared blue of coming."

"Nan—you little idiot!"

"Well, you did say so, Jinny. You said we must expect her to be completely taken up with her lords and ladies."

Conchita gave a dry little laugh. "Well, you wait," she said.

Nan stood still,. gazing up at the noble façade of the great house. "It *is* grand. I'm so glad I'm not afraid of it," she murmured, following the other two up the steps between the mighty urns and columns of the doorway.

It was a relief to the girls—though somewhat of a surprise—that there was no one to welcome them when they entered the big domed hall hung with tall family portraits and moth-eaten trophies of the chase. Conchita, seeing that they hesitated, said: "Come along to your room—you won't see any of the in-laws till dinner"; and they went with her up the stairs, and down a succession of long corridors, glad that the dread encounter was postponed. Miss Jacky March, to whom they had been introduced by Miss Testvalley, had assured them that Lady Brightlingsea was the sweetest and kindest of women; but this did not appear to be Conchita's view, and they felt eager to hear more of her august relatives before facing them at dinner.

In the room with dark heavy bed-curtains and worn chintz armchairs which had been assigned to the sisters, the lady's-maid was already shaking out their evening toilets. Nan had wanted to take Miss Testvalley to All-friars, and had given way to a burst of childish weeping when it was explained to her that girls who were "out" did not go visiting with their governesses. Maids were a new feature in the St George household, and when, with Miss Jacky March's aid, Laura Testvalley had run down a paragon, and introduced her into the family, Mrs. St George was even more terrified than the girls. But Miss Testvalley laughed. "You were afraid of me once," she said to Virginia. "You and Nan must get used to being waited on, and having your clothes kept in order. And don't let the woman see that you're not used to it. Behave as if you'd never combed your own hair or rummaged for your stockings. Try and feel that you're as good as any of these people you're going about with," the dauntless governess ordained.

"I guess we're as good as anybody," Virginia replied haughtily. "But they act differently from us, and we're not used to them yet."

"Well, act in your own way, as you call it—that will amuse them much more than if you try to copy them."

After deliberating with the maid and Conchita over the choice of dinner-dresses, they followed their friend along the corridor to her own bedroom. It was too late to disturb the baby, who was in the night-nursery in the other wing; but in Conchita's big shabby room, after inspecting everything it contained, the sisters settled themselves down happily on a wide sofa with broken springs. Dinner at Allfriars was not till eight, and they had an hour ahead of them before the dressing-gong. "Tell us about everything, Conchita darling," Virginia commanded.

"Well, you'll find only a family party, you know. They

don't have many visitors here, because they have to bleed themselves white to keep the place going, and there's not much left for entertaining. They're terribly proud of it—they couldn't imagine living in any other way. At least my father-in-law couldn't. He thinks God made Allfriars for him to live in, and Frenshaw—the other place, in Essex; but he doesn't understand why God gave him so little money to do it on. He's so busy thinking about that, that he doesn't take much notice of anybody. You mustn't mind. My mother-in-law's good-natured enough; only she never can think of anything to say to people she isn't used to. Dick talks a little when he's here; but he so seldom is, what with racing and fishing and shooting. I believe he's at Newmarket now; but he seldom keeps me informed of his movements." Her aquamarine eyes darkened as she spoke her husband's name.

"But aren't your sisters-in-law here?" Virginia asked.

Conchita smiled. "Oh, yes, poor dears; there's nowhere else for them to go. But they're too shy to speak when my mother-in-law doesn't; sometimes they open their mouths to begin, but they never get as far as the first sentence. You must get used to an ocean of silence, and just swim about in it as well as you can. I haven't drowned yet, and you won't. Oh—and Seadown's here this week. I think you'll like him; only he doesn't say much either."

"Who does talk, then?" Nan broke in, her spirits sinking at this picture of an Allfriars evening.

"Well, I do; too much so, my mother-in-law says. But

243

this evening you two will have to help me out. Oh, and the Rector thinks of something to say every now and then; and so does Jacky March. She's just arrived, by the way. You know her, don't you?"

"That little Miss March with the funny curls, that Miss Testvalley took us to see?"

"Yes. She's an American, you know—but she's lived in England for years and years. I'll tell you something funny—only you must swear not to let on. She was madly in love with Lord Brightlingsea—with my father-in-law. Isn't that a good one?" said Conchita with her easy laugh.

"Mercy! In love? But she must be sixty," cried Virginia, scandalized.

"Well," said Nan gravely, "I can imagine being in love at sixty."

"There's nothing crazy you can't imagine," her sister retorted. "But can you imagine being in love with Miss March?"

"Oh, she wasn't sixty when it happened," Conchita continued. "It was ages and ages ago. She *says* they were actually engaged, and that he jilted her after the wedding-dress was ordered; and I believe he doesn't deny it. But of course he forgot all about her years ago; and after a time she became a great friend of Lady Brightlingsea's, and comes here often, and gives all the children the loveliest presents. Don't you call that funny?"

Virginia drew herself up. "I call it demeaning herself; it shows she hasn't any proper pride. I'm sorry she's an American."

Nan sat brooding in her corner. "I think it just shows she loves him better than she does her pride."

The two elder girls laughed, and she hung her head with a sudden blush. "Well," said Virginia, "if mother heard that she'd lock you up."

The dressing-gong boomed through the passages, and the sisters sprang up and raced back to their room.

The Marquess of Brightlingsea stood with his coat-tails to the monumental mantelpiece of the red drawing-room, and looked severely at his watch. He was still, at sixty, a splendid figure of a man, firm-muscled, well set-up, with the sloping profile and coldly benevolent air associated, in ancestral portraits, with a tie-wig, and ruffles crossed by an Order. Lord Brightlingsea was a just man, and having assured himself that it still lacked five minutes to eight he pocketed his watch with a milder look, and began to turn about busily in the empty shell of his own mind. His universe was a brilliantly illuminated circle extending from himself at its centre to the exact limit of his occupations and interests. These comprised his dealings with his tenantry and his man of business, his local duties as Lord Lieutenant of the County and M.F.H., and participation in the manly sports suitable to his rank and age. The persons ministering to these pursuits were necessarily in the foreground, and the local clergy and magistracy in the middle distance, while his family clung in a precarious half-light on the periphery, and all beyond was blackness. Lady Brightlingsea considered it her duty to fish out of this outer darkness, and drag for a moment into the light, any person or obligation entitled to fix her husband's attention; but they always faded back into night as soon as they had served their purpose.

Lord Brightlingsea had learned from his valet that several guests had arrived that afternoon, his own eldest son among them. Lord Seadown was seldom at Allfriars except in the hunting season, and his father's first thought was that if he had come at so unlikely a time it was probably to ask for money. The thought was excessively unpleasant, and Lord Brightlingsea was eager to be rid of it, or at least to share it with his wife, who was more used to such burdens. He looked about him impatiently; but Lady Brightlingsea was not in the drawing-room, nor in the Vandyke saloon beyond. Lord Brightlingsea, as he glanced down the length of the saloon, said to himself: "Those tapestries ought to be taken down and mended"—but that too was an unpleasant thought, associated with much trouble and expense, and therefore belonging distinctly to his wife's province. Lord Brightlingsea was well aware of the immense value of the tapestries, and knew that if he put them up for sale all the big London dealers would compete for them; but he would have kicked out of the house any one who approached him with an offer. "I'm not sunk as low as Thwarte," he muttered to himself, shuddering at the sacrilege of the Titian carried off from Honourslove to the auction-room.

"Where the devil's your mother?" he asked, as a big-boned girl in a faded dinner-dress entered the drawing-room.

"Mamma's talking with Seadown, I think; I saw him

go into her dressing-room," Lady Honoria Marable replied.

Lord Brightlingsea cast an unfavourable glance on his daughter. ("If her upper teeth had been straightened when she was a child we might have had her married by this time," he thought. But that again was Lady Brightlingsea's affair.)

"It's an odd time for your mother to be talking in her dressing-room. Dinner'll be on the table in a minute."

"Oh, I'm sure Mamma will be down before the others. And Conchita's always late, you know."

"Conchita knows that I won't eat my soup cold on her account. Who are the others?"

"No one in particular. Two American girls who are friends of Conchita's."

"H'm. And why were they invited, may I ask?"

Honoria Marable hesitated. All the girls feared their father less than they did their mother, because she remembered and he did not. Honoria feared him least of all, and when Lady Brightlingsea was not present was almost at her ease with him. "Mamma told Conchita to ask them down, I think. She says they're very rich. I believe their father's in the American army. They call him 'Colonel'."

"The American army? There isn't any. And they call dentists 'Colonel' in the States." But Lord Brightlingsea's countenance had softened. "Seadown..." he thought. If that were the reason for his son's visit, it altered the situation, of course. And, much as he disliked to admit such considerations to his mind, he repeated carelessly: "You say these Americans are very rich?"

"Mamma has heard so. I think Miss March knows them, and she'll be able to tell her more about them. Miss March is here too, you know."

"Miss March?" Lord Brightlingsea's sloping brow was wrinkled in an effort of memory. He repeated: "March —March. Now that's a name I know. . ."

Lady Honoria smiled. "I should think so, Papa!"

"Now why? Do you mean that I know her too?"

"Yes. Mamma told me to be sure to remind you."

"Remind me of what?"

"Why, that you jilted her, and broke her heart. Don't you remember? You're to be particularly nice to her, Papa; and be sure not to ask her if she's ever seen Allfriars before."

"I—what? Ah, yes, of course. . . That old nonsense! I hope I'm 'nice', as you call it, to every one who comes to my house," Lord Brightlingsea rejoined, pulling down the lapels of his dress-coat, and throwing back his head majestically.

At the same moment the drawing-room door opened again, and two girls came into the room. Lord Brightlingsea, gazing at them from the hearth, gave a faint exclamation, and came forward with extended hand. The elder and taller of the two advanced to meet it.

"You're Lord Brightlingsea, aren't you? I'm Miss St George, and this is my sister Annabel," the young lady said, in a tone that was fearless without being familiar.

Lord Brightlingsea fixed on her a gaze of undisguised benevolence. It was a long time since his eyes had rested on anything so fresh and fair, and he found the sensation very agreeable. It was a pity, he reflected, that his eldest son lacked his height, and had freckles and white eye-lashes. "Gad," he thought, "if I were Seadown's age. . ."

But before he could give further expression to his approval another guest had appeared. This time it was some one vaguely known to him; a small elderly lady, dressed with a slightly antiquated elegance, who came toward him reddening under her faint touch of rouge. "Oh, Lord Brightlingsea—" and, as he took her trembling little hand he repeated to himself: "My wife's old friend, of course; Miss March. The name's perfectly familiar to me—what the deuce else did Honoria say I was to remember about her?"

XI

WHEN the St George girls, following candle in hand the bedward procession headed by Lady Brightlingsea, had reached the door of their room, they could hardly believe that the tall clock ticking so loudly in the corner had not gone back an hour or two.

"Why, is it only half past ten?" Virginia exclaimed.

Conchita, who had followed them in, threw herself on the sofa with a laugh. "That's what I always think when I come down from town. But it's not the clocks at Allfriars that are slow; my father-in-law sees to that. It's the place itself." She sighed. "In London the night's just beginning. And the worst of it is that when I'm here I feel as dead with sleep by ten o'clock as if I'd been up till daylight."

"I suppose it's the struggling to talk," said Nan irrepressibly.

"That, and the awful certainty that when anybody does speak nothing will be said that one hasn't heard a million times before. Poor little Miss March! What a fight she put up; but it's no use. My father-in-law can never think of anything to say to her.—Well, Jinny, what did you think of Seadown?"

Virginia coloured; the challenge was a trifle too direct. "Why, I thought he looked pretty sad, too; like all the others."

"Well, he *is* sad, poor old Seedy. The fact is—it's no

mystery—he's tangled up with a rapacious lady who can't afford to let him go; and I suspect he's so sick of it that if any nice girl came along and held out her hand. . ."

Virginia, loosening her bright tresses before the mirror, gave them a contemptuous toss. "In America girls don't have to hold out their hands—"

"Oh, I mean, just be kind; show him a little sympathy. He isn't easy to amuse; but I saw him laugh once or twice at things Nan said."

Nan sat up in surprise. "Me? Jinny says I always say the wrong thing."

"Well, you know, that rather takes in England. They're so tired of the perfectly behaved Americans who are afraid of using even a wrong word."

Virginia gave a slightly irritated laugh. "You'd better hold your hand out, Nan, if you want to be Conchita's sister-in-law."

"Oh, misery! What I like is just chattering with people I'm not afraid of—like that young man we met the other day in London who said he was a friend of yours. He lives somewhere near here, doesn't he?"

"Oh, Guy Thwarte. Rather! He's one of the most fascinating detrimentals in England."

"What's a detrimental?"

"A young man that all the women are mad about, but who's too poor to marry. The only kind left for the married women, in fact—so hands off, please, my dear. Not that I want Guy for myself," Conchita added with her lazy laugh. "Dick's enough of a detrimental for me. What I'm looking for is a friend with a settled income that he doesn't know how to spend."

"Conchita!" Virginia exclaimed, flushed with disapproval.

Lady Richard rose from the sofa. "So sorry! I forgot you little Puritans weren't broken in yet. Goodnight, dears. Breakfast at nine sharp; and don't forget family prayers." She stopped on the threshold to add in a half-whisper: "Don't forget, either, that the day after tomorrow we're going to drive over to call on him—the detrimental, I mean. And even if you don't care about him, you'll see the loveliest place in all England."

"Well, it was true enough, what Conchita said about nobody speaking," Virginia remarked when the two sisters were alone. "Did you ever know anything as awful as that dinner? I couldn't think of a word to say. My voice just froze in my throat."

"I didn't mind so much, because it gave me a chance to look," Nan rejoined.

"At what? All I saw was a big room with cracks in the ceiling, and bits of plaster off the walls. And after dinner, when those great bony girls showed us albums with views of the Rhine, I thought I should scream. I wonder they didn't bring out a magic lantern!"

Nan was silent. She knew that Virginia's survey of the world was limited to people, the clothes they wore, and the carriages they drove in. Her own universe was so crammed to bursting with wonderful sights and sounds that, in spite of her sense of Virginia's superiority—her beauty, her ease, her self-confidence—Nan sometimes felt a shamefaced pity for her. It must be cold and lonely, she thought, in such an empty colourless world as her sister's.

"But the house is terribly grand, don't you think it is? I like to imagine all those people on the walls, in their splendid historical dresses, walking about in the big rooms. Don't you believe they come down at night sometimes?"

"Oh, shut up, Nan. You're too old for baby-talk. . . Be sure you look under the bed before you blow out the candle. . . ."

Virginia's head was already on the pillow, her hair overflowing it in ripples of light.

"Do come to bed, Nan. I hate the way the furniture creaks. Isn't it funny there's no gas? I wish we'd told that maid to sit up for us." She waited a moment, and then went on: "I'm sorry for Lord Seadown. He looks so scared of his father; but I thought Lord Brightlingsea was very kind, really. Did you see how I made him laugh?"

"I saw they couldn't either of them take their eyes off you."

"Oh, well—if they have nobody to look at but those daughters I don't wonder," Virginia murmured complacently, her lids sinking over her drowsy eyes.

Nan was not drowsy. Unfamiliar scenes and faces always palpitated in her long afterward; but the impact of new scenes usually made itself felt before that of new people. Her soul opened slowly and timidly to her kind, but her imagination rushed out to the beauties of the visible world; and the decaying majesty of Allfriars moved her strangely. Splendour neither frightened her, nor made her self-assertive as it did Virginia; she never felt herself matched against things greater than herself, but softly merged in them; and she lay awake, thinking of what Miss Testvalley had told her of the history of the ancient Abbey, which Henry VIII had bestowed on an ancestor of Lord Brightlingsea's, and of the tragic vicissitudes following on its desecration. She lay for a long time listening to the mysterious sounds given forth by old houses at night, the undefinable creakings, rustlings and sighings which would have frightened Virginia had she remained awake, but which sounded to Nan like the long murmur of the past breaking on the shores of a sleeping world.

In a majestic bedroom at the other end of the house the master of Allfriars, in dressing-gown and slippers, appeared from his dressing-room. On his lips was a smile of retrospective satisfaction seldom seen by his wife at that hour.

"Well, those two young women gave us an unexpectedly lively evening—eh, my dear? Remarkably intelligent, that eldest girl; the beauty, I mean. I'm to show her the pictures tomorrow morning. By the way, please send word to the Vicar that I shan't be able to go to the vestry meeting at eleven; he'd better put it off till next week... What are you to tell him? Why—er —unexpected business... And the little one, who looks such a child, had plenty to say for herself too. She seemed to know the whole history of the place. Now, why can't our girls talk like that?"

"You've never encouraged them to chatter," replied

Lady Brightlingsea, settling a weary head on a longed-for pillow; and her lord responded by a growl. As if talk were necessarily chatter! Yet as such Lord Brightlingsea had always regarded it when it issued from the lips of his own family. How little he had ever been understood by those nearest him, he thought; and as he composed himself to slumber in his half of the vast bed, his last conscious act was to murmur over: "The Hobbema's the big black one in the red drawing-room, between the lacquer cabinets; and the portrait of Lady Jane Grey that they were asking about must be the one in the octagon room, over the fire-place." For Lord Brightlingsea was determined to shine as a connoisseur in the eyes of the young lady for whom he had put off the vestry meeting.

The terrace of Honourslove had never looked more beautiful than on the following Sunday afternoon. The party from Allfriars—Lady Richard Marable, her brother-in-law Lord Seadown, and the two young ladies from America—had been taken through the house by Sir Helmsley and his son, and after a stroll along the shady banks of the Love, murmuring in its little glen far below, had returned by way of the gardens to the chapel hooded with ivy at the gates of the park. In the gardens they had seen the lavender-borders, the hundreds of feet of rosy brick hung with peaches and nectarines, the old fig-tree heavy with purple fruit in a sheltered corner; and in the chapel, with its delicately traceried roof and dark oaken stalls, had lingered over kneeling and recumbent Thwartes, Thwartes in cuirass

and ruff, in furred robes, in portentous wigs, their stiffly
farthingaled ladies at their sides, and baby Thwartes
tucked away overhead in little marble cots. And now,
turning back to the house, they were looking out from
the terrace over the soft reaches of country bathed in
afternoon light.

After the shabby vastness of Allfriars everything about
Honourslove seemed to Nan St George warm, cared-for,
exquisitely intimate. The stones of the house, the bricks
of the walls, the very flags of the terrace, were so full
of captured sunshine that in the darkest days they must
keep an inner brightness. Nan, though too ignorant to
single out the details of all this beauty, found herself
suddenly at ease with the soft mellow place, as though
some secret thread of destiny attached her to it.

Guy Thwarte, somewhat to her surprise, had kept at
her side during the walk and the visit to the chapel. He
had not said much, but with him also Nan had felt instantly at ease. In his answers to her questions she had
detected a latent passion for every tree and stone of the
beautiful old place—a sentiment new to her experience,
as a dweller in houses without histories, but exquisitely
familiar to her imagination. They had walked together
to the far end of the terrace before she noticed that the
others, guided by Sir Helmsley, were passing through
the glass doors into the hall. Nan turned to follow, but
her companion laid his hand on her arm. "Stay," he
said quietly.

Without answering she perched herself on the ledge
of the balustrade, and looked up at the long honey-
coloured front of the house, with the great carven shield

above the door, and the quiet lines of cornice and window-frames.

"I wanted you to see it in this light. It's the magic hour," he explained.

She turned her glance from the house to his face. "I see why Conchita says it's the most beautiful place in England."

He smiled. "I don't know. I suppose if one were married to a woman one adored, one would soon get beyond her beauty. That's the way I feel about Honourslove. It's in my bones."

"Oh, then you understand!" she exclaimed.

"Understand—?"

Nan coloured a little; the words had slipped out. "I mean about the *beyondness* of things. I know there's no such word. . ."

"There's such a feeling. When two people have reached it together it's—well, they *are* 'beyond'." He broke off. "You see now why I wanted you to come to Honourslove," he said in an odd new voice.

She was still looking at him thoughtfully. "You knew I'd understand."

"Oh, everything!"

She sighed for pleasure; but then: "No. There's one thing I don't understand. How you go away and leave it all for so long."

He gave a nervous laugh. "You don't know England. That's part of our sense of beyondness: I'd do more than that for those old stones."

Nan bent her eyes to the worn flags on the terrace. "I see; that was stupid of me."

For no reason at all the quick colour rushed to her temples again, and the young man coloured too. "It's a beautiful view," she stammered, suddenly self-conscious. "It depends who looks at it," he said.

She dropped to her feet, and turned to gaze away over the shimmering distances. Guy Thwarte said nothing more, and for a long while they stood side by side without speaking, each seeing the other in every line of the landscape.

Sir Helmsley, after fulminating in advance against the foreign intruders, had been all smiles on their arrival. Guy was used to such sudden changes of the paternal mood, and knew that feminine beauty could be counted on to produce them. His father could never, at the moment, hold out against deep lashes and brilliant lips, and no one knew better than Virginia St George how to make use of such charms.

"That red-haired witch from Brazil has her wits about her," Sir Helmsley mumbled that evening over his after-dinner cigar. "I don't wonder she stirs them up at Allfriars. Gad, I should think Master Richard Marable had found his match... But your St George girl is a goddess ...*patuit dea*—I think I like 'em better like that... divinely dull...just the quiet bearers of their own beauty, like the priestesses in a Panathenaic procession..." He leaned back in his armchair, and looked sharply across the table at his son, who sat with bent head, drawing vague arabesques on the mahogany. "Guy, my boy —that kind are about as expensive to acquire as the Venus of Milo; and as difficult to fit into domestic life."

Guy Thwarte looked up with an absent smile. "I daresay that's what Seadown's thinking, sir."

"Seadown?"

"Well, I suppose your classical analogies are meant to apply to the eldest Miss St George, aren't they?"

Father and son continued to look at each other, the father perplexed, the son privately amused. "What? Isn't it the eldest—?" Sir Helmsley broke out.

Guy shook his head, and his father sank back with a groan. "Good Lord, my boy! I thought I understood you. Sovran beauty . . . and that girl has it. . ."

"I suppose so, sir."

"You *suppose*—?"

Guy held up his head and cleared his throat. "You see, sir, it happens to be the younger one—"

"The younger one? I didn't even notice her. I imagined you were taking her off my hands so that I could have a better chance with the beauties."

"Perhaps in a way I was," said Guy. "Though I think you might have enjoyed talking to her almost as much as gazing at the goddess."

"H'm. What sort of talk?"

"Well, she came to a dead point before the Rossetti in the study, and at once began to quote 'The Blessed Damozel'."

"That child? So the Fleshly School has penetrated to the backwoods! Well, I don't know that it's exactly the best food for the family breakfast-table."

"I imagine she came on it by chance. It appears she has a wonderful governess who's a cousin of the Rossettis."

"Ah, yes. One of old Testavaglia's descendants, I suppose. What a queer concatenation of circumstances, to doom an Italian patriot to bring up a little Miss Jonathan!"

"I think it was rather a happy accident to give her some one with whom she could talk of poetry."

"Well—supposing you were to leave that to her governess? Eh? I say, Guy, you don't mean—?"

His son paused before replying. "I've nothing to add to what I told you the other day, sir. My South American job comes first; and God knows what will have become of her when I get back. She's barely nineteen and I've only seen her twice. . ."

"Well, I'm glad you remember that," his father interjected. "I never should have, at your age."

"Oh, I've given it thought enough, I can assure you," Guy rejoined, still with his quiet smile.

Sir Helmsley rose from his chair. "Shall we finish our smoke on the terrace?"

They went out together into the twilight, and strolled up and down, as their habit was, in silence. Guy Thwarte knew that Sir Helmsley's mind was as crowded as his own with urgent passionate thoughts clamouring to be expressed. And there were only three days left in which to utter them! To the young man his father's step and his own sounded as full of mystery as the tread of the coming years. After a while they made one of their wonted pauses, and stood leaning against the balustrade above the darkening landscape.

"Eh, well—what are you thinking of?" Sir Helmsley broke out, with one of his sudden jerks of interrogation.

Guy pondered. "I was thinking how strange and far-off everything here seems to me already. I seem to see it all as sharply as things in a dream."

Sir Helmsley gave a nervous laugh. "H'm. And I was thinking that the strangest thing about it all was to hear common-sense spoken about a young woman under the roof of Honourslove." He pressed his son's arm, and then turned abruptly away, and they resumed their walk in silence; for in truth there was nothing more to be said.

XII

A DARK-HAIRED girl who was so handsome that the heads nearest her were all turned her way, stood impatiently at a crowded London street-corner. It was a radiant afternoon of July; and the crowd which had checked her advance had assembled to see the fine ladies in their state carriages on the way to the last Drawing-room of the season.

"I don't see why they won't let us through. It's worse than a village circus," the beauty grumbled to her companion, a younger girl who would have been pretty save for that dazzling proximity, but who showed her teeth too much when she laughed. She laughed now.

"What's wrong with just staying where we are, Liz? It beats any Barnum show I ever saw, and the people are ever so much more polite. Nobody shoves you. Look at that antique yellow coach coming along now, with the two powdered giants hanging on at the back. Oh, Liz!— and the old mummy inside! I guess she dates way back beyond the carriage. But look at her jewels, will you? My goodness—and she's got a real live crown on her head!"

"Shut up, Mab—everybody's looking at you," Lizzy Elmsworth rejoined, still sulkily, though in spite of herself she was beginning to be interested in the scene.

The younger girl laughed again. "They're looking at *you*, you silly. It rests their eyes, after all the scare-crows in those circus-chariots. Liz, why do you suppose they dress up like queens at the waxworks, just to go to an afternoon party?"

"It's not an ordinary party. It's the Queen's Drawing-room."

"Well, I'm sorry for the Queen if she has to feast her eyes for long on some of these beauties. . . Oh, good; the carriages are moving! Better luck next time. This next carriage isn't half as grand, but maybe it's pleasanter inside. . . Oh!" Mab Elmsworth suddenly exclaimed, applying a sharp pinch to her sister's arm.

" 'Oh' what? I don't see anything so wonderful—"

"Why, look, Lizzy! Reach up on your tip-toes. In the third carriage—if it isn't the St George girls! Look, *look!* When they move again they'll see us."

"Nonsense. There are dozens of people between us. Besides, I don't believe it is. . . How in the world should they be here?"

"Why, I guess Conchita fixed it up. Or don't they present people through our Legation?"

"You have to have letters to the Minister. Who on earth'd have given them to the St Georges?"

"I don't know; but there they are. Oh, Liz, look at Jinny, will you? She looks like a queen herself—a queen going to her wedding, with that tulle veil and the feathers . . . Oh, mercy, and there's little Nan! Well, the headdress isn't as becoming to her—she hasn't got the *style,* has she? Now, Liz! The carriages are moving. . . I'm not tall enough—you reach up and wave. They're sure to see us if you do."

Lizzy Elmsworth did not move. "I can survive not being seen by the St George girls," she said coldly. "If only we could get out of this crowd."

"Oh, just wait till I squeeze through, and make a sign to them! There—. Oh, thank you so much... Now they see me! Jinny—Nan—do look! It's Mab..."

Lizzy caught her sister by the arm. "You're making a show of us; come away," she whispered angrily.

"Why, Liz... Just wait a second... I'm sure they saw us..."

"I'm sure they didn't want to see us. Can't you understand? A girl screaming at the top of her lungs from the side-walk... Please come when I tell you to, Mabel."

At that moment Virginia St George turned her head toward Mab's gesticulating arm. Her face, under its halo of tulle and arching feathers, was so lovely that the eyes in the crowd deserted Lizzy Elmsworth. "Well, they're not *all* mummies going to Court," a man said good-naturedly; and the group about him laughed.

"Come away, Mabel," Miss Elmsworth repeated. She did not know till that moment how much she would dislike seeing the St George girls in the glory of their Court feathers. She dragged her reluctant sister through a gap in the crowd, and they turned back in the direction of the hotel where they were staying.

"Now I hope you understand that they saw us, *and didn't want to see us!*"

"Why, Liz, what's come over you? A minute ago you said they couldn't possibly see us."

"Now I'm sure they did, and made believe not to.

I should have thought you'd have had more pride than to scream at them that way among all those common people."

The two girls walked on in silence.

Mrs. St George had been bitterly disappointed in her attempt to launch her daughters in New York. Scandalized though she was by Virginia's joining in the wretched practical joke played on the Assembly patronesses by Lord Richard Marable and his future brother-in-law, she could not think that such a prank would have lasting consequences. The difficulty, she believed, lay with Colonel St George. He was too free-and-easy, too much disposed to behave as if Fifth Avenue and Wall Street were one. As a social figure no one took him seriously (except certain women she could have named, had it not demeaned her even to think of them), and by taking up with the Clossons, and forcing her to associate publicly with that divorced foreigner, he had deprived her girls of all chance of social recognition. Miss Testvalley had seen it from the first. She too was terribly upset about the ball; but she did not share Mrs. St George's view that Virginia and Nan, by acting as bridesmaids to Conchita Closson, had increased the mischief. At the wedding their beauty had been much remarked; and, as Miss Testvalley pointed out, Conchita had married into one of the greatest English families, and if ever the girls wanted to do a London season, knowing the Brightlingseas would certainly be a great help.

"A London season?" Mrs. St George gasped, in a

tone implying that her burdens and bewilderments were heavy enough already.

Miss Testvalley laughed. "Why not? It might be much easier than New York; you ought to try," that intrepid woman declared.

Mrs. St George, in her bewilderment, repeated this to her eldest daughter; and Virginia, who was a thoughtful girl, turned the matter over in her mind. The New York experiment, though her mother regarded it as a failure, had not been without its compensations; especially the second winter, when Nan emerged from the school-room. There was no doubt that Nan supplemented her sister usefully; she could always think of something funny or original to say, whereas there were moments when Virginia had to rely on the length of her eyelashes and the lustre of her lips, and trust to them to plead for her. Certainly the two sisters made an irresistible pair. The Assembly ladies might ignore their existence, but the young men did not; and there were jolly little dinners and gay theatre-parties in plenty to console the exiled beauties. Still, it was bitter to be left out of all the most exclusive entertainments, to have not a single invitation to Newport, to be unbidden to the Opera on the fashionable nights. With Mrs. St George it rankled more than with her daughters. With the approach of the second summer she had thought of hiring a house at Newport; but she simply didn't dare—and it was then that Miss Testvalley made her bold suggestion.

"But I've never been to England. I wouldn't know

how to get to know people. And I couldn't face a strange country all alone."

"You'd soon make friends, you know. It's easier sometimes in foreign countries."

Virginia here joined in. "Why shouldn't we try, mother? I'm sure Conchita'd be glad to get us invitations. She's awfully good-natured."

"Your father would think we'd gone crazy."

Perhaps Mrs. St George hoped he would; it was always an added cause for anxiety when her husband approved of holiday plans in which he was not to share. And that summer she knew he intended to see the Cup Races off Newport, with a vulgar drinking crowd, Elmsworth and Closson among them, who had joined him in chartering a steam-yacht for the occasion.

Colonel St George's business association with Mr. Closson had turned out to be an exceptionally fruitful one, and he had not failed to remind his wife that its pecuniary results had already justified him in asking her to be kind to Mrs. Closson. "If you hadn't, how would I have paid for this European trip, I'd like to know, and all the finery for the girls' London season?" he had playfully reminded her, as he pressed the steamer-tickets and a letter of credit into her reluctant hand.

Mrs. St George knew then that the time for further argument was over. The letter of credit, a vaguely understood instrument which she handled as though it were an explosive, proved that his decision was irrevocable. The pact with Mr. Closson had paid for the projected European tour, and would also, Mrs. St George bitterly reflected, help to pay for the charter of the steam-yacht, and the champagne orgies on board, with ladies in pink bonnets. All this was final, unchangeable, and she could only exhale her anguish to her daughters and their governess.

"Now your father's rich his first idea is to get rid of us, and have a good time by himself."

Nan flushed up, longing to find words in defence of the Colonel; and Virginia spoke for her. "How silly, mother! Father feels it's only fair to give us a chance in London. You know perfectly well that if we get on there we'll be invited everywhere when we get back to New York. That's why father wants us to go."

"But I simply couldn't go to England all alone with you girls," Mrs. St George despairingly repeated.

"But we won't be alone. Of course Miss Testvalley'll come too!" Nan interrupted.

"Take care, Nan! If I do, it will be to try to get you on with your Italian," said the governess. But they were all aware that by this time she was less necessary to her pupils than to their mother. And so, they hardly knew how, they had all (with Colonel St George's too-hearty encouragement) drifted, or been whirled, into this wild project; and now, on a hot July afternoon, when Mrs. St George would have been so happy sipping her lemonade in friendly company on the Grand Union verandah, she sat in the melancholy exile of a London hotel, and wondered when the girls would get back from that awful performance they called a Drawing-room.

There had been times—she remembered ruefully—when she had not been happy at Saratoga, had felt uncomfortable in the company of the dubious Mrs. Closson, and irritated by the vulgar exuberance of Mrs. Elmsworth; but such was her present loneliness that she would have welcomed either with open arms. And it was precisely as this thought crossed her mind that the buttons knocked on the door to ask if she would receive Mrs. Elmsworth.

"Oh, my dear!" cried poor Mrs. St George, falling on her visitor's breast; and two minutes later the ladies were mingling their loneliness, their perplexities, their mistrust of all things foreign and unfamiliar, in an ecstasy of interchanged confidences.

The confidences lasted so long that Mrs. Elmsworth did not return to her hotel until after her daughters. She found them alone in the dark shiny sitting-room which so exactly resembled the one inhabited by Mrs. St George, and saw at once that they were out of humour with each other if not with the world. Mrs. Elmsworth disliked gloomy faces, and on this occasion felt herself entitled to resent them, since it was to please her daughters that she had left her lazy pleasant cure at Bad Ems to give them a glimpse of the London season.

"Well, girls, you look as if you were just home from a funeral," she remarked, breathing heavily from her ascent of the hotel stairs, and restraining the impulse to undo the upper buttons of her strongly whale-boned Paris dress.

"Well, we are. We've seen all the old corpses in London dressed up for that circus they call a Drawing-room," said her eldest daughter.

"They weren't all corpses, though," Mab interrupted.

"What do you think, mother? We saw Jinny and Nan St George, rigged out to kill, feathers and all, in the procession!"

Mrs. Elmsworth manifested no surprise. "Yes, I know. I've just been sitting with Mrs. St George, and she told me the girls had gone to the Drawing-room. She said Conchita Marable fixed it up for them. So you see it's not so difficult, after all."

Lizzy shrugged impatiently. "If Conchita has done it for them we can't ask her to do it again for us. Besides, it's too late; I saw in the paper it was the last Drawing-room. I told you we ought to have come a month ago."

"Well, I wouldn't worry about that," said her mother good-naturedly. "There was a Miss March came in while I was with Mrs. St George—such a sweet little woman. An American; but she's lived for years in London, and knows everybody. Well, she said going to a Drawing-room didn't really amount to anything; it just gave the girls a chance to dress up and see a fine show. She says the thing is to be in the Prince of Wales's set. That's what all the smart women are after. And it seems that Miss March's friend, Lady Churt, is very intimate with the Prince and has introduced Conchita to him, and he's crazy about her Spanish songs. Isn't that funny, girls?"

"It may be very funny. But I don't see how it's going to help us," Lizzy grumbled.

Mrs. Elmsworth gave her easy laugh. "Well, it won't, if you don't help yourselves. If you think everybody's against you, they will be against you. But that Miss March has invited you and Mabel to take tea at her house next week—it seems everybody in England takes tea at five. In the country-houses the women dress up for it, in things they call 'tea-gowns'. I wish we'd known that when we were ordering our clothes in Paris. But Miss March will tell you all about it, and a lot more besides."

Lizzy Elmsworth was not a good-tempered girl, but she was too intelligent to let her temper interfere with her opportunities. She hated the St George girls for having got ahead of her in their attack on London, but was instantly disposed to profit by the breach they had made. Virginia St George was not clever, and Lizzy would be able to guide her; they could be of the greatest use to each other, if the St Georges could be made to enter into the plan. Exactly what plan, Lizzy herself did not know; but she felt instinctively that, like their native country, they could stand only if they were united.

Mrs. St George, in her loneliness, had besought Mrs. Elmsworth to return the next afternoon. She didn't dare invite Lizzy and Mab, she explained, because her own girls were being taken to see the Tower of London by some of their new friends (Lizzy's resentment stirred again as she listened); but if Mrs. Elmsworth would just drop in and sit with her, Mrs. St George thought perhaps Miss March would be coming in too, and then they would talk over plans for the rest of the summer. Lizzy understood at once the use to which Mrs. St George's loneliness might be put. Mrs. Elmsworth was lonely too; but this did not greatly concern her daughter. In the St George and Elmsworth circles unemployed mothers were the rule; but Lizzy saw that, by pooling their solitudes, the two ladies might become more contented, and therefore more manageable. And having come to lay siege to London Miss Elmsworth was determined, at all costs, not to leave till the citadel had fallen.

"I guess I'll go with you," she announced, when her mother rose to put on her bonnet for the call.

"Why, the girls won't be there; she told me so. She says they'll be round to see you tomorrow," said Mrs. Elmsworth, surprised.

"I don't care about the girls; I want to see that Miss March."

"Oh, well," her mother agreed. Lizzy was always doing things she didn't understand, but Mab usually threw some light on them afterward. And certainly, Mrs. Elmsworth reflected, it became her eldest daughter to be in one of her mysterious moods. She had never seen Lizzy look more goddess-like than when they ascended Mrs. St George's stairs together.

Miss March was not far from sharing Mrs. Elmsworth's opinion. When the Elmsworth ladies were shown in, Miss March was already sitting with Mrs. St George. She had returned on the pretext of bringing an invitation for the girls to visit Holland House; but in reality she was impatient to see the rival beauty. Miss Testvalley, the day before, had told her all about Lizzy Elmsworth, whom some people thought, in her different way, as handsome as Virginia, and who was certainly cleverer. And here she was, stalking in ahead of her mother, in what appeared to be the new American style, and carrying her slim height and small regal head with an assurance which might well eclipse Virginia's milder light.

Miss March surveyed her with the practised eye of an old frequenter of the marriage-market.

"Very fair girls usually have a better chance here; but Idina Churt is dark—perhaps, for that reason, this girl might be more likely. . ." Miss March lost herself in almost maternal musings. She often said to herself (and sometimes to her most intimate friends) that Lord Seadown seemed to her like her own son; and now, as she looked on Lizzy Elmsworth's dark splendour, she murmured inwardly: "Of course we must find out first what Mr. Elmsworth would be prepared to do. . ."

To Mrs. Elmsworth, whom she greeted with her most persuasive smile, she said engagingly: "Mrs. St George and I have such a delightful plan to suggest to you. Of course you won't want to stay in London much longer. It's so hot and crowded; and before long it will be a dusty desert. Mrs. St George tells me that you're both rather wondering where to go next, and I've suggested that you should join her in hiring a lovely little cottage on the Thames belonging to a friend of mine, Lady Churt. It could be had at once, servants and all—the most perfect servants—and I've stayed so often with Lady Churt that I know just how cool and comfortable and lazy one can be there. But I was thinking more especially of your daughters and their friends. . . The river's a Paradise at their age . . . the punting by moonlight, and all the rest. . ."

Long-past memories of the river's magic brought a sigh to Miss March's lips; but she turned it into a smile as she raised her forget-me-not eyes to Lizzy Elmsworth's imperial orbs. Lizzy returned the look, and the two immediately understood each other.

"Why, mother, that sounds perfectly lovely. You'd love it too, Mrs. St George, wouldn't you?" Lizzy smiled, stooping gracefully to kiss her mother's friend. She had no idea what punting was, but the fact that it was practised by moonlight suggested the exclusion of rheumatic elders, and a free field—or river, rather—for the exercise of youthful arts. And in those she felt confident of excelling.

XIII

THE lawn before Lady Churt's cottage (or bungalow, as the knowing were beginning to say) spread sweetly to the Thames at Runnymede. With its long deck-like verandah, its awnings stretched from every window, it seemed to Nan St George a fairy galleon making, all sails set, for the river. Swans, as fabulous to Nan as her imaginary galleon, sailed majestically on the silver flood; and boats manned by beautiful bare-armed athletes sped back and forth between the flat grass-banks.

At first Nan was the only one of the party on whom the river was not lost. Virginia's attention travelled barely as far as the circles of calceolarias and lobelias dotting the lawn, and the vases of red geraniums and purple petunias which flanked the door; she liked the well-kept flowers and bright turf, and found it pleasant, on warm afternoons, to sit under an ancient cedar and play at the new-fangled tea-drinking into which they had been initiated by Miss March, with the aid of Lady Churt's accomplished parlour-maid. Lizzy Elmsworth and Mab also liked the tea-drinking, but were hardly aware of the great blue-green boughs under which the rite was celebrated. They had grown up between city streets and watering-place hotels, and were serenely unconscious of the "beyondness" of which Nan had confided her mysterious sense to Guy Thwarte.

The two mothers, after their first bewildered contact with Lady Churt's servants, had surrendered themselves to these accomplished guides, and lapsed contentedly into their old watering-place habits. To Mrs. St George and Mrs. Elmsworth the cottage at Runnymede differed from the Grand Union at Saratoga only in its inferior size, and more restricted opportunities for gossip. True, Miss March came down often with racy tit-bits from London, but the distinguished persons concerned were too remote to interest the exiles. Mrs. St George missed even the things she had loathed at Saratoga—the familiarity of the black servants, the obnoxious sociability of Mrs. Closson, and the spectacle of the race-course, with ladies in pink bonnets lying in wait for the Colonel. Mrs. Elmsworth had never wasted her time in loathing anything. She would have been perfectly happy at Saratoga and in New York if her young ladies had been more kindly welcomed there. She privately thought Lizzy hard to please, and wondered what her own life would have been if she had turned up her nose at Mr. Elmsworth, who was a clerk in the village grocery-store when they had joined their lot; but the girls had their own ideas, and since Conchita Closson's marriage (an unhappy affair, as it turned out) had roused theirs with social ambition, Mrs. Elmsworth was perfectly willing to let them try their luck in England, where beauty such as Lizzy's (because it was rarer, she supposed) had been known to raise a girl almost to the throne. It would certainly be funny, she confided to Mrs. St George, to see one of their daughters settled at Windsor Castle (Mrs. St George thought it would be exceedingly funny to see one of Mrs. Elmsworth's); and Miss March, to whom the confidence was passed on, concluded that Mrs. Elmsworth was imperfectly aware of the difference between the ruler of England and her subjects.

"Unfortunately their Royal Highnesses are all married," she said with her instructive little laugh; and Mrs. Elmsworth replied vaguely: "Oh, but aren't there plenty of other Dukes?" If there were, she could trust Lizzy, her tone implied; and Miss March, whose mind was now set on uniting the dark beauty to Lord Seadown, began to wonder if she might not fail again, this time not as in her own case, but because of the young lady's too-great ambition.

Mrs. Elmsworth also missed the friendly bustle of the Grand Union, the gentlemen coming from New York on Saturdays with the Wall Street news, and the flutter caused in the dining-room when it got round that Mr. Elmsworth had made another hit on the market; but she soon resigned herself to the routine of *bézique* with Mrs. St George. At first she too was chilled by the silent orderliness of the household; but though both ladies found the maid-servants painfully unsociable, and were too much afraid of the cook ever to set foot in the kitchen, they enjoyed the absence of domestic disturbances, and the novel experience of having every wish anticipated.

Meanwhile the bungalow was becoming even more attractive than when its owner inhabited it. Parliament sat exceptionally late that year, and many were the younger members of both Houses, chafing to escape to Scotland, and the private secretaries and minor government officials, still chained to their desks, who found

compensations at the cottage on the Thames. Re-
inforced by the guardsmen quartered at Windsor, they
prolonged the river season in a manner unknown to the
oldest inhabitants. The weather that year seemed to be
in connivance with the American beauties, and punting
by moonlight was only one of the midsummer distractions to be found at Runnymede.

To Lady Richard Marable the Thames-side cottage
offered a happy escape from her little house in London,
where there were always duns to be dealt with, and unpaid servants to be coaxed to stay. She came down often,
always bringing the right people with her, and combin-
ing parties, and inventing amusements, which made
invitations to the cottage as sought-after as cards to the
Royal enclosure. There was not an ounce of jealousy in
Conchita's easy nature. She was delighted with the success of her friends, and proud of the admiration they
excited. "We've each got our own line," she said to Lizzy
Elmsworth, "and if we only back each other up we'll
beat all the other women hands down. The men are
blissfully happy in a house where nobody chaperons
them, and they can smoke in every room, and gaze at
you and Virginia, and laugh at my jokes, and join in
my nigger songs. It's too soon yet to know what Nan
St George and Mab will contribute; but they'll probably develop a line of their own, and the show's not a
bad one as it is. If we stick to the rules of the game, and
don't play any low-down tricks on each other," ("Oh,
Conchita!" Lizzy protested, with a beautiful pained
smile) "we'll have all London in our pocket next year."

No one followed the Runnymede revels with a keener

eye than Miss Testvalley. The invasion of England had been her own invention, and from a thousand little signs she already knew it would end in conquest. But from the outset she had put her charges on their guard against a too-easy triumph. The young men were to be allowed as much innocent enjoyment as they chose; but Miss Testvalley saw to it that they remembered the limits of their liberty. It was amusement enough to be with a group of fearless and talkative girls, who said new things in a new language, who were ignorant of tradition and unimpressed by distinctions of rank; but it was soon clear that their young hostesses must be treated with the same respect, if not with the same ceremony, as English girls of good family.

Miss Testvalley, when she persuaded the St Georges to come to England, had rejoiced at the thought of being once more near her family; but she soon found that her real centre of gravity was in the little house at Runnymede. She performed the weekly pilgrimage to Denmark Hill in the old spirit of filial piety; but the old enthusiasm was lacking. Her venerable relatives (thanks to her earnings in America) were now comfortably provided for; but they had grown too placid, too static, to occupy her. Her natural inclination was for action and conflict, and all her thoughts were engrossed by her young charges. Miss March was an admirable lieutenant, supplying the social experience which Miss Testvalley lacked; and between them they administered the cottage at Runnymede like an outpost in a conquered province.

Miss March, who was without Miss Testvalley's breadth of vision, was slightly alarmed by the audacities of the young ladies, and secretly anxious to improve their social education.

"I don't think they understand *yet* what a Duke is," she sighed to Miss Testvalley, after a Sunday when Lord Seadown had unexpectedly appeared at the cottage with his cousin, the young Duke of Tintagel.

Miss Testvalley laughed. "So much the better! I hope they never will. Look at the well brought-up American girls who've got the peerage by heart, and spend their lives trying to be taken for members of the British aristocracy. Don't they always end by marrying curates or army-surgeons—or just not marrying at all?"

A reminiscent pink suffused Miss March's cheek. "Yes . . . sometimes; perhaps you're right. . . But I don't think I shall ever quite get used to Lady Richard's Spanish dances; or to the peculiar words in some of her songs."

"Lady Richard's married, and needn't concern us," said Miss Testvalley. "What attracts the young men is the girls' naturalness, and their not being afraid to say what they think." Miss March sighed again, and said she supposed that was the new fashion; certainly it gave the girls a better chance. . .

Lord Seadown's sudden appearance at the cottage seemed in fact to support Miss Testvalley's theory. Miss March remembered Lady Churt's emphatic words when the lease had been concluded. "I'm ever so much obliged to you, Jacky. You've got me out of an awfully tight place by finding tenants for me, and getting such a good rent out of them. I only hope your American beauties will want to come back next year. But I've forbidden Seadown to set foot in the place while they're there, and if Conchita Marable coaxes him down you must swear you'll let me know, and I'll see it doesn't happen again."

Miss March had obediently sworn; but she saw now that she must conceal Lord Seadown's visits instead of denouncing them. Poor Idina's exactions were obviously absurd. If she chose to let her house she could not prevent her tenants from receiving any one they pleased; and it was clear that the tenants liked Seadown, and that he returned the sentiment, for after his first visit he came often. Lady Churt, luckily, was in Scotland; and Miss March trusted to her remaining there till the lease of the cottage had expired.

The Duke of Tintagel did not again accompany his friend. He was a young man of non-committal appearance and manner, and it was difficult to say what impression the American beauties made on him; but, to Miss March's distress, he had apparently made little if any on them.

"They don't seem in the least to realize that he's the greatest match in England," Miss March said with a shade of impatience. "Not that there would be the least chance... I understand the Duchess has already made her choice; and the young Duke is a perfect son. Still, the mere fact of his coming..."

"Oh, he came merely out of curiosity. He's always been rather a dull young man, and I daresay all the noise and the nonsense simply bewildered him."

"Oh, but you know him, of course, don't you? You were at Tintagel before you went to America. Is it true that he always does what his mother tells him?"

"I don't know. But the young men about whom that

is said usually break out sooner or later," replied the governess with a shrug.

About this time she began to wonder if the atmosphere of Runnymede were not a little too stimulating for Nan's tender sensibilities. Since Teddy de Santos-Dios, who had joined his sister in London, had taken to coming down with her for Sundays, the fun had grown fast and furious. Practical jokes were Teddy's chief accomplishment, and their preparation involved rather too much familiarity with the upper ranges of the house, too much popping in and out of bedrooms, and too many screaming midnight pillow-fights. Miss Testvalley saw that Nan, whose feelings always rushed to extremes, was growing restless and excited, and she felt the need of shielding the girl and keeping her apart. That the others were often noisy, and sometimes vulgar, did not disturb Miss Testvalley; they were obviously in pursuit of husbands, and had probably hit on the best way of getting them. Seadown was certainly very much taken by Lizzy Elmsworth; and two or three of the other young men had fallen victims to Virginia's graces. But it was too early for Nan to enter the matrimonial race, and when she did, Miss Testvalley hoped it would be for different reasons, and in a different manner. She did not want her pupil to engage herself after a night of champagne and song on the river; her sense of artistic fitness rejected the idea of Nan's adopting the same methods as her elders.

Mrs. St George was slightly bewildered when the governess suggested taking her pupil away from the late hours and the continuous excitements at the cottage. It was not so much the idea of parting from Nan, as of losing the moral support of the governess's presence, that troubled Mrs. St George. "But, Miss Testvalley, why do you want to go away? I never know how to talk to those servants, and I never can remember the titles of the young men that Conchita brings down, or what I ought to call them."

"I'm sure Miss March will help you with all that. And I do think Nan ought to get away for two or three weeks. Haven't you noticed how thin she's grown? And her eyes are as big as saucers. I know a quiet little place in Cornwall where she could have some bathing, and go to bed every night at nine."

To every one's surprise, Nan offered no objection. The prospect of seeing new places stirred her imagination, and she seemed to lose all interest in the gay doings at the cottage when Miss Testvalley told her that, on the way, they would stop at Exeter, where there was a very beautiful cathedral.

"And shall we see some beautiful houses too? I love seeing houses that are so ancient and so lovely that the people who live there have them in their bones."

Miss Testvalley looked at her pupil sharply. "What an odd expression! Did you find it in a book?" she asked; for the promiscuity of Nan's reading sometimes alarmed her.

"Oh, no. It was what that young Mr. Thwarte said to me about Honourslove. It's why he's going away for two years—so that he can make a great deal of money, and come back and spend it on Honourslove."

"H'm—from what I've heard, Honourslove could easily swallow a good deal more than he's likely to make in two years, or even ten," said Miss Testvalley. "The father and son are both said to be very extravagant, and the only way for Mr. Guy Thwarte to keep up his ancestral home will be to bring a great heiress back to it."

Nan looked thoughtful. "You mean, even if he doesn't love her?"

"Oh, well, I daresay he'll love her—or be grateful to her, at any rate."

"I shouldn't think gratitude was enough," said Nan with a sigh. She was silent again for a while, and then added: "Mr. Thwarte has read all your cousin's poetry —Dante Gabriel's, I mean."

Miss Testvalley gave her a startled glance. "May I ask how you happened to find that out?"

"Why, because there's a perfectly beautiful picture by your cousin in Sir Helmsley's study, and Mr. Thwarte showed it to me. And so we talked of his poetry too. But Mr. Thwarte thinks there are other poems even more wonderful than 'The Blessed Damozel'. Some of the sonnets in *The House of Life,* I mean. Do you think they're more beautiful, Miss Testvalley?"

The governess hesitated; she often found herself hesitating over the answers to Nan's questions. "You told Mr. Thwarte that you'd read some of those poems?"

"Oh, yes; I told him I'd read every one of them."

"And what did he say?"

"He said . . . he said he'd felt from the first that he and I would be certain to like the same things; and he *loved* my liking Dante Gabriel. I told him he was your cousin, and that you were devoted to him."

"Ah—well, I'm glad you told him that, for Sir Helmsley Thwarte is an old friend of my cousin's, and one of his best patrons. But you know, Nan, there are people who don't appreciate his poetry—don't see how beautiful it is; and I'd rather you didn't proclaim in public that you've read it all. Some people are so stupid that they wouldn't exactly understand a young girl's caring for that kind of poetry. You see, don't you, dear?"

"Oh, yes. They'd be shocked, I suppose, because it's all about love. But that's why I like it, you know," said Nan composedly.

Miss Testvalley made no answer, and Nan went on in a thoughtful voice: "Shall we see some other places as beautiful as Honourslove?"

The governess reflected. She had not contemplated a round of sight-seeing for her pupil, and Cornwall did not seem to have many sights to offer. But at length she said: "Well, Trevennick is not so far from Tintagel. If the family are away I might take you there, I suppose. You know the old Tintagel was supposed to have been King Arthur's castle."

Nan's face lit up. "Where the Knights of the Round Table were? Oh, Miss Testvalley, can we see that too? And the mere where he threw his sword Excalibur? Oh, couldn't we start tomorrow, don't you think?"

Miss Testvalley felt relieved. She had been slightly disturbed by Nan's allusion to Honourslove, and the unexpected glimpse it gave of an exchange of confidences between Guy Thwarte and her pupil; but she saw that in another moment the thought of visiting the scenes celebrated in Tennyson's famous poems had swept away all other fancies. *The Idylls of the King* had been one of Nan's magic casements, and Miss Testvalley smiled to herself at the ease with which the girl's mind flitted from one new vision to another.

"A child still, luckily," she thought, sighing, she knew not why, at what the future might hold for Nan when childish things should be put away.

XIV

THE Duke of Tintagel was a young man burdened with scruples. This was probably due to the fact that his father, the late Duke, had had none. During all his boyhood and youth the heir had watched the disastrous effects of not considering trifles. It was not that his father had been either irresponsible or negligent. The late Duke had no vices; but his virtues were excessively costly. His conduct had always been governed by a sense of the overwhelming obligations connected with his great position. One of these obligations, he held, consisted in keeping up his rank; the other, in producing an heir. Unfortunately the Duchess had given him six daughters before a son was born, and two more afterward in the attempt to provide the heir with a younger brother; and though daughters constitute a relatively small charge on a great estate, still a Duke's daughters cannot (or so their parent thought) be fed, clothed, educated and married at as low a cost as young women of humbler origin. The Duke's other obligation, that of keeping up his rank, had involved him in even heavier expenditure. Hitherto Longlands, the seat in Somersetshire, had been thought imposing enough even for a Duke; but its owner had always been troubled by the fact that the new castle at Tintagel, built for his great-grandfather in the approved Gothic style of the day, and with the avowed intention of surpassing Inveraray, had never been inhabited. The expense of completing it, and living in it in suitable state, appeared to have discouraged its creator; and for years it stood abandoned on its Cornish cliff, a sadder ruin than the other, until it passed to the young Duke's father. To him it became a torment, a reproach, an obsession; the Duke of Tintagel must live at Tintagel as the Duke of Argyll lived at Inveraray, with a splendour befitting the place; and the carrying out of this resolve had been the late Duke's crowning achievement.

His young heir, who had just succeeded him, had as keen a sense as his father of ducal duties. He meant, if possible, to keep up in suitable state both Tintagel and Longlands, as well as Folyat House, his London residence; but he meant to do so without the continual drain on his fortune which his father had been obliged to incur. The new Duke hoped that, by devoting all his time and most of his faculties to the care of his estates and the personal supervision of his budget, he could reduce his cost of living without altering its style; and the indefatigable Duchess, her numerous daughters notwithstanding, found time to second the attempt. She was not the woman to let her son forget the importance of her aid; and though a perfect understanding had always reigned between them, recent symptoms made it appear that the young Duke was beginning to chafe under her regency.

Soon after his visit to Runnymede he and his mother sat together in the Duchess's boudoir in the London house, a narrow lofty room on whose crowded walls authentic Raphaels were ultimately mingled with watercolours executed by the Duchess's maiden aunts, and photographs of shooting-parties at the various ducal estates. The Duchess invariably arranged to have this hour alone with her son, when breakfast was over, and her daughters (of whom death or marriage had claimed all but three) had gone their different ways. The Duchess had always kept her son to herself, and the Ladies Clara, Ermyntrude and Almina Folyat would never have dreamed of intruding on them.

At present, as it happened, all three were in the country, and Folyat House had put on its summer sack-cloth; but the Duchess lingered on, determined not to forsake her son till he was released from his Parliamentary duties.

"I was hoping," she said, noticing that the Duke had twice glanced at the clock, "that you'd manage to get away to Scotland for a few days. Isn't it possible? The Hopeleighs particularly wanted you to go to them at Loch Skarig. Lady Hopeleigh wrote yesterday to ask me to remind you. . ."

The Duchess was small of stature, with firm round cheeks, a small mouth and quick dark eyes under an anxiously wrinkled forehead. She did not often smile, and when, as now, she attempted it, the result was a pucker similar to the wrinkles on her brow. "You know that some one else will be very grieved if you don't go," she insinuated archly.

The Duke's look passed from faint *ennui* to marked severity. He glanced at the ceiling, and made no answer.

"My dear Ushant," said the Duchess, who still called him by the title he had borne before his father's death, "surely you can't be blind to the fact that poor Jean Hopeleigh's future is in your hands. It is a serious thing to have inspired such a deep sentiment. . ."

The Duke's naturally inexpressive face had become completely expressionless, but his mother continued: "I only fear it may cause you a lasting remorse. . ."

"I will never marry any one who hunts me down for the sake of my title," exclaimed the Duke abruptly.

His mother raised her neat dark eyebrows in a reproachful stare. "For your title? But, my dear Ushant, surely Jean Hopeleigh. . ."

"Jean Hopeleigh is like all the others. I'm sick of being tracked like a wild animal," cried the Duke, who looked excessively tame.

The Duchess gave a deep sigh. "Ushant—!"

"Well?"

"You haven't—it's not possible—formed an imprudent attachment? You're not concealing anything from me?" The Duke's smiles were almost as difficult as his mother's; but his muscles made an effort in that direction. "I shall never form an attachment until I meet a girl who doesn't know what a Duke is!"

"Well, my dear, I can't think where one could find a being so totally ignorant of everything on which England's greatness rests," said the Duchess impressively.

"Then I shan't marry."

"Ushant—!"

"I'm sorry, mother—"

She lifted her sharp eyes to his. "You remember that the roof at Tintagel has still to be paid for?"

"Yes."

"Dear Jean's settlements would make all that so easy. There's nothing the Hopeleighs wouldn't do. . ."

The Duke interrupted her. "Why not marry me to a Jewess? Some of those people in the City could buy up the Hopeleighs and not feel it."

The Duchess drew herself up. Her lips trembled, but no word came. Her son stalked out of the room. From the threshold he turned to say: "I shall go down to Tintagel on Friday night to go over the books with Blair." His mother could only bend her head; his obstinacy was beginning to frighten her.

The Duke got into the train on the Friday with a feeling of relief. His high and continuous sense of his rank was combined with a secret desire for anonymity. If he could have had himself replaced in the world of fashion and politics by a mechanical effigy of the Duke of Tintagel, while he himself went obscurely about his private business, he would have been a happier man. He was as firmly convinced as his mother that the greatness of England rested largely on her Dukes. The Dukes of Tintagel had always had a strong sense of public obligation; and the young Duke was determined not to fall below their standard. But his real tastes were for small matters, for the *minutiae* of a retired and leisurely existence. As a little boy his secret longing had been to be a clock-maker; or rather (since their fabrication might have been too delicate a business) a man who sold clocks and sat among them in his little shop, watching them, doctoring them, taking their temperature, feeling their pulse, listening to their chimes, oiling, setting and regulating them. The then Lord Ushant had never avowed this longing to his parents; even in petticoats he had understood that a future Duke can never hope to keep a clock-shop. But often, wandering through the great saloons and interminable galleries of Longlands and Tintagel, he had said to himself with a beating heart: "Some day I'll wind all these clocks myself, every Sunday morning before breakfast."

Later he felt that he would have been perfectly happy as a country squire, arbitrating in village disputes, adjusting differences between vicar and school-master, sorting fishing-tackle, mending broken furniture, doctoring the dogs, re-arranging his collection of stamps; instead of which fate had cast him for the centre front of the world's most brilliant social stage.

Undoubtedly his mother had been a great help. She enjoyed equally the hard work and the pompous ceremonial incumbent on conscientious Dukes; and the poor young Duke was incorrigibly conscientious. But his conscience could not compel him to accept a marriage arranged by his mother. That part of his life he intended to arrange for himself. His departure for Tintagel was an oblique reply to the Duchess's challenge. She had told him to go to Scotland, and he was going to Cornwall instead. The mere fact of being seated in a train which was hurrying westward was a declaration of independence. The Duke longed above all to be free, to decide for himself; and though he was ostensibly going to Tintagel on estate business, his real purpose was to think over his future in solitude.

If only he might have remained unmarried! Not that

he was without the feelings natural to young men; but the kind of marriage he was expected to make took no account of such feelings. "I won't be hunted—I won't!" the Duke muttered as the train rushed westward, seeing himself as a panting quarry pursued by an implacable pack of would-be Duchesses. Was there no escape? Yes. He would dedicate his public life entirely to his country, but in private he would do as he chose. Valiant words, and easy to speak when no one was listening; but with his mother's small hard eyes on him, his resolves had a way of melting. Was it true that if he did not offer himself to Jean Hopeleigh the world might accuse him of trifling with her? If so, the sooner he married some one else the better. The chief difficulty was that he had not yet met any one whom he really wanted to marry.

Well, he would give himself at least three days in which to think it all over, out of reach of the Duchess's eyes. . .

A salt mist was drifting to and fro down the coast as the Duke, the next afternoon, walked along the cliffs toward the ruins of the old Tintagel. Since early morning he had been at work with Mr. Blair, the agent, going into the laborious question of reducing the bills for the roof of the new castle, and examining the other problems presented by the administration of his great domain. After that, with agent and housekeeper, he had inspected every room in the castle, carefully examining floors and ceilings, and seeing to it that Mr. Blair recorded the repairs to be made, but firmly hurrying past the innumerable clocks, large and small, loud and soft, which, from writing-table and mantel-shelf and cabinet-top, cried out to him for attention. "Have you a good man for the clocks?" he had merely asked, with an affectation of indifference; and when the housekeeper replied: "Oh, yes, your Grace. Mr. Trelly from Wadebridge comes once a week, the same that his late Grace always employed," he had passed on with a distinct feeling of disappointment; for probably a man of that sort would resent any one else's winding the clocks—a sentiment the Duke could perfectly appreciate.

Finally, wearied by these labours, which were as much out of scale with his real tastes as the immense building itself, he had lunched late and hastily on bread and cheese, to the despair of the housekeeper, who had despatched a groom before daybreak to scour Wadebridge for delicacies.

The Duke's afternoon was his own, and his meagre repast over he set out for a tramp. The troublesome question of his marriage was still foremost in his mind; for after inspecting the castle he felt more than ever the impossibility of escaping from his ducal burdens. Yet how could the simple-hearted girl of whom he was in search be induced to share the weight of these great establishments? It was unlikely that a young woman too ignorant of worldly advantages to covet his title would be attracted by his responsibilities. Why not remain unmarried, as he had threatened, and let the title and the splendours go to the elderly clergyman who was his heir presumptive? But no—that would be a still worse failure in duty. He must marry, have children, play the great part assigned to him.

THE BUCCANEERS

As he walked along the coast toward the ruined Tintagel he shook off his momentary cowardice. The westerly wind blew great trails of fog in from the sea, and now and then, between them, showed a mass of molten silver, swaying heavily, as though exhausted by a distant gale. The Duke thought of the stuffy heat of London, and the currents of his blood ran less sedately. He would marry, yes; but he would choose his own wife, and choose her away from the world, in some still backwater of rural England. But here another difficulty lurked. He had once, before his father's death, lit on a girl who fitted ideally into his plan: the daughter of a naval officer's widow, brought up in a remote Norfolk village. The Duke had found a friend to introduce him, had called, had talked happily with the widow of parochial matters, had shown her what was wrong with her clock, and had even contrived to be left alone with the young lady. But the young lady could say no more than "Yes" and "No", and she placed even these monosyllables with so little relevance that face to face with her he was struck dumb also. He did not return, and the young lady married a curate.

The memory tormented him now. Perhaps, if he had been patient, had given her time—but no, he recalled her blank bewildered face, and thought what a depressing sight it would be every morning behind the tea-urn. Though he sought simplicity he dreaded dulness. Dimly conscious that he was dull himself, he craved the stimulus of a quicker mind; yet he feared a dull wife less than a brilliant one, for with the latter how could he maintain his superiority? He remembered his discomfort among those loud rattling young women whom his cousin Seadown had taken him to see at Runnymede. Very handsome they were, each in her own way; nor was the Duke insensible to beauty. One especially, the fair one, had attracted him. She was less noisy than the others, and would have been an agreeable sight at the breakfast-table; and she carried her head in a way to show off the Tintagel jewels. But marry an American—? The thought was inconceivable. Besides, supposing she should want to surround herself with all those screaming people, and supposing he had to invite the mother—he wasn't sure which of the two elderly ladies with dyed fringes *was* the mother—to Longlands or Tintagel whenever a child was born? From this glimpse into an alien world the Duke's orderly imagination recoiled. What he wanted was an English bride of ancient lineage and Arcadian innocence; and somewhere in the British Isles there must be one awaiting him. . .

XV

AFTER their early swim the morning had turned so damp and foggy that Miss Testvalley said to Nan: "I believe this would be a good day for me to drive over to Polwhelly and call at the vicarage. You can sit in the garden a little while if the sun comes out."

The vicarage at Polwhelly had been Miss Testvalley's chief refuge during her long lonely months at Tintagel with her Folyat pupils, and Nan knew that she wished to visit her old friends. As for Nan herself, after the swim and the morning walk, she preferred to sit in the inn garden, sheltered by a tall fuchsia hedge, and gazing out over the headlands and the sea. She had not even expressed the wish to take the short walk along the cliffs to the ruins of Tintagel; and she had apparently forgotten Miss Testvalley's offer to show her the modern castle of the same name. She seemed neither listless nor unwell, the governess thought, but lulled by the strong air, and steeped in a lazy beatitude; and this was the very mood Miss Testvalley had sought to create in her.

But an hour or two after Trevennick's only fly had carried off Miss Testvalley, the corner where Nan sat became a balcony above a great sea-drama. A twist of the wind had whirled away the fog, and there of a sudden lay the sea in a metallic glitter, with white clouds storming over it, hiding and then revealing the fiery blue sky between. Sit in the shelter of the fuchsia hedge on such a day? Not Nan! Her feet were already dancing on the sunbeams, and in another minute the gate had swung behind her, and she was away to meet the gale on the downs above the village.

When the Duke of Tintagel reached the famous ruin from which he took his name, another freak of the wind had swept the fog in again. The sea was no more than a hoarse sound on an invisible shore, and he climbed the slopes through a cloud filled with the stormy clash of sea-birds. To some minds the change might have seemed to befit the desolate place; but the Duke, being a good landlord, thought only: "More rain, I suppose; and that is certain to mean a loss on the crops."

But the walk had been exhilarating, and when he reached the upper platform of the castle, and looked down through a break in the fog at the savage coast-line, a feeling of pride and satisfaction crept through him. He liked the idea that a place so ancient and renowned belonged to him, was a mere milestone in his race's long descent; and he said to himself: "I owe everything to England. Perhaps after all I ought to marry as my mother wishes. . ."

He had thought he had the wild place to himself, but as he advanced toward the edge of the platform he perceived that his solitude was shared by a young lady who, as yet unaware of his presence, stood wedged in a coign of the ramparts, absorbed in the struggle between wind and sea.

The Duke gave an embarrassed cough; but between the waves and the gulls the sound did not carry far. The girl remained motionless, her profile turned seaward, and the Duke was near enough to study it in detail.

She had not the kind of beauty to whirl a man off his feet, and his eye was free to note that her complexion, though now warmed by the wind, was naturally pale, that her nose was a trifle too small, and her hair a tawny uncertain mixture of dark and fair. Nothing overpowering in all this; but being overpowered was what the Duke most dreaded. He went in fear of the terrible beauty that is born and bred for the strawberry leaves, and the face he was studying was so grave yet so happy that he felt somehow re-assured and safe. This girl, at any rate, was certainly not thinking of Dukes; and in the eyes she presently turned to him he saw not himself but the sea.

He raised his hat, and she looked at him, surprised but not disturbed. "I didn't know you were there," she said simply.

"The grass deadens one's steps..." the Duke apologized.

"Yes. And the birds scream so—and the wind."

"I'm afraid I startled you."

"Oh, no. I didn't suppose the place belonged to me..." She continued to scrutinize him gravely, and he wondered whether a certain fearless gravity were not what he liked best in woman. Then suddenly she smiled, and he changed his mind.

"But I've seen you before, haven't I?" she exclaimed. "I'm sure I have. Wasn't it at Runnymede?"

"At Runnymede?" he stammered, his heart sinking. The smile, then, had after all been for the Duke!

"Yes. I'm Nan St George. My mother and Mrs. Elmsworth have taken a little cottage there—Lady Churt's cottage. A lot of people come down from London to see my sister Virginia and Liz Elmsworth, and I have an idea you came one day—didn't you? There are so many of them—crowds of young men; and always changing. I'm afraid I can't remember all their names. But didn't Teddy de Santos-Dios bring you down the day we had that awful pillow-fight? I know—you're a Mr. Robinson."

In an instant the Duke's apprehensive mind registered a succession of terrors. First, the dread that he had been recognized and marked down; then the more deadly fear that, though this had actually happened, his quick-witted antagonist was clever enough to affect an impossible ignorance. A Mr. Robinson! For a fleeting second the Duke tried to feel what it would be like to be a Mr. Robinson . . . a man who might wind his own clocks when he chose. It did not feel as agreeable as the Duke had imagined—and he hastily re-became a Duke.

Yet would it not be safer to accept the proffered alias? He wavered. But no; the idea was absurd. If this girl, though he did not remember ever having seen her, had really been at Runnymede the day he had gone there, it was obvious that, though she might not identify him at the moment (a thought not wholly gratifying to his vanity), she could not long remain in ignorance. His face must have betrayed his embarrassment, for she exclaimed: "Oh, then, you're not Mr. Robinson? I'm so sorry! Virginia (that's my sister; I don't believe you've forgotten *her*)—Virginia says I'm always making stupid mistakes. And I know everybody hates being taken for somebody else; and especially for a Mr. Robinson. But won't you tell me your name?"

The Duke's confusion increased. But he was aware that hesitation was ridiculous. There was no help for it; he had to drag himself into the open. "My name's Tintagel."

Nan's eyebrows rose in surprise, and her smile enchanted him again. "Oh, how perfectly splendid! Then of course you know Miss Testvalley?"

The Duke stared. He had never seen exactly that effect produced by the announcement of his name. "Miss Testvalley?"

"Oh, don't you know her? How funny! But aren't you the brother of those girls whose governess she was? They used to live at Tintagel. I mean Clara and Ermie and Mina..."

"Their governess?" It suddenly dawned on the Duke how little he knew about his sisters. The fact of being regarded as a mere appendage to these unimportant females was a still sharper blow to his vanity; yet it gave him the re-assurance that even now the speaker did not know she was addressing a Duke. Incredible as such ignorance was, he was constrained to recognize it. "She knows me only as their brother," he thought. "Or else," he added, "she knows who I am, and doesn't care."

At first neither alternative was wholly pleasing; but after a moment's reflection he felt a glow of relief. "I remember my sisters had a governess they were devoted to," he said, with a timid affability.

"I should think so! She's perfectly splendid. Did you

know she was Dante Gabriel Rossetti's own cousin?"
Nan continued, her enthusiasm rising, as it always did
when she spoke of Miss Testvalley.

The Duke's perplexity deepened; and it annoyed him
to have to grope for his answers in conversing with this
prompt young woman. "I'm afraid I know very few
Italians—"

"Oh, well, you wouldn't know *him;* he's very ill, and
hardly sees anybody. But don't you love his poetry?
Which sonnet do you like best in *The House of Life?*
I have a friend whose favourite is the one that begins:
When do I love thee most, belovèd one?"

"I—the fact is, I've very little time to read poetry," the
Duke faltered.

Nan looked at him incredulously. "It doesn't take
much time if you really care for it. But lots of people
don't—Virginia doesn't. . . Are you coming down soon to
Runnymede? Miss Testvalley and I are going back next
week. They just sent me here for a little while to get a
change of air and some bathing, but it was really because
they thought Runnymede was too exciting for me."

"Ah," exclaimed the Duke, his interest growing, "you
don't care for excitement, then?" (The lovely child!)

Nan pondered the question. "Well, it all depends. . .
Everything's exciting, don't you think so? I mean sunsets
and poetry, and swimming out too far in a rough sea. . .
But I don't believe I care as much as the others for
practical jokes: frightening old ladies by dressing up as
burglars with dark lanterns, or putting wooden rattle-
snakes in people's beds—do *you?*"

It was the Duke's turn to hesitate. "I—well, I must own

that such experiences are unfamiliar to me; but I can hardly imagine being amused by them."

His mind revolved uneasily between the alternatives of disguising himself as a burglar or listening to a young lady recite poetry; and to bring the talk back to an easier level he said: "You're staying in the neighbourhood?"

"Yes. At Trevennick, at the inn. I love it here, don't you? You live somewhere near here, I suppose?"

Yes, the Duke said: his place wasn't above three miles away. He'd just walked over from there. . . He broke off, at a loss how to go on; but his interlocutor came to the rescue.

"I suppose you must know the vicar at Polwhelly? Miss Testvalley's gone to see him this afternoon. That's why I came up here alone. I promised and swore I wouldn't stir out of the inn garden—but how could I help it, when the sun suddenly came out?"

"How indeed?" echoed the Duke, attempting one of his difficult smiles. "Will your governess be very angry, do you think?"

"Oh, fearfully, at first. But afterward she'll understand. Only I do want to get back before she comes in, or she'll be worried. . ." She turned back to the rampart for a last look at the sea; but the deepening fog had blotted out everything. "I must really go," she said, "or I'll never find my way down."

The Duke's gaze followed her. Was this a tentative invitation to guide her back to the inn? Should he offer to do so? Or would the governess disapprove of this even more than of her charge's wandering off alone in the fog? "If you'll allow me—may I see you back to Treven-nick?" he suggested.

"Oh, I wish you would. If it's not too far out of your way?"

"It's—it's on my way," the Duke declared, lying hur-riedly; and they started down the steep declivity. The slow descent was effected in silence, for the Duke's lie had exhausted his conversational resources, and his com-panion seemed to have caught the contagion of his shy-ness. Inwardly he was thinking: "Ought I to offer her a hand? Is it steep enough—or will she think I'm pre-suming?"

He had never before met a young lady alone in a ruined castle, and his mind, nurtured on precedents, had no rule to guide it. But nature cried aloud in him that he must somehow see her again. He was still turning over the best means of effecting another meeting—an in-vitation to the castle, a suggestion that he should call on Miss Testvalley?—when, after a slippery descent from the ruins, and an arduous climb up the opposite cliff, they reached the fork of the path where it joined the lane to Trevennick.

"Thank you so much; but you needn't come any further. There's the inn just below," the young lady said, smiling.

"Oh, really? You'd rather—? Mayn't I—?"

She shook her head. "No; really," she mimicked him lightly; and with a quick wave of dismissal she started down the lane.

The Duke stood motionless, looking irresolutely after her, and wondering what he ought to have said or done.

"I ought to have contrived a way of going as far as the inn with her," he said to himself, exasperated by his own lack of initiative. "It comes of being always hunted, I suppose," he added, as he watched her slight outline lessen down the hill.

Just where the descent took a turn toward the village, Nan encountered a familiar figure panting upward.

"Annabel—I've been hunting for you everywhere!"

Annabel laughed and embraced her duenna. "You weren't expected back so soon."

"You promised me faithfully that you'd stay in the garden. And in this drenching fog—"

"Yes; but the fog blew away after you'd gone, and I thought that let me off my promise. So I scrambled up to the castle—that's all."

"That's all? Over a mile away, and along those dangerous slippery cliffs?"

"Oh, it was all right. There was a gentleman there who brought me back."

"A gentleman—in the ruins?"

"Yes. He says he lives somewhere round here."

"How often have I told you not to let strangers speak to you?"

"He didn't. I spoke to him. But he's not really a stranger, darling; he thinks he knows you."

"Oh, he does, does he?" Miss Testvalley gave a sniff of incredulity.

"I saw he wanted to ask if he could call," Nan continued, "but he was too shy. I never saw anybody so scared. I don't believe he's been around much."

"I daresay he was shocked by your behaviour."

"Oh, no. Why should he have been? He just stayed with me while we were getting up the cliff; after that I said he mustn't come any farther. Why, there he is still—at the top of the lane, where I left him. I suppose he's been watching to see that I got home safely. Don't you call that sweet of him?"

Miss Testvalley released herself from her pupil's arm. Her eyes were not only keen but far-sighted. They followed Nan's glance, and rested on the figure of a young man who stood above them on the edge of the cliff. As she looked he turned slowly away.

"Annabel! Are you sure that was the gentleman?"

"Yes... He's funny. He says he has no time to read poetry. What do you suppose he does instead?"

"But it's the Duke of Tintagel!" Miss Testvalley suddenly declared.

"The Duke? That young man?" It was Nan's turn to give an incredulous laugh. "He said his name was Tintagel, and that he was the brother of those girls at the castle; but I thought of course he was a younger son. He never said he was the Duke."

Miss Testvalley gave an impatient shrug. "They don't go about shouting out their titles. The family name is Folyat. And he has no younger brother, as it happens."

"Well, how was I to know all that? Oh, Miss Testvalley," exclaimed Nan, spinning around on her governess, "but if he's the Duke he's the one Miss March wants Jinny to marry!"

"Miss March is full of brilliant ideas."

"I don't call that one particularly brilliant. At least not if I was Jinny, I shouldn't. I think," said Nan, after a moment's pondering, "that the Duke's one of the stupidest young men I ever met."

"Well," rejoined her governess severely, "I hope he thinks nothing worse than that of you."

XVI

THE Mr. Robinson for whom Nan St George had mistaken the Duke of Tintagel was a young man much more confident of his gifts, and assured as to his future, than that retiring nobleman. There was nothing within the scope of his understanding which Hector Robinson did not know, and mean at some time to make use of. His grandfather had been first a miner and then a mine-owner in the North; his father, old Sir Downman Robinson, had built up one of the biggest cotton industries in Lancashire, and been rewarded with a knighthood, and Sir Downman's only son meant to turn the knighthood into a baronetcy, and the baronetcy into a peerage. All in good time.

Meanwhile, as a partner in his father's big company, and director in various city enterprises, and as Conservative M.P. for one of the last rotten boroughs in England, he had his work cut out for him, and could boast that his thirty-five years had not been idle ones.

It was only on the social side that he had hung fire. In coming out against his father as a Conservative, and thus obtaining without difficulty his election to Lord Saltmire's constituency, Mr. Robinson had flattered himself that he would secure a footing in society as readily as in the City. Had he made a miscalculation? Was it true that fashion had turned toward Liberalism, and

that a young Liberal M.P. was more likely to find favour
in the circles to which Mr. Robinson aspired?

Perhaps it was true; but Mr. Robinson was a Conservative by instinct, by nature, and in his obstinate
self-confidence was determined that he would succeed
without sacrificing his political convictions. And at any
rate, when it came to a marriage, he felt reasonably sure
that his Conservatism would recommend him in the
families from which he intended to choose his bride.

Mr. Robinson, surveying the world as his oyster, had
already (if the figure be allowed) divided it into two
halves, each in a different way designed to serve his purpose. The one, which he labelled Mayfair, held out
possibilities of immediate success. In that set, which had
already caught the Heir to the Throne in its glittering
meshes, there were ladies of the highest fashion who, in
return for pecuniary favours, were ready and even eager
to promote the ascent of gentlemen with short pedigrees
and long purses. As a member of Parliament he had a
status which did away with most of the awkward pre-
liminaries; and he found it easy enough to pick up,
among his masculine acquaintances, an introduction
to that privileged group beginning to be known as "the
Marlborough set".

But it was not in this easy-going world that he meant
to marry. Socially as well as politically Mr. Robinson
was a true Conservative, and it was in the duller half of
the London world, the half he called "Belgravia", that
he intended to seek a partner. But into those uniform
cream-coloured houses where dowdy dowagers ruled, and
flocks of marriageable daughters pined for a suitor ap-

proved by the family, Mr. Robinson had not yet forced his way. The only interior known to him in that world was Lord Saltmire's, and in this he was received on a strictly Parliamentary basis. He had made the immense mistake of not immediately recognizing the fact, and of imagining, for a mad moment, that the Earl of Saltmire, who had been so ready to endow him with a seat in Parliament, would be no less disposed to welcome him as a brother-in-law. But Lady Audrey de Salis, plain, dowdy, and one of five unmarried sisters, had refused him curtly and all too definitely; and the shock had thrown him back into the arms of Mayfair. Obviously he had aspired too high, or been too impatient; but it was in his nature to be aspiring and impatient, and if he was to succeed it must be on the lines of his own character.

So he had told himself as he looked into his glass on the morning of his first visit to the cottage at Runnymede, whither Teddy de Santos-Dios was to conduct him. Mr. Robinson saw in his mirror the energetic reddish features of a young man with a broad short nose, a dense crop of brown hair, and a heavy brown moustache. He had been among the first to recognize that whiskers were going out, and had sacrificed as handsome a pair as the City could show. When Mr. Robinson made up his mind that a change was coming, his principle was always to meet it half way; and so the whiskers went. And it did make him look younger to wear only the fashionable moustache. With that, and a flower in the buttonhole of his Poole coat, he could take his chance with most men, though he was aware that the careless unself-consciousness of the elect was still beyond him. But in time he would achieve that too.

Certainly he could not have gone to a better school than the bungalow at Runnymede. The young guardsmen, the budding M.P.'s and civil servants who frequented it, were all of the favoured caste whose ease of manner Mr. Robinson envied; and nowhere were they so easy as in the company of the young women already familiar to fashionable London as "the Americans". Mr. Robinson returned from that first visit enchanted and slightly bewildered, but with the fixed resolve to go back as often as he was invited. Before the day was over he had lent fifty pounds to Teddy de Santos-Dios, and lost another fifty at poker to the latter's sister, Lady Richard Marable, thus securing a prompt invitation for the following week; and after that he was confident of keeping the foot-hold he had gained.

But if the young ladies enchanted him he saw in the young men his immediate opportunity. Lady Richard's brother-in-law, Lord Seadown, was, for instance, one of the golden youths to whom Mr. Robinson had vainly sought an introduction. Lord Richard Marable, Seadown's younger brother, he did know; but Lord Richard's acquaintance was easy to make, and led nowhere, least of all in the direction of his own family. At Runnymede Lord Richard was seldom visible; but Lord Seadown, who was always there, treated with brotherly cordiality all who shared the freedom of the cottage. There were others too, younger sons of great houses, officers quartered at Windsor or Aldershot, young Parliamentarians and minor Government officials reluctantly detained in town at the season's end, and hailing with joy the novel distractions of Runnymede; there was even—on one memorable day—the young Duke of Tintagel, a shrinking neutral-tinted figure in that highly coloured throng.

"Now if *I* were a Duke—!" Robinson thought, viewing with pity the unhappy nobleman's dull clothes and embarrassed manner; but he contrived an introduction to his Grace, and even a few moments of interesting political talk, in which the Duke took eager refuge from the call to play blindman's-buff with the young ladies. All this was greatly to the good, and Mr. Robinson missed no chance to return to Runnymede.

On a breathless August afternoon he had come down from London, as he did on most Saturdays, and joined the party about the tea-table under the big cedar. The group was smaller than usual. Miss March was away visiting friends in the Lake country, Nan St George was still in Cornwall with her governess, Mrs. St George and Mrs. Elmsworth, exhausted by the heat, had retired to the seclusion of their bedrooms, and only Virginia St George and the two Elmsworth girls, under the doubtful chaperonage of Lady Richard Marable, sat around the table with their usual guests—Lord Seadown, Santos-Dios, Hector Robinson, a couple of young soldiers from Windsor, and a caustic young civil servant, the Honourable Miles Dawnly, who could always be trusted to bring down the latest news from London—or, at that season, from Scotland, Homburg or Marienbad, as the case might be.

Mr. Robinson by this time felt quite at home among

them. He agreed with the others that it was far too hot to play tennis or even croquet, or to go on the river before sunset, and he lay contentedly on the turf under the cedar, thinking his own thoughts, and making his own observations, while he joined in the languid chatter about the tea-table.

Of observations there were always plenty to be made at Runnymede. Robinson, by this time, had in his hands most of the threads running from one to another of these careless smiling young people. It was obvious, for instance, that Miles Dawnly, who had probably never lost his balance before, was head-over-ears in love with Conchita Marable, and that she was "playing" him indolently and amusedly, for want of a bigger fish. But the neuralgic point in the group was the growing rivalry between Lizzy Elmsworth and Virginia St George. Those two inseparable friends were gradually becoming estranged; and the reason was not far to seek. It was between them now, in the person of Lord Seadown, who lay at their feet, plucking up tufts of clover, and gazing silently skyward through the dark boughs of the cedar. It had for some time been clear to Robinson that the susceptible young man was torn between Virginia St George's exquisite profile and Lizzy Elmsworth's active wit. He needed the combined stimulus of both to rouse his slow imagination, and Robinson saw that while Virginia had the advantage as yet, it might at any moment slip into Lizzy's quick fingers. And Lizzy saw this too.

Suddenly Mabel Elmsworth, at whose feet no one was lying, jumped up and declared that if she sat still a minute longer she would take root. "Walk down to the river with me, will you, Mr. Robinson? There may be a little more air there than under the trees."

Robinson had no particular desire to walk to the river, or anywhere else, with Mab Elmsworth. She was jolly and conversable enough, but minor luminaries never interested him when stars of the first magnitude were in view. However, he was still tingling with the resentment aroused by the Lady Audrey de Salis's rejection, and in the mood to compare unfavourably that silent and large-limbed young woman with the swift nymphs of Runnymede. At Runnymede they all seemed to live, metaphorically, from hand to mouth. Everything that happened seemed to be improvised, and this suited his own impetuous pace much better than the sluggish *tempo* of the Saltmire circle. He rose, therefore, at Mabel's summons, wondering what the object of the invitation could be. Was she going to ask him to marry her? A little shiver ran down his spine; for all he knew, that might be the way they did it in the States. But her first words dispelled his fear.

"Mr. Robinson, Lord Seadown's a friend of yours, isn't he?"

Robinson hesitated. He was far too intelligent to affect to be more intimate with any one than he really was, and after a moment he answered: "I haven't known him long; but everybody who comes here appears to be on friendly terms with everybody else."

His companion frowned slightly. "I wish they really were! But what I wanted to ask you was—have you ever noticed anything particular between Lord Seadown and my sister?"

Robinson stopped short. The question took him by surprise. He had already noticed, in these free-mannered young women, a singular reticence about their family concerns, a sort of moral modesty that seemed to constrain them to throw a veil over matters freely enough discussed in aristocratic English circles. He repeated: "Your sister?"

"You probably think it's a peculiar question. Don't imagine I'm trying to pump you. But everybody must have seen that he's tremendously taken with Lizzy, and that Jinny St George is doing her best to come between them."

Robinson's embarrassment deepened. He did not know where she was trying to lead him. "I should be sorry to think that of Miss St George, who appears to be so devoted to your sister."

Mabel Elmsworth laughed impatiently. "I suppose that's the proper thing to say. But I'm not asking you to take sides—I'm not even blaming Virginia. Only it's been going on now all summer, and what I say is it's time he chose between them, if he's ever going to. It's very hard on Lizzy, and it's not fair that he should make two friends quarrel. After all, we're all alone in a strange country, and I daresay our ways are not like yours, and may lead you to make mistakes about us. All I wanted to ask is, if you couldn't drop a hint to Lord Seadown."

Hector Robinson looked curiously at this girl, who might have been pretty in less goddess-like company, and who spoke with such precocious wisdom on subjects delicate to touch. "By Jove, she'd make a good wife for an ambitious man," he thought. He did not mean himself, but he reflected that the man who married her beautiful sister might be glad enough, at times, to have such a counsellor at his elbow.

"I think you're right about one thing, Miss Elmsworth. Your ways are so friendly, so kind, that a fellow, if he wasn't careful, might find himself drawn two ways at once—"

Mabel laughed. "Oh, you mean: we flirt. Well, it's in our blood, I suppose. And no one thinks the worse of a girl for it at home. But over here it may seem undignified; and perhaps Lord Seadown thought he had the right to amuse himself without making up his mind. But in America, when a girl has shown that she really cares, it puts a gentleman on his honour, and he understands that the game has gone on long enough."

"I see."

"Only, we've nobody here to say this to Lord Seadown" (Mabel seemed tacitly to assume that neither mother could be counted on for the purpose—not at least in such hot weather), "and so I thought—"

Mr. Robinson murmured: "Yes—yes—" and after a pause went on: "But Lord Seadown is Lady Richard's brother-in-law. Couldn't she—?"

Mabel shrugged. "Oh, Conchita's too lazy to be bothered. And if she took sides, it would be with Jinny St George, because they're great friends, and she'd want all the money she can get for Seadown. Colonel St George is a very rich man nowadays."

"I see," Mr. Robinson again murmured. It was out of the question that he should speak on such a matter to Lord Seadown, and he did not know how to say this to any one as inexperienced as Mabel Elmsworth. "I'll think it over— I'll see what can be done," he pursued, directing his steps toward the group under the cedar in his desire to cut the conversation short.

As he approached he thought what a pretty scene it was: the young women in their light starched dresses and spreading hats, the young men in flannel boating suits, stretched at their feet on the turf, and the afternoon sunlight filtering through the dark boughs in dapplings of gold.

Mabel Elmsworth walked beside him in silence, clearly aware that her appeal had failed; but suddenly she exclaimed: "There's a lady driving in that I've never seen before. . . She's stopping the carriage to get out and join Conchita. I suppose it's a friend of hers, don't you?"

Calls from ladies, Mr. Robinson had already noticed, were rare and unexpected at the cottage. If a guardsman had leapt from the station fly Mabel, whether she knew him or not, would have remained unperturbed; but the sight of an unknown young woman of elegant appearance filled her with excitement and curiosity. "Let's go and see," she exclaimed.

The visitor, who was dark-haired, with an audaciously rouged complexion, and the kind of nose which the Laureate had taught his readers to describe as tip-tilted, was personally unknown to Mr. Robinson also; but thanks to the Bond Street photographers and the new society journals her features were as familiar to him as her reputation.

"Why, it's Lady Churt—it's your landlady!" he exclaimed, with a quick glance of enquiry at his companion. The tie between Seadown and Lady Churt had long been notorious in their little world, and Robinson instantly surmised that the appearance of the lady might have a far from favourable bearing on what Mabel Elmsworth had just been telling him. But Mabel hurried forward without responding to his remark, and they joined the party just as Lady Churt was exchanging a cordial hand-clasp with Lady Richard Marable.

"Darling!"

"Darling Idina, what a surprise!"

"Conchita, dearest—I'd no idea I should find you here! Won't you explain me, please, to these young ladies—my tenants, I suppose?" Lady Churt swept the group with her cool amused glance, which paused curiously, and as Robinson thought somewhat anxiously, on Virginia St George's radiant face.

"She looks older than in her photographs—and hunted, somehow," Robinson reflected, his own gaze resting on Lady Churt.

"I'm Lady Churt—your landlady, you know," the speaker continued affably, addressing herself to Virginia and Lizzy. "Please don't let me interrupt this delightful party. Mayn't I join it instead? What a brilliant idea to have tea out here in hot weather! I always used to have it on the terrace. But you Americans are so clever at arranging things." She looked about her, mustering the group with her fixed metallic smile. With the exception of Hector Robinson the young men were evidently all known to her, and she found an easy word of greeting for each. Lord Seadown was the last that she named.

"Ah, Seadown—so you're here too? Now I see why you

forgot that you were lunching with me in town today. I must say you chose the better part!" She dropped into the deep basket-chair which Santos-Dios had pushed forward, and held out her hand for a proffered mint-julep. "No tea, thanks—not when one of Teddy's demoralizing mixtures is available... You see, I know what to expect when I come here... A cigarette, Seadown? I hope you've got my special supply with you, even if you've forgotten our engagement?" She smiled again upon the girls. "He spoils me horribly, you know, by always remembering to carry about my particular brand."

Seadown, with flushed face and lowering brow, produced the packet, and Lady Churt slipped the contents into her cigarette-case. "I do hope I'm not interrupting some delightful plan or other? Perhaps you were all going out on the river? If you were, you mustn't let me delay you, for I must be off again in a few minutes."

Every one protested that it was much too hot to move, and Lady Churt continued: "Really—you had no plans? Well, it *is* pleasanter here than anywhere else. But perhaps I'm dreadfully in the way. Seadown's looking at me as if I were..." She turned her glance laughingly toward Virginia St George. "The fact is, I'm not at all sure that landladies have a right to intrude on their tenants unannounced. I daresay it's really against the law."

"Well, if it is, you must pay the penalty by being detained at our pleasure," said Lady Richard gaily; and after a moment's pause Lizzy Elmsworth came forward. "Won't you let me call my mother and Mrs. St George, Lady Churt? I'm sure they'd be sorry not to see you.

It was so hot after luncheon that they went up to their rooms to rest."

"How very wise of them! I wouldn't disturb them for the world." Lady Churt set down her empty glass, and bent over the lighting of a cigarette. "Only you really mustn't let me interfere for a moment with what you were all going to do. You see," she added, turning about with a smile of challenge, "you see, though my tenants haven't yet done me the honour of inviting me down, I've heard what amusing things are always going on here, and what wonderful ways you've found of cheering up the poor martyrs to duty who can't get away to the grouse and the deer—and I may as well confess that I'm dreadfully keen to learn your secrets."

Robinson saw that this challenge had a slightly startling effect on the three girls, who stood grouped together with an air of mutual defensiveness unlike their usual easy attitude. But Lady Richard met the words promptly. "If your tenants haven't invited you down, Idina dear, I fancy it's only because they were afraid to have you see how rudimentary their arts are compared to their landlady's. So many delightful people had already learnt the way to the cottage that there was nothing to do but to leave the door unlatched. Isn't that your only secret, girls? If there's any other—" she too glanced about her with a smile—"well, perhaps it's *this;* but this, remember, *is* a secret, even from the stern Mammas who are taking their siesta upstairs."

As she spoke she turned to her brother. "Come, Teddy —if everybody's had tea, what about lifting the tray and things on to the grass, and putting this table to its real use?" Two of the young men sprang to her aid, and in a moment tray and tea-cloth had been swept away, and the green baize top of the folding table had declared its original purpose.

"Cards? Oh, how jolly!" cried Lady Churt. She drew a seat up to the table, while Teddy de Santos-Dios, who had disappeared into the house, hurried back with a handful of packs. "But this is glorious! No wonder my poor little cottage has become so popular. What—poker? Oh, by all means. The only game worth playing—I took my first lesson from Seadown last week... Seadown, I had a little *porte-monnaie* somewhere, didn't I? Or did I leave it in the fly? Not that I've much hope of finding anything in it but some powder and a few pawn-tickets... Oh, Seadown, will you come to my rescue? Lend me a fiver, there's a darling—I hope I'm not going to lose more than that."

Lord Seadown who, since her arrival, had maintained a look of gloomy detachment, drew forth his note-case with an embarrassed air. She received it with a laugh. "What? *Carte blanche?* What munificence! But let me see—." She took up the note-case, ran her fingers through it, and drew out two or three five-pound notes. "Heavens, Seadown, what wealth! How am I ever to pay you back if I lose? Or even if I win, when I need so desperately every penny I can scrape together?" she slipped the notes into her purse, which the observant Hector Robinson, alert for the chance of making himself known to the newcomer, had hastened to retrieve from the fly. Lady Churt took the purse with a brief nod for the service rendered, and a long and attentive look at the personable Hector; then she handed back Lord Seadown's note-case. "Wish me luck, my dear! Perhaps I may manage to fleece one or two of these hardened gamblers."

The card-players, laughing, settled themselves about the table. Lady Churt and Lady Richard sat on opposite sides, Lord Seadown took a seat next to his sister-in-law, and the other men disposed themselves as they pleased. Robinson, who did not care to play, had casually placed himself behind Lady Churt, and the three girls, resisting a little banter and entreaty, declared that they also preferred to walk about and look on at the players.

The game began in earnest, and Lady Churt opened with the supernaturally brilliant hand which often falls to the lot of the novice. The stakes (the observant Robinson noticed) were higher than usual, the players consequently more intent. It was one of those afternoons when thunder invisibly amasses itself behind the blue, and as the sun drooped slowly westward it seemed as though the card-table under the cedar-boughs were overhung by the same feverish hush as the sultry lawns and airless river.

Lady Churt's luck did not hold. Too quickly elated, she dashed ahead toward disaster. Robinson was not long in discovering that she was too emotional for a game based on dissimulation, and no match for such seasoned players as Lady Richard and Lady Richard's brother. Even the other young men had more experience, or at any rate more self-control, than she could muster; and though her purse had evidently been better supplied than she pretended, the time at length came when it was nearly empty.

But at that very moment her luck turned again. Robinson could not believe his eyes. The hand she held could hardly be surpassed; she understood enough of the game to seize her opportunity, and fling her last notes into the jack-pot presided over by Teddy de Santos-Dios's glossy smile and supple gestures. There was more money in the jack-pot than Robinson had ever seen on the Runnymede card-table, and a certain breathlessness overhung the scene, as if the weight of the thundery sky were in the lungs of the players.

Lady Churt threw down her hand, and leaned back with a sparkle of triumph in eyes and lips. But Miles Dawnly, with an almost apologetic gesture, had spread his cards upon the table.

"Begorra! A royal flush—" a young Irish lieutenant gasped out. The groups about the table stared at each other. It was one of those moments which make even seasoned poker-players gasp. For a short interval of perplexity Lady Churt was silent; then the exclamations of the other players brought home to her the shock of her disaster.

"It's the sort of game that fellows write about in their memoirs," murmured Teddy, almost awestruck; and the lucky winner gave an embarrassed laugh. It was almost incredible to him too.

Lady Churt pushed back her chair, nearly colliding with the attentive Robinson. She tried to laugh. "Well, I've learnt my lesson! Lost Seadown's last copper, as well as my own. Not that he need mind; he's won more than he lent me. But I'm completely ruined—down and out, as I believe you say in the States. I'm afraid you're all too clever for me, and one of the young ladies had better take my place," she added with a drawn smile.

"Oh, come, Idina, don't lose heart!" exclaimed Lady Richard, deep in the game, and annoyed at the interruption.

"Heart, my dear? I assure you I've never minded parting with that organ. It's losing the shillings and pence that I can't afford."

Miles Dawnly glanced across the table at Lizzy Elmsworth, who stood beside Hector Robinson, her keen eyes bent on the game. "Come, Miss Elmsworth, if Lady Churt is really deserting us, won't you replace her?"

"Do, Lizzy," cried Lady Richard; but Lizzy shook her head, declaring that she and her friends were completely ignorant of the game.

"What, even Virginia?" Conchita laughed. "There's no excuse for her, at any rate, for her father is a celebrated poker-player. My respected parent always says he'd rather make Colonel St George a handsome present than sit down at poker with him."

Virginia coloured at the challenge, but Lizzy, always quicker at the uptake, intervened before she could answer.

"You seem to have forgotten, Conchita, that girls don't play cards for money in America."

Lady Churt turned suddenly toward Virginia St George, who was standing behind her. "No. I understand the game you young ladies play has fewer risks, and requires only two players," she said, fixing her vivid

eyes on the girl's bewildered face. Robinson, who had
drawn back a few steps, was still watching her intently.
He said to himself that he had never seen a woman so
angry, and that certain small viperine heads darting
forked tongues behind their glass cases at the Zoo would
in future always remind him of Lady Churt.

For a moment Virginia's bewilderment was shared by
the others about the table; but Conchita, startled out of
her absorption in the game, hastily assumed the air of
one who is vainly struggling to repress a burst of ill-
timed mirth. "How frightfully funny you are, Idina!
I do wish you wouldn't make me laugh so terribly in
this hot weather!"

Lady Churt's colour rose angrily. "I'm glad it amuses
you to see your friends lose their money," she said. "But
unluckily I can't afford to make the fun last much
longer."

"Oh, nonsense, darling! Of course your luck will turn.
It's been miraculous already. Lend her something to go
on with, Seadown, do. . ."

"I'm afraid Seadown can't go on either. I'm sorry to be
a spoil-sport, but I must really carry him off. As he forgot to lunch with me today it's only fair that he should
come back to town for dinner."

Lord Seadown, who had relapsed into an unhappy
silence, did not break it in response to this; but Lady
Richard once more came to his rescue. "We love your
chaff, Idina; and we hope the idea of carrying off Seadown is only a part of it. You say he was engaged to
lunch with you today; but isn't there a mistake about
dates? Seedy, in his family character as my brother-in-

law, brought me down here for the week-end, and I'm
afraid he's got to wait and see me home on Monday.
You wouldn't suppose my husband would mind my travelling alone, would you, considering how much he does
it himself—or professes to; but as a matter of fact he and
my father-in-law, who disagree on so many subjects, are
quite agreed that I'm not to have any adventures if they
can help it. And so you see... But sit down again,
darling, do. Why should you hurry away? If you'll only
stop and dine you'll have an army of heroes to see you
back to town; and Seadown's society at dinner."

The effect of this was to make Lady Churt whiten
with anger under her paint. She glanced sharply from
Lady Richard to Lord Seadown.

"Yes; do, Idina," the latter at length found voice to
say.

Lady Churt threw back her brilliant head with another laugh. "Thanks a lot for your invitation, Conchita
darling—and for yours too, Seadown. It's really rather
amusing to be asked to dine in one's own house... But
today I'm afraid I can't. I've got to carry you back to
London with me, Seadown, whoever may have brought
you here. The fact is—" she turned another of her challenging glances on Virginia St George— "the fact is, it's
time your hostesses found out that you don't go with the
house; at least not when I'm not living in it. That
ought to have been explained to them, perhaps—"

"Idina ..." Lord Seadown muttered in anguish.

"Oh, I'm not blaming anybody! It's such a natural
mistake. Lord Seadown comes down so continually when
I'm here," Lady Churt pursued, her eyes still on Vir-

ginia's burning face, "that I suppose he simply forgot
the house was let, and went on coming from the mere
force of habit. I do hope, Miss St George, his being here
hasn't inconvenienced you? Come along, Seadown, or
we'll miss our train; and please excuse yourself to these
young ladies, who may think your visits were made on
their account—mayn't they?"

A startled silence followed. Even Conchita's ready
tongue seemed to fail her. She cast a look of interrogation at her brother-in-law, but his gaze remained obstinately on the ground, and the other young men had
discreetly drawn back from the scene of action.

Virginia St George stood a little way from her friends.
Her head was high, her cheeks burning, her blue eyes
dark with indignation. Mr. Robinson, intently following the scene, wondered whether it were possible for a
young creature to look more proud and beautiful. But
in another moment he found himself reversing his judg-
ment; for Mr. Robinson was all for action, and suddenly,
swiftly, the other beauty, Virginia's friend and rival, had
flung herself into the fray.

"Virginia! What are you waiting for? Don't you see
that Lord Seadown has no right to speak till you do?
Why don't you tell him at once that he has your permission to announce your engagement?" Lizzy Elmsworth cried with angry fervour.

Mr. Robinson hung upon this dialogue with the
breathless absorption of an experienced play-goer discovering the gifts of an unknown actress. "By Jove—by
Jove," he murmured to himself. His talk with Mabel
Elmsworth had made clear to him the rivalry he had

already suspected between the two beauties, and he could measure the full significance of Lizzy's action.

"By Jove—she knew she hadn't much of a chance with Seadown, and quick as lightning she decided to back up the other girl against the common enemy." His own admiration, which, like Seadown's, had hitherto wavered between the two beauties, was transferred in a flash, and once for all, to Lizzy. "Gad, she looks like an avenging goddess—I can almost hear the arrow whizzing past! What a party-leader she'd make," he thought; and added, with inward satisfaction: "Well, she won't be thrown away on this poor nonentity, at all events."

Virginia St George still stood uncertain, her blue entreating eyes turned with a sort of terror on Lady Churt.

"Seadown!" the latter repeated with an angry smile.

The sound of his name seemed to rouse the tardy suitor. He lifted his head, and his gaze met Virginia's, and detected her tears. He flushed to his pale eyebrows.

"This is all a mistake, a complete mistake... I mean," he stammered, turning to Virginia, "it's just a joke of Lady Churt's—who's such an old friend of mine that I know she'll want to be the first to congratulate me... if you'll only tell her that she may."

He went up to Virginia, and took possession of her trembling hand. Virginia left it in his; but with her other hand she drew Lizzy Elmsworth to her.

"Oh, Lizzy," she faltered.

Lizzy bestowed on her a kiss of congratulation, and drew back with a little laugh. Mr. Robinson, from his secret observatory, guessed exactly what was passing through her mind. "She's begun to realize that she's thrown away her last hope of Seadown; and very likely she repents her rashness. But the defence of the clan before everything; and I daresay he wasn't the only string to her bow."

Lady Churt stood staring at the two girls with a hard bright intensity which, as the silence lengthened, made Mr. Robinson conscious of a slight shiver down his spine. At length she too broke into a laugh. "Really—" she said, "really. . ." She was obviously struggling for the appropriate word. She found it in another moment.

"Engaged? Engaged to Seadown? What a delightful surprise! Almost as great a one, I suspect, to Seadown as to Miss St George herself. Or is it only another of your American jokes—just a way you've invented of keeping Seadown here over Sunday? Well, for my part you're welcome either way. . ." She paused and her quick ironic glance travelled from face to face. "But if it's serious, you know—then of course I congratulate you, Seadown. And you too, Miss St George." She went up to Virginia, and looked her straight in the eyes. "I congratulate you, my dear, on your cleverness, on your good looks, on your success. But you must excuse me for saying that I know Seadown far too well to congratulate you on having caught him for a husband."

She held out a gloved hand rattling with bracelets, just touched Virginia's shrinking fingers, and stalked past Lord Seadown without seeming to see him.

"Conchita, darling, how cleverly you've staged the whole business. We must really repeat it the next time there are *tableaux vivants* at Stafford House." Her eyes took a rapid survey of the young men. "And now I must be off. Mr. Dawnly, will you see me to my fly?"

Mr. Robinson turned from the group with a faint smile as Miles Dawnly advanced to accompany Lady Churt. "What a tit-bit for Dawnly to carry back to town!" he thought. "Poor woman... She'll have another try for Seadown, of course—but the game's up, and she probably knows it. I thought she'd have kept her head better. But what fools the cleverest of them can be..." He had the excited sense of having assisted at a self-revelation such as the polite world seldom offers. Every accent of Lady Churt's stinging voice, every lift of her black eyebrows and tremor of her red lips, seemed to bare her before him in her avidity, her disorder, her social arrogance and her spiritual poverty. The sight curiously re-adjusted Mr. Robinson's sense of values, and his admiration for Lizzy Elmsworth grew with his pity for her routed opponent.

XVII

UNDER the fixed smile of the Folyat Raphael the Duchess of Tintagel sat at breakfast opposite two of her many daughters, the Ladies Almina Folyat and Gwendolen de Lurey.

When the Duke was present he reserved to himself the right to glance through the morning papers between his cup of tea and his devilled kidneys; but in his absence his mother exercised the privilege, and had the *Morning Post* placed before her as one of her jealously guarded rights.

She always went straight to the Court Circular, and thence (guided by her mother's heart) to the Fashionable Marriages; and now, after a brief glance at the latter, she threw down the journal with a sudden exclamation.

"Oh, Mamma, what is it?" both daughters cried in alarm. Lady Almina thought wistfully: "Probably somebody else she had hopes of for Ermie or me is engaged," and Lady Gwendolen de Lurey, who had five children, and an invalid husband with a heavily mortgaged estate, reflected, as she always did when she heard of a projected marriage in high life, that when her own engagement had been anounced every one took it for granted that Colonel de Lurey would inherit within the year the immense fortune of a paralyzed uncle—who after all was still alive. "So there's no use planning in advance," Lady Gwendolen concluded wearily, glancing at the clock to make sure it was not yet time to take her second girl to the dentist (the children always had to draw lots for the annual visit to the dentist, as it was too expensive to take more than one a year).

"What is it, Mamma?" the daughters repeated apprehensively.

The Duchess laid down the newspaper, and looked first at one and then at the other. "It is—it is—that I sometimes wonder what we bring you all up for!"

"Mamma!"

"Yes; the time, and the worry, and the money—"

"But what in the world has happened, Mamma?"

"What has happened? Only that Seadown is going to marry an American! That a—what's the name?—a Miss Virginia St George of New York is going to be premier Marchioness of England!" She pushed the paper aside, and looked up indignantly at the imbecile smile of the Raphael Madonna. "And nobody cares!" she ended bitterly, as though including that insipid masterpiece in her reproach.

Lady Almina and Lady Gwendolen repeated with astonishment: "Seadown?"

"Yes; your cousin Seadown—who used to be at Longlands so often at one time that I *had* hoped. . ."

Lady Almina flushed at the hint, which she took as a personal reproach, and her married sister, seeing her distress, intervened: "Oh, but Mamma, you know perfectly well that for years Seadown has been Idina Churt's property, and nobody has had a chance against her."

The Duchess gave her dry laugh. "Nobody? It seems this girl had only to lift a finger—"

"I daresay, Mamma, they use means in the States that a well-bred English girl wouldn't stoop to."

The Duchess stirred her tea angrily. "I wish I knew what they are!" she declared, unconsciously echoing the words of an American President when his most successful general was accused of intemperance.

Lady Gwendolen, who had exhausted her ammunition, again glanced at the clock. "I'm afraid, Mamma, I must ask you to excuse me if I hurry off with Clare to the dentist. It's half past nine—and in this house I'm always sure Ushant keeps the clocks on time..."

The Duchess looked at her with unseeing eyes. "Oh, Ushant—!" she exclaimed. "If you can either of you tell me where Ushant is—or why he's not in London, when the House has not risen—I shall be much obliged to you!"

Lady Gwendolen had slipped away under cover of this outburst, and the Duchess's unmarried daughter was left alone to weather the storm. She thought: "I don't much mind, if only Mamma lets me alone about Seadown."

Lady Almina Folyat's secret desire was to enter an Anglican Sisterhood, and next to the grievance of her not marrying, she knew none would be so intolerable to her mother as her joining one of these High Church masquerades, as the evangelical Duchess would have called it. "If you want to dress yourself up, why don't you go to a fancy-ball?" the Duchess had parried her daughter's first approach to the subject; and since then Lady Almina had trembled, and bided her time in silence. She had always thought, she could not tell why, that perhaps when Ushant married he might take her side—or at any rate set her the example of throwing off their mother's tyranny.

"Seadown marrying an American! I pity poor Selina Brightlingsea; but she has never known how to manage her children." The Duchess folded the *Morning Post,* and gathered up her correspondence. Her morning duties lay before her, stretching out in a long monotonous perspective to the moment when all Ushant's clocks should simultaneously strike the luncheon hour. She felt a sudden discouragement when she thought of it— she to whom the duties of her station had for over thirty years been what its pleasures would have been to other women. Well—it was a joy, even now, to do it all for Ushant, neglectful and ungrateful as he had lately been; and she meant to go on with the task unflinchingly till the day when she could put the heavy burden into the hands of his wife. And what a burden it seemed to her that morning!

She reviewed it all, as though it lay outlined before her on some vast chart: the treasures, the possessions, the heirlooms: the pictures, the jewels—Raphaels, Correggios, Ruysdaels, Vandykes and Hobbemas, the Folyat rubies, the tiaras, the legendary Ushant diamond, the plate, the great gold service for royal dinners, the priceless porcelain, the gigantic ranges of hot-houses at Longlands; and then the poor, the charities, the immense distribution of coal and blankets, committee-meetings, bazaar-openings, foundation-layings; and last, but not least onerous, the recurring court duties, inevitable as the turn of the seasons. She had been Mistress of the

Robes, and would be so again; and her daughter-in-law, of course, could be no less. The Duchess smiled suddenly at the thought of what Seadown's prospects might have been if he had been a future Duke, and obliged to initiate his American wife into the official duties of her station! "It will be bad enough for his poor mother as it is—but fancy having to prepare a Miss St George of New York for her duties as Mistress of the Robes. But no—the Queen would never consent. The Prime Minister would have to be warned... But what nonsense I'm inventing!" thought the Duchess, pushing back her chair, and ringing to tell the butler that she would see the groom-of-the-chambers that morning before the housekeeper.

"No message from the Duke, I suppose?" she asked, as the butler backed toward the threshold.

"Well, your Grace, I was about to mention to your Grace that his Grace's valet has just received a telegram instructing him to take down a couple of portmanteaux to Tintagel, where his Grace is remaining for the present."

The door closed, and the Duchess sat looking ahead of her blindly. She had not noticed that her second daughter had also disappeared, but now a sudden sense of being alone—quite alone and unwanted—overwhelmed her, and her little piercing black eyes grew dim.

"I hope," she murmured to herself, "this marriage will be a warning to Ushant." But this hope had no power to dispel her sense of having to carry her immense burden alone.

When the Duke finally joined his mother at Longlands he had surprisingly little to say about his long stay at Tintagel. There had been a good many matters to go into with Blair; and he had thought it better to remain till they were settled. So much he said, and no more; but his mere presence gradually gave the Duchess the comfortable feeling of slipping back with him into the old routine.

The shooting-parties had begun, and as usual, in response to long-established lists of invitations, the guns were beginning to assemble. The Duchess always made out these lists; her son had never expressed any personal preference in the matter. Though he was a moderately good shot he took no interest in the sport, and, as often as he could, excused himself on the ground of business. His cousins Seadown and Dick Marable, both ardent sportsmen and excellent shots, used often to be asked to replace him on such occasions; and he always took it for granted that Seadown would be invited, though Dick Marable no longer figured on the list.

After a few days, therefore, he said to his mother: "I'm afraid I shall have to go up to town tomorrow morning for a day or two."

"To town? Are you never going to allow yourself a proper holiday?" she protested.

"I shan't be away long. When is Seadown coming? He can replace me."

The Duchess's tight lips grew tighter. "I doubt if Seadown comes. In fact, I've done nothing to remind him. So soon after his engagement, I could hardly suggest it, could I?"

The Duke's passive countenance showed a faint surprise. "But surely, if you invite the young lady—"

"And her Mamma? And her sister? I understand there's a sister—" the Duchess rejoined ironically.

"Yes," said the Duke, the slow blood rising to his face, "there's a sister."

"Well, you know how long in advance our shooting-parties are made up; even if I felt like adding three unknown ladies to my list, I can't think where I could put them."

Knowing the vast extent of the house, her son received this in a sceptical silence. At length he said: "Has Seadown brought Miss St George to see you?"

"No. Selina Brightlingsea simply wrote me a line. I fancy she's not particularly eager to show off the future Marchioness."

"Miss St George is wonderfully beautiful," the Duke murmured.

"My dear Ushant, nothing will convince me that our English beauties can be surpassed.—But since you're here will you glance at the seating of tonight's dinner-table. The Hopeleighs, you remember, are arriving. . ."

"I'm afraid I'm no good at dinner-tables. Hadn't you better consult one of the girls?" replied the Duke, ignoring the mention of the expected guests; and as he turned to leave the room his mother thought, with a sinking heart: "I might better have countermanded the Hopeleighs. He has evidently got wind of their coming, and now he's running away from them."

The cottage at Runnymede stood dumb and deserted-looking as the Duke drove up to it. The two mothers, he knew, were in London, with the prospective bride and her friends Lizzy and Mab, who were of course to be among her bridesmaids. In view of the preparations for her daughter's approaching marriage, Mrs. St George had decided to take a small house in town for the autumn, and, as the Duke also knew, she had chosen Lady Richard Marable's, chiefly because it was near Miss Jacky March's modest dwelling, and because poor Conchita was more than ever in need of ready money.

The Duke of Tintagel was perfectly aware that he should find neither Mrs. St George nor her eldest daughter at Runnymede; but he was not in quest of either. If he had not learned, immediately on his return to Longlands, that Jean Hopeleigh and her parents were among the guests expected there, he might never have gone up to London, or taken the afternoon train to Staines. It took the shock of an imminent duty to accelerate his decisions; and to run away from Jean Hopeleigh had become his most urgent duty.

He had not returned to the cottage since the hot summer day when he had avoided playing blindman's-buff with a bevy of noisy girls only by letting himself be drawn into a tiresome political discussion with a pushing young man whose name had escaped him.

Now the whole aspect of the place was changed. The house seemed empty, the bright awnings were gone, and a cold gray mist hung in the cedar-boughs and hid the river. But the Duke found nothing melancholy in the scene. He had a healthy indifference to the worst vagaries of the British climate, and the mist reminded him of the day when, in the fog-swept ruins of Tintagel, he had come on the young lady whom it had been his exquisite privilege to guide back to Trevennick. He had called at the inn the next day, to re-introduce himself to the young lady's governess, and to invite them both to the new Tintagel; and for a fortnight his visits to the inn at Trevennick, and theirs to the ducal seat, had been frequent and protracted. But, though he had spent with them long hours which had flown like minutes, he had never got beyond saying to himself: "I shan't rest till I've found an English girl exactly like her." And to be sure of not mistaking the copy he had continued his study of the original.

Miss Testvalley was alone in the little upstairs sitting-room at Runnymede. For some time past she had craved a brief respite from her arduous responsibilities, but now that it had come she was too agitated to profit by it.

It was startling enough to be met, on returning home with Nan, by the announcement of Virginia's engagement; and when she had learned of Lady Churt's dramatic incursion she felt that the news she herself had to impart must be postponed—the more so as, for the moment, it was merely a shadowy affair of hints, apprehensions, divinations.

If Miss Testvalley could have guessed the consequences of her proposal to give the St George girls a season in England, she was not sure she would not have steered Mrs. St George back to Saratoga. Not that she had lost her taste for battle and adventure; but she had

developed a tenderness for Nan St George, and an odd
desire to shelter her from the worldly glories her governess's rash advice had thrust upon the family. Nan
was different, and Miss Testvalley could have wished a
different future for her; she felt that Belgravia and Mayfair, shooting-parties in great country-houses, and the
rest of the fashionable routine to which Virginia and
the Elmsworth girls had taken so promptly, would leave
Nan bewildered and unsatisfied. What kind of life
would satisfy her, Miss Testvalley did not profess to
know. The girl, for all her flashes of precocity, was in
most ways immature, and the governess had a feeling
that she must shape her own fate, and that only unhappiness could come of trying to shape it for her. So
it was as well that at present there was no time to deal
with Nan.

Virginia's impending marriage had thrown Mrs. St
George into a state of chaotic despair. It was too much
for her to cope with—too complete a revenge on the
slights of Mrs. Parmore and the cruel rebuff of the Assembly ladies. "We might better have stayed in New
York," Mrs. St George wailed, aghast at the practical
consequences of a granted prayer.

Miss Jacky March and Conchita Marable soon laughed
her out of this. The trembling awe with which Miss
March spoke of Virginia's privilege in entering into one
of the greatest families in England woke a secret response in Mrs. St George. She, who had suffered because
her beautiful daughters could never hope to marry into
the proud houses of Eglinton or Parmore, was about to
become the mother-in-law of an earl, who would one

day (in a manner as unintelligible to Mrs. St George as the development of the embryo) turn into the premier Marquess of England. The fact that it was all so unintelligible made it seem more dazzling. "At last Virginia's beauty will have a worthy setting," Miss March exulted; and when Mrs. St George anxiously murmured: "But look at poor Conchita. Her husband drinks, and behaves dreadfully with other women, and she never seems to have enough money—" Miss March calmed her with the remark: "Well, you ask her if she'd rather be living in Fifth Avenue, with more money than she'd know how to spend."

Conchita herself confirmed this. "Seadown's always been the good boy of the family. He'll never give Jinny any trouble. After all, that hateful entanglement with Idina Churt shows how quiet and domestic he really is. That was why she held him so long. He likes to sit before the same fire every evening... Of course with Dick it's different. The family shipped him off to South America because they couldn't keep him out of scrapes. And if I took a sentimental view of marriage I'd sit up crying half the night... But I'll tell you what, Mrs. St George; even that's worth while in London. In New York, if a girl's unhappily married there's nothing to take her mind off it; whereas here there's never really time to think about it. And of course Jinny won't have my worries, and she'll have a position that Dick wouldn't have given me even if he'd been a model son and husband."

Most of this was beyond Mrs. St George's grasp; but the gist of it was consoling, and even flattering. After all, if it was the kind of life Jinny wanted, and if even poor Conchita, and that wretched Jacky March, who'd been so cruelly treated, agreed that London was worth the price—well, Mrs. St George supposed it must be; and anyhow Mrs. Parmore and Mrs. Eglinton must be rubbing their eyes at this very minute over the announcement of Virginia's engagement in the New York papers. All that London could give, in rank, in honours, in social glory, was only, to Mrs. St George, a knife to stab New York with—and that weapon she clutched with feverish glee. "If only her father rubs the Brightlingseas into those people he goes with at Newport," she thought vindictively.

The bell rung by the Duke tinkled languidly and long before a flurried maid appeared; and the Duke, accustomed to seeing double doors fly open on velvet carpets at his approach, thought how pleasant it would be to live in a cottage with too few servants, and have time to notice that the mat was shabby, and the brass knocker needed polishing.

Mrs. St George and Mrs. Elmsworth were up in town. Yes, he knew that; but might he perhaps see Miss Testvalley? He muttered his name as if it were a term of obloquy, and the dazzled maid curtsied him into the drawing-room and rushed up to tell the governess.

"Did you tell his Grace that Miss Annabel was in London too?" Miss Testvalley asked.

No, the maid replied; but his Grace had not asked for Miss Annabel.

"Ah—" murmured the governess. She knew her man

well enough by this time to be aware that this looked serious. "It was me he asked for?" And the maid, evidently sharing her astonishment, declared that it was.

"Oh, your Grace, there's no fire!" Miss Testvalley exclaimed, as she entered the drawing-room a moment later and found her visitor standing close to the icy grate. "No, I won't ring. I can light a fire at least as well as any house-maid."

"Not for me, please," the Duke protested. "I dislike over-heated rooms." He continued to stand near the hearth. "The—the fact is, I was just noticing, before you came down, that this clock appears to be losing about five minutes a day; that is, supposing it to be wound on Sunday mornings."

"Oh, your Grace—would you come to our rescue? That clock has bothered Mrs. St George and Mrs. Elmsworth ever since we came here—"

But the Duke had already opened the glass case, and with his ear to the dial was sounding the clock as though it were a human lung. "Ah—I thought so!" he exclaimed in a tone of quiet triumph; and for several minutes he continued his delicate manipulations, watched attentively by Miss Testvalley, who thought: "If ever he nags his wife—and I should think he might be a nagger— she will only have to ask him what's wrong with the drawing-room clock. And how many clocks there must be, at Tintagel and Longlands and Folyat House!"

"There—but I'm afraid it ought to be sent to a professional," said the Duke modestly, taking the seat designated by Miss Testvalley.

"I'm sure it will be all right. Your Grace is so wonderful with clocks." The Duke was silent, and Miss Testvalley concluded that doctoring the time-piece had been prompted less by an irrepressible impulse than by the desire to put off weightier matters. "I'm so sorry," she said, "that there's no one here to receive you. I suppose the maid told you that our two ladies have taken a house in town for a few weeks, to prepare for Miss St George's wedding."

"Yes, I've heard of that," said the Duke, almost solemnly. He cast an anxious glance about him, as if in search of something; and Miss Testvalley thought proper to add: "And your young friend Annabel has gone to London with her sister."

"Ah—" said the Duke laboriously.

He stood up, walked back to the hearth, gazed at the passive face of the clock, and for a moment followed the smooth movement of the hands. Then he turned to Miss Testvalley. "The wedding is to take place soon?"

"Very soon; in about a month. Colonel St George naturally wants to be present, and business will take him back to New York before December. In fact, it was at first intended that the wedding should take place in New York—"

"Oh—" murmured the Duke, in the politely incredulous tone of one who implies: "Why attempt such an unheard-of experiment?"

Miss Testvalley caught his meaning and smiled. "You know Lord and Lady Richard were married in New York. It seems more natural that a girl should be married from her own home."

The Duke looked doubtful. "Have they the necessary churches?" he asked.

"Quite adequate," said Miss Testvalley drily.

There was another and heavier silence before the Duke continued: "And does Mrs. St George intend to remain in London, or will she take a house in the country?"

"Oh, neither. After the wedding Mrs. St George will go to her own house in New York. She will sail immediately with the Colonel."

"Immediately—" echoed the Duke. He hesitated. "And Miss Annabel—?"

"Naturally goes home with her parents. They wish her to have a season in New York."

This time the silence closed in so oppressively that it seemed as though it had literally buried her visitor. She felt an impulse to dig him out, but repressed it.

At length the Duke spoke in a hoarse unsteady voice. "It would be impossible for me—er—to undertake the journey to New York."

Miss Testvalley gave him an amused glance. "Oh, it's settled that Lord Seadown's wedding is to be in London."

"I—I don't mean Seadown's. I mean—my own," said the Duke. He stood up again, walked the length of the room, and came back to her. "You must have seen, Miss Testvalley... It has been a long struggle, but I've decided..."

"Yes?"

"To ask Miss Annabel St George—"

Miss Testvalley stood up also. Her heart was stirred

with an odd mixture of curiosity and sympathy. She really liked the Duke—but could Annabel ever be brought to like him?

"And so I came down today, in the hope of consulting with you—"

Miss Testvalley interrupted him. "Duke, I must remind you that arranging marriages for my pupils is not included in my duties. If you wish to speak to Mrs. St George—"

"But I don't!" exclaimed the Duke. He looked so startled that for a moment she thought he was about to turn and take flight. It would have been a relief to her if he had. But he coughed nervously, cleared his throat, and began again.

"I've always understood that in America it was the custom to speak first to the young lady herself. And knowing how fond you are of Miss St George, I merely wished to ask—"

"Yes, I am very fond of her," Miss Testvalley said gravely.

"Quite so. And I wished to ask if you had any idea whether her . . . her feelings in any degree corresponded with mine," faltered the anxious suitor.

Miss Testvalley pondered. What should she say? What could she say? What did she really wish to say? She could not, at the moment, have answered any of these questions; she knew only that, as life suddenly pressed closer to her charge, her impulse was to catch her fast and hold her tight.

"I can't reply to that, your Grace. I can only say that I don't know."

"You don't know?" repeated the Duke in surprise.

"Nan in some ways is still a child. She judges many things as a child would—"

"Yes! That's what I find so interesting . . . so unusual. . ."

"Exactly. But it makes your question unanswerable. How can one answer for a child who can't yet answer for herself?"

The Duke looked crestfallen. "But it's her childish innocence, her indifference to money and honours and—er—that kind of thing, that I value so immensely. . ."

"Yes. But you can hardly regard her as a rare piece for your collection."

"I don't know, Miss Testvalley, why you should accuse me of such ideas. . ."

"I don't accuse you, your Grace. I only want you to understand that Nan is one thing now, but may be another, quite different, thing in a year or two. Sensitive natures alter strangely after their first contact with life."

"Ah, but I should make it my business to shield her from every contact with life!"

"I'm sure you would. But what if Nan turned out to be a woman who didn't want to be shielded?"

The Duke's countenance expressed the most genuine dismay. "Not want to be shielded? I thought you were a friend of hers," he stammered.

"I am. A good friend, I hope. That's why I advise you to wait, to give her time to grow up."

The Duke looked at her with a hunted eye, and she suddenly thought: "Poor man! I daresay he's trying to marry her against some one else. Running away from the fatted heiress. . . But Nan's worth too much to be used as an alternative."

"To wait? But you say she's going back to the States immediately."

"Well, to wait till she returns to England. She probably will, you know."

"Oh, but I can't wait!" cried the Duke, in the astonished tone of the one who has never before been obliged to.

Miss Testvalley smiled. "I'm afraid you must say that to Annabel herself, not to me."

"I thought you were my friend. I hoped you'd advise me. . ."

"You don't want me to advise you, Duke. You want me to agree with you."

The Duke considered this for some time without speaking; then he said: "I suppose you've no objection to giving me the London address?" and the governess wrote it down for him with her same disciplined smile.

XVIII

To Sir Helmsley Thwarte, Bart.
Honourslove, Lowdon, Glos.

MY DEAR SIR HELMSLEY,

It seems an age since you have given Ushant and me the pleasure of figuring among the guns at Longlands; but I hope next month you will do us that favour.

You are, as you know, always a welcome guest; but I will not deny that this year I feel a special need for your presence. I suppose you have heard that Selina Brightlingsea's eldest boy is marrying an American—so that there will soon be two daughters-in-law of that nationality in the family. I make no comment beyond saying that I fail to see why the virtue and charms of our English girls are not sufficient to satisfy the hearts of our young men. It is useless, I suppose, to argue such matters with the interested parties; one can only hope that when experience has tested the more showy attractions of the young ladies from the States, the enduring qualities of our own daughters will re-assert themselves. Meanwhile I am selfishly glad that it is poor Selina, and not I, on whom such a trial has been imposed.

But to come to the point. You know Ushant's exceptionally high standards, especially in family matters, and will not be surprised to hear that he feels we ought to do our cousinly duty toward the Brightlingseas by inviting Seadown, his fiancée, and the latter's family (a Colonel and Mrs. St George, and a younger daughter), to Longlands. He says it would not matter half as much if Seadown were marrying one of our own kind; and though I do not quite fol-

349

low this argument, I respect it, as I do all my dear son's decisions. You see what is before me, therefore; and though you may not share Ushant's view, I hope your own family feeling will prompt you to come and help me out with all these strange people.

The shooting is especially good this year, and if you could manage to be with us from the 10th to the 18th of November, Ushant assures me the sport will be worthy of your gun.

Believe me

Yours very sincerely

BLANCHE TINTAGEL

Longlands House, November 15

To Guy Thwarte Esqre
Care of the British Consulate General
Rio Janeiro
(To be forwarded)

MY DEAR BOY,

Look on the above address and marvel! You who know how many years it is since I have allowed myself to be dragged into a Longlands shooting-party will wonder what can have caused me to succumb at last.

Well—queerly enough, a sense of duty! I have, as you know, my (rare) moments of self-examination and remorse. One of these penitential phases coincided with Blanche Tintagel's invitation, and as it was re-inforced by a moving appeal to my tribal loyalty, I thought I ought to respond, and I did. After all, Tintagel is our Duke, and Longlands is our Dukery, and we local people ought all to back each other up in subversive times like these.

The reason of Blanche's cry for help will amuse you. Do you remember, one afternoon just before you left for Brazil, having asked me to invite to Honourslove two American young ladies, friends of Lady Dick Marable's, who were staying at Allfriars? You were so urgent that my apprehensions were aroused; and I imagine rightly. But being soft-

350

hearted I yielded, and Lady Richard appeared with an enchantress, and the enchantress's younger sister, who seemed to me totally eclipsed by her elder, though you apparently thought otherwise. I've no doubt you will recall the incident.

Well—Seadown is to marry the beauty, a Miss St George, of New York. Rumours, of course, are rife about the circumstances of the marriage. Seadown is said to have been trapped by a clever manœuvre; but as this report probably emanates from Lady Churt—the Ariadne in the case—it need not be taken too seriously. We know that American business men are "smart", but we also know that their daughters are beautiful; and having seen the young lady who has supplanted Ariadne, I have no difficulty in believing that her "beaux yeux" sufficed to let Seadown out of prison—for friends and foes agree that the affair with the relentless Idina had become an imprisonment. They also say that Papa St George is very wealthy, and that consideration must be not without weight—its weight in gold—to the Brightlingseas. I hope they will not be disappointed, but as you know I am no great believer in transatlantic fortunes— though I trust, my dear fellow, that the one you are now amassing is beyond suspicion. Otherwise I should find it hard to forego your company much longer.

It's an odd chance that finds me in an atmosphere so different from that of our shabby old house, on the date fixed for the despatch of my monthly chronicle. But I don't want to miss the South American post, and it may amuse you to have a change from the ordinary small beer of Honourslove. Certainly the contrast is not without interest; and perhaps it strikes me the more because of my disintegrating habit of seeing things through other people's eyes, so that at this moment I am viewing Longlands, not as a familiar and respected monument, but as the unheard-of and incomprehensible phenomenon that a great English country-seat offers to the unprejudiced gaze of the American backwoodsman and his females. I refer to the St George party, who arrived the day before yesterday, and are still in the first flush of their bewilderment.

The Duchess and her daughters are of course no less bewildered. They have no conception of a society not based on aristocratic institutions, with Inveraray, Welbeck, Chatsworth, Longlands and so forth as its main supports; and their guests cannot grasp the meaning of such institutions or understand the hundreds of minute observances forming the texture of an old society. This has caused me, for the first time in my life, to see from the outside at once the absurdity and the impressiveness of our great ducal establishments, the futility of their domestic ceremonial, and their importance as custodians of historical tradition and of high (if narrow) social standards. My poor friend Blanche would faint if she knew that I had actually ventured to imagine what an England without Dukes might be, perhaps may soon be; but she would be restored to her senses if she knew that, after weighing the evidence for and against, I have decided that, having been afflicted with Dukes, we'd better keep 'em. I need hardly add that such problems do not trouble the St Georges, who have not yet reached the stage of investigating social origins.

I can't imagine how the Duchess and the other ladies deal with Mrs. St George and her daughters during the daily absence of the guns; but I have noticed that American young ladies cannot be kept quiet for an indefinite time by being shown views of Vesuvius and albums of family watercolours.

Luckily it's all right for the men. The shooting has never been better, and Seadown, who is in his element, has had the surprise of finding that his future father-in-law is not precisely out of his. Colonel St George is a good shot; and it is not the least part of the joke that he is decidedly bored by covert shooting, an institution as new to him as dukedoms, and doesn't understand how a man who respects himself can want to shoot otherwise than over a dog. But he accommodates himself well enough to our effete habits, and is in fact a big good-natured easy-going man, with a kind of florid good looks, too new clothes, and a collection of funny stories, some of which are not new enough.

As to the ladies, what shall I say? The beauty *is* a beauty, as I discovered (you may remember) the moment she appeared at Honourslove. She is precisely what she was then: the obvious, the finished exemplar, of what she professes to be. And, as you know, I have always had a preference for the icily regular. Her composure is unshakeable; and under a surface of American animation I imagine she is as passive as she looks. She giggles with the rest, and says: "Oh, girls", but on her lips such phrases acquire a classic cadence. I suspect her of having a strong will and knowing all the arts of exaction. She will probably get whatever she wants in life, and will give in return only her beautiful profile. I don't believe her soul has a full face. If I were in Seadown's place I should probably be as much in love with her as he is. As a rule I don't care for interesting women; I mean in the domestic relation. I prefer a fine figure-head embodying a beautiful form a solid bulk of usage and conformity. But I own that figure-heads lack conversation. . .

Your little friend is not deficient in this respect; and she is also agreeable to look upon. Not beautiful; but there is a subtler form of loveliness, which the unobservant confuse with beauty, and which this young Annabel is on the way to acquire. I say "on the way" because she is still a bundle of engaging possibilities rather than a finished picture. Of the mother there is nothing to say, for that excellent lady evidently requires familiar surroundings to bring out such small individuality as she possesses. In the unfamiliar she becomes invisible; and Longlands and she will never be visible to each other.

Most amusing of all is to watch our good Blanche, her faithful daughters, and her other guests, struggling with the strange beings suddenly thrust upon them. Your little friend (the only one with whom one can converse, by the way) told me that when Lady Brightlingsea heard of Dick

Marable's engagement to the Brazilian beauty she cabled
to the St Georges' governess: "Is she black?" Well, the attitude of Longlands toward its transatlantic guests is not
much more enlightened than Selina Brightlingsea's. Their
bewilderment is so great that, when one of the girls spoke
of archery clubs being fashionable in the States, somebody
blurted out: "I suppose the Indians taught you?"; and I am
constantly expecting them to ask Mrs. St George how she
heats her wigwam in winter.

The only exceptions are Seadown, who contributes little
beyond a mute adoration of the beauty, and—our host,
young Tintagel. Strange to say, he seems curiously alert and
informed about his American visitors; so much so that I'm
wondering if his including them in the party is due only to
a cousinly regard for Seadown. My short study of the case
has almost convinced me that his motives are more interested. His mother, of course, has no suspicion of this—when
did our Blanche ever begin to suspect anything until it was
emblazoned across the heavens? The first thing she said to
me (in explaining the presence of the St Georges) was that,
since so many of our young eligibles were beginning to make
these mad American marriages, she thought that Tintagel
should see a few specimens at close quarters. *Sancta sim-
plicitas!* If this is her object, I fear the specimens are not
well-chosen. I suspect that Tintagel had them invited because he's very nearly, if not quite, in love with the younger
girl, and being a sincere believer in the importance of
Dukes, wants her family to see what marriage with an English Duke means.

How far the St Georges are aware of all this, I can't say.
The only one I suspect of suspecting it is the young Annabel; but these Americans, under their forth-coming manner,
their surface-gush, as some might call it, have an odd
reticence about what goes on underneath. At any rate the
young lady seems to understand something of her environ-
ment, which is a sealed book to the others. She has been
better educated than her sister, and has a more receptive

mind. It seems as though some one had sown in a bare field a sprinkling of history, poetry and pictures, and every seed had shot up in a flowery tangle. I fancy the sower is the little brown governess of whom you spoke (her pupil says she is little and brown). Miss Annabel asks so many questions about English life in town and country, about rules, customs, traditions, and their why and wherefore, that I sometimes wonder if she is not preparing for a leading part on the social stage; then a glimpse of utter simplicity dispels the idea, and I remember that all her country-people are merciless questioners, and conclude that she has the national habit, but exercises it more intelligently than the others. She is intensely interested in the history of this house, and has an emotional sense at least of its beauties; perhaps the little governess—that odd descendant of old Testavaglia's—has had a hand in developing this side also of her pupil's intelligence.

Miss Annabel seems to be devoted to this Miss Testvalley, who is staying on with the family though both girls are out, and one on the brink of marriage, and who is apparently their guide in the world of fashion—odd as such a rôle seems for an Italian revolutionary. But I understood she had learned her way about the great world as governess in the Brightlingsea and Tintagel households. Her pupil, by the way, tells me that Miss Testvalley knows all about the circumstances in which my D. G. Rossetti was painted, and knows also the mysterious replica with variants which is still in D.G.'s possession, and which he has never been willing to show me. The girl, the afternoon she came to Honourslove, apparently looked closely enough at my picture to describe it in detail to her governess, who says that in the replica the embroidered border of the cloak is *peach-coloured* instead of blue. . .

All this has stirred up the old collector in me, and when the St Georges go to Allfriars, where they have been asked to stay before the wedding, Miss Annabel has promised to try to have the governess invited, and to bring her to

Honourslove to see the picture. What a pity you won't be there to welcome them! The girl's account of the Testavaglia and her family excites my curiosity almost as much as this report about the border of the cloak.

After the above, which reads, I flatter myself, not unlike a page of Saint Simon, the home chronicle will seem tamer than ever. Mrs. Bolt has again upset everything in my study by having it dusted. The chestnut mare has foaled, and we're getting on with the ploughing. We are having too much rain—but when haven't we too much rain in England? The new grocer at Little Ausprey threatens to leave, because he says his wife and the non-conformist minister—but there, you always pretend to hate village scandals, and as I have, for the moment, none of my own to tempt your jaded palate, I will end this confession of an impenitent but blameless parent.

Your aff^{te}

H.T.

P.S. The good Blanche asked anxiously about you—your health, plans and prospects, the probable date of your return; and I told her I would give a good deal to know myself. Do you suppose she has her eye on you for Ermie or Almina? Seadown's defection was a hard blow; and if I'm right about Tintagel, Heaven help her!

BOOK III

XIX

THE windows of the Correggio room at Longlands overlooked what was known as the Duchess's private garden, a floral masterpiece designed by the great Sir Joseph Paxton, of Chatsworth and Crystal Palace fame. Beyond an elaborate cast-iron fountain swarmed over by chaste divinities, and surrounded by stars and crescents of bedding plants, an archway in the wall of yew and holly led down a grass avenue to the autumnal distances of the home park. Mist shrouded the slopes dotted with mighty trees, the bare woodlands, the lake pallidly reflecting a low uncertain sky. Deer flitted spectrally from glade to glade, and on remoter hill-sides blurred clusters of sheep and cattle were faintly visible. It had rained heavily in the morning, it would doubtless rain again before night; and in the Correggio room the drip of water sounded intermittently from the long reaches of roof-gutter and from the creepers against the many-windowed house-front.

The Duchess, at the window, stood gazing out over what seemed a measureless perspective of rain-sodden acres. Then, with a sigh, she turned back to the writing-table and took up her pen. A sheet of paper lay before her, carefully inscribed in a small precise hand:

To a Dowager Duchess.
To a Duchess.
To a Marchioness.

THE BUCCANEERS

To the wife of a Cabinet Minister who has no rank
   by birth.
To the wife of a Bishop.
To an Ambassador.

The page was inscribed: "Important", and under each
head-line was a brief formula for beginning and ending
a letter. The Duchess scrutinized this paper attentively;
then she glanced over another paper bearing a list of
names, and finally, with a sigh, took from a tall mahogany stand a sheet of note-paper with "Longlands
House" engraved in gold under a ducal coronet, and
began to write.

After each note she struck a pencil line through one
of the names on the list, and then began another note.
Each was short, but she wrote slowly, almost laboriously,
like a conscientious child copying out an exercise; and
at the bottom of the sheet she inscribed her name, after
assuring herself once more that the formula preceding
her signature corresponded with the instructions before
her. At length she reached the last note, verified the
formula, and for the twentieth time wrote out underneath: "Annabel Tintagel".

There before her, in orderly sequence, lay the invitations to the first big shooting-party of the season at
Longlands, and she threw down her pen with another
sigh. For a minute or two she sat with her elbows on the
desk, her face in her hands; then she uncovered her eyes,
and looked again at the note she had just signed.

"Annabel Tintagel," she said slowly: "who *is* Annabel
Tintagel?"

The question was one which she had put to herself

more than once during the last months, and the answer was always the same: she did not know. Annabel Tintagel was a strange figure with whom she lived, and whose actions she watched with a cold curiosity, but with whom she had never arrived at terms of intimacy, and never would. Of that she was now sure.

There was another perplexing thing about her situation. She was now, to all appearances, Annabel Tintagel, and had been so for over two years; but before that she had been Annabel St George, and the figure of Annabel St George, her face and voice, her likes and dislikes, her memories and moods, all that made up her tremulous little identity, though still at the new Annabel's side, no longer composed the central Annabel, the being with whom this strange new Annabel of the Correggio room at Longlands, and the Duchess's private garden, felt herself really one. There were moments when the vain hunt for her real self became so perplexing and disheartening that she was glad to escape from it into the mechanical duties of her new life. But in the intervals she continued to grope for herself, and to find no one.

To begin with, what had caused Annabel St George to turn into Annabel Tintagel? That was the central problem! Yet how could she solve it, when she could no longer question that elusive Annabel St George, who was still so near to her, yet as remote and unapproachable as a plaintive ghost?

Yes—a ghost. That was it. Annabel St George was dead, and Annabel Tintagel did not know how to question the dead, and would therefore never be able to find out why and how that mysterious change had come about. . .

"The greatest mistake," she mused, her chin resting on her clasped hands, her eyes fixed unseeingly on the dim reaches of the park, "the greatest mistake is to think that we ever know why we do things. . . I suppose the nearest we can ever come to it is by getting what old people call 'experience'. But by the time we've got that we're no longer the persons who did the things we no longer understand. The trouble is, I suppose, that we change every moment; and the things we did stay."

Of course she could have found plenty of external reasons; a succession of incidents, leading, as a trail leads across a desert, from one point to another of the original Annabel's career. But what was the use of recapitulating these points, when she was no longer the Annabel whom they had led to this splendid and lonely room set in the endless acres of Longlands?

The curious thing was that her uncertainty and confusion of mind seemed to have communicated themselves to the new world into which she found herself transplanted—and that she was aware of the fact. "They don't know what to make of me, and why should they, when I don't know what to make of myself?" she had once said, in an unusual burst of confidence, to her sister Virginia, who had never really understood her confidences, and who had absently rejoined, studying herself while she spoke in her sister's monumental cheval glass, and critically pinching her waist between thumb and fore-finger: "My dear, I've never yet met an Englishman or an Englishwoman who didn't know what to make of a Duchess, if only they had the chance to try. The trouble is you don't give them the chance."

Yes; Annabel supposed it was that. Fashionable London had assimilated with surprising rapidity the lovely transatlantic invaders. Hostesses who only two years ago would have shuddered at the clink of tall glasses and the rattle of cards, now threw their doors open to poker-parties, and offered intoxicating drinks to those to whom the new-fangled afternoon tea seemed too reminiscent of the school-room. Hands trained to draw from a Broadwood the dulcet cadences of "La Sonnambula" now thrummed the banjo to "Juanita" or "The Swanee River". Girls, and even young matrons, pinned up their skirts to compete with the young men in the new game of lawn-tennis on lordly lawns, smoking was spreading from the precincts reserved for it to dining-room and library (it was even rumoured that "the Americans" took sly whiffs in their bedrooms!), Lady Seadown was said to be getting up an amateur nigger-minstrel performance for the Christmas party at Allfriars, and as for the wild games introduced into country-house parties, there was no denying that, even after a hard day's hunting or shooting, they could tear the men from their after-dinner torpor.

A blast of outer air had freshened the stagnant atmosphere of Belgravian drawing-rooms, and while some sections of London society still shuddered (or affected to shudder) at "the Americans", others, and the uppermost among them, openly applauded and imitated them. But in both groups the young Duchess of Tintagel remained a figure apart. The Dowager Duchess spoke of her as "my perfect daughter-in-law", but praise from the Dowager Duchess had about as much zest as a Sunday-school diploma. In the circle where the pace was set by Conchita Marable, Virginia Seadown and Lizzy Elmsworth (now married to the brilliant young Conservative member of Parliament, Mr. Hector Robinson), the circle to which, by kinship and early associations, Annabel belonged, she was as much a stranger as in the straitest fastnesses of the peerage. "Annabel has really managed," Conchita drawled with her slow smile, "to be considered unfashionable among the unfashionable—" and the phrase clung to the young Duchess, and catalogued her once for all.

One side of her loved, as much as the others did, dancing, dressing up, midnight romps, practical jokes played on the pompous and elderly; but the other side, the side which had dominated her since her arrival in England, was passionately in earnest and beset with vague dreams and ambitions, in which a desire to better the world alternated with a longing for solitude and poetry.

If her husband could have kept her company in either of these regions she might not have given a thought to the rest of mankind. But in the realm of poetry the Duke had never willingly risked himself since he had handed up his Vale at Eton, and a great English nobleman of his generation could hardly conceive that he had anything to learn regarding the management of his estates from a little American girl whose father appeared to be a cross between a stock-broker and a professional gambler, and whom he had married chiefly because she seemed too young and timid to have any opinions on any subject whatever.

"The great thing is that I shall be able to form her," he had said to his mother, on the dreadful day when he had broken the news of his engagement to the horrified Duchess; and the Duchess had replied, with a flash of unwonted insight: "You're very skilful, Ushant; but women are not quite as simple as clocks."

As simple as clocks. How like a woman to say that! The Duke smiled. "Some clocks are not at all simple," he said with an air of superior knowledge.

"Neither are some women," his mother rejoined; but there both thought it prudent to let the discussion drop.

Annabel stood up and looked about the room. It was large and luxurious, with walls of dark green velvet framed in heavily carved and gilded oak. Everything about its decoration and furnishings—the towering malachite vases, the ponderous writing-table supported on winged geniuses in ormolu, the heavily foliaged wall-lights, the Landseer portrait, above the monumental chimney-piece, of her husband as a baby, playing with an elder sister in a tartan sash—all testified to a sumptuous "re-doing", doubtless dating from the day when the present Dowager had at last presented her lord with an heir. A stupid oppressive room—somebody else's room, not Annabel's... But on three of the velvet-panelled walls hung the famous Correggios; in the half-dusk of an English November they were like rents in the clouds, tunnels of radiance reaching to pure sapphire distances. Annabel looked at the golden limbs, the parted lips gleaming with laughter, the abandonment of young bodies under shimmering foliage. On dark days—and there were many—these pictures were her sunlight. She speculated about them, wove stories around them, and hung them with snatches of verse from Miss Testvalley's poet-cousin. How was it they went?

Beyond all depth away
The heat lies silent at the brink of day:
Now the hand trails upon the viol-string
That sobs, and the brown faces cease to sing,
Sad with the whole of pleasure.

Were there such beings anywhere, she wondered, save in the dreams of poets and painters, such landscapes, such sunlight? The Correggio room had always been the reigning Duchess's private boudoir, and at first it had surprised Annabel that her mother-in-law should live surrounded by scenes before which Mrs. St George would have veiled her face. But gradually she understood that in a world as solidly buttressed as the Dowager Duchess's by precedents, institutions and traditions, it would have seemed far more subversive to displace the pictures than to hear the children's Sunday-school lessons under the laughter of those happy pagans. The Correggio room had always been the Duchess's boudoir, and the Correggios had always hung there. "It has always been like that," was the Dowager's invariable answer to any suggestion of change; and she had conscientiously brought up her son in the same creed.

Though she had been married for over two years it

was for her first big party at Longlands that the new Duchess was preparing. The first months after her marriage had been spent at Tintagel, in a solitude deeply disapproved of by the Duke's mother, who for the second time found herself powerless to influence her son. The Duke gave himself up with a sort of dogged abandonment to the long dreamed-of delights of solitude and domestic bliss. The ducal couple (as the Dowager discovered with dismay, on her first visit to them) lived like any middle-class husband and wife, tucked away in a wing of the majestic pile where two butlers and ten footmen should have been drawn up behind the dinner-table, and a groom-of-the-chambers have received the guests in the great hall. Groom-of-the-chambers, butlers and footmen had all been relegated to Longlands, and to his mother's dismay only two or three personal servants supplemented the understudies who had hitherto sufficed for Tintagel's simple needs on his trips to Cornwall.

Even after their return to London and Longlands the young couple continued to disturb the Dowager Duchess's peace of mind. The most careful and patient initiation into the functions of the servants attending on her had not kept Annabel from committing what seemed to her mother-in-law inexcusable, perhaps deliberate blunders; such as asking the groom-of-the-chambers to fetch her a glass of water, or bidding one of the under house-maids to lace up her dinner-dress when her own maid was accidentally out of hearing.

"It's not that she's *stupid*, you know, my dear," the Dowager avowed to her old friend Miss Jacky March, "but she puts one out, asking the reason of things that have nothing to do with reasons—such as why the housekeeper doesn't take her meals with the upper servants, but only comes in for dessert. What would happen next, as I said to her, in a house where the housekeeper *did* take her meals with the upper servants? That sort of possibility never occurs to the poor child; yet I really can't call her stupid. I often find her with a book in her hand. I think she thinks too much about things that oughtn't to be thought about," wailed the bewildered Duchess. "And the worst of it is that dear Ushant doesn't seem to know how to help her . . ." her tone implying that, in any case, such a task should not have been laid on him. And Miss Jacky March murmured her sympathy.

XX

THOSE quiet months in Cornwall, which already seemed so much more remote from the actual Annabel than her girlhood at Saratoga, had been of her own choosing. She did not admit to herself that her first sight of the ruins of the ancient Tintagel had played a large part in her wooing; that if the Duke had been only the dullest among the amiable but dull young men who came to the bungalow at Runnymede she would hardly have given him a second thought. But the idea of living in that magic castle by the sad western sea had secretly tinged her vision of the castle's owner; and she had thought that he and she might get to know each other more readily there than anywhere else. And now, in looking back, she asked herself if it were not her own fault that the weeks at Tintagel had not brought the expected understanding. Instead, as she now saw, they had only made husband and wife more unintelligible to each other. To Annabel, the Cornish castle spoke with that rich low murmur of the past which she had first heard in its mysterious intensity the night when she had lain awake in the tapestried chamber at Allfriars, beside the sleeping Virginia, who had noticed only that the room was cold and shabby. Though the walls of Tintagel were relatively new, they were built on ancient foundations, and crowded with the treasures of the past; and near by was the mere of

Excalibur, and from her windows she could see the dark gray sea, and sometimes, at night-fall, the mysterious barge with black sails putting out from the ruined castle to carry the dead King to Avalon.

Of all this, nothing existed for her husband. He saw the new Tintagel only as a costly folly of his father's, which family pride obliged him to keep up with fitting state, in spite of the unfruitful acres that made its maintenance so difficult. In shouldering these cares, however, he did not expect his wife to help him, save by looking her part as a beautiful and angelically pure young Duchess, whose only duties consisted in bestowing her angelic presence on entertainments for the tenantry and agricultural prize-givings. The Duke had grown up under the iron rod of a mother who, during his minority, had managed not only his property, but his very life, and he had no idea of letting her authority pass to his wife. Much as he dreaded the duties belonging to his great rank, deeply as he was oppressed by them, he was determined to perform them himself, were it ever so hesitatingly and painfully, and not to be guided by any one else's suggestions.

To his surprise such suggestions were not slow in coming from Annabel. She had not yet learned that she was expected to remain a lovely and adoring looker-on, and in her daily drives over the estate (in the smart pony-chaise with its burnished trappings and gay piebald ponies) she often, out of sheer loneliness, stopped for a chat at toll-gates, farm-houses and cottages, made purchases at the village shops, scattered toys and lollipops among the children, and tried to find out from their mothers what she could do to help them. It had filled her with wonder to learn that for miles around, both at Longlands and Tintagel, all these people in the quaint damp cottages and the stuffy little shops were her husband's tenants and dependents; that he had the naming of the rectors and vicars of a dozen churches, and that even the old men and women in the mouldy almshouses were there by virtue of his bounty. But when she had grasped the extent of his power it seemed to her that to help and befriend those who depended on him was the best service she could render him. Nothing in her early bringing-up had directed her mind toward any kind of organized beneficence, but she had always been what she called "sorry for people", and it seemed to her that there was a good deal to be sorry about in the lot of these people who depended solely, in health and sickness, on a rich man's whim.

The discovery that her interest in them was distasteful to the Duke came to her as a great shock, and left a wound that did not heal. Coming in one day, a few months after their marriage, from one of her exploring expeditions, she was told that his Grace wished to speak to her in his study, and she went in eagerly, glad to seize the chance of telling him at once about the evidences of neglect and poverty she had come upon that very afternoon.

"Oh, Ushant, I'm so glad you're in! Could you come with me at once to the Linfrys' cottage, down by St Gildas's; you know, that damp place under the bridge, with the front covered with roses? The eldest boy's down with typhoid, and the drains ought to be seen to at once if all the younger ones are not to get it." She spoke in haste, too much engrossed in what she had to say to notice the Duke's expression. It was his silence that roused her; and when she looked at him she saw that his face wore what she called its bolted look—the look she most disliked to see on it. He sat silent, twisting an ivory paper-cutter between his fingers.

"May I ask who told you this?" he said at length, in a voice like his mother's when she was rebuking an upper house-maid.

"Why, I found it out myself. I've just come from there."

The Duke stood up, knocking the paper-cutter to the floor.

"You've been there? Yourself? To a house where you tell me there is typhoid fever? In your state of health? I confess, Annabel—" His lips twitched nervously under his scanty blond moustache.

"Oh, bother my state of health! I feel all right, really I do. And you know the doctors have ordered me to walk and drive every day."

"But not go and sit with Mrs. Linfry's sick children, in a house reeking with disease."

"But, Ushant, I just had to ! There was no one else to see about them. And if the house reeks with disease, whose fault is it but ours? They've no sick-nurse, and nobody to help the mother, or tell her what to do; and the doctor comes only every other day."

"Is it your idea, my dear, that I should provide every cottage on my estates, here and elsewhere, with a hospital nurse?" the Duke asked ironically.

"Well, I wish you would! At least there ought to be

a nurse in every village, and two in the bigger ones; and the doctor ought to see his patients every day; and the drains— Ushant, you must come with me *at once* and smell the drains!" cried Nan in a passion of entreaty.

She felt the Duke's inexpressive eyes fixed coldly on her.

"If your intention is to introduce typhoid fever at Tintagel, I can imagine no better way of going about it," he began. "But perhaps you don't realize that, though it may not be as contagious as typhus, the doctors are by no means sure. . ."

"Oh, but they *are* sure; only ask them! Typhoid comes from bad drains and infected milk. It can't hurt you in the least to go down and see what's happening at the Linfrys'; and you ought to, because they're your own tenants. Won't you come with me now? The ponies are not a bit tired, and I told William to wait—"

"I wish you would not call Armson by his Christian name; I've already told you that in England head grooms are called by their surnames."

"Oh, Ushant, what *can* it matter? I call you by your surname, but I never can remember about the others. And the only thing that matters now. . ."

The Duke walked to the hearth, and pulled the embroidered bell-rope beside the chimney. To the footman who appeared he said: "Please tell Armson that her Grace will not require the pony-chaise any longer this afternoon."

"But—" Annabel burst out; then she stood silent till the door closed on the servant. The Duke remained silent also.

"Is that your answer?" she asked at length, her breath coming quickly.

He lifted a more friendly face. "My dear child, don't look so tragic. I'll see Blair; he shall look into the drains. But do try to remember that these small matters concern my agent more than they do me, and that they don't concern you at all. My mother was very much esteemed and respected at Tintagel, but though she managed my affairs so wisely, it never occurred to her to interfere directly with the agent's business, except as regards Christmas festivities, and the annual school-treat. Her holding herself aloof increased the respect that was felt for her; and my wife could not do better than to follow her example."

Annabel stood staring at her husband without speaking. She was too young to understand the manifold inhibitions, some inherited, some peculiar to his own character, which made it impossible for him to act promptly and spontaneously; but she knew him to be by nature not an unkind man, and this increased her bewilderment.

Suddenly a flood of words burst from her. "You tell me to be careful about my health in the very same breath that you say you can't be bothered about these poor people, and that their child's dying is a small matter, to be looked after by the agent. It's for the sake of your own child that you forbid me to go to see them— but I tell you I don't want a child if he's to be brought up with such ideas, if he's to be taught, as you have been, that it's right and natural to live in a palace with fifty servants, and not care for the people who are slav·

ing for him on his own land, to make his big income bigger! I'd rather be dead than see a child of mine taught to grow up as—as you have!"

She broke down and dropped into a seat, hiding her face in her hands. Her husband looked at her without speaking. Nothing in his past experience had prepared him for such a scene, and the consciousness that he did not know how to deal with it increased his irritation. Had Annabel gone mad—or was it only what the doctors called her "condition"? In either case he felt equally incapable of resolute and dignified action. Of course, if he were told that it was necessary, owing to her "condition", he would send these Linfrys—a shiftless lot— money and food, would ask the doctor to see the boy oftener; though it went hard with him to swallow his own words, and find himself again under a woman's orders. At any rate, he must try to propitiate Annabel, to get her into a more amenable mood; and as soon as possible must take her back to Longlands, where she would be nearer a London physician, accustomed to bringing Dukes into the world.

"Annabel," he said, going up to her, and laying his hand on her bent head.

She started to her feet. "Let me alone," she exclaimed, and brushed past him to the door. He heard her cross the hall and go up the stairs in the direction of her own rooms; then he turned back to his desk. One of the drawing-room clocks stood there before him, disembowelled; and as he began (with hands that still shook a little) to put it cautiously together, he remembered his mother's comment: "Women are not always as simple as clocks." Had she been right?

After a while he laid aside the works of the clock and sat staring helplessly before him. Then it occurred to him that Annabel, in her present mood, was quite capable of going contrary to his orders, and sending for a carriage to drive her back to the Linfrys'—or Heaven knew where. He rang again, and asked for his own servant. When the man came the Duke confided to him that her Grace was in a somewhat nervous state, and that the doctors wished her to be kept quiet, and not to drive out again that afternoon. Would Bowman therefore see the head coachman at once, and explain that, even if her Grace should ask for a carriage, some excuse must be found . . . they were not, of course, to say anything to implicate the Duke, but it must be so managed that her Grace should not be able to drive out again that day.

Bowman acquiesced, with the look of respectful compassion which his face often wore when he was charged with his master's involved and embarrassed instructions; and the Duke, left alone, continued to sit idly at his writing-table.

Annabel did not re-appear that afternoon; and when the Duke, on his way up to dress for dinner, knocked at her sitting-room door, she was not there. He went on to his own dressing-room, but on the way met his wife's maid, and asked if her Grace were already dressing.

"Oh, no, your Grace. I thought the Duchess was with your Grace. . ."

A little chill caught him about the heart. It was nearly

eight o'clock, for they dined late at Tintagel; and the maid had not yet seen her mistress! The Duke said with affected composure: "Her Grace was tired this afternoon. She may have fallen asleep in the drawing-room—" though he could imagine nothing less like the alert and restless Annabel.

Oh, no, the maid said again; her Grace had gone out on foot two or three hours ago, and had not yet returned.

"On foot?"

"Yes, your Grace. Her Grace asked for her pony-carriage; but I understood there were orders—"

The Duke interrupted irritably: "The doctor's orders were that her Grace should not go out at all today."

The maid lowered her lids as if to hide her incredulous eyes, and he felt that she was probably acquainted with every detail of the day's happenings. The thought sent the blood up to the roots of his pale hair, and he challenged her nervously. "You must at least know which way her Grace said she was going."

"The Duchess said nothing to me, your Grace. But I understand she sent to the stables, and finding she could not have a carriage walked away through the park."

"That will do . . . there's been some unfortunate misunderstanding about her Grace's orders," stammered the Duke, turning away to his dressing-room.

The day had been raw and cloudy, and with the dusk rain had begun, and was coming down now in a heavy pour that echoed through the narrow twisting passages of the castle and made their sky-lights rattle. And in this icy down-pour his wife, his Duchess, the expectant mother of future Dukes, was wandering somewhere on foot, alone and unprotected. Anger and alarm contended in the Duke. If any one had told him that marrying a simple unworldly girl, hardly out of the school-room, would add fresh complications to a life already overburdened with them, he would have scoffed at the idea. Certainly he had done nothing to deserve such a fate. And he wondered now why he had been so eager to bring it upon himself. Though he had married for love only a few months before, he was now far more concerned with Annabel as the mother of his son than for her own sake. The first weeks with her had been very sweet—but since then her presence in his house had seemed only to increase his daily problems and bothers. The Duke rang and ordered Bowman to send to the stables for the station-brougham, and when it arrived he drove down at break-neck speed to the Linfrys' cottage. But Nan was not there. The Duke stared at Mrs. Linfry blankly. He did not know where to go next, and it mortified him to reveal his distress and uncertainty to the coachman. "Home!" he ordered angrily, getting into the carriage again; and the dark drive began once more. He was half way back when the carriage stopped with a jerk, and the coachman, scrambling down from the box, called to him in a queer frightened voice.

The Duke jumped out and saw the man lifting a small dripping figure into the brougham. "By the mercy of God, your Grace... I think the Duchess has fainted..."

"Drive like the devil... stop at the stables to send a groom for the doctor," stammered the Duke, pressing his wife in his arms. The rest of the way back was as indistinct to him as to the girl who lay so white on his breast. Bowed over her in anguish, he remembered nothing till the carriage drove under the echoing gate-tower at Tintagel, and lights and servants pressed confusedly about them. He lifted Annabel out, and she opened her eyes and took a few steps alone across the hall. "Oh—am I here again?" she said, with a little laugh; then she swayed forward, and he caught her as she fell...

To the Duchess of Tintagel who was signing the last notes of invitation for the Longlands shooting-party, the scene at Tintagel and what had followed now seemed as remote and legendary as the tales that clung about the old ruins of Arthur's castle. Annabel had put herself hopelessly in the wrong. She had understood it without being told, she had acknowledged it and wept over it at the time; but the irremediable had been done, and she knew that never, in her husband's eyes, would any evidence of repentance atone for that night's disaster.

The miscarriage which had resulted from her mad expedition through the storm had robbed the Duke of a son; of that he was convinced. He, the Duke of Tintagel, wanted a son, he had a right to expect a son, he would have had a son, if this woman's criminal folly had not destroyed his hopes. The physicians summoned in consultation spoke of the necessity of many months of repose... even they did not seem to understand that a Duke must have an heir, that it is the purpose for which Dukes make the troublesome effort of marrying.

It was now more than a year since that had happened, and after long weeks of illness a new Annabel—a third Annabel—had emerged from the ordeal. Life had somehow, as the months passed, clumsily re-adjusted itself. As far as words went, the Duke had forgiven his wife; they had left the solitude of Tintagel as soon as the physicians thought it possible for the Duchess to be moved; and now, in their crowded London life, and at Longlands, where the Dowager had seen to it that all the old ceremonial was re-established, the ducal pair were too busy, too deeply involved in the incessant distractions and obligations of their station, to have time to remember what was over and could not be mended.

But Annabel gradually learned that it was not only one's self that changed. The ceaseless mysterious flow of days wore down and altered the shape of the people nearest one, so that one seemed fated to be always a stranger among strangers. The mere fact, for instance, of Annabel St George's becoming Annabel Tintagel had turned her mother-in-law, the Duchess of Tintagel, into a Dowager Duchess, over whose diminished head the mighty roof of Longlands had shrunk into the modest shelter of a lovely little rose-clad dower-house at the gates of the park. And every one else, as far as Annabel's world reached, seemed to have changed in the same way.

That, at times, was the most perplexing part of it. When, for instance, the new Annabel tried to think herself back on to the verandah of the Grand Union Hotel, waiting for her father and his stock-broker friends to return from the races, or in the hotel ball-room with the red damask curtains, dancing with her sister, with Conchita Closson and the Elmsworth girls, or with the obscure and infrequent young men who now and then turned up to partner their wasted loveliness—when she thought, for instance, of Roy Gilling, and the handkerchief she had dropped, and he had kissed and hidden in his pocket—it was like looking at the flickering figures of the magic lanterns she used to see at children's parties. What was left, now, of those uncertain apparitions, and what relation, say, did the Conchita Closson who had once seemed so ethereal and elusive, bear to Lady Dick Marable, beautiful still, though she was growing rather too stout, but who had lost her lovely indolence and detachment, and was now perpetually preoccupied about money, and immersed in domestic difficulties and clandestine consolations; or to Virginia, her own sister Virginia, who had seemed to Annabel so secure, so aloof, so disdainful of everything but her own pleasures, but who, as Lady Seadown, was enslaved to that dull half-asleep Seadown, absorbed in questions of rank and precedence, and in awe—actually in awe—of her father-in-law's stupid arrogance, and of Lady Brightlingsea's bewildered condescensions?

Yes; changed, every one of them, vanished out of recognition, as the lost Annabel of the Grand Union had vanished. As she looked about her, the only figures which seemed to have preserved their former outline were those of her father and his business friends; but that, perhaps, was because she so seldom saw them, because when they appeared, at long intervals, for a hurried look at transatlantic daughters and grandchildren, they brought New York with them, solidly and loudly, remained jovially unconscious of any change of scene and habits greater than that between the east and west shores of the Hudson, and hurried away again, leaving behind them cheques and christening mugs, and unaware to the last that they had been farther from Wall Street than across the ferry.

Ah, yes—and Laura Testvalley, her darling old Val! She too had remained her firm sharp-edged self. But then she too was usually away, she had not suffered the erosion of daily contact. The real break with the vanished Annabel had come, the new Annabel sometimes thought, when Miss Testvalley, her task at the St Georges' ended, had vanished into the seclusion of another family which required "finishing". Miss Testvalley, since she had kissed the bride after the great Tintagel wedding, nearly three years ago, had re-appeared only at long intervals, and as it were under protest. It was one of her principles—as she had often told Annabel —that a governess should not hang about her former pupils. Later they might require her—there was no knowing, her subtle smile implied; but once the school-room was closed, she should vanish with the tattered lesson-books, the dreary school-room food, the cod-liver oil and the chilblain cures.

Perhaps, Annabel thought, if her beloved Val had remained with her, they might between them have rescued the old Annabel, or at least kept up communications with her ghost—a faint tap now and then against the walls which had built themselves up about the new Duchess. But as it was, there was the new Duchess isolated in her new world, no longer able to reach back to her past, and not having yet learned how to communicate with her present.

She roused herself from these vain musings, and took

up her pen. A final glance at the list had shown her that one invitation had been forgotten—or, if not forgotten, at least postponed.

DEAR MR. THWARTE,

The Duke tells me you have lately come back to England, and he hopes so much that you can come to Longlands for our next shooting-party, on the 18th. He asks me to say that he is anxious to have a talk with you about the situation at Lowdon. He hopes you intend to stand if Sir Hercules Loft is obliged to resign, and wishes you to know that you will have his full support.

Yours sincerely
ANNABEL TINTAGEL

Underneath she added: "P.S. Perhaps you'd remember me if I signed Nan St George." But what was the sense of that, when there was no longer any one of that name? She tore the note up, and re-wrote it without adding the postscript.

XXI

GUY THWARTE had not been back at Honourslove long enough to expect a heavy mail beside
his breakfast plate. His four years in Brazil had cut him
off more completely than he had realized from his
former life; and he was still in the somewhat painful
stage of picking up the threads.

"Only one letter? Lucky devil, I envy you!" grumbled
Sir Helmsley, taking his seat at the other end of the
table and impatiently pushing aside a stack of newspapers, circulars and letters.

The young man glanced with a smile at his father's
correspondence. He knew so well of what it consisted:
innumerable bills, dunning letters, urgent communications from book-makers, tradesmen, the chairman of political committees or art-exhibitions, scented notes from
enamoured ladies, or letters surmounted by mysterious
symbols from astrologers, palmists or alchemists—for Sir
Helmsley had dabbled in most of the arts, and bent
above most of the mysteries. But today, as usual, his son
observed, the bills and the dunning letters predomi-
nated. Guy would have to put some order into that; and
probably into the scented letters too.

"Yes, I'm between two worlds yet—'powerless to be
born' kind of feeling," he said as he took up the solitary
note beside his own plate. The writing was unknown to
him, and he opened the envelope with indifference.

"Oh, my dear fellow—don't say that; don't say 'power-less'," his father rejoined, half-pleadingly, but with a laugh. "There's such a lot waiting to be done; we all expect you to put your hand to the plough without losing a minute. I was lunching at Longlands the other day and had a long talk with Ushant. With old Sir Hercules Loft in his dotage for the last year, there's likely to be a vacancy at Lowdon at any minute, and the Duke's anxious to have you look over the ground without losing any time, especially as that new millionaire from Glasgow is said to have some chance of getting in."

"Oh, well—" Guy was glancing over his letter while his father spoke. He knew Sir Helmsley's great desire was to see him in the House of Commons, an ambition hitherto curbed by the father's reduced fortune, but brought into the foreground again since the son's return from exile with a substantial bank account.

Guy looked up from his letter. "Tintagel's been talking to you about it, I see."

"You see? Why—has he written to you already?"

"No. But she has. The new American Duchess—the little girl I brought here once, you remember?" He handed the letter to his father, whose face expressed a growing satisfaction as he read.

"Well—that makes it plain sailing. You'll go to Longlands, of course?"

"To Longlands?" Guy hesitated. "I don't know. I'm not sure I want to."

"But if Tintagel wants to see you about the seat? You ought to look over the ground. There may not be much time to lose."

"Not if I'm going to stand—certainly."

"*If!*" shouted Sir Helmsley, bringing down his fist with a crash that set the Crown Derby cups dancing. "Is that what you're not sure of? I thought we were agreed before you went away that it was time there was a Thwarte again in the House of Commons."

"Oh—before I went away," Guy murmured. His father's challenge, calling him back suddenly to his old life, the traditional life of a Thwarte of Honourslove, had shown him for the first time how far from it all he had travelled in the last years, how remote had become the old sense of inherited obligations which had once seemed the very marrow of his bones.

"Now you've made your pile, as they say out there," Sir Helmsley continued, attempting a lighter tone, but unable to disguise his pride in the incredible fact of his son's achievement—a Thwarte who had made money!— "now that you've made your pile, isn't it time to think of a career? In my simplicity, I imagined it was one of your principal reasons for exiling yourself."

"Yes; I suppose it was," Guy acquiesced.

After this, for a while, father and son faced one another in silence across the breakfast-table, each, as is the way of the sensitive, over-conscious of the other's thoughts. Guy, knowing so acutely what was expected of him, was vainly struggling to become again the young man who had left England four years earlier; but strive as he would he could not yet fit himself into his place in the old scheme of things. The truth was, he was no longer the Guy Thwarte of four years ago, and would probably never recover that lost self. The break had been too violent, the disrupting influences too powerful. Those dark rich stormy years of exile lay like a raging channel between himself and his old life, and his father's summons only drove him back upon himself.

"You'll have to give me time, sir—I seem to be on both sides of the globe at once," he muttered at length with bent head.

Sir Helmsley stood up abruptly, and walking around the table laid a hand on his son's shoulder. "My dear fellow, I'm so sorry. It seems so natural to have you back that I'd forgotten the roots you've struck over there... I'd forgotten the grave..."

Guy's eyes darkened, and he nodded. "All right, sir..." He stood up also. "I think I'll take a turn about the stables." He put the letter from Longlands into his pocket, and walked out alone onto the terrace. As he stood there, looking out over the bare November landscape, and the soft blue hills fading into a low sky, the sense of kinship between himself and the soil began to creep through him once more. What a power there was in these accumulated associations, all so low-pitched, soft and unobtrusive, yet which were already insinuating themselves through his stormy Brazilian years, and sapping them of their reality! He felt himself becoming again the school-boy who used to go nutting in the hazel-copses of the Red Farm, who fished and bathed in the dark pools of the Love, stole nectarines from the walled gardens, and went cub-hunting in the autumn dawn with his father, glorying in Sir Helmsley's horsemanship, and racked with laughter at his jokes—the school-boy whose heart used to beat to bursting at that bend of the road from the station where you first sighted the fluted chimney-stacks of Honourslove.

He walked across the terrace, and turning the flank of the house passed under the sculptured lintel of the chapel. A smell of autumn rose from the cold paving, where the kneeling Thwartes elbowed each other on the narrow floor, and under the recumbent effigies the pillows almost mingled their stony fringes. How many there were, and how faithfully hand had joined hand in the endless work of enlarging and defending the family acres! Guy's glance travelled slowly down the double line, from the armoured effigy of the old fighting Thwarte who had built the chapel to the Thornycroft image of his own mother, draped in her marble slumber, just as the boy had seen her, lying with drawn lids, on the morning when his father's telegram had called him back from Eton. How many there were—and all these graves belonged to him, all were linked to the same soil and to one another in an old community of land and blood; together for all time, and kept warm by each other's nearness. And that far-off grave which also belonged to him—the one to which his father had alluded —how remote and lonely it was, off there under tropic skies, among other graves that were all strange to him!

He sat down and rested his face against the back of the bench in front of him. The sight of his mother's grave had called up that of his young Brazilian wife, and he wanted to shut out for a moment all those crowding Thwartes, and stand again beside her far-off headstone. What would life at Honourslove have been if he had brought Paquita home with him instead of leaving her among the dazzling white graves at Rio? He sat for a long time, thinking, remembering, trying to strip his mind of conventions and face the hard reality underneath. It was inconceivable to him now that, in the first months of his marriage, he had actually dreamed of severing all ties with home, and beginning life anew as a Brazilian mine-owner. He saw that what he had taken for a slowly matured decision had been no more than a passionate impulse; and its resemblance to his father's headlong experiments startled him as he looked back. His mad marriage had nearly deflected the line of his life—for a little pale face with ebony hair and curving black lashes he would have sold his birth-right. And long before the black lashes had been drawn down over the quiet eyes he had known that he had come to the end of that adventure...

All his life, and especially since his mother's death, Guy Thwarte had been fighting against his admiration for his father, and telling himself that it was his duty to be as little like him as possible; yet more than once he had acted exactly as Sir Helmsley would have acted, or snatched himself back just in time. But in Brazil he had not been in time...

"One brilliant man's enough in a family," he said to himself as he stood up and left the chapel.

Forgetting his projected visit to the stables, he turned back to the house, and crossing the hall, opened the door of his father's study. There he found Sir Helmsley seated at his easel, re-touching a delicately drawn water-colour copy of the little Rossetti Madonna above his desk. Sir Helmsley, whose own work was incurably amateurish, excelled in the art of copying, or rather interpreting, the work of others; and his water-colour glowed with the deep brilliance of the original picture.

As his son entered he laid down his palette with an embarrassed laugh. "Well, what do you think of it—eh?"

"Beautiful. I'm glad you've not given up your painting."

"Eh—? Oh, well, I don't do much of it nowadays. But I'd promised this little thing to Miss Testvalley," the baronet stammered, reddening handsomely above his auburn beard.

Guy echoed, bewildered: "Miss Testvalley?"

Sir Helmsley coughed and cleared his throat. "That governess, you know—or perhaps you don't. She was with the little new Duchess of Tintagel before her marriage; came here with her one day to see my Rossettis. She's Dante Gabriel's cousin; didn't I tell you? Remarkable woman—one of the few relations the poet is always willing to see. She persuaded him to sell me a first study of the 'Bocca Baciata', and I was doing this as a way of thanking her. She's with Augusta Glenloe's girls; I see her occasionally when I go over there."

Sir Helsmley imparted this information in a loud, almost challenging voice, as he always did when he had to communicate anything unexpected or difficult to account for. Explaining was a nuisance, and somewhat of a derogation. He resented anything that made it necessary, and always spoke as if his interlocutor ought to have known beforehand the answer to the questions he was putting.

After his bad fall in the hunting-field, the year before

Guy's return from Brazil, the county had confidently
expected that the lonely widower would make an end
by marrying either his hospital nurse or the Gaiety girl
who had brightened his solitude during his son's absence. One or the other of these conclusions to a career
over-populated by the fair sex appeared inevitable in
the case of a brilliant and unsteady widower. Coroneted
heads had been frequently shaken over what seemed a
foregone conclusion; and Guy had shared these fears.
And behold, on his return, he found the nurse gone, the
Gaiety girl expensively pensioned off, and the baronet,
slightly lame, but with youth renewed by six months of
enforced seclusion, apparently absorbed in a little brown
governess who wore violet poplin and heavy brooches of
Roman mosaic, but who (as Guy was soon to observe)
had eyes like torches, and masses of curly-edged dark
hair which she was beginning to braid less tightly, and to
drag back less severely from her broad forehead.

Guy stood looking curiously at his father. The latter's
bluster no longer disturbed him; but he was uncomfortably reminded of certain occasions when Sir Helmsley, on the brink of an imprudent investment or an
impossible marriage, had blushed and explained with
the same volubility. Could this outbreak be caused by
one of the same reasons? But no! A middle-aged governess? It was unthinkable. Sir Helmsley had always
abhorred the edifying, especially in petticoats; and with
his strong well-knit figure, his handsome auburn head,
and a complexion clear enough for blushes, he still
seemed, in spite of his accident, built for more alluring
prey. His real interest, Guy concluded, was no doubt in

the Rossetti kinship, and all that it offered to his insatiable imagination. But it made the son wonder anew what other mischief his inflammable parent had been up to during his own long absence. It would clearly be part of his business to look into his father's sentimental history, and keep a sharp eye on his future. With these thoughts in his mind, Guy stood smiling down paternally on his father.

"Well, sir, it's all right," he said. "I've thought it over, and I'll go to Longlands; when the time comes I'll stand for Lowdon."

His father returned the look with something filial and obedient in his glance. "My dear fellow, it's all right indeed. That's what I've always expected of you."

Guy wandered out again, drawn back to the soil of Honourslove as a sailor is drawn to the sea. He would have liked to go over all its acres by himself, yard by yard, inch by inch, filling his eyes with the soft slumbrous beauty, his hands with the feel of wrinkled treeboles, the roughness of sodden autumnal turf, his nostrils with the wine-like smell of dead leaves. The place was swathed in folds of funereal mist shot with watery sunshine, and he thought of all the quiet women who had paced the stones of the terrace on autumn days, worked over the simple-garden and among the roses, or sat in the oak parlour at their accounts or their needle-work, speaking little, thinking much, dumb and nourishing as the heaps of faded leaves which mulched the soil for coming seasons.

The "little Duchess's" note had evoked no very clear

memory when he first read it; but as he wandered down the glen through the fading heath and bracken he suddenly recalled their walk along the same path in its summer fragrance, and how they had stayed alone on the terrace when the rest of the party followed Sir Helmsley through the house. They had leaned side by side on the balustrade, he remembered, looking out over that dear scene, and speaking scarcely a word; and yet, when she had gone, he knew how near they had been... He even remembered thinking, as his steamer put out from the docks at Liverpool, that on the way home, after he had done his job in Brazil, he would stop a few days in New York to see her. And then he had heard—with wonder and incredulity—the rumour of her ducal marriage; a rumour speedily confirmed by letters and newspapers from home.

That girl—and Tintagel! She had given Guy the momentary sense of being the finest instrument he had ever had in his hand; an instrument from which, when the time came, he might draw unearthly music. Not that he had ever seriously considered the possibility of trying his chance with her; but he had wanted to keep her image in his heart, as something once glimpsed, and giving him the measure of his dreams. And now it was poor little Tintagel who was to waken those melodies; if indeed he could! For a few weeks after the news came it had blackened Guy's horizon; but he was far away, he was engrossed in labours and pleasures so remote from his earlier life that the girl's pale image had become etherealized, and then had faded out of existence. He sat down on the balustrade of the terrace, in the corner where they had stood together, and pulling out her little note, re-read it.

"The writing of a school-girl . . . and the language of dictation," he thought; and the idea vaguely annoyed him. "How on earth could she have married Tintagel? That girl! . . . One would think from the wording of her note that she'd never seen me before. . . She might at least have reminded me that she'd been here. But perhaps she'd forgotten—as I had!" he ended with a laugh and a shrug. And he turned back slowly to the house, where the estate agent was awaiting him with bills and estimates, and long lists of repairs. Already Sir Helmsley had slipped that burden from his shoulders.

XXII

WHEN their Graces were in residence at Longlands the Dowager did not often come up from the dower-house by the gate. But she had the awful gift of omnipresence, of exercising her influence from a distance; so that while the old family friends and visitors at Longlands said: "It's wonderful, how tactful Blanche is—how she keeps out of the young people's way," every member of the household, from its master to the last boots and scullion and gardener's boy, knew that her Grace's eye was on them all, and the machinery of the tremendous establishment still moving in obedience to the pace and pattern she had set.

But at Christmas the Dowager naturally could not remain aloof. If she had not participated in the Christmas festivities the county would have wondered, the servants gossiped, the tradesmen have thought the end of the world had come.

"I hope you'll do your best to persuade my mother to come next week. You know she thinks you don't like her," Tintagel had said to his wife, a few days before Christmas.

"Oh, why?" Nan protested, blushing guiltily; and of course she had obediently persuaded, and the Duchess had responded by her usual dry jerk of acquiescence.

For the same reason, the new Duchess's family, and her American friends, had also to be invited; or at least so the Duke thought. The Dowager was not of the same mind; but thirty years of dealings with her son ("from his birth the most obstinate baby in the world,") had taught her when to give way; and she did so now.

"It does seem odd, though, Ushant's wanting all those strange people here for Christmas," she confided to her friend Miss March, who had come up with her from the dower-house, "for I understand the Americans make nothing of any of our religious festivals—do they?"

Miss March, who could not forget that she was the daughter of a clergyman of the Episcopal Church of America, protested gently, as she so often had before: "Oh, but, Duchess, that depends, you know; in our church the feasts and observances are exactly the same as in yours. . ." But what, she reflected, have such people as the St Georges to do with the Episcopal Church? They might be Seventh Day Baptists, or even Mormons, for all she knew.

"Well, it's very odd," murmured the Dowager, who was no longer listening to her.

The two ladies had seated themselves after dinner on a wide Jacobean settee at one end of the "double-cube" saloon, the great room with the Thornhill ceiling and the Mortlake tapestries. The floor had been cleared of rugs and furniture—another shock this to the Dowager, but also accepted with her small stiff smile—and down the middle of the polished *parquet* spun a long line of young (and some more than middle-aged) dancers, led, of course, by Lady Dick Marable and her odd Brazilian brother, whose name the Dowager could never remember, but who looked so dreadfully like an Italian hair-dresser. (A girl who had been a close friend of the Dowager's youth had rent society asunder by breaking her engagement to a young officer in the Blues, and running away with her Italian hair-dresser; and when the Dowager's eyes had first rested on Teddy de Santos-Dios she had thought with a shudder: *"Poor Florrie's man must have looked like that."*)

Close in Lady Dick's wake (and obviously more interested in her than in his partner) came Miles Dawnly, piloting a bewildered Brightlingsea girl. It was the custom to invite Dawnly wherever Conchita was invited; and even strait-laced hostesses, who had to have Lady Dick because she "amused the men", were so thankful not to be obliged to invite her husband that they were glad enough to let Dawnly replace him. Every one knew that he was Lady Dick's chosen attendant, but every one found it convenient to ignore the fact, especially as Dawnly's own standing, and his fame as a dancer and a shot, had long since made him a welcome guest.

The Dowager had always thought it a pity that a man with such charming manners, and an assured political future, should seem in no hurry to choose a wife; but when she saw that he had taken for his partner a Marable rather than a Folyat, she observed tartly to Miss March that she did not suppose Mr. Dawnly would ever marry, and hoped Selina Brightlingsea had no illusions on that point.

At the farther end of the great saloon, the odd little Italian governess who used to be at Longlands with the Duchess's younger daughters, and was now "finishing" the Glenloe girls, sat at the piano rattling off a noisy reel which she was said to have learnt in the States; and down the floor whirled the dancers, in pursuit of Lady Richard and the Brazilian.

"Virginia reel, you say they call it? It's all so unusual," repeated the Dowager, lifting her long-handled eye-glass to study the gyrations of the troop.

Yes; it certainly was unusual to see old Lord Brightlingsea pirouetting heavily in the wake of his beautiful daughter-in-law Lady Seadown, and Sir Helmsley Thwarte, incapacitated for pirouetting since his hunting accident, standing near the piano, clapping his hands and stamping his sound foot in time with Lady Dick's Negro chant—they said it was Negro. All so very unusual, especially when associated with Christmas. . . Usually that noisy sort of singing was left to the waits, wasn't it? But under this new rule the Dowager's enquiring eye-glass was really a window opening into an unknown world—a world in whose reality she could not bring herself to believe. "Ushant might better have left me down at the dower-house," she murmured with a strained smile to Miss March.

"Oh, Duchess, don't say that! See how they're all enjoying themselves," replied her friend, wondering, deep down under the old Mechlin which draped her bosom, whether Lord Brightlingsea, when the dance swept him close to her sofa, might not pause before her with his inimitable majesty, lift her to her feet, and carry her off into the reel whose familiar rhythm she felt even now running up from her trim ankles. . . But Lord Brightlingsea pounded past her unseeingly. . . Certainly, as men grew older, mere youth seemed to cast a stronger spell over them; the fact had not escaped Miss March.

Lady Brightlingsea was approaching the Dowager's sofa, bearing down on her obliquely and hesitatingly, like a sailing-vessel trying to make a harbour-mouth on a windless day.

"Do come and sit with us, Selina dear," the Dowager welcomed her. "No, no, don't run away, Jacky... Jacky," she explained, "has been telling me about this odd American dance, which seems to amuse them all so much."

"Oh, yes, do tell us," exclaimed Lady Brightlingsea, coming to anchor between the two. "It's called the Virginia reel, isn't it? I thought it was named after my daughter-in-law—Seadown's wife is called Virginia, you know. But she says no: she used to dance it as a child. It's an odd coincidence, isn't it?"

The Dowager was always irritated by Lady Brightlingsea's vagueness. She said, in her precise tone: "Oh, no, it's a very old dance. The Wild Indians taught it to the Americans, didn't they, Jacky?"

"Well, I'm sure it's wild enough," Lady Brightlingsea murmured, remembering the scantily clad savages in the great tapestry at Allfriars, and thankful that the dancers had not so completely unclothed themselves—though the *décolletage* of the young American ladies went some way in that direction.

Miss March roused herself to reply, with a certain impatience. "But no, Duchess; this dance is not Indian. The early English colonists brought it with them from England to Virginia—Virginia was one of the earliest

English colonies (called after the Virgin Queen, you know), and the Virginia reel is just an old English or Scottish dance."

The Dowager never greatly cared to have her statements corrected; and she particularly disliked its being done before Selina Brightlingsea, whose perpetual misapprehensions were a standing joke with everybody.

"I daresay there are two theories. I was certainly told it was a Wild Indian war-dance."

"It seems much more likely; such a very odd performance," Lady Brightlingsea acquiesced; but neither lady cared to hazard herself farther on the unknown ground of American customs.

"It's like their *valse*—that's very odd too," the Dowager continued, after a silence during which she had tried in vain to think up a new topic.

"The *valse?* Oh, but surely the *valse* is familiar enough. My girls were all taught it as a matter of course—weren't yours? I can't think why it shocked our grandparents, can you?"

The Dowager narrowed her lips. "Not *our* version, certainly. But this American *valse*—'waltz' I think they call it there—"

"Oh, is it different? I hadn't noticed, except that I don't think the young ladies carry themselves with quite as much dignity as ours."

"I should say not! How can they, when every two minutes they have to be prepared to be turned upside down by their partners?"

"*Upside down?*" echoed Lady Brightlingsea, in startled

italics. "What in the world, Blanche, do you mean by *upside down?*"

"Well, I mean—not exactly, of course. But turned round. Surely you must have noticed? Suddenly whizzed around and made to dance backward. Jacky, what is it they call it in the States?"

"Reversing," said Miss March, between dry lips. She felt suddenly weary of hearing her compatriots discussed and criticized and having to explain them; perhaps because she had had to do it too often.

"Ah—'reversing'. Such a strange word too. I don't think it's English. But the thing itself is so strange—suddenly pushing your partner backward. I can't help thinking it's a little indelicate."

The dowager, with reviving interest, rejoined: "Don't you think these new fashions make all the dances seem —er—rather indelicate? When crinolines were worn the movements were not as—as visible as now. These tight skirts, with the gathers up the middle of the front—of course one can't contend against the fashion. But one can at least not exaggerate it, as they appear to do in America."

"Yes—I'm afraid they exaggerate everything in America... My dear," Lady Brightlingsea suddenly interrupted herself, "what in the world can they be going to do next?"

The two long rows facing each other (ladies on one side of the room, gentlemen opposite) had now broken up, and two by two, in dancing pairs, forming a sort of giant caterpillar, were spinning off down the double-cube saloon and all the length of the Waterloo room

401

adjoining it, and the Raphael drawing-room beyond, in the direction of the Classical Sculpture gallery.

"Oh, my dear, where *can* they be going?" Lady Brightlingsea cried.

The three ladies, irresistibly drawn by the unusual sight, rose together and advanced to the middle of the Raphael drawing-room. From there they could see the wild train, headed by Lady Dick's rhythmic chant, sweeping ahead of them down the length of the Sculpture gallery, back again to the domed marble hall which formed the axis of the house, and up the state staircase to the floor above.

"My dear—my dear Jacky," gasped Lady Brightlingsea.

"They'll be going into the bedrooms next, I suppose," said the Dowager with a dry laugh.

But Miss March was beyond speech. She had remembered that the fear of being late for dinner, and the agitation she always felt on great occasions, had caused her to leave on her dressing-table the duplicate set of fluffy curls which should have been locked up with her modest cosmetics. And in the course of this mad flight Lord Brightlingsea might penetrate to her bedroom, and one of those impious girls might cry out: "Oh, look at Jacky March's curls on her dressing-table!" She felt too faint to speak...

Down the upper gallery spun the accelerated reel, song and laughter growing louder to the accompaniment of hurrying feet. Teddy de Santos-Dios had started "John Peel", and one hunting song followed on another in rollicking chorus. Door after door was flung open, whirled through, and passed out of again, as the train pursued its turbulent way. Now and then a couple fell out, panting and laughing, to rejoin the line again when it coiled back upon itself—but the Duchess and Guy Thwarte did not rejoin it.

Annabel had sunk down on a bench at the door of the Correggio room. Guy Thwarte stood at her side, leaning against the wall and looking down at her. He thought how becomingly the dance had flushed her cheeks and tossed her hair. "Poor little thing! Fun and laughter are all she needs to make her lovely—but how is she ever to get them, at Longlands and Tintagel?" he thought.

The door of the Correggio room stood wide as the dance swept on, and he glanced in, and saw the candle-lit walls, and the sunset glow of the pictures. "By Jove! There are the Correggios!"

Annabel stood up. "You know them, I suppose?"

"Well, rather—but I'd forgotten they were in here."

"In my sitting-room. Come and look. They're so mysterious in this faint light."

He followed her, and stood before the pictures, his blood beating high, as it always did at the sight of beauty.

"It sounds funny," he murmured, "to call the Earthly Paradise a sitting-room."

"I thought so too. But it's always been the Duchess's sitting-room."

"Ah, yes. And that 'always been'—." He smiled and broke off, turning away from her to move slowly about from picture to picture. In the pale amber candle-glow they seemed full of mystery, as though withdrawn into their own native world of sylvan loves and revels; and for a while he too was absorbed into that world, and almost unconscious of his companion's presence. When at last he turned he saw that her face had lost the glow of the dance, and become small and wistful, as he had seen it on the day of his arrival at Longlands.

"You're right. They're even more magical than by daylight."

"Yes. I often come here when it's getting dark, and sit among them without making a sound. Perhaps some day, if I'm very patient, I'll tame them, and they'll come down to me. . ."

Guy Thwarte stood looking at her. "Now what on earth," he thought, "does Tintagel do when she says a thing like that to him?"

"They must make up to you for a great deal," he began imprudently, heedless of what he was saying.

"For a good deal—yes. But it's rather lonely sometimes, when the only things that seem real are one's dreams."

The young man flushed up, and made a movement toward her. Then he paused, and looked at the pictures with a vague laugh. She was only a child, he reminded himself—she didn't measure what she was saying.

"Oh, well, you'll go to *them,* some day, in their Italian palaces."

"I don't think so. Ushant doesn't care for travelling."

"How does he know? He's never been out of England," broke from Guy impatiently.

"That doesn't matter. He says all the other places

are foreign. And he hates anything foreign. There are lots of things he's never done that he feels quite sure he'd hate."

Guy was silent. Again he seemed to himself to be eaves-dropping—unintentionally leading her on to say more than she meant; and the idea troubled him.

He turned back to his study of the pictures. "Has it ever occurred to you," he began again after a pause, "that to enjoy them in their real beauty—"

"I ought to persuade Ushant to send them back where they belong?"

"I didn't mean anything so drastic. But did it never occur to you that if you had the courage to sweep away all those . . . those touching little—er . . . family mementoes—" His gesture ranged across the closely covered walls, from illuminated views of Vesuvius in action to landscapes by the Dowager Duchess's great-aunts, funereal monuments worked in hair on faded silk, and photographs in heavy oak frames of ducal relatives, famous race-horses, Bishops in lawn sleeves, and undergraduates grouped about sporting trophies.

Annabel coloured, but with amusement, not annoyance. "Yes; it did occur to me; and one day I smuggled in a ladder and took them all down—every one."

"By jove, you did? It must have been glorious."

"Yes; that was the trouble. The Duchess—"

She broke off, and he interposed, with an ironic lift to the brows: "But you're the Duchess."

"Not the real one. You must have seen that already. I don't know my part yet, and I don't believe I ever shall. And my mother-in-law was so shocked that every single picture I'd taken down had to be put back the same day."

"Ah, that's natural too. We're built like that in this tight little island. We fight like tigers against change, and then one fine day accept it without arguing. You'll see: Ushant will come round, and then his mother will, because he has. It's only a question of time—and luckily you've plenty of that ahead of you." He looked at her as he spoke, conscious that he was not keeping the admiration out of his eyes, or the pity either, as he had meant to.

Her own eyes darkened, and she glanced away. "Yes; there's plenty of time. Years and years of it." Her voice dragged on the word, as if in imagination she were struggling through the long desert reaches of her own future.

"You don't complain of that, do you?"

"I don't know; I can't tell. I'm not as sure as Ushant how I shall feel about things I've never tried. But I've tried this—and I sometimes think I wasn't meant for it. . ." She broke off, and he saw the tears in her eyes.

"My dear child—" he began; and then, half-embarrassed: "For you *are* a child still, you know. Have you any idea how awfully young you are?"

As soon as he had spoken he reflected that she was too young not to resent any allusion to her inexperience. She laughed. "Please don't send me back to the nursery! 'Little girls shouldn't ask questions. You'll understand better when you're grown up'. . . How much longer am I to be talked to like that?"

"I'm afraid that's the most troublesome question of all. The truth is—" He hesitated. "I rather think grow-

ing up's largely a question of climate—of sunshine. . .
Perhaps our moral climate's too chilly for you young
creatures from across the globe. After all, New York's
in the latitude of Naples."

She gave him a perplexed look, and then smiled. "Oh,
I know—those burning hot summers. . ."

"You want so much to go back to them?"

"Do I? I can't tell. . . I don't believe so. . . But somehow it seems as if this were wrong—my being here. . .
If you knew what I'd give to be able to try again . . .
somewhere where I could be myself, you understand, not
just an unsuccessful Duchess. . ."

"Yes; I do understand—"

"Annabel!" a voice called from the threshold, and
Miss Testvalley stood before them, her small brown
face full of discernment and resolution.

"My dear, the Duke's asking for you. Your guests are
beginning to leave, and I must be off with Lady Glenloe
and my girls." Miss Testvalley, with a nod and a smile
at young Thwarte, had linked her arm through Annabel's. She paused a moment on the threshold. "Wasn't I
right, Mr. Thwarte, to insist on your coming up with
us to see the Correggios? I told the Duke it was my
doing. They're wonderful by candle-light. But I'm afraid
we ought not to have carried off our hostess from her
duties."

Laughing and talking, the three descended together
to the great hall, where the departing guests were assembled.

XXIII

THE house-party at Longlands was not to break up for another week; but the morning after the Christmas festivities such general lassitude prevailed that the long galleries and great drawing-rooms remained deserted till luncheon.

The Dowager Duchess had promised her son not to return to the dower-house until the day after Boxing Day. By that time, it was presumed, the new Duchess would be sufficiently familiar with the part she had to play; but meanwhile a vigilant eye was certainly needed, if only to regulate the disorganized household service.

"These Americans appear to keep such strange hours; and they ask for such odd things to be sent to their rooms—such odd things to eat and drink. Things that Boulamine has never even heard of. It's just as well, I suppose, that I should be here to keep him and Mrs. Gillings and Manning from losing their heads," said the Dowager to her son, who had come to her sitting-room before joining the guns, who were setting out late on the morning after the dance (thereby again painfully dislocating the domestic routine).

The Duke made no direct answer to his mother's comment. "Of course you must stay," he said, in a sullen tone, and without looking at her.

The Duchess pursed up her lips. "There's nothing I wouldn't do to oblige you, Ushant; but last night I really felt for a moment—well, rather out of place; and so, I think, did Selina Brightlingsea."

The Duke was gazing steadily at a spot on the wall above his mother's head. "We must move with the times," he remarked sententiously.

"Well—we were certainly doing that last night. Moving faster than the times, I should have thought. At least almost all of us. I believe you didn't participate. But Annabel—"

"Annabel is very young," her son interrupted.

"Don't think that I forget that. It's quite natural that she should join in one of her native dances... I understand they're very much given to these peculiar dances in the States."

"I don't know," said the Duke coldly.

"Only I should have preferred that, having once joined the dancers, she should have remained with them, instead of obliging people to go hunting all over the house for her and her partner—Guy Thwarte, wasn't it? I admit that hearing her name screamed up and down the passages, and in and out of the bedrooms... when she ought naturally to have been at her post in the Raphael room... where I have always stood when a party was breaking up..."

The Duke twisted his fingers nervously about his watch-chain. "Perhaps you could tell her," he suggested.

The Dowager's little eyes narrowed doubtfully. "Don't you think, Ushant, a word from *you*—?"

He glanced at his watch. "I must be off to join the guns... No, decidedly—I'd rather you explained... make her understand..."

His hand on the door, he turned back. "I want, just at present, to say nothing that could ... could in any way put her off..." The door closed, and his mother stood staring blankly after him. That chit—and he was afraid of—what did he call it? "Putting her off"? Was it possible that he did not know his rights? In the Dowager's day, the obligations of a wife—more especially the wife of a Duke—had been as clear as the Ten Commandments. She must give her husband at least two sons, and if in fulfillment of this duty a dozen daughters came uninvited, must receive them with suitably maternal sentiments, and see that they were properly clothed and educated. The Duchess of Tintagel had considered herself lucky in having only eight daughters, but had grieved over Nature's inexorable resolve to grant her no second son.

"Ushant must have two sons—three, if possible. But his wife doesn't seem to understand her duties. Yet she has only to look into the prayer-book ... but I've never been able to find out to what denomination her family belong. Not Church people, evidently, or these tiresome explanations would be unnecessary..."

After an interval of uneasy cogitation the Dowager rang, and sent to enquire if her daughter-in-law could receive her. The reply was that the Duchess was still asleep (at midday—the Dowager, all her life, had been called at a quarter to seven!), but that as soon as she rang she should be given her Grace's message.

The Dowager, with a sigh, turned back to her desk, which was piled, as usual, with a heavy correspondence. If only Ushant had listened to her, had chosen an English wife in his own class, there would probably have been two babies in the nursery by this time, and a third on the way. And none of the rowdy galloping in and out of people's bedrooms at two in the morning. Ah, if sons ever listened to their mothers...

The luncheon hour was approaching when there was a knock on the Dowager's door and Annabel entered. The older woman scrutinized her attentively. No—it was past understanding! If the girl had been a beauty one could, with a great effort of the imagination, have pictured Ushant's infatuation, his subjection; but this pale creature with brown hair and insignificant features, without height, or carriage, or that look of authority given by inherited dignities even to the squat and the round—what right had she to such consideration? Yet it was clear that she was already getting the upper hand of her husband.

"My dear—do come in. Sit here; you'll be more comfortable. I hope," continued the Dowager with a significant smile, as she pushed forward a deep easy-chair, "that we shall soon have to be asking you to take care of yourself... not to commit any fresh imprudence—"

Annabel, ignoring the suggestion, pulled up a straight-backed chair, and seated herself opposite her mother-in-law. "I'm not at all tired," she declared.

"Not consciously, perhaps... But all that wild dancing last night—and in fact into the small hours... must have been very exhausting..."

"Oh, I've had a good sleep since. It's nearly luncheon-time, isn't it?"

"Not quite. And I so seldom have a chance of saying

a word to you alone that I ... I want to tell you how much I hope, and Ushant hopes, that you won't run any more risks. I know it's not always easy to remember; but last night, for instance, from every point of view, it might have been better if you had remained at your post." The Dowager forced a stiff smile. "Duchesses, you know, are like soldiers; they must often be under arms while others are amusing themselves. And when your guests were leaving, Ushant was naturally—er—surprised at having to hunt over the house for you. . ."

Annabel looked at her thoughtfully. "Did he ask you to tell me so?"

"No; but he thinks you don't realize how odd it must have seemed to your guests that, in a middle of a party, you should have taken Mr. Thwarte upstairs to your sitting-room—"

"But we didn't go on purpose. We were following the reel, and I dropped out because I was tired; and as Mr. Thwarte wanted to see the Correggios I took him in."

"That's the point, my dear. Guy Thwarte ought to have known better than to take you away from your guests and go up to your sitting-room with you after midnight. His doing so was—er—tactless, to say the least. I don't know what your customs are in the States, but in England—" the Dowager broke off, as if waiting for an interruption which did not come.

Annabel remained silent, and her mother-in-law continued with gathering firmness: "In England such behaviour might be rather severely judged."

Annabel's eyes widened, and she stood up with a slight

smile. "I think I'm tired of trying to be English," she pronounced.

The Dowager rose also, drawing herself up to her full height. "Trying to be? But you *are* English. When you became my son's wife you acquired his nationality. Nothing can change that now."

"Nothing?"

"Nothing. Remember what you promised in the marriage service. 'To love and to obey—till death us do part.' Those are words not to be lightly spoken."

"No; but I think I did speak them lightly. I made a mistake."

"A mistake, my dear? What mistake?"

Annabel drew a quick breath. "Marrying Ushant," she said.

The Dowager received this with a gasp. "My dear Annabel—"

"I think it might be better if I left him; then he could marry somebody else, and have a lot of children. Wouldn't that be best?" Annabel continued hurriedly.

The Dowager, rigid with dismay, stood erect, her strong plump hands grasping the rim of her writing-table. Words of wrath and indignation, scornful annihilating phrases, rushed to her lips, but were checked by her son's warning. "I want to do nothing to put her off." If Ushant said that, he meant it; meant, poor misguided fellow, that he was still in love with this thankless girl, this chit, this barren upstart, and that his mother, though authorized to coax her back into the right path, was on no account to drive her there by threats or reproaches.

But the mother's heart spoke louder than she meant it to. "If you can talk of your own feelings in that way, even in jest, do you take no account of Ushant's?"

Annabel looked at her musingly. "I don't think Ushant has very strong feelings—about me, I mean."

The Dowager rejoined with some bitterness: "You have hardly encouraged him to, have you?"

"I don't know—I can't explain...I've told Ushant that I don't think I want to be a mother of Dukes."

"You should have thought of that before becoming the wife of one. According to English law you are bound to obey your husband implicitly in...er...all such matters...But, Annabel, we mustn't let our talk end in a dispute. My son would be very grieved if he thought I'd said anything to offend you—and I've not meant to. All I want is your happiness and his. In the first years of marriage things don't always go as smoothly as they might, and the advice of an older woman may be helpful. Marriage may not be all roses—especially at first; but I know Ushant's great wish is to see you happy and contented in the lot he has offered you—a lot, my dear, that most young women would envy," the Dowager concluded, lifting her head with an air of wounded majesty.

"Oh, I know; that's why I'm so sorry for my mistake."

"Your mistake? But there's been no mistake. Your taking Guy Thwarte up to your sitting-room was quite as much his fault as yours; and you need only show him, by a slightly more distant manner, that he is not to misinterpret it. I daresay less importance is attached to such things in your country—where there are no Dukes, of course..."

"No! That's why I'd better go back there," burst from Annabel.

The Dowager stared at her in incredulous wrath. Really, it was beyond her powers of self-control to listen smilingly to such impertinence—such blasphemy, she had almost called it. Ushant himself must stamp out this senseless rebellion...

At that moment the luncheon-gong sent its pompous call down the corridors, and at the sound the Dowager, hurriedly composing her countenance, passed a shaking hand over her neatly waved *bandeaux*. "The gong, my dear! You must not keep your guests waiting... I'll follow you at once..."

Annabel turned obediently to the door, and went down to join the assembled ladies, and the few men who were not out with the guns.

Her heart was beating high after the agitation of her talk with her mother-in-law, but as she descended the wide shallow steps of the great staircase (up and down which it would have been a profanation to gallop, as one used to up and down the steep narrow stairs at home) she reflected that the Dowager, though extremely angry, and even scandalized, had instantly put an end to their discussion when she heard the summons to luncheon. Annabel remembered the endless wordy wrangles between her mother, her sister and herself, and thought how little heed they would have paid to a luncheon-gong in the thick of one of their daily disputes. Here it was different: everything was done by rule, and according to tradition, and for the Duchess of Tintagel to keep her guests waiting for luncheon would have been an offence against the conventions almost as great as that of not being at her post when the company were leaving the night before. A year ago Annabel would have laughed at these rules and observances: now, though they chafed her no less, she was beginning to see the use of having one's whims and one's rages submitted to some kind of control. "It did no good to anybody to have us come down with red noses to a stone-cold lunch, and go upstairs afterward to sulk in our bed-rooms," she thought, and she recalled how her father, when regaled with the history of these domestic dis-agreements, used to say with a laugh: "What a lot of nonsense it would knock out of you women to have to hoe a potato-field, or spend a week in Wall Street."

Yes; in spite of her anger, in spite of her desperate sense of being trapped, Annabel felt in a confused way that the business of living was perhaps conducted more wisely at Longlands—even though Longlands was the potato-field she was destined to hoe for life.

XXIV

THAT evening before dinner, as Annabel sat over her dressing-room fire, she heard a low knock. She had half expected to see her husband appear, after a talk with his mother, and had steeled herself to a repetition of the morning's scene. But she had an idea that the Dowager might have taken her to task only because the Duke was reluctant to do so; she had already discovered that one of her mother-in-law's duties was the shouldering of any job her son wished to be rid of.

The knock, moreover, was too light to be a man's, and Annabel was not surprised to have it followed by a soft hesitating turn of the door-handle.

"Nan dear—not dressing yet, I hope?" It was Conchita Marable, her tawny hair loosely tossed back, her plump shoulders draped in a rosy dressing-gown festooned with swansdown. It was a long way from Conchita's quarters to the Duchess's, and Annabel was amused at the thought of the Dowager's dismay had she encountered, in the stately corridors of Longlands, a lady with tumbled auburn curls, red-heeled slippers, and a pink deshabille with a marked tendency to drop off the shoulders. A headless ghost would have been much less out of keeping with the traditions of the place.

Annabel greeted her visitor with a smile. Ever since Conchita's first appearance on the verandah of the Grand Union, Annabel's admiration for her had been based on a secret sympathy. Even then the dreamy indolent girl had been enveloped in a sort of warm haze unlike the cool dry light in which Nan's sister and the Elmsworths moved. And Lady Dick, if she had lost something of that early magic, and no longer seemed to Nan to be made of rarer stuff, had yet ripened into something more richly human than the others. A warm fruity fragrance, as of peaches in golden sawdust, breathed from her soft plumpness, the tawny spirals of her hair, the smile which had a way of flickering between her lashes without descending to her lips.

"Darling—you're all alone? Ushant's not lurking anywhere?" she questioned, peering about the room with an air of mystery.

Annabel shook her head. "No. He doesn't often come here before dinner."

"Then he's a very stupid man, my dear," Lady Dick rejoined, her smile resting approvingly on her hostess. "Nan, do you know how awfully lovely you're growing? I always used to tell Jinny and the Elmsworths that one of these days you'd beat us all; and I see the day's approaching. . ."

Annabel laughed, and her friend drew back to inspect her critically. "If you'd only burn that alms-house dressing-gown, with the horrid row of horn buttons down the front, which looks as if your mother-in-law had chosen it—ah, she *did?* To discourage midnight escapades, I suppose? Darling, why don't you strike, and let me order your clothes for you—and especially your underclothes? It would be a lovely excuse for running over to Paris, and with your order in my pocket I could get the dress-makers to pay all my expenses, and could bring you back a French maid who'd do your hair so that it wouldn't look like a bun just out of the baking-pan. Oh, Nan—fancy having all you've got—the hair and the eyes, and the rank, and the power, and the money..."

Annabel interrupted her. "Oh, but, Conchie, I haven't got much money."

Lady Dick's smiling face clouded, and her clear gray eyes grew dark. "Now why do you say that? Are you afraid of being asked to help an old friend in a tight place, and do you want to warn me off in advance?"

Annabel looked at her in surprise. "Oh, Conchita, what a beastly question! It doesn't sound a bit like you... Do sit down by the fire. You're shaking all over —why, I believe you're crying!"

Annabel put an arm around her friend's shoulder, and drew her down into an armchair near the hearth, pulling up a low stool for herself, and leaning against Lady Dick's knee with low sounds of sympathy. "Tell me, Conchie darling—what's wrong?"

"Oh, my child, pretty nearly everything." Drawing out a scrap of lace and cambric, Lady Dick applied it to her beautiful eyes; but the tears continued to flow, and Annabel had to wait till they had ceased. Then Lady Dick, tossing back her tumbled curls, continued with a rainbow smile: "But what's the use? They're all things you wouldn't understand. What do you know about being head over ears in debt, and in love with one man while you're tied to another—tied tight in one of these awful English marriages, that strangle you in a noose when you try to pull away from them?"

A little shiver ran over Annabel. What indeed did she know of these things? And how much could she admit to Conchita—or for that matter to any one—that she did know? Something sealed her lips, made it, for the moment, impossible even to murmur the sympathy she longed to speak out. She was benumbed, and could only remain silent, pressing Conchita's hands, and deafened by the reverberation of Conchita's last words: "These awful English marriages, that strangle you in a noose when you try to pull away from them." If only Conchita had not put that into words!

"Well, Nan—I suppose now I've horrified you past forgiveness," Lady Dick continued, breaking into a nervous laugh. "You never imagined things of that sort could happen to anybody you knew, did you? I suppose Miss Testvalley told you that only wicked Queens in history books had lovers. That's what they taught us at school... In real life everything ended at the church door, and you just went on having babies and being happy ever after—eh?"

"Oh, Conchie, Conchie," Nan murmured, flinging her arms about her friend's neck. She felt suddenly years older than Conchita, and mistress of the bitter lore the latter fancied she was revealing to her. Since the tragic incident of the Linfry child's death, Annabel had never asked her husband for money, and he had never informed himself if her requirements exceeded the modest allowance traditionally allotted to Tintagel

Duchesses. It had always sufficed for his mother, and why suggest to his wife that her needs might be greater? The Duke had never departed from the rule inculcated by the Dowager on his coming of age: "In dealing with tenants and dependents, always avoid putting ideas into their heads"—which meant, in the Dowager's vocabulary, giving them a chance to state their needs or ventilate their grievances; and he had instinctively adopted the same system with his wife. "People will always think they want whatever you suggest they might want," his mother had often reminded him; an axiom which had not only saved him thousands of pounds, but protected him from the personal importunities which he disliked even more than the spending of money. He was always reluctant to be drawn into unforeseen expenditure, but he shrank still more from any emotional outlay, and was not sorry to be known (as he soon was) as a landlord who referred all letters to his agents, and resolutely declined personal interviews.

All this flashed through Annabel, but was swept away by Conchita's next words: "In love with one man and married to another..." Yes; that was a terrible fate indeed... and yet, and yet... might one perhaps not feel less lonely with such a sin on one's conscience than in the blameless isolation of an uninhabited heart?

"Darling, can you tell me... anything more? Of course I want to help you; but I must find out ways. I'm almost as much of a prisoner as you are, I fancy; perhaps more. Because Dick's away a good deal, isn't he?"

"Oh, yes, almost always; but his duns are not. The bills keep pouring in. What little money there is is mine, and of course those people know it... But I'm stone-broke at present, and I don't know what I shall do if you can't help me out with a loan." She drew back, and looked at Nan beseechingly. "You don't know how I hate talking to you about such sordid things... You seem so high above it all, so untouched by anything bad."

"But, Conchie, it's not being bad to be unhappy—"

"No, darling; and goodness knows I'm unhappy enough. But I suppose it's wrong to try to console myself—in the way I have. You must think so, I know; but I can't live without affection, and Miles is so understanding, so tender..."

Miles Dawnly, then— Two or three times Nan had wondered—had noticed things which seemed to bespeak a tender intimacy; but she had never been sure... The blood rushed to her forehead. As she listened to Conchita she was secretly transposing her friend's words to her own use. "Oh, I know, I know, Conchie—"

Lady Dick lifted her head quickly, and looked straight into her friend's eyes. "You know—?"

"I mean, I can imagine... how hard it must be not to..."

There was a long silence. Annabel was conscious that Conchita was waiting for some word of solace—material or sentimental, or if possible both; but again a paralyzing constraint descended on her. In her girlhood no one had ever spoken to her of events or emotions below the surface of life, and she had not yet acquired words to express them. At last she broke out with sudden passion: "Conchie—it's all turned out a dreadful mistake, hasn't it?"

"A dreadful mistake—you mean my marriage?"

"I mean all our marriages. I don't believe we're any of us really made for this English life. At least I suppose not, for they seem to take so many things for granted here that shock us and make us miserable; and then they're horrified by things we do quite innocently —like that silly reel last night."

"Oh—you've been hearing about the reel, have you? I saw the old ladies putting their heads together on the sofa."

"If it's not that it's something else. I sometimes wonder—" She paused again, struggling for words. "Conchie, if we just packed up and went home to live, would they really be able to make us come back here, as my mother-in-law says? Perhaps I could cable to father for our passage-money—"

She broke off, perceiving that her suggestion had aroused no response. Conchita threw herself back in her armchair, her eyes wide with an unfeigned astonishment. Suddenly she burst out laughing.

"You little darling! Is that your panacea? Go back to Saratoga and New York—to the Assemblies and the Charity balls? Do you really imagine you'd like that better?"

"I don't know... Don't you, sometimes?"

"Never! Not for a single minute!" Lady Dick continued to gaze up laughingly at her friend. She seemed to have forgotten her personal troubles in the vision of this grotesque possibility. "Why, Nan, have you forgotten those dreary endless summers at the Grand Union, and the Opera boxes sent on off-nights by your father's business friends, and the hanging round, fishing for invitations to the Assemblies and knowing we'd never have a look-in at the Thursday Evening dances? ... Oh, if we were to go over on a visit, just a few weeks' splash in New York or Newport, then every door would fly open, and the Eglintons and Van der Luydens, and all the other old toadies, would be fighting for us, and fawning at our feet; and I don't say I shouldn't like that—for a while. But to be returned to our families as if we'd been sent to England on 'appro', and hadn't suited—no, thank you! And I wouldn't go for good and all on any terms—not for all the Astor diamonds! Why, you dear little goose, I'd rather starve and freeze here than go back to all the warm houses and the hot baths, and the emptiness of everything—people and places. And as for you, an English Duchess, with everything the world can give heaped up at your feet—you may not know it now, you innocent infant, but you'd have enough of Madison Avenue and Seventh Regiment balls inside of a week—and of the best of New York and Newport before your first season was over.—There— does the truth frighten you? If you don't believe me, ask Jacky March, or any of the poor little American old maids, or wives or widows, who've had a nibble at it, and have hung on at any price, because London's London, and London life the most exciting and interesting in the world, and once you've got the soot and the fog in your veins you simply can't live without them; and all the poor hangers-on and left-overs know it as well as we do."

Annabel received this in silence. Lady Dick's tirade filled her with a momentary scorn, followed by a prolonged searching of the heart. Her values, of course, were not Conchita's values; that she had always known. London society, of which she knew so little, had never had any attraction for her save as a splendid spectacle; and the part she was expected to play in that spectacle was a burden and not a delight. It was not the atmosphere of London but of England which had gradually filled her veins and penetrated to her heart. She thought of the thinness of the mental and moral air in her own home; the noisy quarrels about nothing, the paltry preoccupations, her mother's feverish interest in the fashions and follies of a society which had always ignored her. At least life in England had a background, layers and layers of rich deep background, of history, poetry, old traditional observances, beautiful houses, beautiful landscapes, beautiful ancient buildings, palaces, churches, cathedrals. Would it not be possible, in some mysterious way, to create for one's self a life out of all this richness, a life which should somehow make up for the poverty of one's personal lot? If only she could have talked of it all with a friend . . . Laura Testvalley, for instance, of whom her need was so much greater now than it had ever been in the school-room. Could she not perhaps persuade Ushant to let her old governess come back to her—?

Her thoughts had wandered so far from Lady Dick

and her troubles that she was almost startled to hear her friend speak.

"Well, my dear, which do you think worse—having a lover, or owing a few hundred pounds? Between the two I've shocked you hopelessly, haven't I? As much as even your mother-in-law could wish. The Dowager doesn't like me, you know. I'm afraid I'll never be asked to Longlands again." Lady Dick stood up with a laugh, pushing her curls back into their loosened coil. Her face looked pale and heavy.

"You haven't shocked me—only made me dreadfully sorry, because I don't know what I can do. . ."

"Oh, well; don't lie awake over it, my dear," Lady Dick retorted with a touch of bitterness. "But wasn't that the dressing-bell? I must hurry off and be laced into my dinner-gown. They don't like unpunctuality here, do they? And tea-gowns wouldn't be tolerated at dinner."

"Conchie—wait!" Annabel was trembling with the sense of having failed her friend, and been unable to make her understand why. "Don't think I don't care— Oh, please don't think that! The way we live makes it look as if there wasn't a whim I couldn't gratify; but Ushant doesn't give me much money, and I don't know how to ask for it."

Conchita turned back and gave her a long look. "The skinflint! No, I suppose he wouldn't; and I suppose you haven't learnt yet how to manage him."

Annabel blushed more deeply: "I'm not clever at managing, I'm afraid. You must give me time to look about, to find out—" It had suddenly occurred to her, she hardly knew why, that Guy Thwarte was the one person she could take into her confidence in such a matter. Perhaps he would be able to tell her how to raise the money for her friend. She would pluck up her courage, and ask him the next day.

"Conchie, dear, by tomorrow evening I promise you..." she began; and found herself instantly gathered to her friend's bosom.

"Two hundred pounds would save my life, you darling—and five hundred make me a free woman..."

Conchita loosened her embrace. The velvet glow suffused her face again, and she turned joyfully toward the door. But on the threshold she paused, and coming back laid her hands on Annabel's shoulders.

"Nan," she said, almost solemnly, "don't judge me, will you, till you find out for yourself what it's like."

"What what is like? What do you mean, Conchita?"

"Happiness, darling," Lady Dick whispered. She pressed a quick kiss on her friend's cheek; then, as the dressing-bell crashed out its final call, she picked up her rosy draperies and fled down the corridor.

XXV

THE next morning Annabel, after a restless night, stood at her window watching the dark return of day. Dawn was trying to force a way through leaden mist; every detail, every connecting link, was muffled in folds of rain-cloud. That was England, she thought; not only the English scene but the English life was perpetually muffled. The links between these people and their actions were mostly hidden from Annabel; their looks, their customs, their language, had implications beyond her understanding.

Sometimes fleeting lights, remote and tender, shot through the fog; then the blanket of incomprehension closed in again. It was like that day in the ruins of Tintagel, the day when she and Ushant had met... As she looked back on it, the scene of their meeting seemed symbolical: in a ruin and a fog... Lovers ought to meet under limpid skies and branches dripping with sunlight, like the nymphs and heroes of Correggio.

The thought that she had even imagined Ushant as a lover made her smile, and she turned away from the window... Those were dreams, and the reality was: what? First that she must manage to get five hundred pounds for Conchita; and after that, must think about her own future. She was glad she had something active and helpful to do before reverting once more to that dreary problem.

Through her restless night she had gone over and over every possible plan for getting the five hundred pounds. The idea of consulting Guy Thwarte had faded before the first hint of daylight. Of course he would offer to lend her the sum; and how could she borrow from a friend money she saw no possibility of re-paying? And yet, to whom else could she apply? The Dowager? Her mind brushed past the absurd idea . . . and past that of her sisters-in-law. How bewildered, how scandalized the poor things would be! Annabel herself, she knew, was bewilderment enough to them: a wife who bore no children, a Duchess who did not yet clearly understand the duties of a groom-of-the-chambers, or know what the Chiltern Hundreds were! To all his people it was as if Ushant had married a savage. . .

There was her own family, of course; her sister, her friends the Elmsworths. Annabel knew that in the dizzy up-and-down of Wall Street, which ladies were not expected to understand, Mr. Elmsworth was now "on top", as they called it. The cornering of a heavy block of railway shares, though apparently necessary to the development of another line, had temporarily hampered her father and Mr. Closson, and Annabel was aware that Virginia had already addressed several unavailing appeals to Colonel St George. Certainly, if he had cut down the girls' allowances it was because the poor Colonel could not help himself; and it seemed only fair that his first aid, whenever it came, should go to Virginia, whose husband's income had to be extracted from the heavily burdened Brightlingsea estate, rather than to the wife of one of England's wealthiest Dukes.

One of England's wealthiest Dukes! That was what Ushant was; and it was naturally to him that his wife should turn in any financial difficulty. But Annabel had never done so since the Linfry incident, and though she knew the sum she wanted was nothing to a man with Ushant's income, she was as frightened as though she had been going to beg for the half of his fortune.

The others, of course—Virginia, the Elmsworths and poor Conchita—had long since become trained borrowers and beggars. Money—or rather the want of it—loomed before them at every turn, and they had mastered most of the arts of extracting it from reluctant husbands or parents. This London life necessitated so many expenditures unknown to the humdrum existence of Madison Avenue and the Grand Union Hotel: Court functions, Royal Ascot, the Cowes season, the entertaining of royalties, the heavy cost of pheasant-shooting, deer-stalking and hunting, above all (it was whispered) the high play and extravagant luxury prevailing in the inner set to which the lovely newcomers had been so warmly welcomed. You couldn't, Virginia had over and over again explained to Annabel, expect to keep your place in that jealously guarded set if you didn't dress up, live up, play up, to its princely standards. But Annabel had lent an inattentive ear to these hints. She wanted nothing of what her sister and her sister's friends were fighting for; their needs did not stir her imagination, and they soon learned that, beyond occasionally letting them charge a dress, or a few yards of lace, to her account, she could give them little aid.

It was Conchita's appeal which first roused her sympathy. "You don't know what it is," Lady Dick had said, "to be in love with one man and tied to another"; and instantly the barriers of Nan's indifference had broken down. It was wrong—it was no doubt dreadfully wrong—but it was human, it was understandable, it made her frozen heart thaw in soft participation. "It must be less wicked to love the wrong person than not to love anybody at all," she thought, considering her own desolate plight...

But such thoughts were pure self-indulgence; her immediate business was the finding of the five hundred pounds to lift Conchita's weight of debt.

When there was a big shooting-party at Longlands every hour of the Duke's day was disposed of in advance, and Nan had begun to regard this as a compensation for the boredom associated with such occasions. She was resolved never again to expose herself to the risks of those solitary months at Tintagel, with an Ushant at leisure to dissect his grievances as he did his clocks...
After much reflexion she scribbled a note to him: "Please let me know after breakfast when I can see you—" and to her surprise, when the party rose from the sumptuous repast which always fortified the guns at Longlands, the Duke followed her into the east drawing-room, where the ladies were accustomed to assemble in the mornings, with their needle-work and correspondence.

"If you'll come to my study for a moment, Annabel."

"Now—?" she stammered, not expecting so prompt a response.

The Duke consulted his watch. "I have a quarter of

an hour before we start." She hesitated, and then, reflecting that she might have a better chance of success
if there were no time to prolong the discussion, she rose
and followed him.

The Duke's study at Longlands had been created by
a predecessor imbued with loftier ideas of his station,
and the glories befitting it, than the present Duke could
muster. In size, and splendour of ornament, it seemed
singularly out of scale with the nervous little man pacing
its stately floor; but it had always been "the Duke's
study", and must therefore go on being so to the end of
time.

Ushant had seated himself behind his monumental
desk, as if to borrow from it the authority he did not
always know how to assert unaided. His wife stood before him without speaking. He lifted his head, and
forced one of the difficult smiles he had inherited from
his mother. "Yes—?"

"Oh, Ushant—I don't know how to begin; and this
room always frightens me. It looks as if people came
here only when you send for them to be sentenced."

The Duke met this with a look of genuine bewilderment. Could it be, the look implied, that his wife imagined there was some link between the peerage and the
magistracy? "Well, my dear—?"

"Oh, you wouldn't understand... But what I've actually come for is to ask you to let me have five hundred
pounds."

There, it was out—about as lightly as if she had hurled
a rock at him through one of the tall windows! He

frowned and looked down, picking up an emblazoned paper-cutter to examine it.

"Five hundred pounds?" he repeated slowly.

"Yes."

"Do I understand that you are asking me for that sum?"

"Yes."

There was another heavy silence, during which she strained her eyes to detect any change in his guarded face. There was none.

"Five hundred pounds?"

"Oh, please, Ushant—yes!"

"Now—at once?"

"At once," she faltered, feeling that each syllable of his slow interrogatory was draining away a drop of her courage.

The Duke again attempted a smile. "It's a large sum —a very large sum. Has your dress-maker led you on rather farther than your means would justify?"

Nan reddened. Her dress-maker! She wondered if Ushant had ever noticed her clothes? But might he not be offering her the very pretext she needed? She hated having to use one, but since she could think of no other way of getting what she wanted, she resolved to surmount her scruples.

"Well, you see, I've never known exactly what my means were . . . but I do want this money. . ."

"Never known what your means were? Surely it's all clearly enough written down in your marriage settlements."

"Yes; but sometimes one is tempted to spend a trifle more..."

"You must have been taught very little about the value of money to call five hundred pounds a trifle."

Annabel broke into a laugh. "You're teaching me a lot about it now."

The Duke's temples grew red under his straw-coloured hair, and she saw that her stroke had gone home.

"It's my duty to do so," he remarked drily. Then his tone altered, and he added, on a conciliatory note: "I hope you'll bear the lesson in mind; but of course if you've incurred this debt it must be paid."

"Oh, Ushant—"

He raised his hand to check her gratitude. "Naturally... If you'll please tell these people to send me their bill." He rose stiffly, with another glance at his watch. "I said a quarter of an hour—and I'm afraid it's nearly up."

Nan stood crestfallen between her husband and the door. "But you don't understand..." (She wondered whether it was not a mistake to say that to him so often?) "I mean," she hurriedly corrected herself, "it's really no use your bothering... If you'll just make out the cheque to me I'll—"

The Duke stopped short. "Ah—" he said slowly. "Then it's *not* to pay your dress-maker that you want it?"

Nan's quick colour flew to her forehead. "Well, no— it's not. I—I want it for...my private charities..."

"Your private charities? Is your allowance not paid regularly? All your private expenditures are supposed to

be included in it. My mother was always satisfied with
that arrangement."

"Yes; but did your mother never have unexpected
calls—? Sometimes one has to help in an emergency. . ."

The two faced each other in a difficult silence. At
length the Duke straightened himself, and said with an
attempt at ease: "I'm willing to admit that emergencies
may arise; but if you ask me to advance five hundred
pounds at a moment's notice it's only fair that I should
be told why you need it."

Their eyes met, and a flame of resistance leapt into
Nan's. "I've told you it's for a *private* charity."

"My dear, there should be nothing private between
husband and wife."

She laughed impatiently. "Are you trying to say you
won't give me the money?"

"I'm saying quite the contrary. I'm ready to give it if
you'll tell me what you want it for."

"Ushant—it's a long time since I've asked you a
favour, and you can't go on forever ordering me about
like a child."

The Duke took a few steps across the room; then he
turned back. His complexion had faded to its usual
sandy pallor, and his lips twitched a little. "Perhaps,
my dear, you forget how long it is since *I* have asked for
a favour. I'm afraid you must make your choice. If I'm
not, as you call it, to order you about like a child, you
may force me to order you about as a wife." The words
came out slowly, haltingly, as if they had cost him a
struggle. Nan had noticed before now that anger was
too big a garment for him: it always hung on him in

uneasy folds. "And now my time is up. I can't keep the
guns waiting any longer," he concluded abruptly, turning toward the door.

Annabel stood silent; she could find nothing else to
say. She had failed, as she had foreseen she would, for
lack of the arts by which cleverer women gain their
ends. "You can't force me . . . no one can force me . . ."
she cried out suddenly, hardly knowing what she said;
but her husband had already crossed the threshold, and
she wondered whether the closing of the door had not
drowned her words.

The big house was full of the rumour of the departing sportsmen. Gradually the sounds died out, and the
hush of boredom and inactivity fell from the carved
and gilded walls. Annabel stood where the Duke left
her. Now she went out into the long vaulted passage on
which the study opened. The passage was empty, and so
was the great domed and pillared hall beyond. Under
such lowering skies the ladies would remain grouped
about the fire in the east drawing-room, trying to cheat
the empty hours with gossip and embroidery and letter-
writing. It was not a day for them to join the sportsmen,
even had their host encouraged this new-fangled habit;
but it was well known that the Duke, who had no great
taste for sport, and practised it only as one of the duties
of his station, did not find the task lightened by feminine companionship.

In the lobby of one of the side entrances Annabel
found an old garden hat and cloak. She put them on
and went out. It would have been impossible for her,

just then, to join the bored but placid group in the east drawing-room. The great house had become like a sepulchre to her; under its ponderous cornices and cupolas she felt herself reduced to a corpse-like immobility. It was only in the open that she became herself again—a stormy self, reckless and rebellious. "Perhaps," she thought, "if Ushant had ever lived in smaller houses he would have understood me better." Was it because all the great people secretly felt as Ushant did—oppressed, weighed down under a dead burden of pomp and precedent—that they built these gigantic palaces to give themselves the illusion of being giants?

Now, out of doors, under the lowering skies, she could breathe and even begin to think. But for the moment all her straining thoughts were arrested by the same insurmountable barrier: she was the Duchess of Tintagel, and knew no way of becoming any one else...

She walked across the gardens opening out from the west wing, and slowly mounted the wooded hill-side beyond. It was beginning to rain, and she must find a refuge somewhere—a solitude in which she could fight out this battle between herself and her fate. The slope she was climbing was somewhat derisively crowned by an octagonal temple of Love, with rain-streaked walls of peeling stucco. On the summit of the dome the neglected god spanned his bow unheeded, and underneath it a door swinging loose on broken hinges gave admittance to a room stored with the remnants of derelict croquet-sets and disabled shuttlecocks and grace-rings. It was evidently many a day since the lords of

Longlands had visited the divinity who is supposed to rule the world.

Nan, certain of being undisturbed in this retreat, often came there with a book or writing-materials; but she had not intruded on its mouldy solitude since the beginning of winter.

As she entered, a chill fell on her; but she sat down at the stone table in the centre of the dilapidated mosaic floor, and rested her chin on her hands. "I must think it all out," she said aloud, and closing her eyes she tried to lose herself in an inner world of self-examination.

But think out what? Does a life-prisoner behind iron bars take the trouble to think out his future? What a waste of time, what a cruel expenditure of hope. . . Once more she felt herself sinking into depths of childish despair—one of those old benumbing despairs without past or future which used to blot out the skies when her father scolded her or Miss Testvalley looked disapproving. Her face dropped into her hands, and she broke into sobs of misery.

The sobs murmured themselves out; but for a long time she continued to sit motionless, her face hidden, with a child's reluctance to look out again on a world which has wounded it. Her back was turned to the door, and she was so sunk in her distress that she was unconscious of not being alone until she felt a touch on her shoulder, and heard a man's voice: "Duchess—are you ill? What's happened?"

She turned, and saw Guy Thwarte bending over her. "What is it—what has made you cry?" he continued, in the compassionate tone of a grown person speaking to a frightened child.

Nan jumped up, her wet handkerchief crumpled against her eyes. She felt a sudden anger at this intrusion. "Where did you come from? Why aren't you out with the guns?" she stammered.

"I was to have been; but a message came from Lowdon to say that Sir Hercules is worse, and Ushant has asked me to prepare some notes in case the election comes on sooner than we expected. So I wandered up the hill to clear my ideas a little."

Nan stood looking at him with a growing sense of resentment. Hitherto his presence had roused only friendly emotions; his nearness had even seemed a vague protection against the unknown and the inimical. But in her present mood that nearness seemed a deliberate intrusion—as though he had forced himself upon her out of some unworthy curiosity, had seized the chance to come upon her unawares.

"Won't you tell me why you are crying?" he insisted gently.

Her childish anger flamed. "I'm not crying," she retorted, hurriedly pushing her handkerchief into her pocket. "And I don't know why you should follow me here. You must see that I want to be alone."

The young man drew back, surprised. He too, since the distant day of their first talk at Honourslove, had felt between them the existence of a mysterious understanding which every subsequent meeting had renewed, though in actual words so little had passed between them. He had imagined that Annabel was glad he should feel this, and her sudden rebuff was like a blow. But her distress was so evident that he did not feel obliged to take her words literally.

"I had no idea of following you," he answered. "I didn't even know you were here; but since I find you in such distress, how can I help asking if there's nothing I can do?"

"No, no, there's nothing!" she cried, humiliated that this man of all others should surprise her in her childish wretchedness. "Well, yes—I *am* crying . . . now. . . . You can see I am, I suppose?" She groped for the handkerchief. "But if anybody could do anything for me, do you suppose I'd be sitting here and just bearing it? It's because there's nothing . . . nothing . . . any one can do, that I've come here to get away from people, to get away from everything. . . . Can't you understand that?" she ended passionately.

"I can understand your feeling so—yes. I've often thought you must." She gave him a startled look, and her face crimsoned. "But can't you see," he pursued, "that it's hard on a friend—a man who's ventured to think himself your friend—to be told, when he sees you in trouble, that he's not wanted, that he can be of no use, that even his sympathy's unwelcome?"

Annabel continued to look at him with resentful eyes. But already the mere sound of his voice was lessening the weight of her loneliness, and she answered more gently: "You're very kind—"

"Oh, *kind!*" he echoed impatiently.

"You've always been kind to me. I wish you hadn't been away for so many years. I used to think sometimes that if only I could have asked you about things..."

"But—but if you've really thought that, why do you want to drive me away now that I *am* here?" He went up to her with outstretched hands; but she shook her head.

"Because I'm not the Annabel you used to know. I'm a strange woman, strange even to myself, who goes by my name. I suppose in time I'll get to know her, and learn how to live with her."

The angry child had been replaced by a sad but self-controlled woman, who appeared to Guy infinitely farther away and more inaccessible than the other. He had wanted to take the child in his arms and comfort her with kisses; but this newcomer seemed to warn him to be circumspect, and after a pause he rejoined, with a smile: "And can't I be of any use, even to the strange woman?"

Her voice softened. "Well, yes; you can. You are of use... Thinking of you as a friend does help me ... it often has..." She went up to him and put her hand in his. "Please believe that. But don't ask me anything more; don't even say anything more now, if you really want to help me."

He held her hand without attempting to disregard either her look or her words. Through the loud beat of his blood a whisper warned him that the delicate balance of their friendship hung on his obedience.

"I want it above all things, but I'll wait," he said, and lifted the hand to his lips.

XXVI

AS long as the Dowager ruled at Longlands she had found her chief relaxation from ducal drudgery in visiting the immense collection of rare and costly exotic plants in the Duke's famous conservatories. But when she retired to the dower-house, and the sole command of the one small glass-house attached to her new dwelling, she realized the insipidity of inspecting plants in the company of a severe and suspicious head gardener compared with the joys of planting, transplanting, pruning, fertilizing, writing out labels, pressing down the earth about outspread roots, and compelling an obedient underling to do in her own way what she could not manage alone. The Dowager, to whom life had always presented itself in terms of duty, to whom even the closest human relations had come draped in that pale garb, had found her only liberation in gardening; and since amateur horticulture was beginning to be regarded in the highest circles not only as an elegant distraction but almost as one of a great lady's tasks, she had immersed herself in it with a guilty fervour, still doubting if anything so delightful could be quite blameless.

Her son, aware of this passion, which equalled his own for dismembering clocks, was in the habit of going straight to the conservatory when he visited her; and there he found her on the morning after his strange conversation with his wife.

The Dowager was always gratified by his visits, which were necessarily rare during the shooting-parties; but it would have pleased her better had he not come at the exact moment when, gauntleted and aproned, she was transferring some new gloxinia seedlings from one pan to another.

She laid down her implements, scratched a few words in a note-book at her elbow, and dusted the soil from her big gloves.

"Ah, Ushant—." She broke off, struck by his unusual pallor, and the state of his hair. "My dear, you don't look well. Is anything wrong?" she asked, in the tone of one long accustomed to being told every morning of some new wrongness in the course of things.

The Duke stood looking down at the long shelf, the heaps of upturned soil and the scattered labels. It occurred to him that, for ladies, horticulture might prove a safe and agreeable pastime.

"Have you ever tried to interest Annabel in this kind of thing?" he asked abruptly. "I'm afraid I'm too ignorant to do it myself—but I sometimes think she would be happier if she had some innocent amusement like gardening. Needle-work doesn't seem to appeal to her."

The Dowager's upper lip lengthened. "I've not had much chance of discussing her tastes with her; but of course, if you wish me to...Do you think, for instance, she might learn to care for grafting?"

It was inconceivable to the Duke that any one should care for grafting; but not wishing to betray his complete ignorance of the subject, he effected a diversion by proposing a change of scene. "Perhaps we could talk more comfortably in the drawing-room," he suggested.

His mother laid down her tools. She was used to interruptions, and did not dare to confess how trying it was to be asked to abandon her seedlings at that critical stage. She also weakly regretted having to leave the pleasant temperature of the conservatory for an icy drawing-room in which the fire was never lit till the lamps were brought. Such economies were necessary to a Dowager with several daughters whose meagre allowances were always having to be supplemented; but the Duchess, who was almost as hardened to cold as her son, led the way to the drawing-room without apology.

"I'm sorry," she said, as she seated herself near the lifeless hearth, "that you think dear Annabel lacks amusements."

The Duke stood before the chimney, his hands thrust despondently in his pockets. "Oh—I don't say that. But I suppose she's been used to other kinds of amusement in the States; skating, you know, and dancing—they seem to do a lot of dancing over there; and even in England I suppose young ladies expect more variety and excitement nowadays than they had in your time."

The Dowager, who had taken up her alms-house knitting, dropped a sigh into its harsh folds.

"Certainly in my time they didn't expect much— luckily, for they wouldn't have got it."

The Duke made no reply, but moved uneasily back and forth across the room, as his way was when his mind was troubled.

"Won't you sit down, Ushant?"

"Thanks. No." He returned to his station on the hearth-rug.

"You're not joining the guns?" his mother asked.

"No. Seadown will replace me. The fact is," the Duke continued in an embarrassed tone, "I wanted a few minutes of quiet talk with you."

He paused again, and his mother sat silent, automatically counting her stitches, though her whole mind was centred on his words. She was sure some pressing difficulty had brought him to her, but she knew that any visible sign of curiosity, or even sympathy, might check his confidence.

"I—I have had a very—er—embarrassing experience with Annabel," he began; and the Dowager lifted her head quickly, but without interrupting the movement of her needles.

The Duke coughed and cleared his throat. ("At the last minute," his mother thought, "he's wondering whether he might not better have held his tongue." She knitted on.)

"A—a really incomprehensible experience." He threw himself into the chair opposite hers. "And completely unexpected. Yesterday morning, just as I was leaving the house, Annabel asked me for a large sum of money —a very large sum. For five hundred pounds."

"Five hundred pounds?" The needles dropped from the Dowager's petrified fingers.

Her son gave a dry laugh. "It seems to me a considerable amount."

The Dowager was thinking hurriedly: "That chit! *I* shouldn't have dared to ask him for a quarter of that amount—much less his father. . ." Aloud she said: "But what does she want it for?"

"That's the point. She refuses to tell me."

"Refuses—?" the Dowager gasped.

"Er—yes. First she hinted it was for her dress-maker; but on being pressed she owned it was not."

"Ah—and then?"

"Well—then . . . I told her I'd pay the debt if she'd incurred it; but only if she would tell me to whom the money was owing."

"Of course. Very proper."

"So I thought; but she said I'd no right to cross-examine her—"

"Ushant! She called it that?"

"Something of the sort. And as the guns were waiting, I said that was my final answer—and there the matter ended."

The Dowager's face quivered with an excitement she had no means of expressing. This woman—he'd offered her five hundred pounds! And she'd refused it. . .

"It could hardly have ended otherwise," she approved, thinking of the many occasions when a gift of five hundred pounds from the late Duke would have eased her daily load of maternal anxieties.

Her son made no reply, and as he began to move uneasily about the room, it occurred to her that what he wanted was not her approval but her dissent. Yet how could she appear to encourage such open rebellion? "You certainly did right," she repeated.

"Ah, there I'm not sure," the Duke muttered.

"Not sure—?"

"Nothing's gained, I'm afraid, by taking that tone with Annabel." He reddened uncomfortably, and turned his head away from his mother's scrutiny.

"You mean you think you were too lenient?"

"Lord, no—just the contrary. I . . . oh, well, you wouldn't understand. These American girls are brought up differently from our young women. You'd probably say they were spoilt. . ."

"I should," the Dowager assented drily.

"Well—perhaps. Though in a country where there's no primogeniture I suppose it's natural that daughters should be more indulged. At any rate, I . . . I thought it all over during the day—I thought of nothing else, in fact; and after she'd gone down to dinner yesterday evening I slipped into her room and put an envelope with the money on her dressing-table."

"Oh, Ushant—how generous, how noble!"

The Duchess's hard little eyes filled with sudden tears. Her mind was torn between wrath at her daughter-in-law's incredible exactions, and the thought of what such generosity on her own husband's part might have meant to her, with those eight girls to provide for. But Annabel had no daughters—and no sons—and the Dowager's heart had hardened again before her eyes were dry. Would there be no limit to Ushant's weakness, she wondered?

"You're the best judge, of course, in any question between your wife and yourself; but I hope Annabel will never forget what she owes you."

The Duke gave a short laugh. "She's forgotten it already."

"Ushant—!"

He crimsoned unhappily and again averted his face from his mother's eyes. He felt a nervous impulse to possess himself of the clock on the mantel-shelf and take it to pieces; but he turned his back on the temptation. "I'm sorry to bother you with these wretched details ... but ... perhaps one woman can understand another where a man would fail..."

"Yes—?"

"Well, you see, Annabel has been rather nervous and uncertain lately; I've had to be patient. But I thought —I thought when she found she'd gained her point about the money...she...er...would wish to show her gratitude..."

"Naturally."

"So, when the men left the smoking-room last night, I went up to her room. It was not particularly late, and she had not undressed. I went in, and she did thank me ...well, very prettily... But when I...when I proposed to stay, she refused, refused absolutely—"

The Dowager's lips twitched. "Refused? On what ground?"

"That she hadn't understood I'd been driving a bargain with her. The scene was extremely painful," the Duke stammered.

"Yes; I understand." The Dowager paused, and then added abruptly: "So she handed back the envelope—?"

Her son hung his head. "No; there was no question of that."

"Ah—her pride didn't prevent her accepting the bribe, though she refused to stick to the bargain?"

"I can't say there was an actual bargain; but—well, it was something like that. . ."

The Dowager sat silent, her needles motionless in her hands. This, she thought, was one of the strangest hours of her life, and not the least strange part of it was the light reflected back on her own past, and on the weary nights when she had not dared to lock her door. . .

"And then—?"

"Then—well, the end of it was that she said she wanted to go away."

"Go away?"

"She wants to go off somewhere—she doesn't care where—alone with her old governess. You know; the little Italian woman who's with Augusta Glenloe and came over the other night with the party from Champions. She seems to be the only person Annabel cares for, or who, at any rate, has any influence over her."

The Dowager meditated. Again the memory of her own past thrust itself between her and her wrath against her daughter-in-law. Ah, if she had ever dared to ask the late Duke to let her off—to let her go away for a few days, she didn't care where! Even now, she trembled inwardly at the thought of what his answer would have been. . .

"Do you think this governess's influence is good?" she asked at length.

"I've always supposed it was. She's very much attached to Annabel. But how can I ask Augusta Glenloe to lend me her girls' governess to go—I don't know where—with my wife?"

"It's out of the question, of course. Besides, a Duchess

of Tintagel can hardly wander about the world in that way. But perhaps—if you're sure it's wise to yield to this ... this fancy of Annabel's. . ."

"Yes, I am," the Duke interrupted uncomfortably.

"Then why not ask Augusta Glenloe to invite her to Champions for a few weeks? I could easily explain ... putting it on the ground of Annabel's health. Augusta will be glad to do what she can. . ."

The Duke heaved a deep sigh, at once of depression and relief. It was clear that he wished to put an end to the talk, and escape as quickly as possible from the questions in his mother's eyes.

"It might be a good idea."

"Very well. Shall I write?"

The Duke agreed that she might—but of course without giving the least hint. . .

Oh, of course; naturally the Dowager understood that. Augusta would accept her explanation without seeing anything unusual in it. . . It wasn't easy to surprise Augusta.

The Duke, with a vague mutter of thanks, turned to the door; and his mother, following him, laid her hand on his arm. "You've been very long-suffering, Ushant; I hope you'll have your reward."

He stammered something inaudible, and went out of the room. The Dowager, left alone, sat down by the hearth and bent over her scattered knitting. She had forgotten even her haste to get back to the gloxinias. Her son's halting confidences had stirred in her a storm of unaccustomed emotion, and memories of her own past crowded about her like mocking ghosts. But the

Dowager did not believe in ghosts, and her grim realism made short work of the phantoms. "There's only one way for an English Duchess to behave—and the wretched girl has never learnt it. . ." Smoothing out her knitting, she restored it to the basket reserved for pauper industries; then she stood up, and tied on her gardening apron. There were still a great many seedlings to transplant, and after that the new curate was coming to discuss arrangements for the next Mothers' Meeting . . . and then—

"There's always something to be done next. . . I daresay that's the trouble with Annabel—she's never assumed her responsibilities. Once one does, there's no time left for trifles." The Dowager, half way across the room, stopped abruptly. "But what in the world can she want with those five hundred pounds? Certainly not to pay her dress-maker—that was a stupid excuse," she reflected; for even to her untrained eye it was evident that Annabel, unlike her sister and her American friends, had never dressed with the elegance her rank demanded. Yet for what else could she need this money —unless indeed (the Dowager shuddered at the thought) to help some young man out of a scrape? The idea was horrible; but the Dowager had heard it whispered that such cases had been known, even in their own circle; and suddenly she remembered the unaccountable incident of her daughter-in-law's taking Guy Thwarte upstairs to her sitting-room in the course of that crazy reel. . .

XXVII

AT Champions, the Glenloe place in Gloucestershire, a broad-faced amiable brick house with regular windows and a pillared porch replaced the ancestral towers which had been destroyed by fire some thirty years earlier, and now, in ivy-draped ruin, invited the young and romantic to mourn with them by moonlight.

The family did not mourn; least of all Lady Glenloe, to whom airy passages and plain square rooms seemed infinitely preferable to rat-infested moats and turrets, a troublesome over-crowded muniment-room, and the famous family portraits that were continually having to be cleaned and re-backed; and who, in rehearsing the saga of the fire, always concluded with a sigh of satisfaction: "Luckily they saved the stuffed birds."

It was doubtful if the other members of the family had ever noticed anything about the house but the temperature of the rooms, and the relative comfort of the armchairs. Certainly Lady Glenloe had done nothing to extend their observations. She herself had accomplished the unusual feat of having only two daughters and four sons: and this achievement, and the fact that Lord Glenloe had lived for years on a ranch in Canada, and came to England but briefly and rarely, had obliged his wife to be a frequent traveller, going from the soldier sons in Canada and India to the gold-miner in South Africa and the Embassy attaché at St Petersburg, and returning home via the Northwest and the marital ranch.

Such travels, infrequent in Lady Glenloe's day, had opened her eyes to matters undreamed-of by most ladies of the aristocracy, and she had brought back from her wanderings a mind tanned and toughened like her complexion by the healthy hardships of the road. Her two daughters, though left at home, and kept in due subordination, had caught a whiff of the gales that whistled through her mental rigging, and the talk at Champions was full of easy allusions to Thibet, Salt Lake City, Tsarskoë or Delhi, as to all of which Lady Glenloe could furnish statistical items, and facts on plant and bird distribution. In this atmosphere Miss Testvalley breathed more freely than in her other educational prisons, and when she appeared on the station platform to welcome the young Duchess, the latter, though absorbed in her own troubles, instantly noticed the change in her governess. At Longlands, during the Christmas revels, there had been no time or opportunity for observation, much less for private talk; but now Miss Testvalley took possession of Annabel as a matter of course.

"My dear, you won't mind there being no one but me to meet you? The girls and their brothers from Petersburg and Ottawa are out with the guns, and Lady Glenloe sent you all sorts of excuses, but she had an important parish meeting—something to do with almshouse sanitation; and she thought you'd probably be tired by the journey, and rather glad to rest quietly till dinner."

Yes—Annabel was very glad. She suspected that the informal arrival had been planned with Lady Glenloe's connivance, and it made her feel like a girl again to be springing up the stairs on Miss Testvalley's arm, with no groom-of-the-chambers bowing her onward, or housekeeper curtseying in advance. "Everything's pot-luck at Champions." Lady Glenloe had a way of saying it that made pot-luck sound far more appetizing than elaborate preparations; and Annabel's spirits rose with every step.

She had left Longlands with a heavy mind. After a scene of tearful gratitude, Lady Dick, her money in her pocket, had fled to London by the first train, ostensibly to deal with her more pressing creditors; and for another week Annabel had continued to fulfill her duties as hostess to the shooting-party. She had wanted to say a word in private to Guy Thwarte, to excuse herself for her childish outbreak when he had surprised her in the temple; but the day after Conchita's departure he too had gone, called to Honourslove on some local business, and leaving with a promise to the Duke that he would return for the Lowdon election.

Without her two friends, Annabel felt herself more than ever alone. She knew that the Duke, according to his lights, had behaved generously to her; and she would have liked to feel properly grateful. But she was conscious only of a bewildered resentment. She was sure she had done right in helping Conchita Marable, and she could not understand why an act of friendship should have to be expiated like a crime, and in a way so painful to her pride. She felt that she and her husband would never be able to reach an understanding, and this being so it did not greatly matter which of the two was at fault. "I guess it was our parents, really, for making us so different," was her final summing up to Laura Testvalley, in the course of that first unbosoming.

The astringent quality of Miss Testvalley's sympathy had always acted on Annabel like a tonic. Miss Testvalley was not one to weep with you, but to show you briskly why there was no cause for weeping. Now, however, she remained silent for a long while after listening to her pupil's story; and when she spoke, it was with a new softness. "My poor Nan, life makes ugly faces at us sometimes, I know."

Annabel threw herself on the brown cashmere bosom which had so often been her refuge. "Of course you know, you darling old Val. I think there's nothing in the world you don't know." And her tears broke out in a releasing shower.

Miss Testvalley let them flow; apparently she had no bracing epigram at hand. But when Nan had dried her eyes, and tossed back her hair, the governess remarked quietly: "I'd like you to try a change of air first; then we'll talk this all over. There's a good deal of fresh air in this house, and I want you to ventilate your bewildered little head."

Annabel looked at her with a certain surprise. Though Miss Testvalley was often kind, she was seldom tender; and Nan had a sudden intuition of new forces stirring under the breast-plate of brown cashmere. She looked again, more attentively, and then said: "Val, your hair's grown ever so much thicker; and you do it in a new way."

"I—do I?" For the first time since Annabel had known her, Miss Testvalley's brown complexion turned to a rich crimson. The colour darted up, flamed and faded, all in a second or two; but it left the governess's keen little face suffused with a soft inner light like—why, yes, Nan perceived with a start, like that velvety glow on Conchita's delicate cheek. For a moment, neither of the women spoke; but some quick current of understanding seemed to flash between them.

Miss Testvalley laughed. "Oh, my hair . . . you think? Yes; I have been trying a new hair-lotion—one of those wonderful French things. You didn't know I was such a vain old goose? Well, the truth is, Lady Churt was staying here (you know she's a cousin); and after she left, one of the girls found a bottle of this stuff in her room, and just for fun we—that is, I . . . well, there's my silly secret. . ." She laughed again, and tried to flatten her upstanding ripples with a pedantic hand. But the ripples sprang up defiantly, and so did her colour. Nan kept an intent gaze on her.

"You look ten years younger, you look *young,* I mean, Val dear," she corrected herself with a smile.

"Well, that's the way I want you to look, my child—. No; don't ring for your maid—not yet! First let me look through your dresses, and tell you what to wear this evening. You know, dear, you've never thought enough about the little things; and one fine day, if one doesn't, they may suddenly grow into tremendously big ones." She lowered her fine lids. "That's the reason I'm letting my hair wave a little more. Not *too* much, you think? . . . Tell me, Nan, is your maid clever about hair?"

Nan shook her head, "I don't believe she is. My mother-in-law found her for me," she confessed, remembering Conchita's ironic comment on the horn buttons of her dressing-gown.

Presently Lady Glenloe appeared, brisk and brown, in rough tweed and shabby furs. She was as insensible to heat and cold as she was to most of the finer shades of sensation, and her dress always conformed to the calendar, without taking account of such unimportant trifles as latitudes.

"Ah, I'm glad you've got a good fire. They tell me it's very cold this evening. So delighted you've come, my dear; you must need a change and a rest after a series of those big Longlands parties. I've always wondered how your mother-in-law stood the strain... Here you'll find only the family; we don't go in for any ceremony at Champions—but I hope you'll like being with my girls... By the way, dinner may be a trifle late; you won't mind? The fact is, Sir Helmsley Thwarte sent a note this morning to ask if he might come and dine, and bring his son, who's at Honourslove. You know Sir Helmsley, of course? And Guy—he's been with you at Longlands, hasn't he? We must all drive over to Honourslove... Sir Helmsley's a most friendly neighbour; we see him here very often, don't we, Miss Testvalley?"

The governess's head was bent to the grate, from which a coal had fallen. "When Mr. Thwarte's there, Sir Helmsley naturally likes to take him about, I suppose," she murmured to the tongs.

"Ah, just so!—Guy ought to marry," Lady Glenloe announced. "I must get some young people to meet him the next time he comes. . . You know there was an unfortunate marriage at Rio—but luckily the young woman died . . . leaving him a fortune, I believe. Ah, I must send word at once to the cook that Sir Helmsley likes his beef rather underdone. . . Sir Helmsley's very particular about his food. . . But now I'll leave you to rest, my dear. And don't make yourself too fine. We're used to pot-luck at Champions."

Annabel, left alone, stood pondering before her glass. She was to see Guy Thwarte that evening—and Miss Testvalley had reproached her for not thinking enough about the details of her dress and hair. Hair-dressing had always been a much-discussed affair among the St George ladies, but something winged and impatient in Nan resisted the slow torture of adjusting puffs and curls. Regarding herself as the least noticeable in a group where youthful beauty carried its torch so high, and convinced that, wherever they went, the other girls would always be the centre of attention, Nan had never thought it worth while to waste much time on her inconspicuous person. The Duke had not married her for her beauty—how could she imagine it, when he might have chosen Virginia? Indeed, he had mentioned, in the course of his odd wooing, that beautiful women always frightened him, and that the qualities he especially valued in Nan were her gentleness and her inexperience— "And certainly I was inexperienced enough," she meditated, as she stood before the mirror; "but

I'm afraid he hasn't found me particularly gentle."

She continued to study her reflection critically, wondering whether Miss Testvalley was right, and she owed it to herself to dress her hair more becomingly, and wear her jewels as if she hadn't merely hired them for a fancy-ball. (The comparison was Miss Testvalley's.) She could imagine taking an interest in her hair, even studying the effect of a flower or a ribbon skilfully placed; but she knew she could never feel at ease under the weight of the Tintagel heirlooms. Luckily the principal pieces, ponderous coronets and tiaras, massive necklaces and bracelets hung with stones like rocs' eggs, were locked up in a London bank, and would probably not be imposed upon her except at Drawing-rooms or receptions for foreign sovereigns; yet even the less ceremonious ornaments, which Virginia or Conchita would have carried off with such an air, seemed too imposing for her slight presence.

But now, for the first time, she felt a desire to assert herself, to live up to her opportunities. "After all, I'm Annabel Tintagel, and as I can't help myself I might as well try to make the best of it." Perhaps Miss Testvalley was right. Already she seemed to breathe more freely, to feel a new air in her lungs. It was her first escape from the long oppression of Tintagel and Longlands, and the solemn London house; and freed from the restrictions they imposed, and under the same roof with her only two friends in the great lonely English world, she felt her spirits rising. "I know I'm always too glad or too sad—like that girl in the German play that **Miss** Testvalley read to me," she said to herself; and wondered whether Guy Thwarte knew Clärchen's song, and would think her conceited if she told him she had always felt that a little bit of herself was Clärchen. "There are so many people in me," she thought; but tonight the puzzling idea of her multiplicity cheered instead of bewildering her. . . "There can't be too many happy Nans," she thought with a smile, as she drew on her long gloves.

That evening her maid had had to take her hair down twice before each coil and ripple was placed to the best advantage of her small head, and in proper relation to the diamond briar-rose on the shoulder of her coral pink *poult-de-soie.*

When she entered the drawing-room she found it empty; but the next moment Guy Thwarte appeared, and she went up to him impulsively.

"Oh, I'm so glad you're here. I've been wanting to tell you how sorry I am to have behaved so stupidly the day you found me in the temple—" "of Love," she had been about to add; but the absurdity of the designation checked her. She reddened and went on: "I wanted to write and tell you; but I couldn't. I'm not good at letters."

Guy was looking at her, visibly surprised at the change in her appearance, and the warm animation of her voice. "This is better than writing," he rejoined, with a smile. "I'm glad to see you so changed—looking so . . . so much happier. . ."

("Already?" she reflected guiltily, remembering that she had been away from Longlands only a few hours!)

"Yes; I am happier. Miss Testvalley says I'm always going up and down. . . And I wanted to tell you—do you remember Clärchen's song?" she began in an eager voice, feeling her tongue loosened and her heart at ease with him again.

Lady Glenloe's ringing accents interrupted them. "My dear Duchess! You've been looking for us? I'm so sorry. I had carried everybody off to my son's study to see this extraordinary new thing—this telephone, as they call it. I brought it back with me the other day from the States. It's a curious toy; but to you, of course, it's no novelty. In America they're already talking from one town to another—yes actually! Mine goes only as far as the lodge, but I'm urging Sir Helmsley Thwarte to put one in at Honourslove, so that we can have a good gossip together over the crops and the weather. . . But he says he's afraid it will unchain all the bores in the county. . . Sir Helmsley, I think you know the Duchess? I'm going to persuade her to put in a telephone at Longlands. . . We English are so backward. They have them in all the principal hotels in New York; and when I was in St Petersburg last winter they were actually talking of having one between the Imperial Palace and Tsarskoë—"

The old butler appeared to announce dinner, and the procession formed itself, headed by Annabel on the arm of the son from the Petersburg Embassy.

"Yes, at Tsarskoë I've seen the Empress talking over it herself. She uses it to communicate with the nurseries," the diplomatist explained impressively; and Nan wondered why they were all so worked up over an object already regarded as a domestic utensil in America. But it was all a part of the novelty and excitement of being at Champions, and she thought with a smile how much less exhilarating the subjects of conversation at a Longlands dinner would have been.

XXVIII

THE Champions party chose a mild day of February for the drive to Honourslove. The diplomatic son conducted the Duchess, his mother and Miss Testvalley in the wagonette, and the others followed in various vehicles piloted by sons and daughters of the house. For two hours they drove through the tawny winter landscape bounded by hills veiled in blue mist, traversing villages clustered about silver-gray manor-houses, and a little market-town with a High Street bordered by the wool-merchants' stately dwellings, and guarded by a sturdy church-tower. The dark green of rhododendron plantations made autumn linger under the bare woods; on house-fronts sheltered from the wind the naked jasmine was already starred with gold. This merging of the seasons, so unlike the harsh break between summer and winter in America, had often touched Nan's imagination; but she had never felt as now the mild loveliness of certain winter days in England. It all seemed part of the unreality of her sensations, and as the carriage turned in at the gates of Honourslove, she recalled her only other visit there, when she and Guy Thwarte had stood alone on the terrace before the house, and found not a word to say. Poor Nan St George—so tongue-tied and bewildered by the surge of her feelings; why had no one taught her the words for them? As the carriage drew up before the door she seemed to see her own pitiful figure of four years ago flit by like a ghost; but in a moment it vanished in the warm air of the present.

The day was so soft that Lady Glenloe insisted on a turn through the gardens before luncheon; and, as usual when a famous country-house is visited, the guests found themselves following the prescribed itinerary— saying the proper things about the view from the terrace, descending the steep path to the mossy glen of the Love, and returning by the walled gardens and the chapel.

Their host, heading the party with the Duchess and Lady Glenloe, had begun his habitual and slightly ironic summary of the family history. Lady Glenloe lent it an inattentive ear; but Annabel hung on his words, and always quick to discover an appreciative listener, he soon dropped his bantering note to unfold the romantic tale of the old house. Annabel felt that he understood her questions, and sympathized with her curiosity, and as they turned away from the chapel he said, with his quick smile: "I see Miss Testvalley was right, Duchess—she always is. She told me you were the only foreigner she'd ever known who cared for the real deep-down England, rather than the sham one of the London drawing-rooms."

Nan flushed with pride; it still made her as happy to be praised by Miss Testvalley as when the little brown governess had sniffed appreciatively at the posy her pupil had brought her on her first evening at Saratoga.

"I'm afraid I shall always feel strange in London drawing-rooms," Nan answered; "but that hidden-away life of England, the old houses and their histories, and all the far-back things the old people hand on to their grandchildren—they seem so natural and home-like. And Miss Testvalley, who's a foreigner too, has shown me better than anybody how to appreciate them."

"Ah—that's it. We English are spoilt; we've ceased to feel the beauty, to listen to the voices. But you and she come to it with fresh eyes and fresh imaginations—you happen to be blessed with both. I wish more of our Englishwomen felt it all as you do. After luncheon you must go through the old house, and let it talk to you. . . My son, who knows it all even better than I do, will show it to you. . ."

"You spoke the other day about Clärchen's song; the evening my father and I drove over to dine at Champions," Guy Thwarte said suddenly.

He and Annabel, at the day's end, had drifted out again to the wide terrace. They had visited the old house, room by room, lingering long over each picture, each piece of rare old furniture or tapestry, and already the winter afternoon was fading out in crimson distances overhung by twilight. In the hall Lady Glenloe had collected her party for departure.

"Oh, Clärchen? Yes—when my spirits were always jumping up and down Miss Testvalley used to call me Clärchen, just to tease me."

"And doesn't she, any longer? I mean, don't your spirits jump up and down any more?"

"Well, I'm afraid they do sometimes. Miss Testvalley

says things are never as bad as I think, or as good as I expect—but I'd rather have the bad hours than not believe in the good ones, wouldn't you? What really frightens me is not caring for anything any more. Don't you think that's worse?"

"That's the worst, certainly. But it's never going to happen to you, Duchess."

Her face lit up. "Oh, do you think so? I'm not sure. Things seem to last so long—as if in the end they were bound to wear people out. Sometimes life seems like a match between one's self and one's gaolers. The gaolers, of course, are one's mistakes; and the question is, who'll hold out longest? When I think of that, life, instead of being too long, seems as short as a winter day... Oh, look, the lights already, over there in the valley... this day's over. And suddenly you find you've missed your chance. You've been beaten..."

"No, no; for there'll be other days soon. And other chances. Goethe was a very young man when he wrote Clärchen's song. The next time I come to Champions I'll bring *Faust* with me, and show you some of the things life taught him."

"Oh, are you coming back to Champions? When? Before I leave?" she asked eagerly; and he answered: "I'll come whenever Lady Glenloe asks me."

Again he saw her face suffused with one of its Clärchen-like illuminations, and added, rather hastily: "The fact is, I've got to hang about here on account of the possible bye-election at Lowdon. Ushant may have told you—"

The illumination faded. "He never tells me anything

about politics. He thinks women oughtn't to meddle with such things."

Guy laughed. "Well, I rather believe he's right. But meanwhile, here I am, waiting rather aimlessly until I'm called upon to meddle...And as soon as Champions wants me I'll come."

In Sir Helmsley's study he and Miss Testvalley were standing together before Sir Helmsley's copy of the little Rossetti Madonna. The ladies of the party had been carried off to collect their wraps, and their host had seized the opportunity to present his water-colour to Miss Testvalley. "If you think it's not too bad—"

Miss Testvalley's colour rose becomingly. "It's perfect, Sir Helmsley. If you'll allow me, I'll show it to Dante Gabriel the next time I go to see the poor fellow." She bent appreciatively over the sketch. "And you'll let me take it off now?"

"No. I want to have it framed first. But Guy will bring it to you. I understand he's going to Champions in a day or two for a longish visit."

Miss Testvalley made no reply, and her host, who was beginning to know her face well, saw that she was keeping back many comments.

"You're not surprised?" he suggested.

"I—I don't know."

Sir Helmsley laughed. "Perhaps we shall all know soon. But meanwhile let's be a little indiscreet. Which of the daughters do you put your money on?"

Miss Testvalley carefully replaced the water-colour on its easel. "The...the daughters?"

467

"Corisande or Kitty... Why, you must have noticed. The better pleased Lady Glenloe is, the more off-hand her manner becomes. And just now I heard her suggesting to my son to come back to Champions as soon as he could, if he thought he could stand a boring family party."

"Ah—yes." Miss Testvalley remained lost in contemplation of her water-colour. "And you think Lady Glenloe approves?"

"Intensely, judging from her indifferent manner." Sir Helmsley stroked his short beard reflectively. "And I do too. Whichever of the young ladies it is, *cela sera de tout repos.* Cora's eyes are very small; but her nose is straighter than Kitty's. And that's the kind of thing I want for Guy: something safe and unexciting. Now that he's managed to scrape together a little money—the first time a Thwarte has ever done it by the work of his hands or his brain—I dread his falling a victim to some unscrupulous woman."

"Yes," Miss Testvalley acquiesced, a faint glint of irony in her fine eyes. "I can imagine how anxious you must be."

"Oh, desperately; as anxious as the mother of a flirtatious daughter—"

"I understand that."

"And you make no comment?"

"I make no comment."

"Because you think in this particular case I'm mistaken?"

"I don't know."

Sir Helmsley glanced through the window at the darkening terrace. "Well, here he is now. And a lady with him. Shall we toss a penny on which it is—Corisande or Kitty? Oh—no! Why, it's the little Duchess, I believe. . ."

Miss Testvalley still remained silent.

"Another of your pupils!" Sir Helmsley continued, with a teasing laugh. He paused, and added tentatively: "And perhaps the most interesting—eh?"

"Perhaps."

"Because she's the most intelligent—or the most unhappy?"

Miss Testvalley looked up quickly. "Why do you suggest that she's unhappy?"

"Oh," he rejoined, with a slight shrug, "because you're so incurably philanthropic that I should say your swans would often turn out to be lame ducks."

"Perhaps they do. At any rate, she's the pupil I was fondest of and should most wish to guard against unhappiness."

"Ah—" murmured Sir Helmsley, on a half-questioning note.

"But Lady Glenloe must be ready to start; I'd better go and call the Duchess," Miss Testvalley added, moving toward the door. There was a sound of voices in the hall, and among them Lady Glenloe's, calling out: "Cora, Kitty—has any one seen the Duchess? Oh, Mr. Thwarte, we're looking for the Duchess, and I see you've been giving her a last glimpse of your wonderful view. . ."

"Not the last, I hope," said Guy smiling, as he came forward with Annabel.

"The last for today, at any rate; we must be off at once on our long drive. Mr. Thwarte, I count on you for next Saturday. Sir Helmsley, can't we persuade you to come too?"

The drive back to Champions passed like a dream. To secure herself against disturbance, Nan had slipped her hand into Miss Testvalley's, and let her head droop on the governess's shoulder. She heard one of the Glenloe girls whisper: "The Duchess is asleep," and a conniving silence seemed to enfold her. But she had no wish to sleep: her wide-open eyes looked out into the falling night, caught the glint of lights flashing past in the High Street, lost themselves in the long intervals of dusk between the villages, and plunged into deepening night as the low glimmer of the west went out. In her heart was a deep delicious peace such as she had never known before. In this great lonely desert of life stretching out before her she had a friend—a friend who understood not only all she said, but everything she could not say. At the end of the long road on which the regular rap of the horses' feet was beating out the hours, she saw him standing, waiting for her, watching for her through the night.

XXIX

D O you know, I think Nan's coming to stay next week!"

Mrs. Hector Robinson laid down the letter she had been perusing and glanced across the funereal architecture of the British breakfast-table at her husband, who, plunged in *The Times,* sat in the armchair facing her. He looked up with the natural resentment of the male Briton disturbed by an untutored female in his morning encounter with the news. "Nan—?" he echoed interrogatively.

Lizzy Robinson laughed—and her laugh was a brilliant affair, which lit up the mid-winter darkness of the solemn pseudo-gothic breakfast-room at Belfield.

"Well, Annabel, then; Annabel Duchess—"

"The—not the Duchess of Tintagel?"

Mr. Robinson had instantly discarded *The Times.* He sat gazing incredulously at the face of his wife, on which the afterglow of her laugh still enchantingly lingered. Certainly, he thought, he had married one of the most beautiful women in England. And now his father was dead, and Belfield and the big London house, and the Scottish shooting-lodge, and the Lancashire mills which fed them—all for the last year had been his. Everything he had put his hand to had succeeded. But he had never pictured the Duchess of Tintagel at a Belfield house-party, and the vision made him a little dizzy.

The afterglow of his wife's amusement still lingered. "The—Duchess—of—Tintagel," she mimicked him. "Has there never been a Duchess at Belfield before?"

Mr. Robinson stiffened slightly. "Not *this* Duchess. I understood the Tintagels paid no visits."

"Ushant doesn't, certainly—luckily for us! But I suppose he can't keep his wife actually chained up, can he, with all these new laws, and the police prying in everywhere? At any rate, she's been at Lady Glenloe's for the last month; and now she wants to know if she can come here."

Mr. Robinson's stare had the fixity of a muscular contraction. "She's written to ask—?"

His wife tossed the letter across the monuments in Sheffield plate. "There—if you don't believe me."

He read the short note with a hurriedly assumed air of detachment. "Dear me—who else is coming? Shall you be able to fit her in, do you think?" The detachment was almost too perfect, and Lizzy felt like exclaiming: "Oh, come, my dear—don't over-do it!" But she never gave her husband such hints except when it was absolutely necessary.

"Shall I write that she may come?" she asked, with an air of wifely compliance.

Mr. Robinson coughed—in order that his response should not be too eager. "That's for you to decide, my dear. I don't see why not; if she can put up with a rather dull hunting crowd," he said, suddenly viewing his other guests from a new angle. "Let me see—there's old Dashleigh—I'm afraid he *is* a bore—and Hubert Clyde, and Colonel Beagles, and of course Sir Blasker Tripp for Lady Dick Marable—eh?" He smiled suggestively. "And Guy Thwarte; is the Duchess likely to object to Guy Thwarte?"

Lizzy Robinson's smile deepened. "Oh, no; I gather she won't in the least object to him."

"Why—what do you mean? You don't—"

In his surprise and agitation Mr. Robinson abandoned all further thought of *The Times.*

"Well—it occurs to me that she may conceivably have known he was coming here next week. I know he's been at Champions a good deal during the month she's been spending there. And I—well, I should certainly have risked asking him to meet her, if he hadn't already been on your list."

Mr. Robinson looked at his wife's smile, and slowly responded to it. He had always thought he had a prompt mind, as quick as any at the uptake; but there were times when this American girl left him breathless, and even a little frightened. Her social intuitions were uncannily swift; and in his rare moments of leisure from politics and the mills he sometimes asked himself if, with such gifts of divination, she might not some day be building a new future for herself. But there was a stolid British baby upstairs in the nursery, and Mr. Robinson was richer than anybody she was likely to come across, except old Blasker Tripp, who of course belonged to Conchita Marable. And she certainly seemed happy, and absorbed in furthering their joint career... But his chief reason for feeling safe was the fact that her standard of values was identical with his own. Strangely enough, this lovely alien who had been swept into his life on a brief gust of passion, proved to have a respect as profound as his for the concrete realities, and his sturdy unawareness of everything which could not be expressed in terms of bank accounts or political and social expediency. It was as if he had married Titania, and she had brought with her a vanload of ponderous mahogany furniture exactly matching what he had grown up with at Belfield. And he knew she had her eye on a peerage. . .

Yes; but meanwhile—. He picked up *The Times,* and began to smooth it out with deliberation, as though seeking a pretext for not carrying on the conversation.

"Well, Hector—?" his wife began impatiently. "I suppose I shall have to answer this." She had recovered Annabel's letter.

Her husband still hesitated. "My dear—I should be only too happy to see the Duchess here. . . But. . ." The more he reflected, the bigger grew the But suddenly looming before him. "Have you any way of knowing if —er—the Duke approves?"

Lizzy again sounded her gay laugh. "Approves of Nan's coming here?"

Her husband nodded gravely, and as she watched him her own face grew attentive. She had learned that Hector's ideas were almost always worth considering.

"You mean . . . he may not like her inviting herself here?"

"Her doing so is certainly unconventional."

"But she's been staying alone at Champions for a month."

Mr. Robinson was still dubious. "Lady Glenloe's a relative. And besides, her visit to Champions is none of our business. But if you have any reason to think—"

His wife interrupted him. "What I think is that Nan's

dying of boredom, and longing for a change; and if the Duke let her go to Champions, where she was among strangers, I don't see how he can object to her coming here, to an old friend from her own country. I'd like to see him refuse to let her stay with me," cried Lizzy in what her husband called her "Hail Columbia voice".

Mr. Robinson's frown relaxed. Lizzy so often found the right note. This was probably another instance of the advantage, for an ambitious man, of marrying some one by nationality and up-bringing entirely detached from his own social problems. He now regarded as a valuable asset the breezy independence of his wife's attitude, which at first had alarmed him. "It's one of the reasons of their popularity," he reflected. There was no doubt that London society was getting tired of pretences and compliances, of conformity and uniformity. The free and easy Americanism of this little band of invaders had taken the world of fashion by storm, and Hector Robinson was too alert not to have noted the renovation of the social atmosphere. "Wherever the men are amused, fashion is bound to follow," was one of Lizzy's axioms; and certainly, from their future sovereign to his most newly knighted subject, the men *were* amused in Mayfair's American drawing-rooms.

[The text of the novel breaks off at this point. The scenario that follows outlines Edith Wharton's overall purpose and her conclusion. Judging from the way her original plan corresponds to the completed part of the novel, we may assume that, however she would have worked out in detail the projected final chapters, she would have followed her scenario generally without altering her basic conception and ending.]

This novel deals with the adventures of three American families with beautiful daughters who attempt the London social adventure in the 'seventies—the first time the social invasion had ever been tried in England on such a scale.

The three mothers—Mrs. St George, Mrs. Elmsworth, and Mrs. Closson—have all made an attempt to launch their daughters in New York, where their husbands are in business, but have no social standing (the families, all of very ordinary origin, being from the south-west, or from the northern part of the state of New York). The New York experiment is only partly successful, for though the girls attract attention by their beauty they are viewed distrustfully by the New York hostesses whose verdict counts, their origin being hazy and their appearance what was then called "loud." So, though admired at Saratoga, Long Branch and the White Sulphur Springs, they fail at Newport and in New York, and the young men flirt with them but do not offer marriage.

Mrs. St George has a governess for her youngest daughter, Nan, who is not yet out. She knows that governesses are fashionable, and is determined that Nan shall have the same advantages as the daughters of the New York aristocracy, for she suspects that her daughter Virginia's lack of success, and the failure of Lizzy and Mabel Elmsworth, may have been due to lack of social training. Mrs. St George therefore engages a governess who has been in the best houses in New York and London, and a highly competent middle-aged woman named Laura Testvalley (she is of Italian origin

—the name is corrupted from Testavaglia) arrives in the family. Laura Testvalley has been in several aristocratic families in England, but after a run of bad luck has come to the States on account of the great demand for superior "finishing" governesses, and the higher salaries offered. Miss Testvalley is an adventuress, but a great-souled one. She has been a year with the fashionable Mrs. Parmore of New York, who belongs to one of the oldest Knickerbocker families, but she finds the place dull, and is anxious for higher pay and a more lavish household. She recognizes the immense social gifts of the St George girls, and becomes in particular passionately attached to Nan.

She says to Mrs. St George: "Why try Newport again? Go straight to England first, and come back to America with the prestige of a brilliant London season."

Mrs. St George is dazzled, and persuades her husband to let her go. The Closson and Elmsworth girls are friends of the oldest St George girl, and they too persuade their parents to let them try London.

The three families embark together on the adventure, and though furiously jealous of each other, are clever enough to see the advantage of backing each other up; and Miss Testvalley leads them all like a general.

In each particular family the sense of solidarity is of course even stronger than it is between members of the group, and as soon as Virginia St George has made a brilliant English marriage she devotes all her energies to finding a husband for Nan.

But Nan rebels—or at least is not content with the

prizes offered. She is, or thinks she is, as ambitious as
the others, but it is for more interesting reasons; intellectual, political and artistic. She is the least beautiful
but by far the most brilliant and seductive of them all;
and to the amazement of the others (and adroitly
steered by Miss Testvalley) she suddenly captures the
greatest match in England, the young Duke of Tintagel.

But though she is dazzled for the moment her heart
is not satisfied. The Duke is kindly but dull and arrogant, and the man she really loves is young Guy
Thwarte, a poor officer in the Guards, the son of Sir
Helmsley Thwarte, whose old and wonderfully beautiful place in Gloucestershire, Honourslove, is the scene
of a part of the story.

Sir Helmsley Thwarte, the widowed father of Guy,
a clever, broken-down and bitter old worldling, is cap-
tivated by Miss Testvalley, and wants to marry her; but
meanwhile the young Duchess of Tintagel has suddenly
decided to leave her husband and go off with Guy, and
it turns out that Laura Testvalley, moved by the youth
and passion of the lovers, and disgusted by the medio-
cre Duke of Tintagel, has secretly lent a hand in the
planning of the elopement, the scandal of which is to
ring through England for years.

Sir Helmsley Thwarte discovers what is going on,
and is so furious at his only son's being involved in such
an adventure that, suspecting Miss Testvalley's complicity, he breaks with her, and the great old adventuress, seeing love, deep and abiding love, triumph for
the first time in her career, helps Nan to join her lover,

who has been ordered to South Africa, and then goes back alone to old age and poverty.

The Elmsworth and Closson adventures will be interwoven with Nan's, and the setting will be aristocratic London in the season, and life in the great English country-houses as they were sixty years ago.

Notes *for* Fast and Loose

2.1–3   *"Let woman beware. . . ."* From *Lucile* (1860), a novel in verse by Edward Robert Bulwer-Lytton (1831–1891), better known as Robert Lytton, perhaps in order not to be confused with his father, the novelist Edward Bulwer, First Lord of Lytton (1803–1873). *Lucile,* published under the pseudonym "Owen Meredith," was immensely popular in the United States, reaching a fifth edition in 1893.

2.6   *Cornélie.* Almost certainly Emelyn Washburn, the only child of the rector of Calvary Church in New York. The quotation, partially obliterated from having been covered by a tape or a strip of paper, now removed, is probably from Dante's *Inferno,* canto 2, line 53, preceding Beatrice's first appearance in the poem: "e donna mi chiamò beata e bella" (A blessed and beautiful lady called me). Edith's friendship with Emelyn began in Newport the summer of 1875. The quotation may be a pleasant allusion to the occasions when they reach Dante aloud to each other.

3.4–5   *"'Tis best to be off. . . ."* An Anglicized version of a Scots song, the first verse of which is:

> It's gude to be merry and wise,
> It's gude to be honest and true;
> And afore ye're off wi' the auld love,
> It's best to be on wi' the new.

This is as it appears in *The Songs of England and Scotland* (1835). The last two lines are also quoted in Scott's *The Bride of Lammermoor* (1819) and Trollope's *Barchester Towers* (1855).

483

5.6	*The ballad to Celia.* Ben Jonson's lyric poem "Come my Celia" set to music by Alphonso Ferrabosco the Younger. It is the wooing song in Jonson's play *Volpone* (1606).
11.2	*"Auld Robin Gray. . . ."* From the ballad of that name by Lady Anne Barnard, written about 1772. This story of a May-December marriage has a happy ending: Auld Robin Gray opportunely dies, but not before blessing his young wife and reuniting her with her first love.
20.3	*"the least little . . ."* From Tennyson's *Maud, A Monodrama* (1855) 2, l. 87.
21.8	*"drowning dull care."* From the anonymous song, "Begone, dull care!"
21.12–13	*Guy Fawkes.* A facetious allusion to the conspirator in the Gunpowder Plot to blow up the British houses of Parliament on November 5, 1605.
21.20	*Fortunatus.* A hero in medieval legend of Eastern origin, Fortunatus possessed an inexhaustible purse.
21.26–27	*Knight of the Dolorous Visage.* Don Quixote de la Mancha, the hero of Cervantes' novel (1605), so called by his "squire," Sancho Panza.
25.2–3	*"Through you, whom once. . . ."* Slightly misquoted from "The Letters," Tennyson, ll. 35–36: "And you, whom I loved so well / Thro' you my life will be accurst."
26.26	*Swift's Club, Regent St.* The earlier address, St. James St., page 17, for Guy's club is more suitable than this one, which must be an error in transcription.
27.15	*with a bust of Pallas.* A parodic echo of Poe's "The Raven." Though Egerton does not perch on the "bust of Pallas," his "sharp, short rap at the door of [Guy's] sanctum" and misogynistic

pronouncements recall the raven and his "nevermore."

28.19   *Telemachus.* An allusion not to Homer's *Odyssey* but to Fénélon's *The Adventures of Telemachus,* in which the hero, cautioned by Mentor, resists Calypso's advances. Mentor not only counsels flight (as Egerton does to Guy) to escape the temptress, but finally pushes Telemachus from a rock into the sea, making return to the island rather difficult.

29.2   *"Every woman is at heart a rake!"* From *Moral Epistles,* "Epistle to a Lady," l. 216: "Men, some to bus'ness, some to pleasure take; / But ev'ry woman is at heart a rake."

31.6   *Salvandy.* Narcisse Achille Salvandy (1795–1856), a conservative French statesman and author of *Revolution and the Revolutionaries* (1830).

32.3   *Bismarck-coloured.* A dull yellowish brown color called bismarck-brown. Its etymology unknown, it probably derives from Prince Otto von Bismarck (1815–1898). More specifically, it may come from the color of the uniforms worn by German troops in the Franco-Prussian War. It was an innovation for soldiers to wear uniforms that blended into the terrain.

32.20   *Lady Bountiful.* The charitable wealthy widow in George Farquhar's play *The Beaux' Stratagem* (1707) whose name became a byword for benevolence.

33.19   *Miss Ingelow.* Jean Ingelow (1820–1897), English poet and children's writer, is now best remembered for her children's book *Mopsa the Fairy* (1869). In her own day her verse, blending Wordsworth with Tennyson, was widely read, especially in the United States.

36.15   *hundred-eyed maid.* In Greek mythology, the hundred-eyed giant Argus under Hera's direction spied on Io, one of Zeus's favorites.

37.2   *"I & he, Brothers in art."* From Tennyson's "The Gardener's Daughter: or, the Pictures," ll. 3–4.

39.5   *Le jeu. . . .* (The play is not worth the cost of the candle) French version of an old saying first cited in the late sixteenth century in a work by Montaigne.

45.2   *"Oh, to be in England. . . ."* The opening lines of "Home Thoughts from Abroad," in Browning's *Dramatic Lyrics.*

46.2   *melancholy Jacques.* An attendant lord in Shakespeare's *As You Like It* (1599), Jaques was a solitary, cynical malcontent who could "suck melancholy out of a song, such as a weasel sucks eggs."

48.11   *"tip-tilted."* See "Notes to *The Buccaneers*," 317.25.

48.16   *Benedick.* The perennial bachelor in Shakespeare's *Much Ado about Nothing* (1598). He vows not to marry but falls in love with Beatrice and marries her.

54.25–26   *"The roses had shuddered. . . ."* From chapter 13 of Thackeray's *History of Henry Esmond;* in full, the sentence is "The roses had shuddered out of her cheeks; her eyes were glaring; she looked quite old."

57.2   *"The lady, in truth, was young. . . ."* This refers to Mathilda, Madeline's counterpart in *Lucile* (part 2, canto 2, stanza 3).

60.11   *"The Gardener's Daughter."* In this poem by Tennyson the speaker, a painter like Guy, falls in love with the gardener's golden-haired daughter Rose at first sight when he sees her tending her flowers.

64.2–3   *"Through those days. . . ."* This quotation and

others that follow attributed to old plays or songs suggest that where memory failed, invention stepped in—a not uncommon nineteenth-century practice with epigraphs. Although variants of these quotations are to be found in dictionaries of proverbs and quotations, I have been unable to trace exact sources, not even in the plays Edith Jones read or in Robert Chambers's *Cyclopaedia of English Literature,* a compilation of British authors from Anglo-Saxon times to her present, which was her basic text for her English studies.

64.10–11   *"Dieu dispose."* The French version of the English proverb "Man proposes but God disposes."

71.2–3   *"Adieu, bal, plaisir, amour. . . ."* (Adieu, balls, pleasure, love.) Probably from a work by the French dramatist Germain Delavigne (1790–1868), known for his vaudevilles, comedies, and libretti.

75.29   *Queen Mab.* Queen of the fairies, the midwife who delivers men of their dreams, most famously described in Shakespeare's *Romeo and Juliet* (1595) act 1, scene 4.

79.2   *"When pain & anguish. . . ."* From canto 6, stanza 30, of *Marmion.* The preceding lines are:
O, Woman! in our hours of ease,
Uncertain, coy, and hard to please,
And variable as the shade
By light quivering aspen made;

88.1–2   *Robert Spencer's bright words.* William Robert Spencer (1769–1834) was a translator and fashionable author of light verse.

89.16   *"Gather ye roses. . . ."* Lyric poem by Robert Herrick (1591–1674), set to music by William Lawes (1602–1645).

95.12   *awfully sorry.* "Awfully" in the sense of "very" came into colloquial usage in England in the mid-nineteenth century. Its use in the phrase "too awfully nice" was satirized in *Punch* in 1877.

99.2–3   *"Could ye come back. . . ."* From the poem "Too Late," by Dinah Maria Mulock [Craik] (1826–1887), British novelist, poet, and children's writer. Her rags-to-riches novel *John Halifax, Gentleman* (1856) was a best-seller; it is now only a footnote in histories of Victorian novels of social reform. Her poetry proved to be even more ephemeral. Unlike Georgie, the fickle young lady in this poem is not reconciled with her lover in this world; she remorsefully begs him to "drop forgiveness from heaven like dew."

108.27–28   *"to where, beyond these voices. . . ."* The last line of Tennyson's "Guinevere," from *Idylls of the King.*

117.8   *"Goodbye Sweetheart."* A novel (1872) by the British author Rhoda Broughton (1840–1920). As her books in this period of high Victorian prudishness were considered bold and improper reading for young ladies, the yoking of this novel with Sand's and Goethe's would not have seemed as incongruous then as it does to us now.

Notes for The Buccaneers

124.5   *crinoline:* a dome-shaped or pyramidal cagelike structure made up of graduated hoops of whalebone or of steel wire worn as a petticoat to distend a full skirt. A style introduced in the late 1850s, it was out-of-date within the decade.

124.11–13   Eugénie (1826–1920), empress of the French (1853–1870) and consort of Napoleon III, set fashions throughout the capitals of Europe and in New York as well. She is represented as wearing a porkpie (a hat with a low flat crown and a narrow turned-up brim) in Eugène-Louis Boudin's painting (1863) of her and her suite on the beach at Trouville. She was more closely associated with Biarritz, where she had a house and spent part of each year.

141.31   *Timeo Danaos . . . :* "The Greeks I fear; and most when gifts they bring." Virgil, *Aeneid*, 2:49.

144.16–18   Edith Wharton's play on the proverbial expression "Gaming, women, and wine, / while they laugh, they make men pine," as recorded by George Herbert in *Outlandish Proverbs* (1640).

145.3   Long Branch, New Jersey, was a seaside resort popular especially with presidents—Grant, Garfield, and Wilson had summer houses there or nearby.

149.2   *and her heart grew like water:* an expression meaning to feel weak from apprehension, as in "The hearts of all the French were turned to water" (Charles Kingsley, *Hereward the Wake*, 1866, ch. 20).

160.4–10   Gabriele Pasquale Giuseppe Rossetti (1783–1854), father of the poet and painter Dante Gabriel Rossetti (1828–1882), was a political exile from the kingdom of Naples and the author of patriotic verse in Italian. A revolutionary in the cause of Italian unification, he fled to England in 1824. The fictional Gennaro Testavaglia bears a family resemblance not only to the elder Rossetti but to other literary and patriot figures such as Massimo Taparelli, marchese d'Azeglio (1798–1866) and Giovanni Battista Niccolini (1782–1861). Azeglio was the author of two historical novels; Niccolini was a Tuscan dramatist whose masterpiece was the play *Arnaldo da Brescia* (1843). *La Donna della Fortezza* is a fictional title.

161.19   *Exeter Hall:* philanthropic fervor characteristic of the Evangelical wing of the Church of England, derived from the name of the London building on the Strand used for religious and humanitarian meetings from 1831 to 1907.

161.21   *Carbonari:* members of a secret society in Spain, France, and Italy originating in the kingdom of Naples in the early nineteenth century. The Italian Carbonari took part in the Naples uprising in 1820 and after 1830 were absorbed into the Risorgimento movement.

161.28   *dolman:* a short mantle with wide capelike sleeves. As beaded trimming was a style of the late 1860s, Laura's beaded dolman was quite out of fashion.

163.3–4   *"Whence came ye . . .":* John Keats, *Endymion* (1818).

163.11–12   *Nita, Juanita, . . . :* from "Juanita," a Spanish air with words by Caroline E. S. Norton.

172.29   Frederick Denison Maurice (1805–1872), English clergyman, author of many religious works, and a leader of the Christian Socialist movement.

173.7   *Le mie prigioni* (1832, trans. *My Prisons*) by Silvio Pellico (1789–1854). One of the most influential and celebrated works of the Italian romantic movement and the Risorgimento, it is an account of the author's experiences of ten years imprisonment for his participation in the Carbonari movement.

175.23   Light, low shoes in bronze-colored kid were fashionable especially for indoor wear from the 1860s to the turn of the century.

180.3   The comic song "Champagne Charlie Was His Name" (1867), words by H. J. Whymark and music by Alfred Lee.

182.12   The Pompeian style in interior decoration was inspired by the wall colors, especially red and black, and the ornamentation of the houses of Pompeii. It began in the eighteenth century with the chromocolor publication of pictures of the excavated ruins but remained periodically fashionable through the 1870s.

188.9   The allusion is to the Babylonian captivity of the Jews, 586–38 B.C.

208.6   *Poems* (1870) by Dante Gabriel Rossetti, in which "The Blessed Damozel" was first published in book form; he composed the first version of this poem and others in 1846–48.

217.18–19   A Russian countess in the novel *A Diplomat's Diary* (1890) by Julien Gordon (pseudonym of Julie van Rensselaer Cruger) also thinks Brazil is in the southern part of the United States. Paul Bourget in *Outre-Mer: Impressions of America* (1895) singled out her novels for their rendering of American drawing-room conversation. It seems likely, especially given Bourget's recommendation, that Edith Wharton derived her idea of Lady Brightlingsea's blunder from this novel.

227.31   Sophocles' tragedy *Oedipe-roi*, translated by J. Lacroix, opened at the Théâtre-Français on September 18, 1858.

235.11   *M.F.H.:* master of the foxhounds, a member of the hunt in charge of the kennels and hunting arrangements. It is a position of great importance in fox-hunting country.

236.14–16   Afternoon or five o'clock tea came into being in the 1840s as a light meal when the dinner hour was moved from six-thirty or seven to an hour or so later. By the 1850s it was a custom in fashionable houses, and by the 1870s an established feature of British country life. Even if Sir Helmsley is old-fashioned, this and later allusions to the novelty of afternoon tea are anachronistic.

238.8   Sir John Everett Millais (1829–1896), English painter, was one of the founders of the Pre-Raphaelite Brotherhood in 1848 and subsequently was highly successful as a portrait painter and book illustrator.

239.4–5   Wilton House, Wiltshire, is the prototype of Allfriars. The original Palladian design of about 1633 is attributed to Isaac de Caus (1590–1648), but was strongly influenced by the famous English architect and designer Inigo Jones (1573–1652).

253.14   By 1876, gas-lighting was widespread in the United States, whereas in Great Britain many but not all country houses had gaslights. Aristocratic landowners tended to resist technological progress in plumbing, lighting, and heating.

254.4   Wilton House, the model for Allfriars, was

built on the site of an abbey bestowed on the Pembrokes by Henry VIII.

255.8–9   The work of the Dutch landscape painter Meindert Hobbema (1638–1709) was much admired and collected in England beginning in the eighteenth century.

258.23–25   *patuit dea:* visible goddess. *Panathenaic procession:* a great procession following the Panathenaea, the festival at Athens held annually in honor of Athena. The Parthenon frieze is generally taken to be a representation of the Panathenaic procession. The surviving slabs depicting priestesses, girls, and goddesses are among the Elgin Marbles placed in the British Museum in 1816.

259.26   *the Fleshly School:* epithet for the Pre-Raphaelites coined by the British novelist Robert Buchanan. His notorious article published in 1871 under the heading "The Fleshly School of Poetry" attacked mainly Rossetti.

260.3–4   *Jonathan:* nickname for patriots in the American Revolution, later applied to Americans of the United States generally.

262.7   *Drawing-room:* a court reception at which women were presented to the queen.

263.25–26   A tulle veil and a headdress with three feathers (representing the fleur-de-lis and the ancient British claim to the French throne) were required dress for the presentation at court.

272.23   Holland House in Kensington (built in 1607, destroyed in 1940) was in the first half of the nineteenth century celebrated as a center of Whig political and literary society. A private residence, its collection of memorabilia and paintings was open to visitors by invitation only.

275.3   Runnymede, in Surrey bordering Windsor Great Park, is listed in the 1875 *Pascoe's London Guide and Directory for American Travellers* under the heading "Rural and Holiday Resorts." It was notable as the place where King John signed the Magna Charta and for its scenic woodlands.

284.22   Rossetti's sonnet sequence *The House of Life* was first published in 1870; in its final, expanded form it appeared in 1881.

288.7   The duke of Argyll referred to was George Douglas Campbell (1823–1900). Inveraray Castle in Scotland is the seat of the dukes of Argyll. The dukes of Tintagel and the new castle were imaginary.

299.9–10 *terrible beauty that is born:* an anachronistic pun on William Butler Yeats's famous line in his poem "Easter 1916."

299.10   *strawberry leaves:* an allusion to the representation of strawberry leaves on the coronet of a duke, marquis, or earl.

309.23–24 *the Marlborough set:* the social circle of the Prince of Wales after his London residence, Marlborough House (1710), where he and his friends congregated.

317.25   Alfred, Lord Tennyson (1809–1892), poet laureate (1850–1892). The *OED* cites his poem *Gareth and Lynette* (1872) as the origin of the word *tip-tilted:* "And lightly was her slender nose / Tip-tilted like the petal of a flower."

333.1–6 In response to a delegation urging Abraham Lincoln to remove General Grant from his position, the president was said to have asked the reason.

    "Why," replied the spokesman, "he drinks too much whisky."

"Ah!" rejoined Mr. Lincoln, dropping his lower lip. "By the way, gentlemen, can either of you tell me where General Grant procures his whisky? because, if I can find out, I will send every general in the field *a barrel of it!*"

(*Anecdotes of Abraham Lincoln,* ed. J. B. McClure [Chicago: Rhodes & McClure, 1884], p. 94.)

334.31–335.1   *Mistress of the Robes:* a woman traditionally of high rank in charge of the queen's wardrobe.

351.10   In Greek mythology, Theseus married Ariadne after she had delivered him from the Minotaur, but he abandoned her on the island of Naxos. According to some versions, she took her own life out of grief; in others, under the influence of the wine god Dionysus, she regained her good spirits.

356.6   The memoirs of the French diplomat and courtier Louis de Rouvroy (1675–1755), duc de Saint-Simon, give an insider's vivid and often scathing picture of life at the court of Louis XIV.

356.6   The memoirs of the French diplomat and courtier Louis de Rouvroy (1675–1755), duc de Saint-Simon, give an insider's vivid and often scathing picture of life at the court of Louis XIV.

363.10–13   *Broadwood:* an old-fashioned piano. *Ah, non credea mirarti,* the sleepwalking aria from Vincenzo Bellini's *La Sonnambula,* was a Victorian favorite both as sung and as arranged for the piano. *Swanee River:* minstrel song by Stephen Collins Foster (1826–1864), first published in *Old Folks at Home* (1851).

365.20   Sir Edwin Henry Landseer (1802–1873), one

of the most popular and prolific painters of his time, was most famous for his sentimental animal paintings, especially of dogs, but he also painted portraits of the royal family and the nobility.

365.27   There is no such series by Correggio, but the description of the imaginary paintings here and subsequently (pp. 403–4) is evocative of his actual mythological works. *The Earthly Paradise,* the name Wharton gave these paintings, is the title of a poem by William Morris, published in four volumes in two installments, 1868 and 1870. See Adeline Tintner, "Pre-Raphaelite Painting and Poetry in Edith Wharton's *The Buccaneers* (1938)," *Journal of Pre-Raphaelite Studies,* forthcoming 1994.

366.7–11   The passage quoted is from Rossetti's "For a Venetian Pastoral by Giorgione (in the Louvre)," in his *Sonnets for Pictures . . .* (1881).

384.23–24   An echo of Matthew Arnold's "Stanzas from the Grande Chartreuse" (1855), ll. 85–86.

388.13   Thomas Thornycroft (1815–1885), English sculptor, whose most important works included a bust of Albert, the Prince Consort.

390.20   The title of Rossetti's oil painting *Bocca Baciata* (1859) comes from Boccaccio's "Bocca Baciata non perda ventura" (The mouth that has been kissed loses not its freshness). Rossetti painted an enlarged replica of this painting in watercolor titled *La Bionda del Balcone* (The fair-haired woman on the balcony, 1868). The original, now in a private collection, is reproduced in Virginia Surtees, *The Paintings and Drawings of Dante Gabriel Rossetti (1828–1882)* (Oxford: at the Clarendon Press, 1971), 2:186.

396.22–24   Longlands has the features of the late-seventeenth and early-eighteenth century great country houses of which Blenheim Palace, designed by Sir John Vanbrugh, is the most monumental example. The floor plan as traced by the course of the dancers of the reel is strikingly close to Blenheim's. At Blenheim the ceiling painted by the English painter Sir James Thornhill (1675–1734) was that of the great hall rather than of the saloon. The Blenheim tapestries were woven in Belgium; those at Longlands were made by seventeenth-century Flemish tapestry makers at Mortlake in Surrey.

398.25 Apparently she was wearing a mantilla of a delicate type of handmade lace called *Mechlin,* after the city in Belgium noted for its lace making.

429.14 *Chiltern Hundreds:* Administrative districts in Buckinghamshire, of which the stewardship (a merely formal office) is applied for by members of parliament wishing to resign their seats. In other words, it is a method of resignation peculiar to the British Parliament and not likely to be known to a foreigner.

459.30–460.4 The play is Goethe's *Egmont* (1788), and Clärchen's song appears in act 3, scene 2:

> Blissful
> And tearful,
> With thought-teeming brain;
> Hoping
> And fearing
> In passionate pain;
> Now shouting in triumph,
> Now sunk in despair;—
> With love's thrilling rapture.
> What joy can compare!
> (trans. Anna Swanwick)

472.7–9 In this context, the most relevant "new laws"

of the 1870s were those extending women's rights, most importantly the Married Woman's Property Act of 1870, which gave women the right to ownership of property after marriage, and the Matrimonial Clauses Act of 1878, which allowed abused women to obtain legal separation from their husbands as well as financial support.

A Note on the Texts

The text for this edition of *Fast and Loose* is the manuscript in the Clifton Waller Barrett Collection of the Alderman Library, University of Virginia. The manuscript is in ink and in a finely formed Spencerian handwriting, the hallmark of feminine gentility of the period. It takes up 119 pages, mistakenly misnumbered 129, of lined paper in a notebook 6½ inches by 8½ inches. The numbering error occurs at page 89, the verso of which is numbered 100; the numbering continues in sequence from there. "Fast and Loose, A Novelette by David Olivieri" appears both on the first page, in the author's handwriting, and on a Bristol board label the size of a visiting card affixed to the cover, probably in the author's lettering. The quotation and dedication are on the inside cover. As reproduced here, the table of contents is at the end of the text. The concluding inscription—"Begun in the Autumn of 1876 at Pencraig, Newport; finished January 7th 1877 at New York"—is in the more fluent and expansive handwriting of Edith Wharton's maturity. The manuscript is mostly a clean copy; the revisions in the original handwriting suggest that this was a final copy of a previous draft. Some pages have been removed but without loss of text. The manuscript of the reviews, now in the Wharton collection, Lilly Library, Indiana University, Bloomington, in the same handwriting as the text and also in ink, consists of loose sheets, one for each review.

To keep the flavor of Edith Wharton's youthful style, I have followed her revised text in paragraphing, punctuation, capitalization, and spelling. A printed text reproducing all her idiosyncracies would be, however, virtually un-readable, and a misrepresentation of her intentions, for the handwritten draft is not a manuscript prepared for publication. Her dashes present the main problem: although sometimes used conventionally for emphasis or interrupted speech, they not only vary in length from little more than an extended period to half a line but often appear inexpressively beneath, or instead of, other forms of punctuation.

Concluding that literal transcription would be impracticable and at best faithful only to her handwriting, I have made conventional substitutions or deletions where the dashes seemed to me clearly unintended. I have also silently corrected a few obvious mechanical errors, such as missing commas or quotation marks, using as my guide her own practice elsewhere in the text. For a few other matters I have followed the practice of her first published book of fiction, *The Greater Inclination:* I have normalized as "Mr.," "Mrs.," and "Dr." titles appearing in the original with the *r* or *rs* raised and underlined; such words as *anybody* and *everybody* written unconventionally as two words, are spelled normally; the use of many dots to indicate ellipsis has been modernized.

Modern practice has also been followed in the handling of correspondence within the text in that letters run in, in the manuscript, are printed here in extract form. In the placing of quotation marks with a dash to represent interrupted speech, the author's "— appears here as —."

A list of the author's stylistic revisions is appended. Not listed are the author's changes or corrections that were purely mechanical.

The text of *The Buccaneers* and the scenario are a reprint in facsimile of the first and only edition, published posthumously in 1938 under the direction of Gaillard Lapsley, the first executor of Edith Wharton's literary estate. As a memorandum dated November 15, 1932, of her publisher Appleton-Century indicates, she planned to write a novel titled *The Buccaneers* after finishing her memoirs, *A Backward Glance* (published in 1934). The contract for publication of the novel was dated April 19, 1934, and the book was scheduled to come out in the fall of 1935. When she wrote her scenario or preliminary plan is not known, but probably sometime in the late summer of 1934, she sent it to her editor at Appleton's, John L. B. Williams, primarily, it seems, for the purpose of arranging for publication in serial form. In June of 1935, Williams at her request sent the scenario and all of the manuscript he had in hand to her New York agent, Eric S. Pinker, who was to take over the arrangements for magazine publication. The editor of the *Woman's Home Companion,* the magazine most interested in publishing it, had refused to commit herself to publication without seeing the whole book, particularly to see how the author treated the moral question of Nan's elopement. (She was worried—according to Williams in an unpublished letter in the Beinecke collection—that "the conservative element" among the magazine's readers would be offended by Nan's leaving her husband to run away with her lover "since Nan's character is depicted as rather finer than that of any of the other persons in the story.") As a result, Pinker decided not to try to place the book for serialization until it was completed.

Despite this added pressure to complete the book, Wharton devoted her creative energy, diminished as it was by illness, to revision of what (judging from the scenario and surviving notes) was the first three-fourths of the book rather than forging ahead to complete it. A protégé of hers to whom she had given her novel in progress to read counted five sets of revisions. According to his foreword to the first edition, Lapsley based his text on what he considered her latest version: "The novel is printed from the manuscript which she kept by her for reference and revision and gives, therefore, the last word she was able to say as to the form and phrasing of the text. It is a consequence of her method . . . that at the stage she had reached this was at many points not the final word; nevertheless apart from the correction of the press and certain verbal emendations required by sense or consistency the manuscript is printed exactly as Mrs. Wharton left it."

Given the palimpsest of Edith Wharton's revisions, Lapsley must have used the singular *the* and *it* in a manner of speaking, for the book follows the author's revised text successively in *two* manuscripts. As Lapsley observed, in the course of writing, Edith Wharton "moved on an irregular front, and was as often engaged in consolidating or developing a position already won as in actual advance." The manuscripts of the novel in the Edith Wharton collection at the Beinecke Library of Yale University and in the Appleton-Century archives at the Lilly Library of the University of Indiana conform to this description of Mrs. Wharton's method of composition all too well.

The Beinecke manuscripts, apart from thirty-two miscellaneous pages with additional revisions, consist of: (1) the initial version on blue paper written by hand, with revisions, paginated 1 to 510, breaking off at the same point as the book (in this edition, p. 475) and (2) a typed version (henceforth called Ms2) incorporating the revisions of the preceding and containing two sets of further revisions in the author's hand, pages 1 to 271, followed by clean copy (pp. 272 to 287), breaking off at the same point as the book. A third version of the text (henceforth called Ms3), which is in the Lilly Library, paginated 1 to 284, breaks off earlier, at page 465 of the book. Up to chapter 25 (p. 253 of the ms.; p. 428 of the book) the text corresponds to that of the book, with exceptions that can be accounted for either as printing errors and corrections or as changes Lapsley made for the sake of "sense or consistency." This portion of Ms3 incorporates the revisions of Ms2 as well as other changes *not* in Ms2 (derived from what must have been a manuscript subsequent to it) and also contains a few revisions in the author's hand. Ms3 does not incorporate the second set of revisions made on Ms2 from chapter 25 onward, which were evidently made after Ms3 was typed and apparently no longer in Wharton's possession. While it is possible there was another working copy from which Lapsley derived his text, collation of the manuscripts with the book indicates that Lapsley most probably based his text on Ms3 up to page 428 of the book and on Ms2 from page 428 to the end.

Limitations of space precludes listing all of Edith Wharton's emendations, which were almost always made for the sake of brevity, concreteness, and precision. The list below of revisions to *The Buccaneers* offers a glimpse into her painstaking search for the right word, for sound as well as sense. Its main purpose, however, is to record inadvertent errors in the book (for example, the omission of the closing parenthesis on page 202, line 30) and changes or omissions in the text made either deliberately for the sake of "sense or consistency" (174.10) or accidentally (217.4). On the assumption that the text was based on Ms2 and Ms3, as just described, the list comprises primarily the instances in which the book deviates from both Ms2 and Ms3 or from the author's usual practice, as when italics are omitted (264.6). Changes due to press conventions (*defence* instead of *defense*) and obvious typographical errors in the manuscripts, unless reproduced in the book, are not included.

Revisions to FAST AND LOOSE

3.9   Holly] *above deleted* 'Pine'

5.25   still] *followed by deleted* 'abou'

7.18   on] *over erased* 'onto'

8.7   if] *followed by deleted* 'my'

8.11   shopping] *above deleted* 'marketing'

8.16   First] *over erased* 'Lord B'

14.19   opposite] *comma inserted and followed by deleted* '& leaned'

18.3   emotions] *preceded by deleted* 'refle'

18.7   member] *preceded by deleted* 'man in'

19.3   them] *preceded by deleted* 'it'

20.4   people] *preceded by deleted* 'men'

20.7   talent] *followed by deleted* 'a love of'

20.8   bewitching] *preceded by erased* 'fine'

21.10   was leaving] *preceded by deleted* 'turned away'

22.11   woes] *interlined above deleted* 'himself'

22.22   glared] *interlined above deleted* 'stared'

23.4   His] *preceded by deleted* 'the'

23.8   slowly] *interlined above deleted* 'deliberately'

23.10   we were] *interlined above deleted* 'she was'

24.11   kindly] *interlined above deleted* 'unutterable'

25.7   in] *preceded by deleted* 'fr'

25.12   Georgie] *preceded by deleted* 'She'

25.23   for] *interlined above deleted* 'but'

27.4   apartment] *interlined above deleted* 'room'

27.9   in] *preceded by deleted* 'at'

28.14   pitied] *preceded by deleted* 'sym' *and followed by deleted* 'his friend' *and* '[Guy]'s sorrow'

28.17   unbelieving] 'un' *interlined above deleted* 'mis'

28.25   Egerton] *preceded by deleted* 'his friend Jack sharply; but'

28.30   the same] *preceded by deleted* 'like that'

30.6   four] *interlined above deleted* 'three'

31.5   needed] *preceded by deleted* 'it tak'

31.13   A] *over partially erased* 'Two'
32.7   rolled] *preceded by deleted* 'passed'
32.23   passing] *preceded by deleted* 'overrated pleasures'
33.2   out] *preceded by deleted* 'anything else'
33.18   Altogether] *preceded by deleted* 'never'
33.19   Ingelow] *preceded by deleted* 'Je'
34.10   Is] *preceded by deleted* 'Has the'
35.24   at] *preceded by deleted* 'for'
36.8   heavy] *preceded by deleted* 'the'
37.16   made] *interlined above deleted* 'gave'
38.10   hinted] *preceded by deleted* 'obs'
38.13   but] *preceded by deleted* 'sublimely'
39.11   16] *superimposed on* '17'
40.29   palette] *preceded by deleted* 'colours'
41.21   take] *preceded by deleted* 'wou'
42.1   met] *preceded by deleted* 'spot'
42.26   we] *preceded by deleted* 'you will'
43.6   do] *interlined above deleted* 'commit'
48.4   Hebe's] *preceded by deleted* 'nymph's'
48.10   &] *followed by deleted* 'made'
49.16   reveal] *preceded by deleted* 'disclose'
50.8   bosom] *interlined above deleted* 'throat & neck'
50.23   with] *preceded by deleted* 'beside a'
51.22   orders] *preceded by* 'obliges to'
52.22   in] *preceded by deleted* 'as she'
53.14   & it] *preceded by deleted* 'that'
55.9   thoroughly] *preceded by deleted* 'not'
58.8   whatever] *preceded by deleted* 'all'
58.9   April] *interlined above and between* 'one' *and* 'morning'
58.11   Giovanni] *preceded by deleted* 'Baptis'
58.14   went] *preceded by deleted* 'ga'
58.16   wrote to] *interlined above deleted* 'told'
58.18   &] *followed by deleted* 'only'
59.1   parasol.] *followed by deleted* 'on the'
59.18   fashionable] *interlined above deleted* 'lesser'
60.4   woman-kind] *preceded by deleted* 'human-natu'

60.6	among . . . classes] *interlined above and after* 'beauty.'
61.8	smile.] *followed by deleted* 'half holding out her hand.'
61.14	Mr. Graham] *interlined above deleted* 'her father'
61.14	Madeline] *interlined above deleted* 'she'
61.24	apartments] *interlined above deleted* 'rooms'
62.9	an hour] *preceded by deleted* 'half'
66.25	perfectly] *interlined above deleted* 'quite'
67.20	fair] *preceded by deleted* 'sweet'
68.3	When] *preceded by deleted* 'But'
68.14	braids] *superimposed over* 'hair'
68.25	weary] *preceded by deleted* 'sadness'
69.3	days were] *interlined and over deleted* 'life was'
72.14	had] *interlined above deleted* 'might'
72.28	place] *preceded by deleted* 'affection she had'
74.24	expressively] *preceded by deleted* 'obser'
74.29	continually] *interlined above deleted* 'with everyone'
75.21	on the threshold] *interlined above with caret*
75.23	from] *interlined above deleted* 'through'
75.26	ceiling] *preceded by deleted* 'roof'
76.2	as] *preceded by deleted* 'like th'
76.9	specimens] *preceded by deleted* 'rare'
76.17	crowded] *preceded by deleted* 'qu'
76.18	cannot] *preceded by deleted* 'do'
77.7	wooed] *preceded by deleted* 'met'
77.24	but] *preceded by deleted* 'or get'
78.11	suffering] *preceded by deleted* 'face &'
78.17	a] *written over deleted* 'an' *and followed by deleted* 'un-used'
78.18	his] *preceded by deleted* 'the'
79.24	given in] *deleted* 'to' *interlined above; followed by deleted* 'the big lonely studio' *with* 'big' *interlined above* 'lonely'
80.1	honour] *followed by deleted* 'in the big studio in the Via'
80.4	grew] *preceded by deleted* 'dis'
80.5–6	discover] *preceded by deleted* 'fas'
80.9	effect] *followed by* 'of this change' *interlined above*
80.18	&] *preceded by deleted* 'to meet'

80.23   at] *preceded by deleted* 'he'
80.25   against a] *followed by deleted* 'the wall'; 'a' *interlined above* 'the'
80.27   &] *preceded by deleted* '& as he'
81.28   glancing] *preceded by deleted* 'surprised.'
81.29   maid] *preceded by deleted* 'Engli'
82.26   they] *preceded by deleted* '& seen Teresina laid on a bed'
83.15   shawls] *preceded by deleted* 'clo'
83.18   suffering] *interlined above deleted* 'grief'
84.5   have] *preceded by deleted* 'are'
84.14   harsh] *preceded by deleted* 'cr'
84.17   Teresina] *preceded by deleted* 'at last'
84.28   would] *preceded by deleted* 'ca'
85.8   Few] *preceded by deleted* 'Indeed,'
85.11   shy] *interlined above deleted* 'quiet'
87.26   & then] *interlined above deleted* 'sitt'
88.8   &] *preceded by deleted* 'with her'
88.28   he] *preceded by deleted* 'talking shyly'
89.9   I] *preceded by deleted* '"Look," said'
90.5   in] *preceded by deleted* 'presently'
90.24   burning] *preceded by deleted* 'flaming'
91.17   weeping] *preceded by deleted* 'hiding'
92.2   can] *preceded by deleted* 'knows'
93.12   passage] *interlined above deleted* 'journey'
93.13   poorly] *preceded by deleted* 'feeb'
93.18   several] *interlined above deleted* 'a'
94.4   did not] *interlined above deleted* 'never'; 'red' *deleted from* 'occurred'
94.5   March] *interlined with caret above* 'day'
94.17   failed] *preceded by deleted* 'not'
94.23   cheek] *preceded by deleted* 'eyes'
94.26   harmonious] *preceded by deleted* 'mysterious'
94.26   the ends] 'the' *interlined above deleted* 'her'
94.28   cherished—] *followed by deleted* 'she s'
95.14   this] *superimposed on partially deleted* 'these'
95.14   sympathy] *preceded by deleted* 'words were'
97.10   truth] *preceded by deleted* 'realit'

97.24	&] *preceded by deleted* '& would hav'
97.28	nearly] *preceded by deleted* 'more'
98.5	& haughty] *preceded by deleted* 'he was &'
100.17	until in] *interlined with caret above deleted* 'In'
100.26	A] *preceded by deleted* 'The dawn'
102.2	bed] *preceded by deleted* 'lounge b'
102.11	as . . . fancied] *interlined above deleted* 'able to take a step,'
102.19	afternoon] *interlined above deleted* 'morning'
102.19	four] *preceded by deleted* 'twelve o'clock'
102.25	absorbing] *revised from* 'absorption' *by deleting* 'ption' *and adding* 'bing'
104.20	&] *preceded by deleted* 'to'
105.19	Then] *preceded by deleted* 'You may'
105.29	Guy] *preceded by deleted* 'him'
106.12	voice] *preceded by deleted* 'low'
106.28	still] *preceded by deleted* 'laying her'
107.17	trembling] *preceded by deleted* 'little,'
111.3	nearly five] *interlined above deleted* 'four'
111.9	He] *preceded by deleted* 'but'
111.13	efface] *preceded by deleted* 'alter'
114.28	representatives] *preceded by deleted* 'heroes'
115.9	a] *preceded by deleted* 'such'

Revisions to THE BUCCANEERS

Book page/line	*Book*	*Ms 2*	*Ms 3*
134.11–12	That Eglinton girl had.	That Eglinton girl had.	That Eglinton girl there.
135.26	here?" Nan	here?" Nan] *preceded by paragraph sign*	here?" Nan
167.21	chose his	chose, his	chose, his
174.10	Quarter of an hour	Half an hour	Half an hour
180.15	crimping-pins	hairpins	hairpins
184.23	to many clubs. Their	to so many clubs: the Manhattan, the Athletic, the Players. Their	to so many clubs: the Manhattan, the Athletic, the Players. Their
189.5	let	letting	letting
202.30	boxes,	boxes),	boxes),
203.20	Parmore	Eglinton	Eglinton
215.4	exclusive	elusive	elusive
217.4	re-animate	reanimate	re-animate [*end-of-line hyphen*]
219.29	Marables,	Marables;	Marables,
242.18	act	set	set
264.6	do look	*do* look	do look
267.25	further	farther	farther

Book *page/line*	*Book*	*Ms 2*	*Ms 3*
270.6	Drawing-room. She	Drawing-room with a Lady Somebody—I never can get their names. She	Drawing-room with a Lady Somebody—I never can get their names. She
270.21–22	seems that Miss March's friend, Lady Churt,	seems Lady Churt's	seems Lady Churt's
270.31	next week	tomorrow	tomorrow
282.19–20	Lizzy Elmsworth	Virginia St George	Virginia St George
282.21	Virginia's graces	Lizzy Elmsworth's dark radiance	Lizzy Elmsworth's dark radiance
289.11	had put on	in] *over deleted* 'had put on'	in
366.29–31	*No single line space between* 'same creed' *and* 'Though she had,' *to indicate change of scene*	*Single line space between* 'same creed' *and* 'though she had'	*Single line space between* 'same creed' *and* 'though she had'
368.1	puts one out	does so put one out	puts one out so
371.6	rectors and vicars of	vicars and curates in	curates and vicars in
372.4	what she called its bolted look—the look she	what she called its bolted look—the expression	the cautious and distrustful look she

511

Book page/line	*Book*	*Ms 2*	*Ms 3*
390.21	with Augusta	with your aunt Augusta	with your aunt Augusta
391.8	what seemed a	such] *inserted above deleted* 'what seemed'	such a
393.9	had been...He even	had been...After that he had met her two or three times, at Allfriars, and again in London; and each time, though they had said so little to each other, he had the same sense of their close communion.	*same as Ms 2, but* 'of close communion'
394.13	that burden	that uneasy burden	that uneasy burden
397.1	A girl	A young girl	A young girl
399.5	vessel trying	(canvas)] *over deleted* 'flapping sails' *followed by* 'trying'	vessel with flapping canvas trying
401.15	dowager	Dowager	Dowager

Book page/line	Book	Ms 2	Ms 3
403.4–5	but the Duchess and Guy Thwarte did not rejoin it.	but they did not all rejoin it.	but they did not all rejoin it.
405.23–24	Yes; it did occur to me; and one day I smuggled in a ladder and took them all down—every one.	Yes; that has occurred to me. And I went so far, one day, as to smuggle in a ladder and take them all down myself—every one.	Yes; it did occur to me; and one day I went so far as to smuggle in a ladder and take them all down—every one.
405.25	jove,	Jove,	Jove,
407.28–29	were assembled	were already assembled] *above deleted* 'being cloaked for departure'	were already being cloaked for departure.
410.14	eight	seven	seven
437.16	was the Duchess	was Duchess	was Duchess
443.11	the state of his hair	rumpled hair	the rumpled state of his hair
447.22	eight	seven	seven
453.14	this atmosphere	air] *above deleted* 'cosmopolitan air'	cosmopolitan atmosphere
456.11	I have been	I *have* been	I've been
456.13	Lady Churt	Lady Idina Churt	Lady Idina Churt

Book *page/line*	*Book*	*Ms 2*	*Ms 3*
459.5	merely hired them	hired them merely	hired them that morning
467.5	I'm	*I'm*	[*no text for Ms 3*]